VOLUME
TEN

IMAGE COMICS, INC.

Robert Kirkman
CHIEF OPERATING OFFICER

Erik Larsen
CHIEF FINANCIAL OFFICER

Todd McFarlane
PRESIDENT

Marc Silvestri
CHIEF EXECUTIVE OFFICER

Jim Valentino
VICE PRESIDENT

Eric Stephenson
PUBLISHER / CHIEF CREATIVE OFFICER

Nicole Lapalme
VICE PRESIDENT OF FINANCE

Leanna Caunter
ACCOUNTING ANALYST

Sue Korpela
ACCOUNTING & HR MANAGER

Matt Parkinson
VICE PRESIDENT OF SALES & PUBLISHING PLANNING

Lorelei Bunjes
VICE PRESIDENT OF DIGITAL STRATEGY

Dirk Wood
VICE PRESIDENT OF INTERNATIONAL SALES & LICENSING

Ryan Brewer
INTERNATIONAL SALES & LICENSING MANAGER

Alex Cox
DIRECTOR OF DIRECT MARKET SALES

Chloe Ramos
BOOK MARKET & LIBRARY SALES MANAGER

Emilio Bautista
DIGITAL SALES COORDINATOR

Jon Schlaffman
SPECIALTY SALES COORDINATOR

Kat Salazar
VICE PRESIDENT OF PR & MARKETING

Deanna Phelps
MARKETING DESIGN MANAGER

Drew Fitzgerald
MARKETING CONTENT ASSOCIATE

Heather Doornink
VICE PRESIDENT OF PRODUCTION

Drew Gill
ART DIRECTOR

Hilary DiLoreto
PRINT MANAGER

Tricia Ramos
TRAFFIC MANAGER

Melissa Gifford
CONTENT MANAGER

Erika Schnatz
SENIOR PRODUCTION ARTIST

Wesley Griffith
PRODUCTION ARTIST

Rich Fowlks
PRODUCTION ARTIST

www.imagecomics.com

BRIAN K. VAUGHAN
WRITER

FIONA STAPLES
ARTIST

FONOGRAFIKS
LETTERING + DESIGN

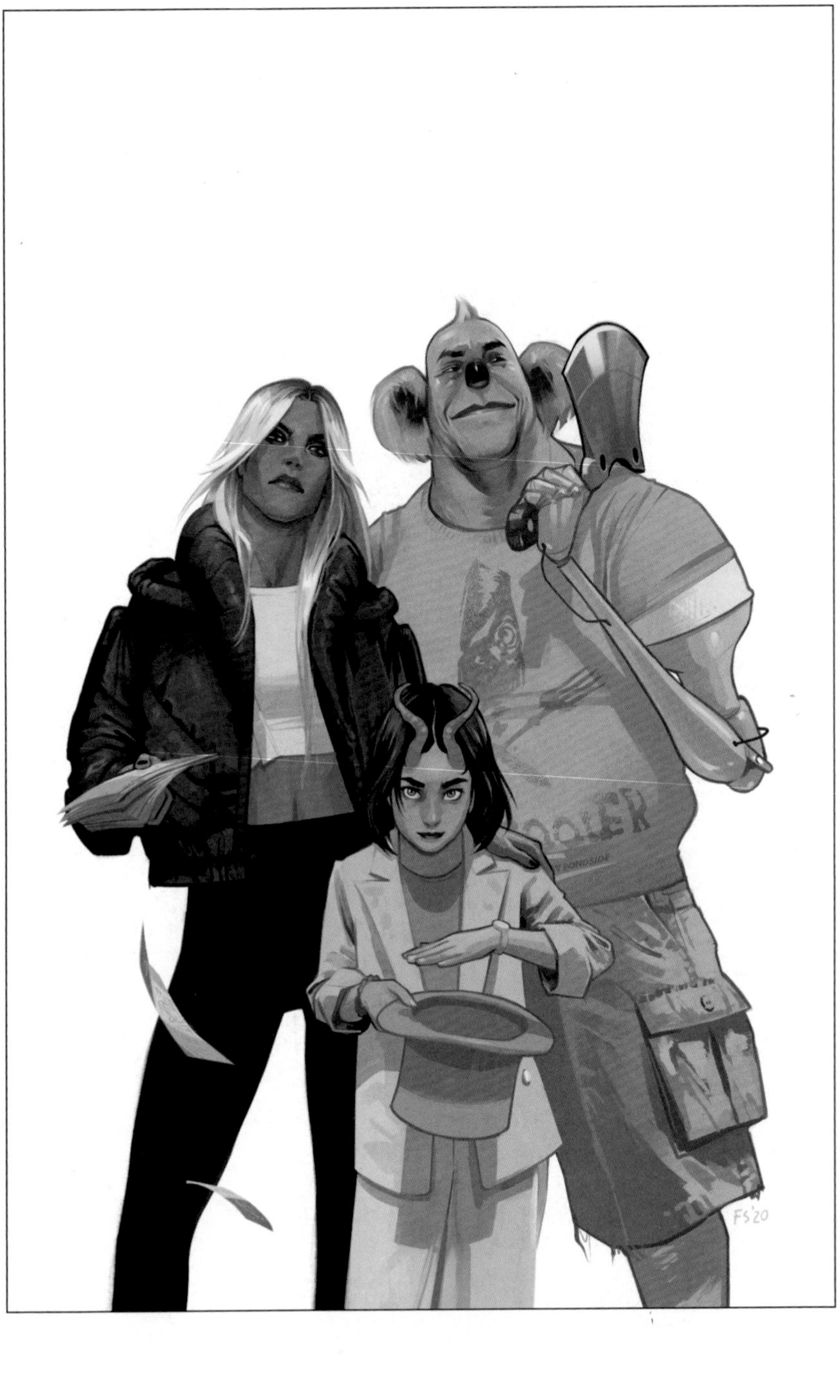
FS'20

CHAPTER

FIFTY-FIVE

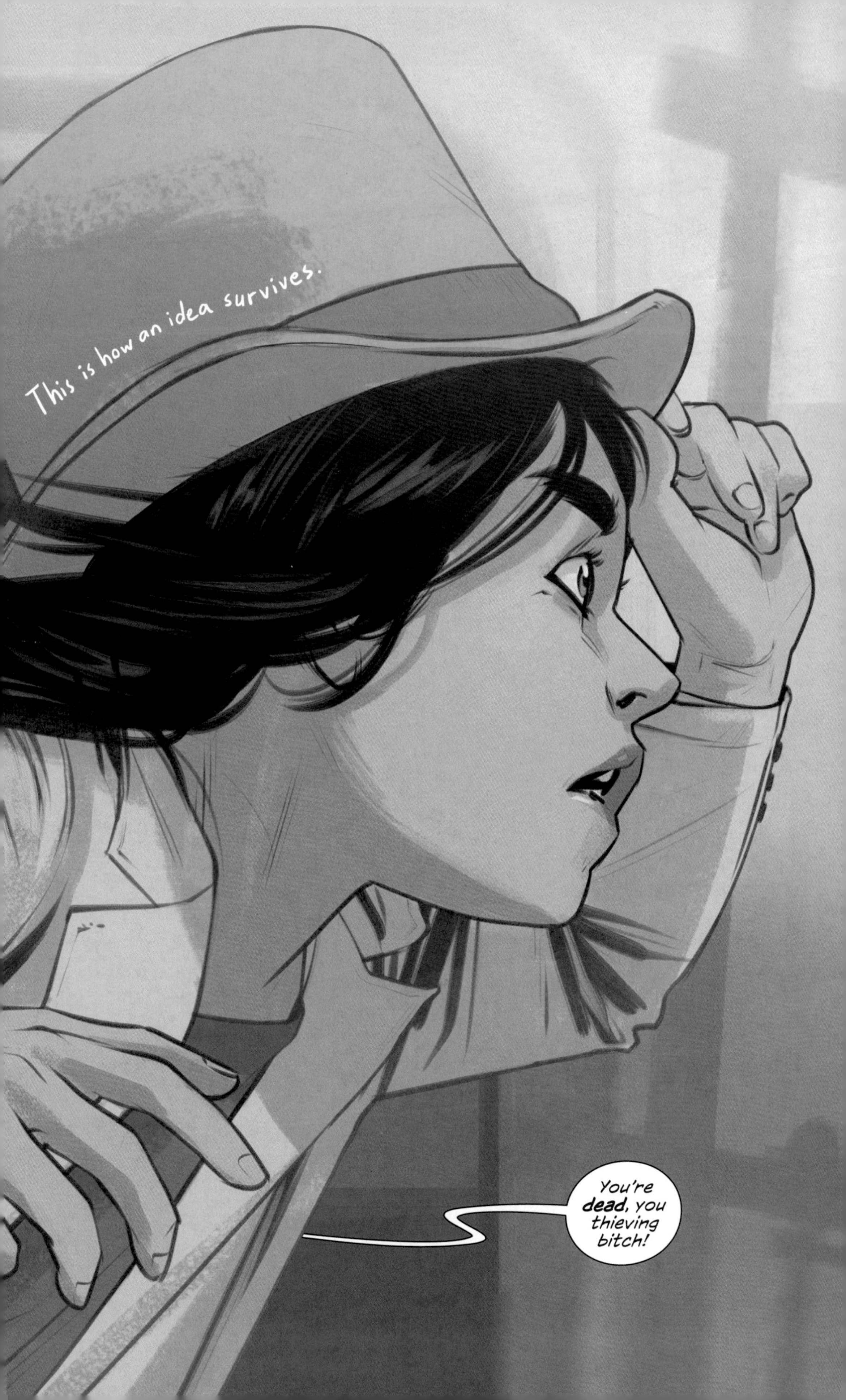
This is how an idea survives.
You're dead, you thieving bitch!

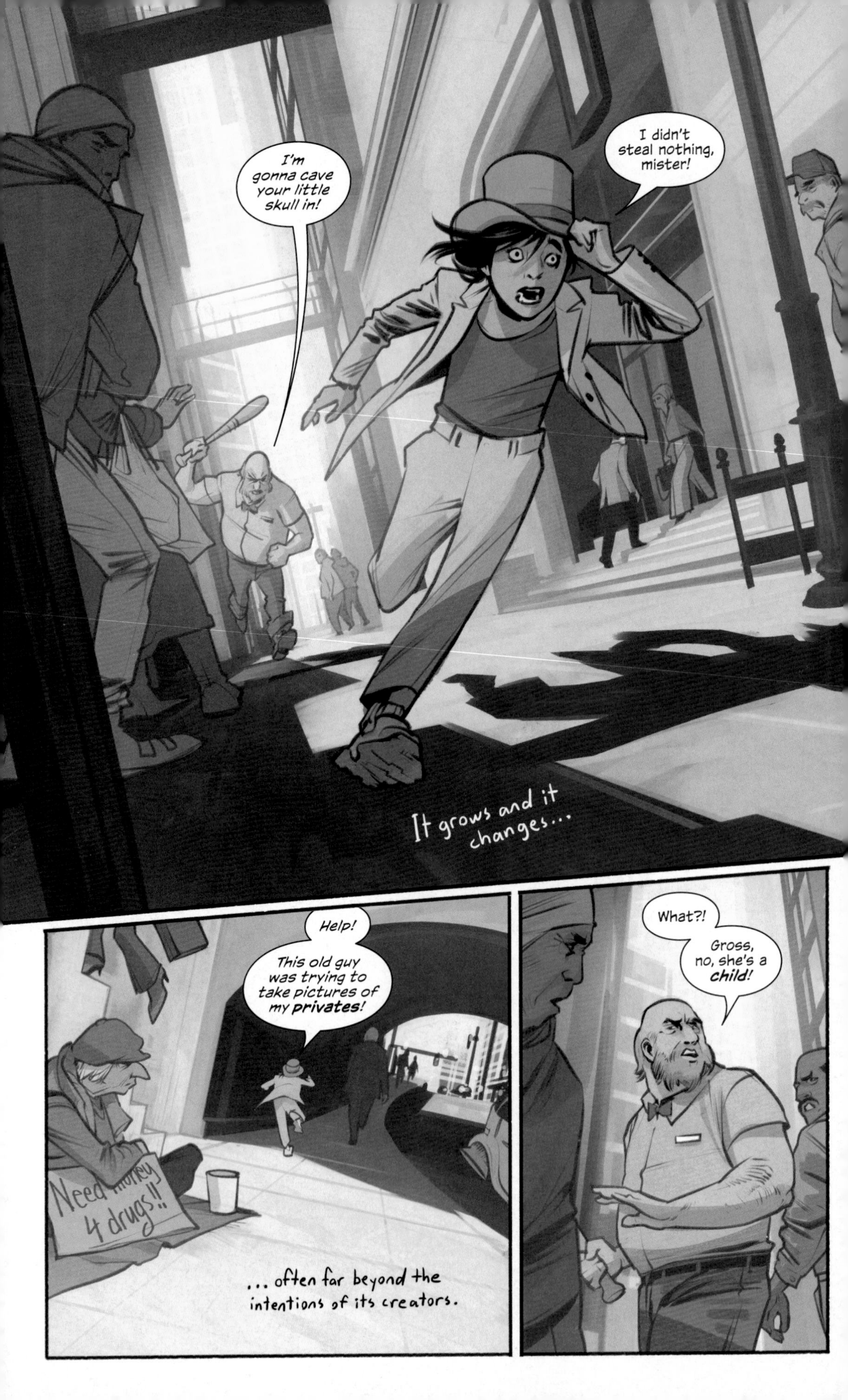
I'm gonna cave your little skull in!
I didn't steal nothing, mister!
It grows and it changes...
Help!
This old guy was trying to take pictures of my **privates**!
Need money 4 drugs!!
... often far beyond the intentions of its creators.
What?!
Gross, no, she's a **child**!

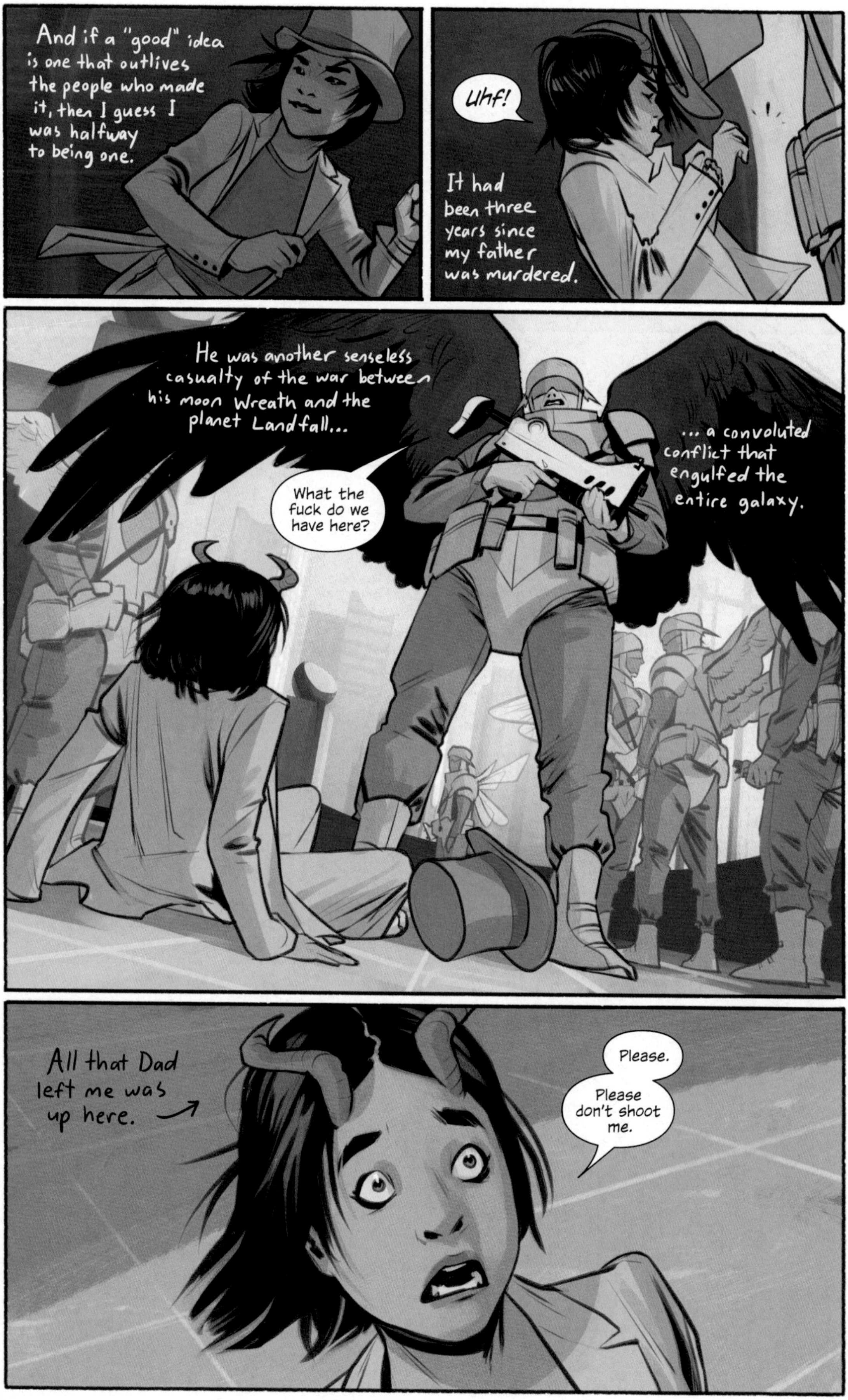
And if a "good" idea is one that outlives the people who made it, then I guess I was halfway to being one.
Uhf!
It had been three years since my father was murdered.
He was another senseless casualty of the war between his moon Wreath and the planet Landfall...
What the fuck do we have here?
...a convoluted conflict that engulfed the entire galaxy.
All that Dad left me was up here.
Please.
Please don't shoot me.

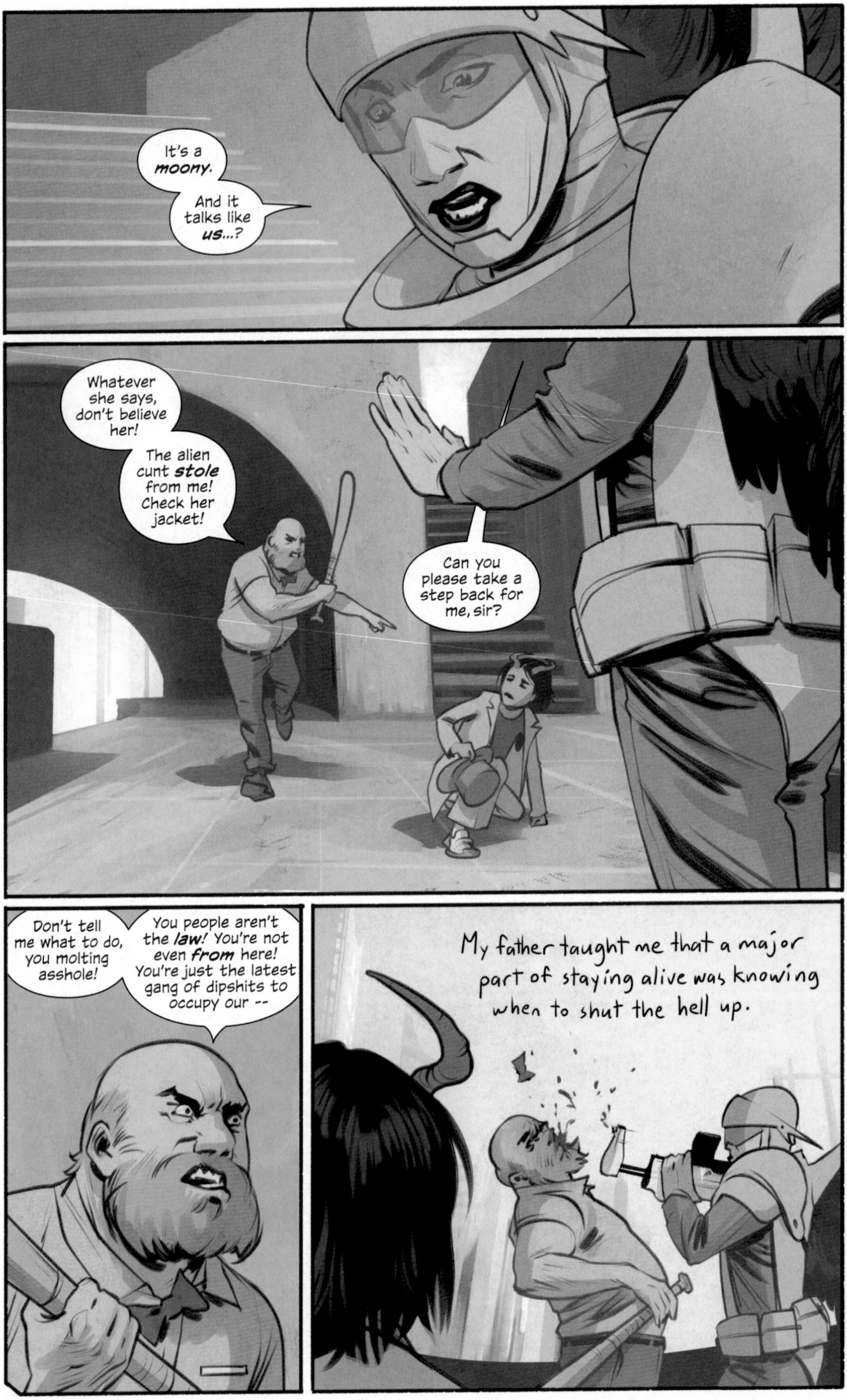
It's a *moony*.
And it talks like *us*...?
Whatever she says, don't believe her!
The alien cunt *stole* from me! Check her jacket!
Can you please take a step back for me, sir?
Don't tell me what to do, you molting asshole!
You people aren't the *law!* You're not even *from* here! You're just the latest gang of dipshits to occupy our --
My father taught me that a major part of staying alive was knowing when to shut the hell up.

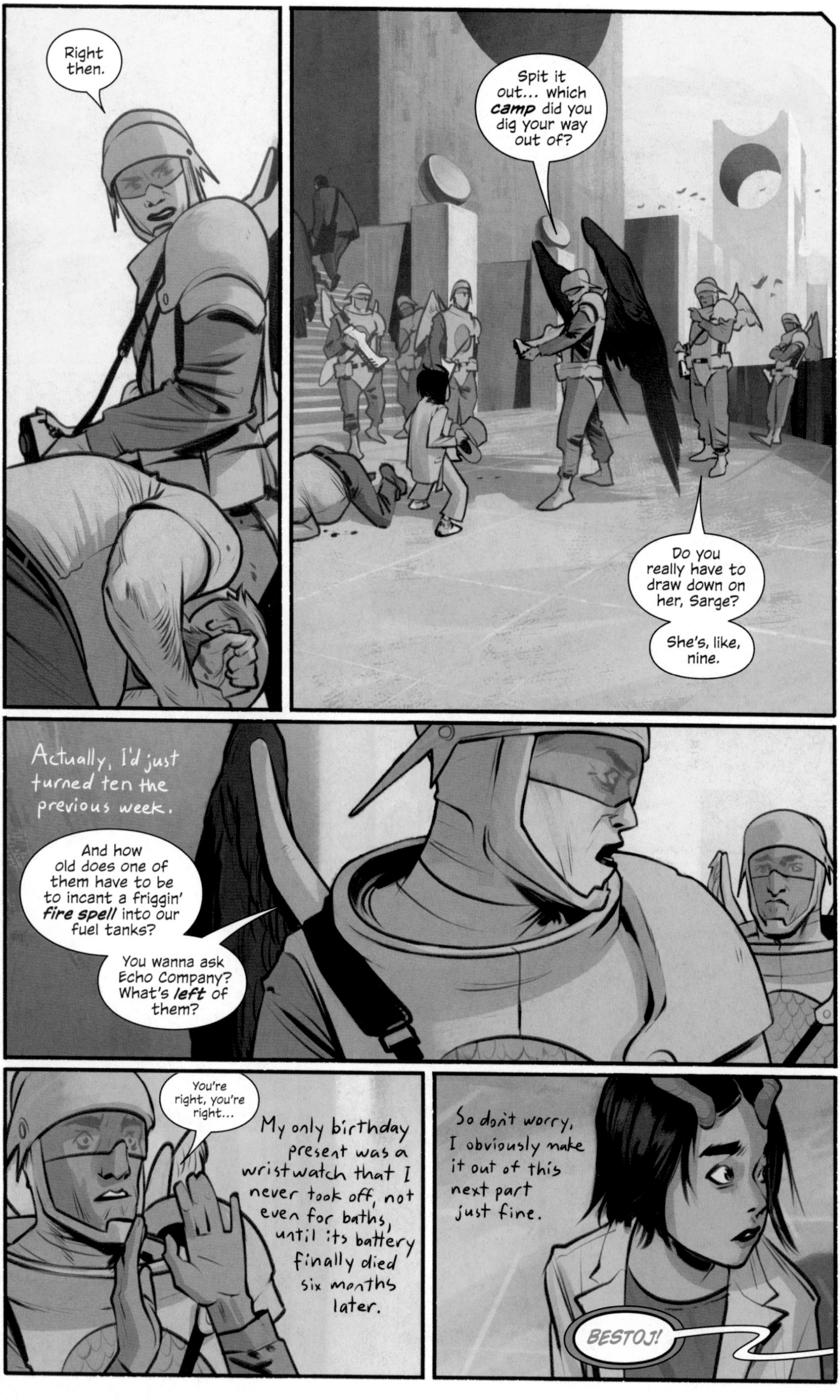
Right then.
Spit it out... which camp did you dig your way out of?
Do you really have to draw down on her, Sarge?
She's, like, nine.
Actually, I'd just turned ten the previous week.
And how old does one of them have to be to incant a friggin' fire spell into our fuel tanks?
You wanna ask Echo Company? What's left of them?
You're right, you're right...
My only birthday present was a wristwatch that I never took off, not even for baths, until its battery finally died six months later.
So don't worry, I obviously make it out of this next part just fine.
BESTOJ!

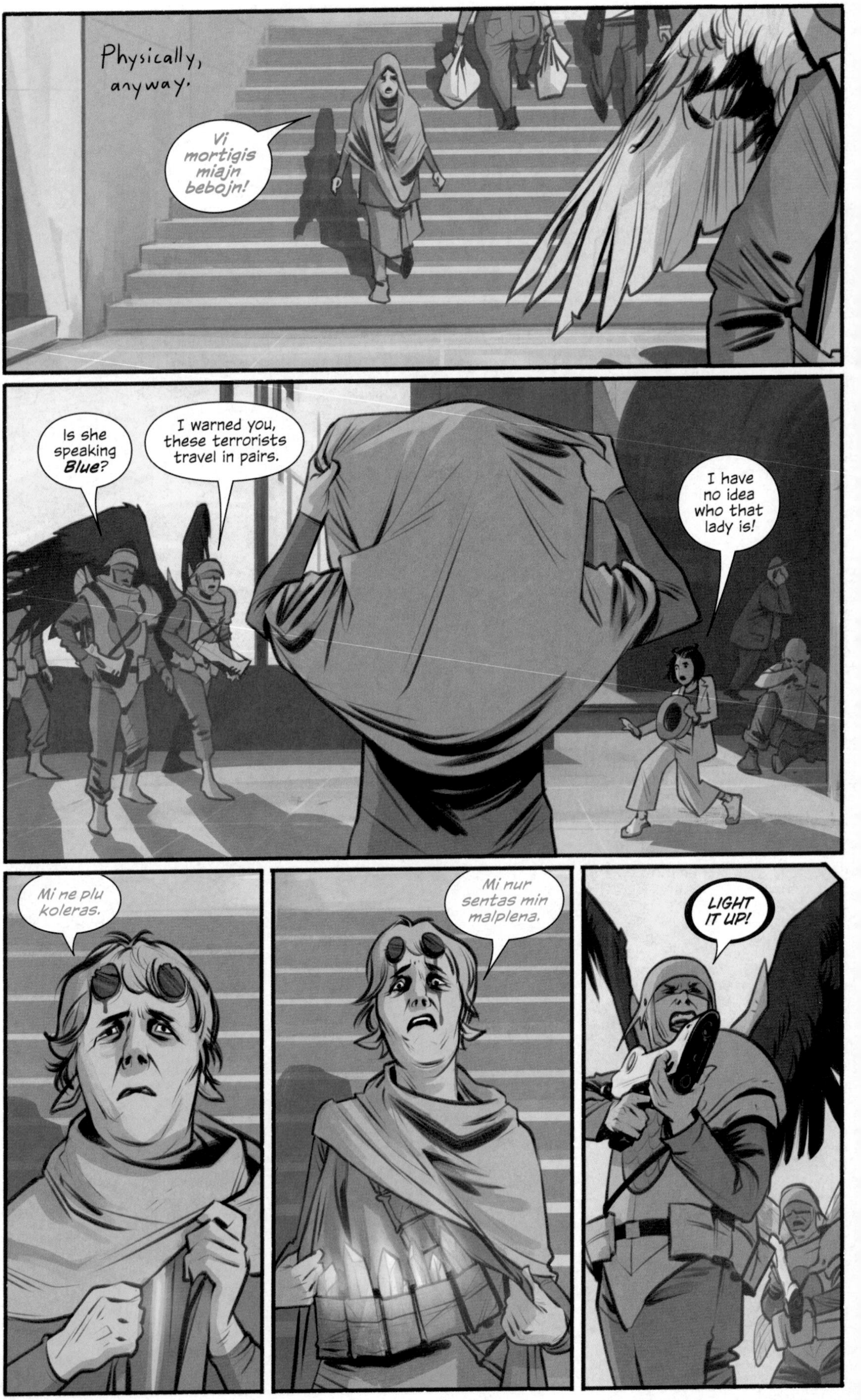

Physically, anyway.
Vi mortigis miajn bebojn!
Is she speaking Blue?
I warned you, these terrorists travel in pairs.
I have no idea who that lady is!
Mi ne plu koleras.
Mi nur sentas min malplena.
LIGHT IT UP!

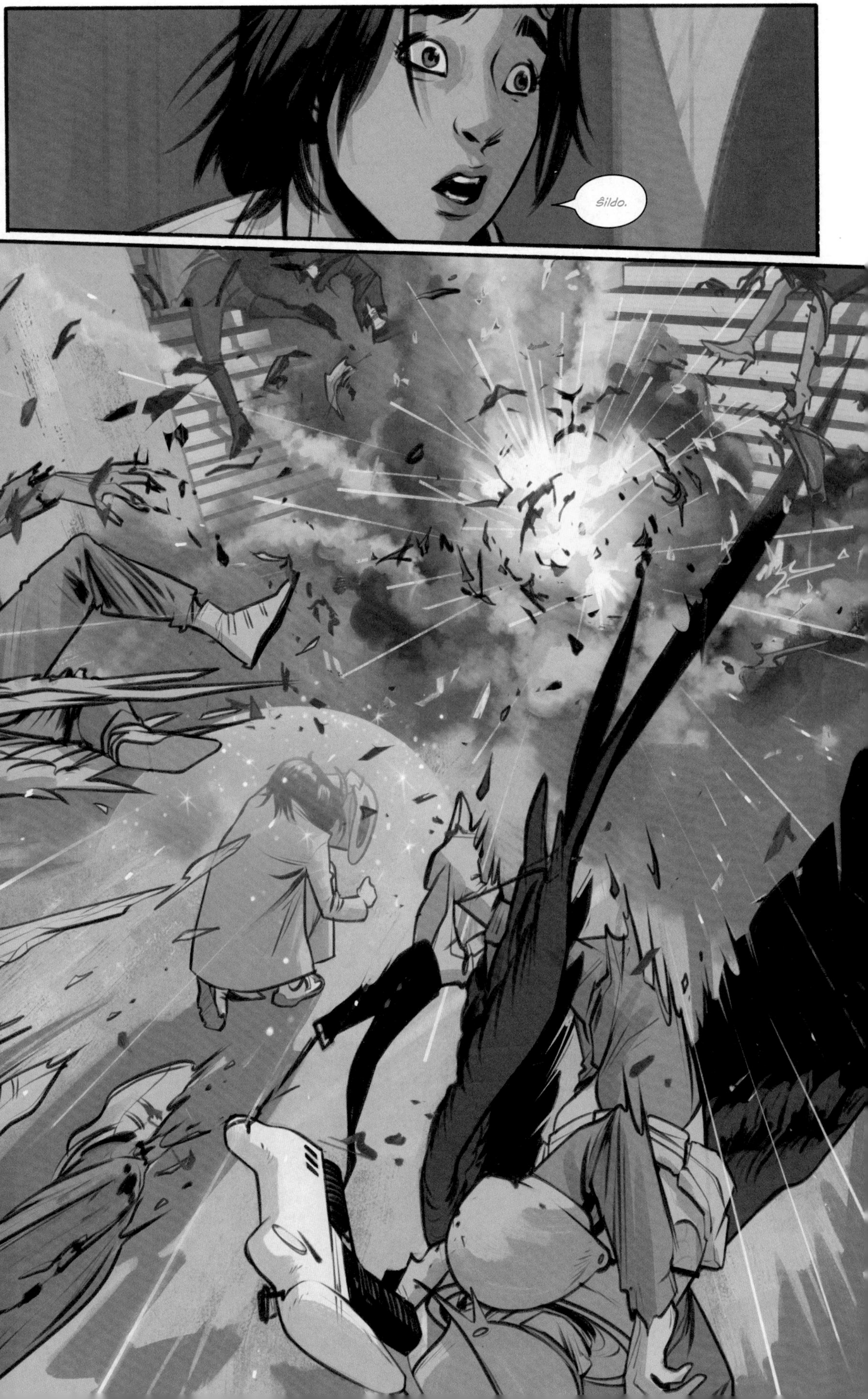
Ŝildo.

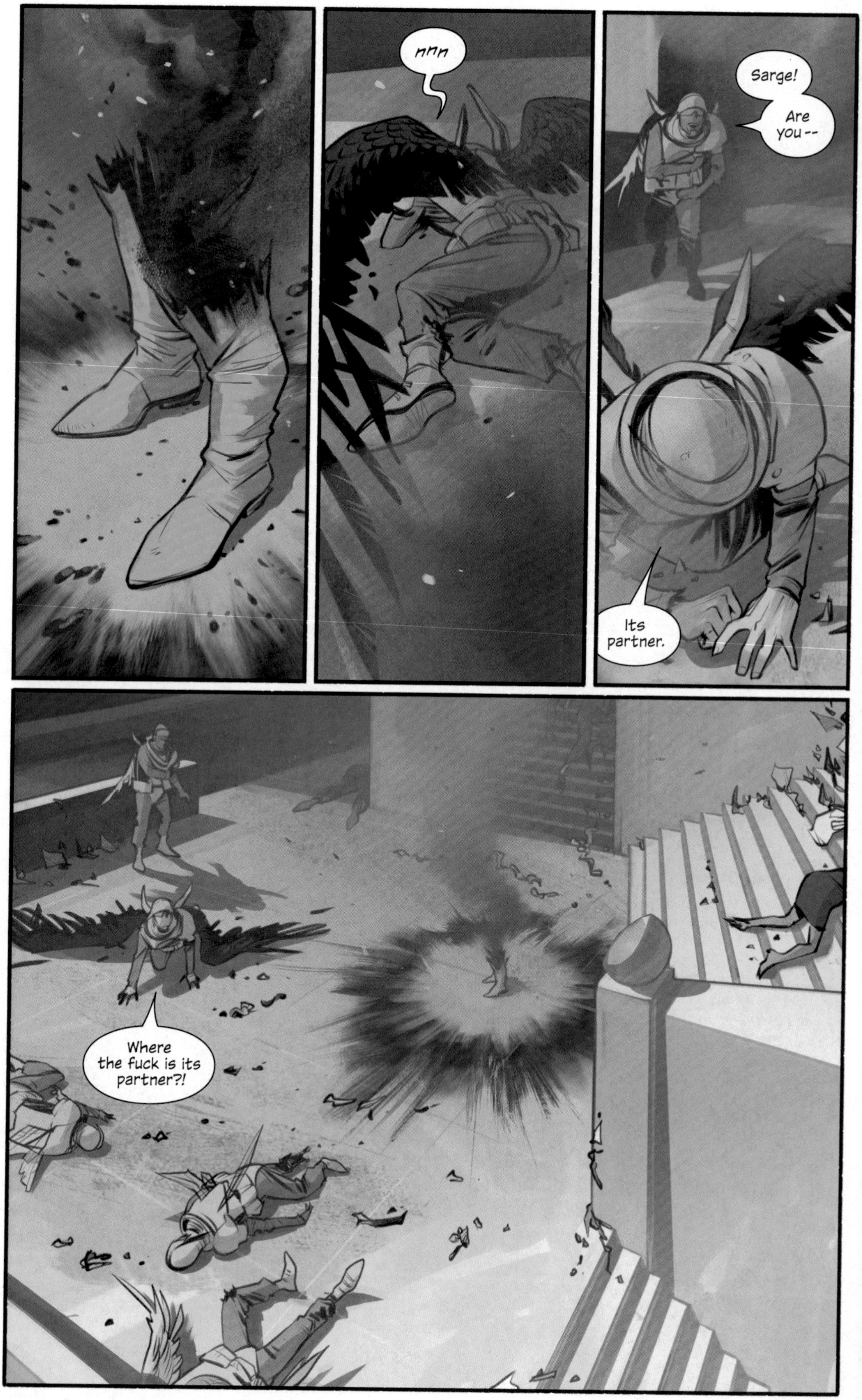
nnn
Sarge!
Are you --
Its partner.
Where the fuck is its partner?!

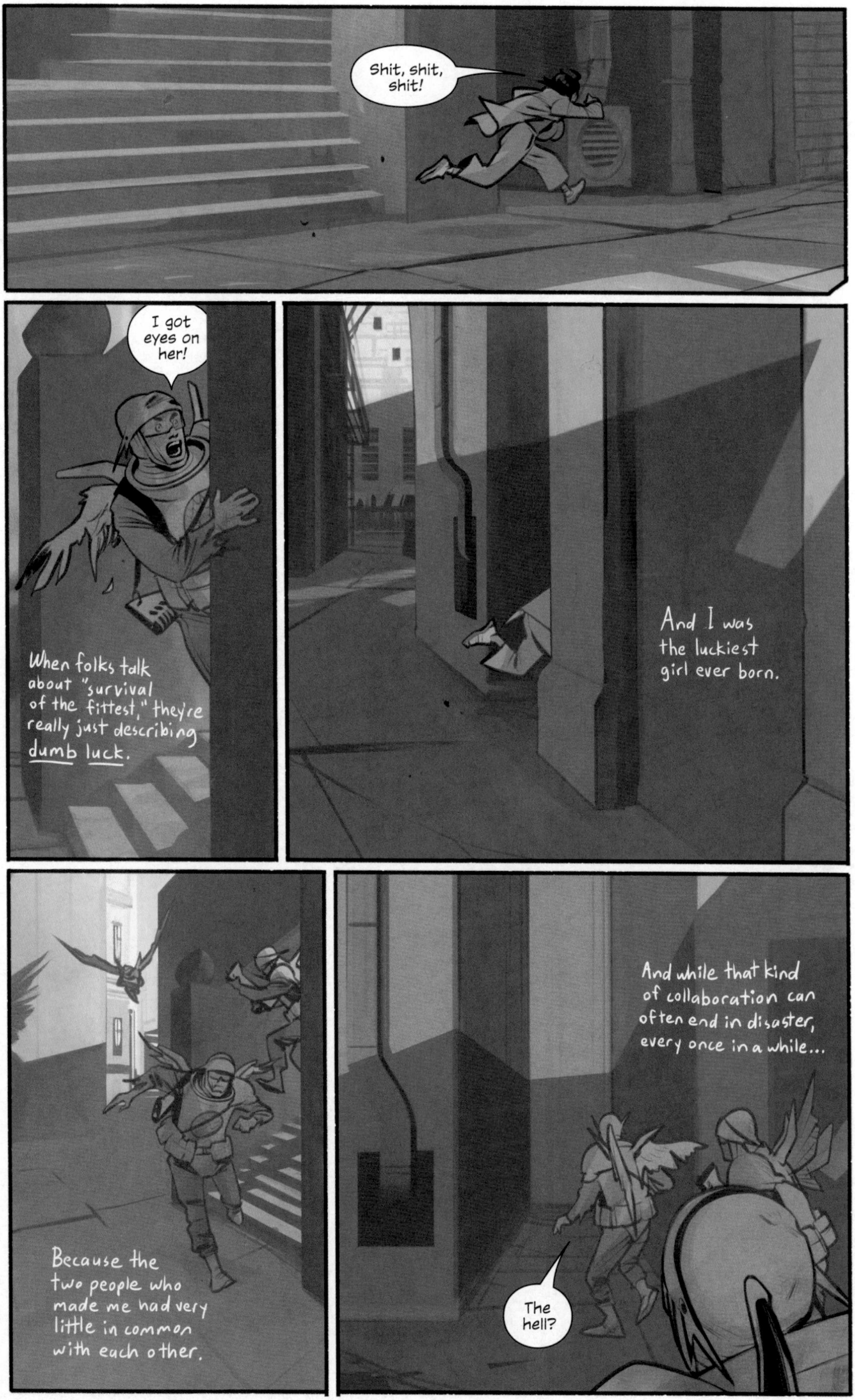
Shit, shit, shit!
I got eyes on her!
When folks talk about "survival of the fittest," they're really just describing dumb luck.
And I was the luckiest girl ever born.
Because the two people who made me had very little in common with each other.
And while that kind of collaboration can often end in disaster, every once in a while...
The hell?

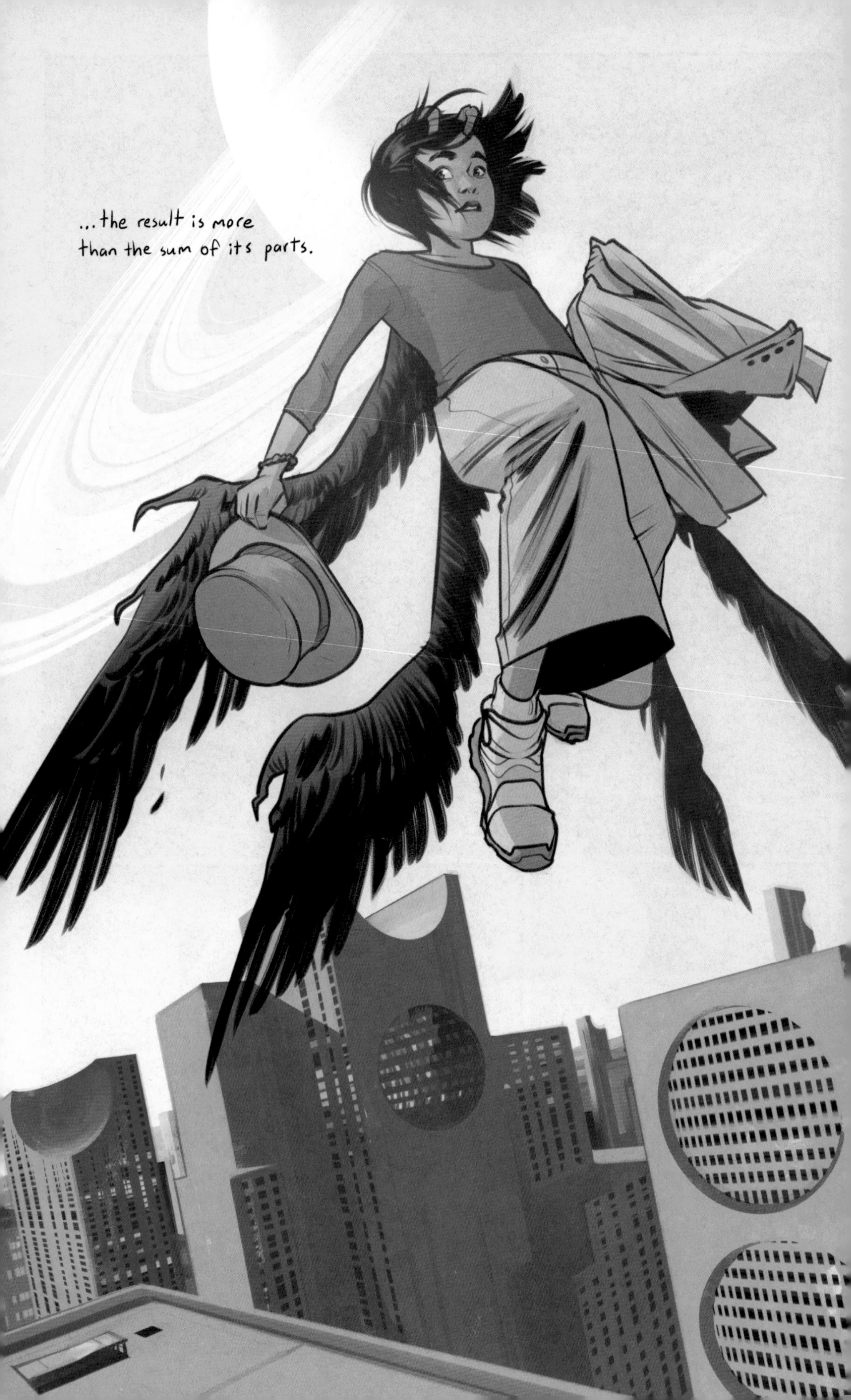
...the result is more
than the sum of its parts.

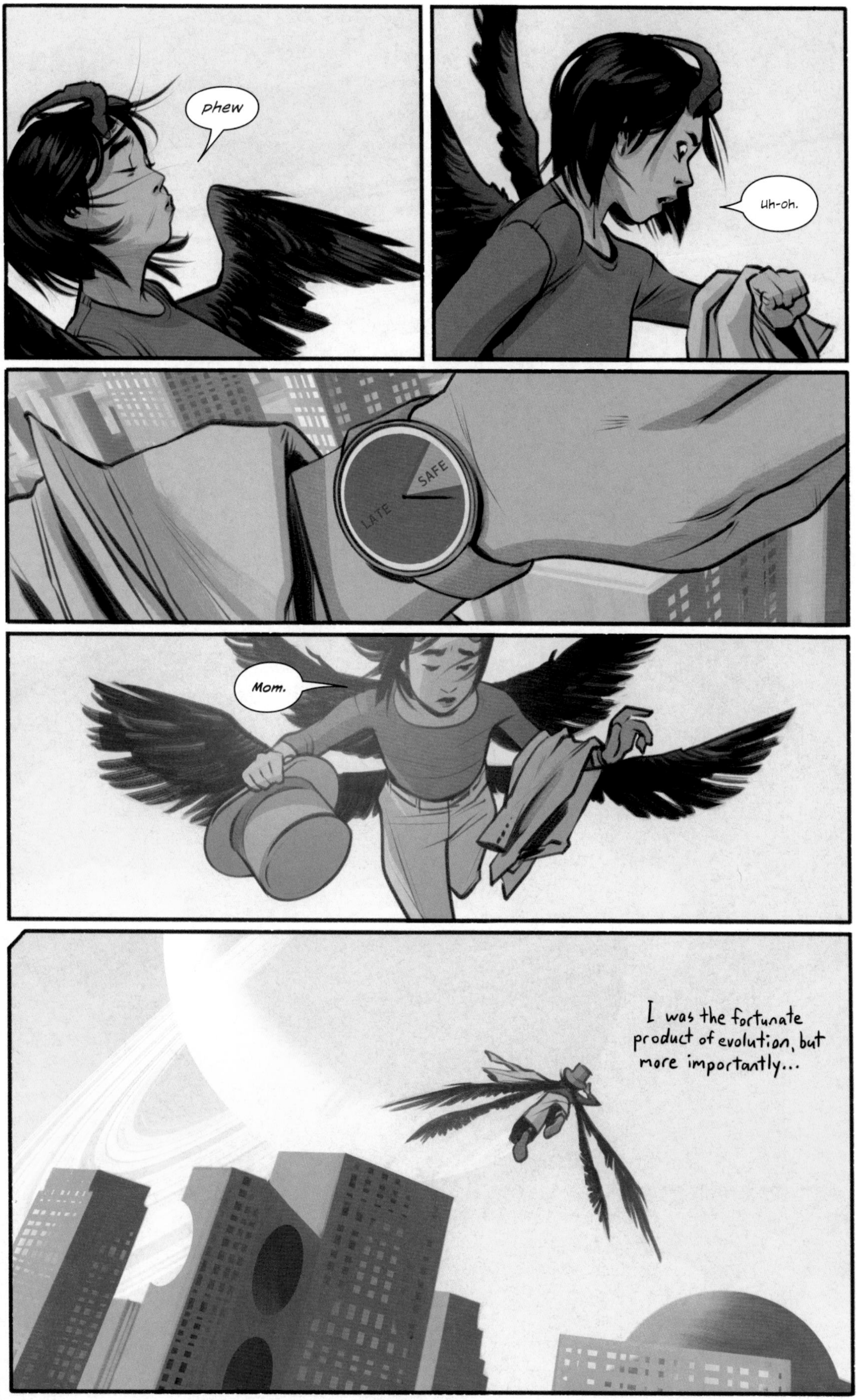
phew
uh-oh.
SAFE
LATE
Mom.
I was the fortunate product of evolution, but more importantly...

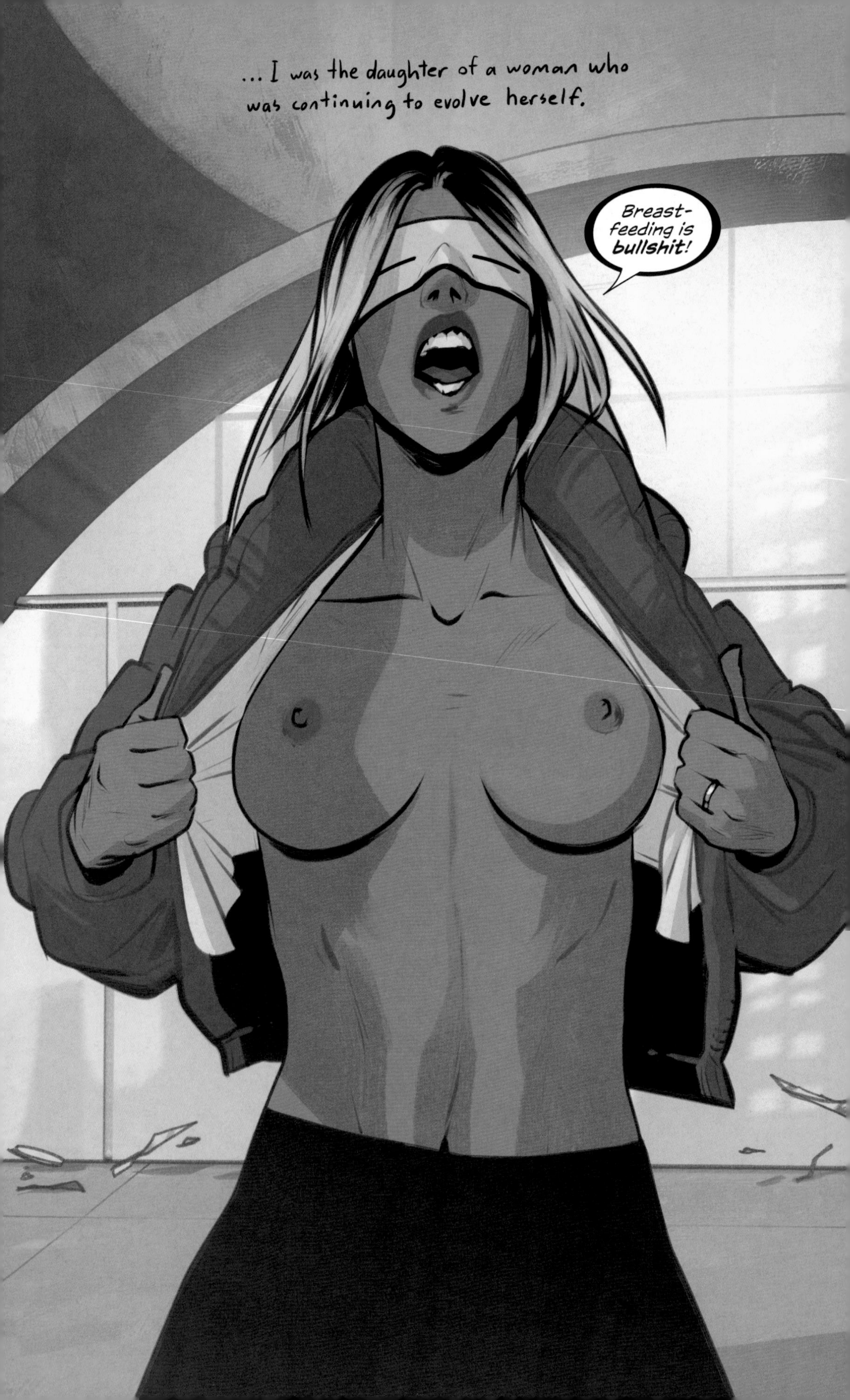
...I was the daughter of a woman who was continuing to evolve herself.
Breast-feeding is bullshit!

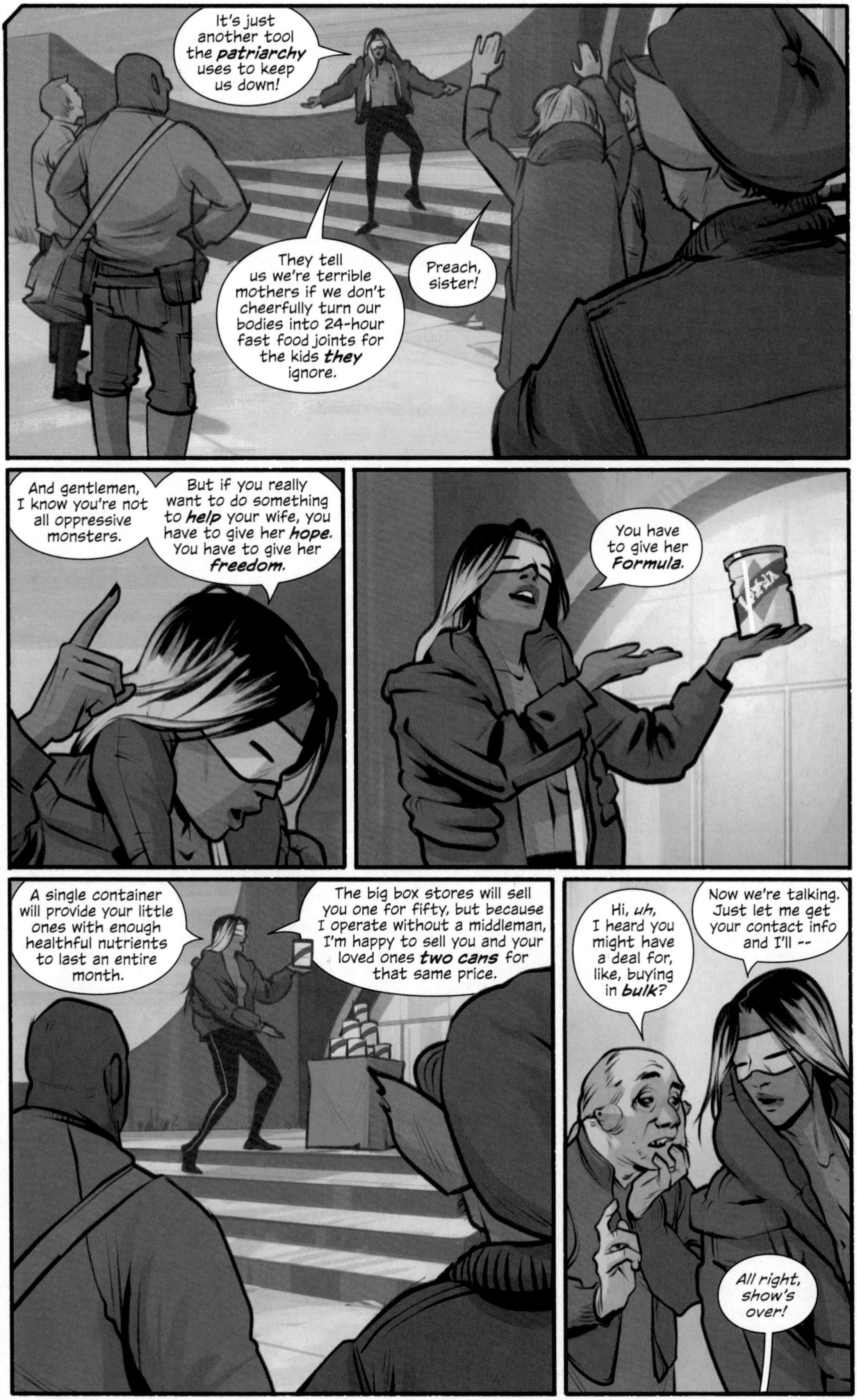

It's just another tool the patriarchy uses to keep us down!
They tell us we're terrible mothers if we don't cheerfully turn our bodies into 24-hour fast food joints for the kids they ignore.
Preach, sister!
And gentlemen, I know you're not all oppressive monsters.
But if you really want to do something to help your wife, you have to give her hope. You have to give her freedom.
You have to give her Formula.
A single container will provide your little ones with enough healthful nutrients to last an entire month.
The big box stores will sell you one for fifty, but because I operate without a middleman, I'm happy to sell you and your loved ones two cans for that same price.
Hi, uh, I heard you might have a deal for, like, buying in bulk?
Now we're talking. Just let me get your contact info and I'll --
All right, show's over!

Move it along, pervs.

You, too, sweet-heart.

This is blatant discrimination!

I have exactly the same right to show my nipples in public as any--

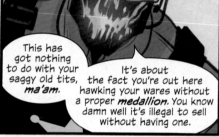

This has got nothing to do with your *saggy old tits*, ma'am.

It's about the fact you're out here hawking your wares without a proper *medallion*. You know damn well it's illegal to sell without having one.

You mean without *buying* one, from the same people who pay you? Yeah, I know how this shakedown goes.

Whatever, I'm done here anyway.

Nah, you blew your chance to get out of this with a warning. Let's see some identification.

Guys, come on.

I'm just trying to take care of my family.

And what, you think we're out here risking our lives for the fun of it?

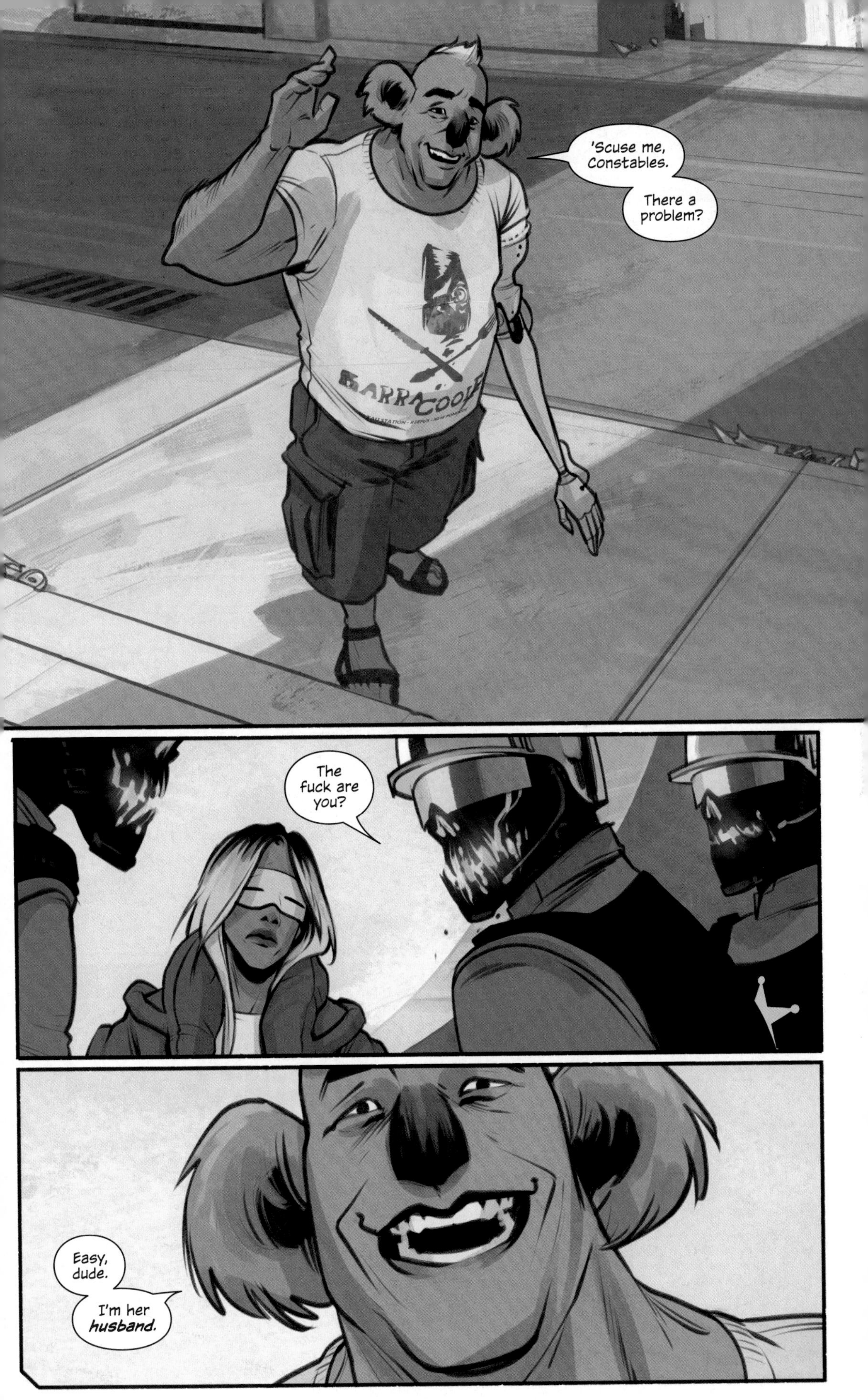
'Scuse me, Constables.
There a problem?
The fuck are you?
Easy, dude.
I'm her *husband*.

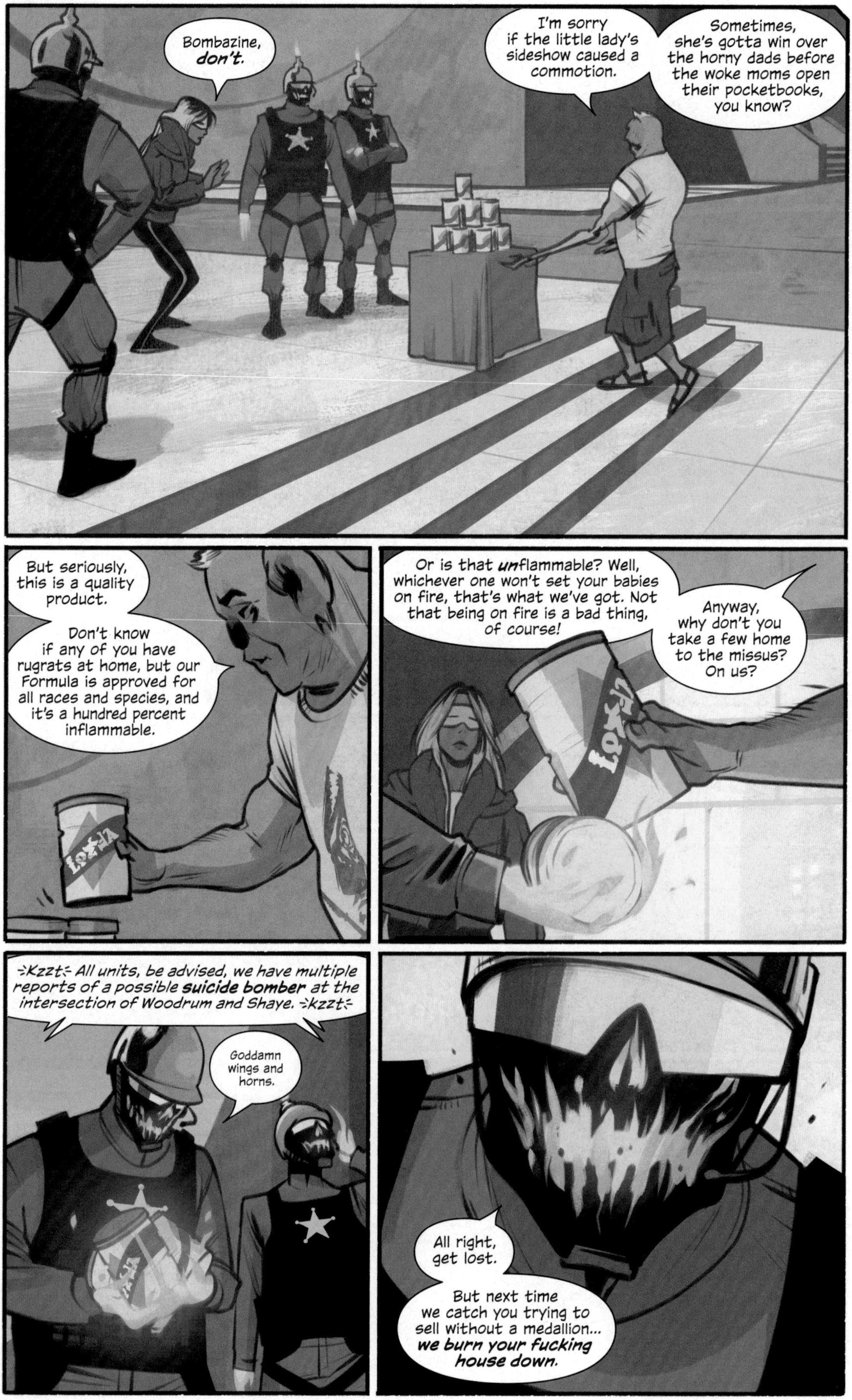

Bombazine, *don't*.
I'm sorry if the little lady's sideshow caused a commotion.
Sometimes, she's gotta win over the horny dads before the woke moms open their pocketbooks, you know?
But seriously, this is a quality product.
Don't know if any of you have rugrats at home, but our Formula is approved for all races and species, and it's a hundred percent inflammable.
Or is that *un*flammable? Well, whichever one won't set your babies on fire, that's what we've got. Not that being on fire is a bad thing, of course!
Anyway, why don't you take a few home to the missus? On us?
*-Kzzt- All units, be advised, we have multiple reports of a possible **suicide bomber** at the intersection of Woodrum and Shaye. -kzzt-*
Goddamn wings and horns.
All right, get lost.
But next time we catch you trying to sell without a medallion... ***we burn your fucking house down.***

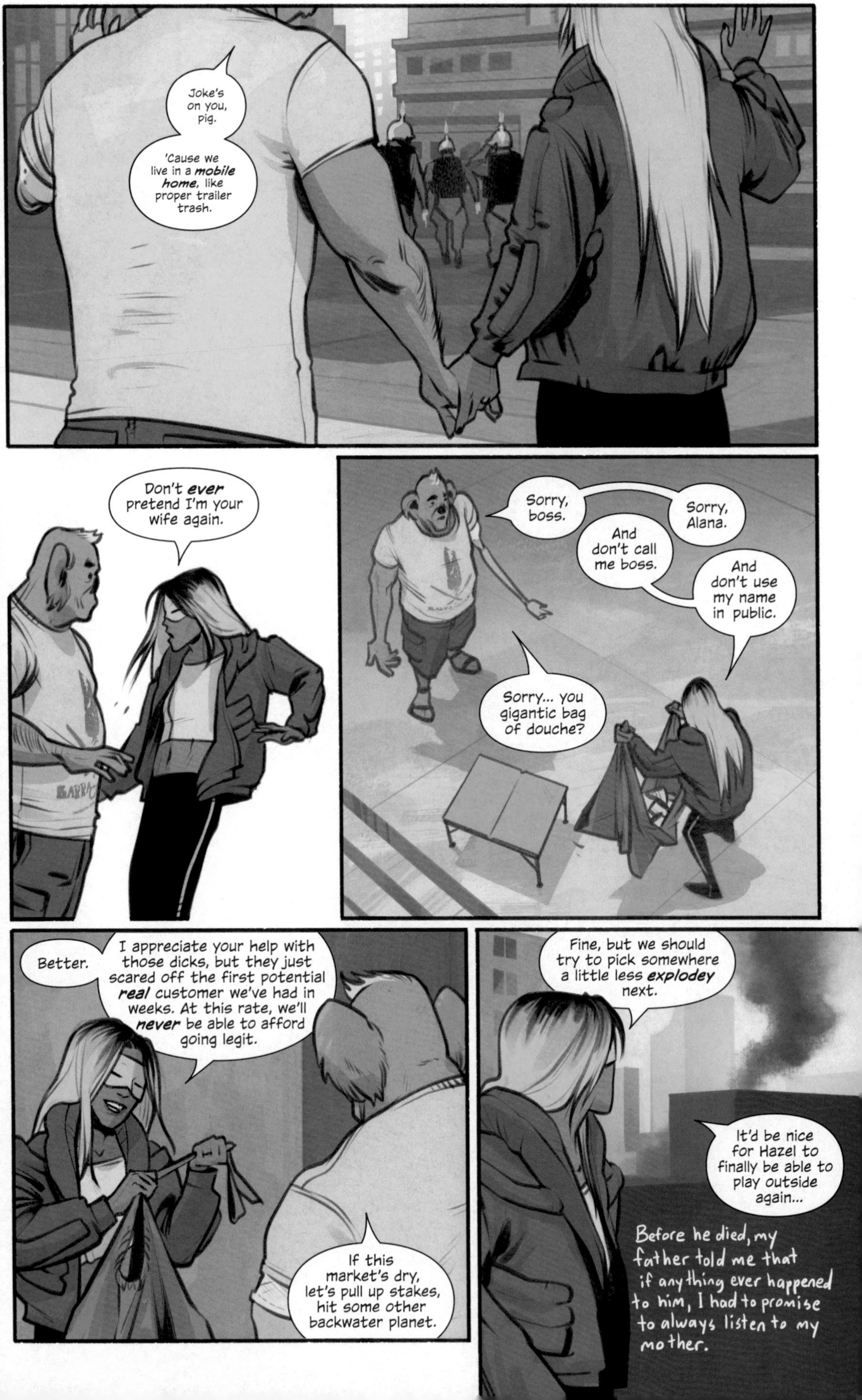

Joke's on you, pig.
'Cause we live in a ***mobile home***, like proper trailer trash.
Don't ***ever*** pretend I'm your wife again.
Sorry, boss.
Sorry, Alana.
And don't call me boss.
And don't use my name in public.
Sorry... you gigantic bag of douche?
Better.
I appreciate your help with those dicks, but they just scared off the first potential ***real*** customer we've had in weeks. At this rate, we'll ***never*** be able to afford going legit.
If this market's dry, let's pull up stakes, hit some other backwater planet.
Fine, but we should try to pick somewhere a little less ***explodey*** next.
It'd be nice for Hazel to finally be able to play outside again...
Before he died, my father told me that if anything ever happened to him, I had to promise to always listen to my mother.

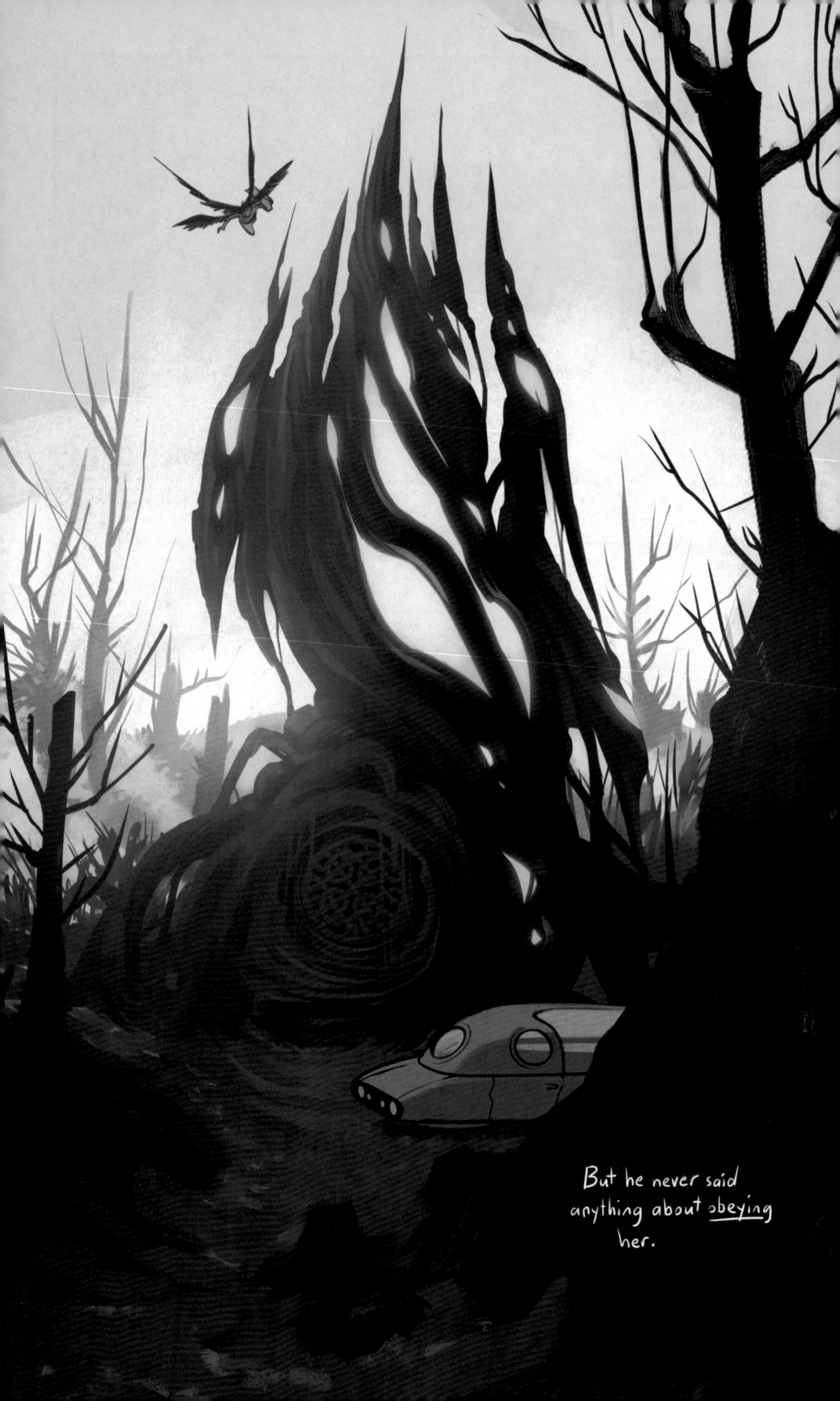
But he never said anything about obeying her.

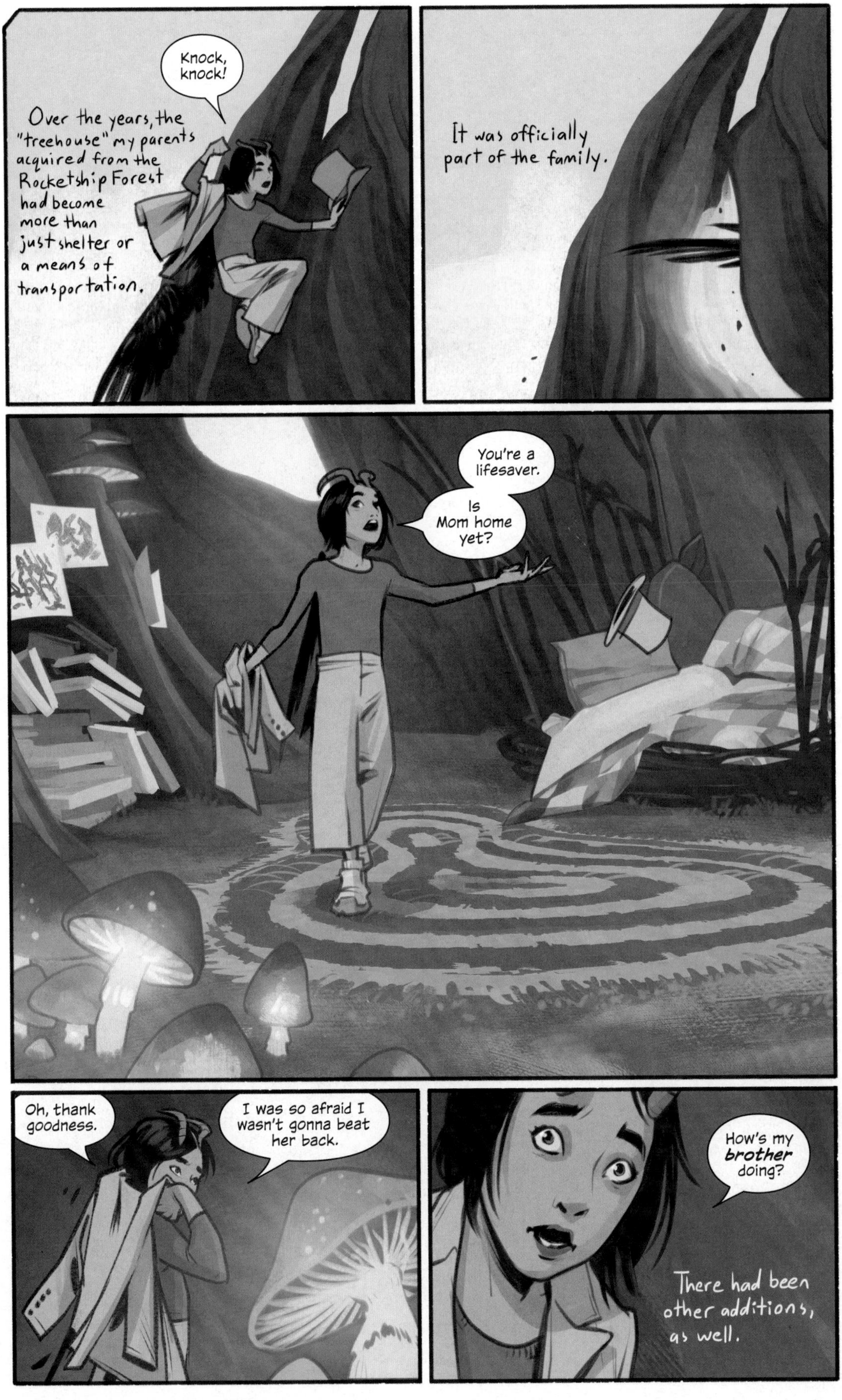

Knock, knock!
Over the years, the "treehouse" my parents acquired from the Rocketship Forest had become more than just shelter or a means of transportation.
It was officially part of the family.
You're a lifesaver.
Is Mom home yet?
Oh, thank goodness.
I was so afraid I wasn't gonna beat her back.
How's my **brother** doing?
There had been other additions, as well.

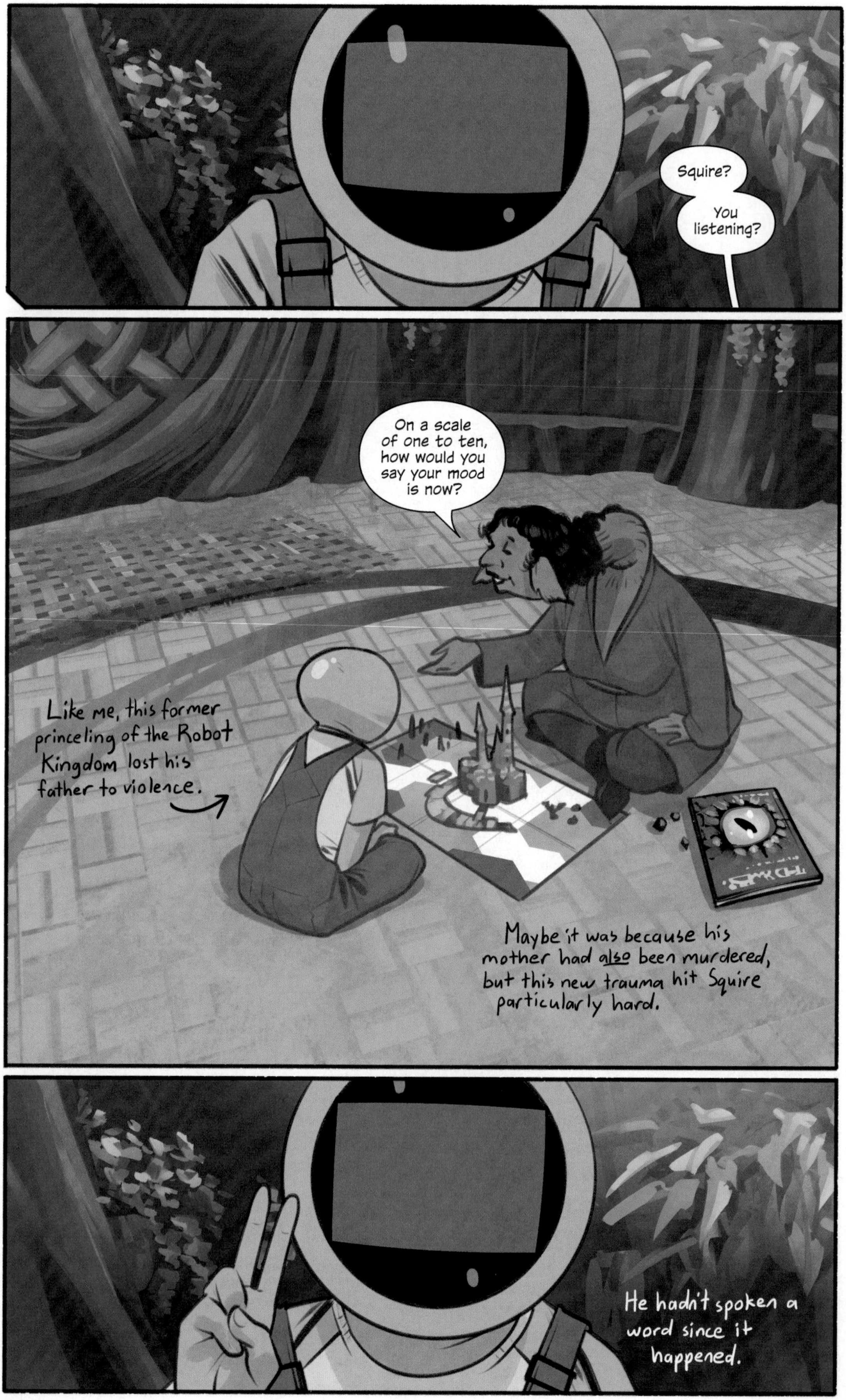

Squire?
You listening?
On a scale of one to ten, how would you say your mood is now?
Like me, this former princeling of the Robot Kingdom lost his father to violence.
Maybe it was because his mother had also been murdered, but this new trauma hit Squire particularly hard.
He hadn't spoken a word since it happened.

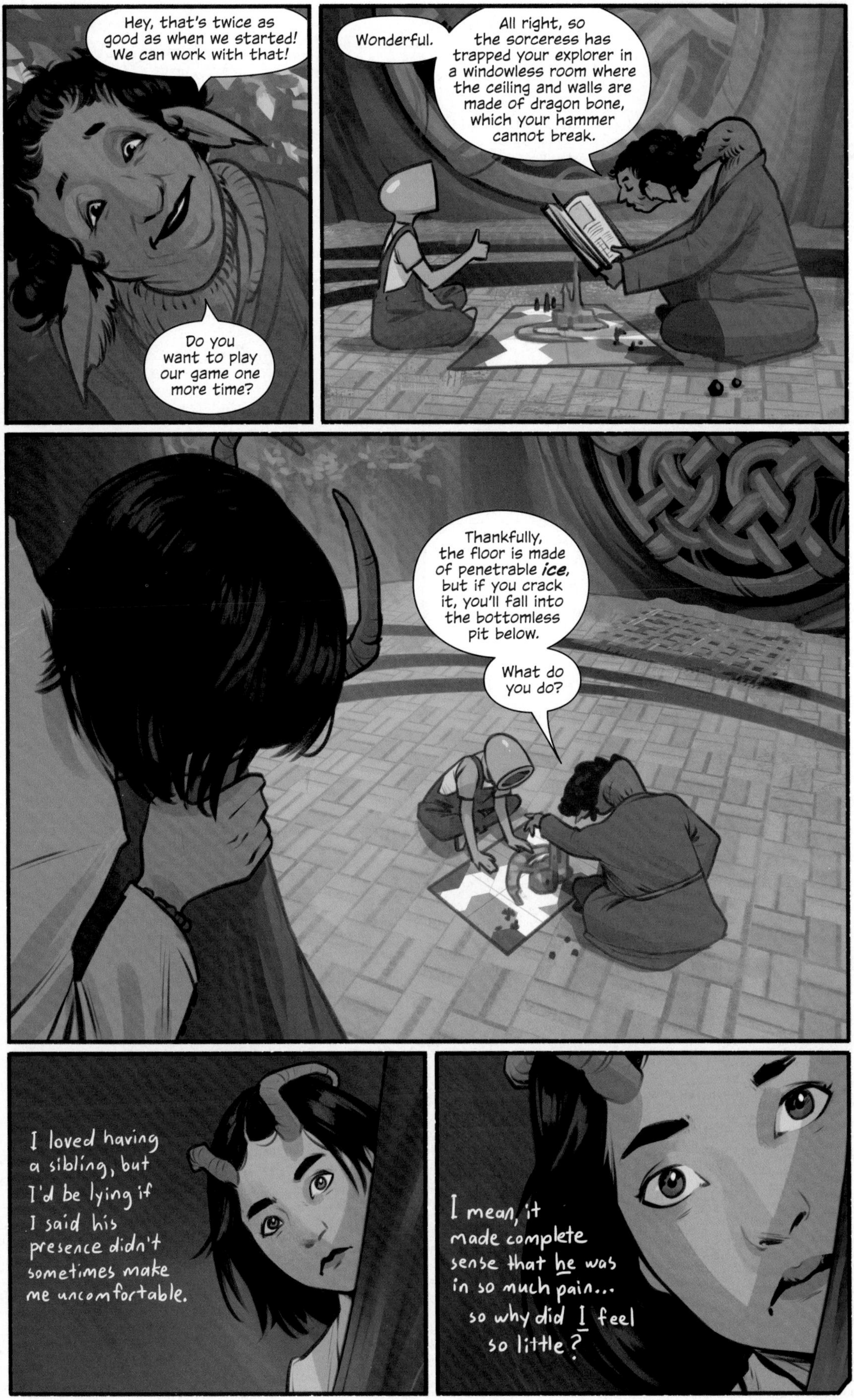
Hey, that's twice as good as when we started! We can work with that!
Do you want to play our game one more time?
Wonderful.
All right, so the sorceress has trapped your explorer in a windowless room where the ceiling and walls are made of dragon bone, which your hammer cannot break.
Thankfully, the floor is made of penetrable *ice*, but if you crack it, you'll fall into the bottomless pit below.
What do you do?
I loved having a sibling, but I'd be lying if I said his presence didn't sometimes make me uncomfortable.
I mean, it made complete sense that he was in so much pain... so why did I feel so little?

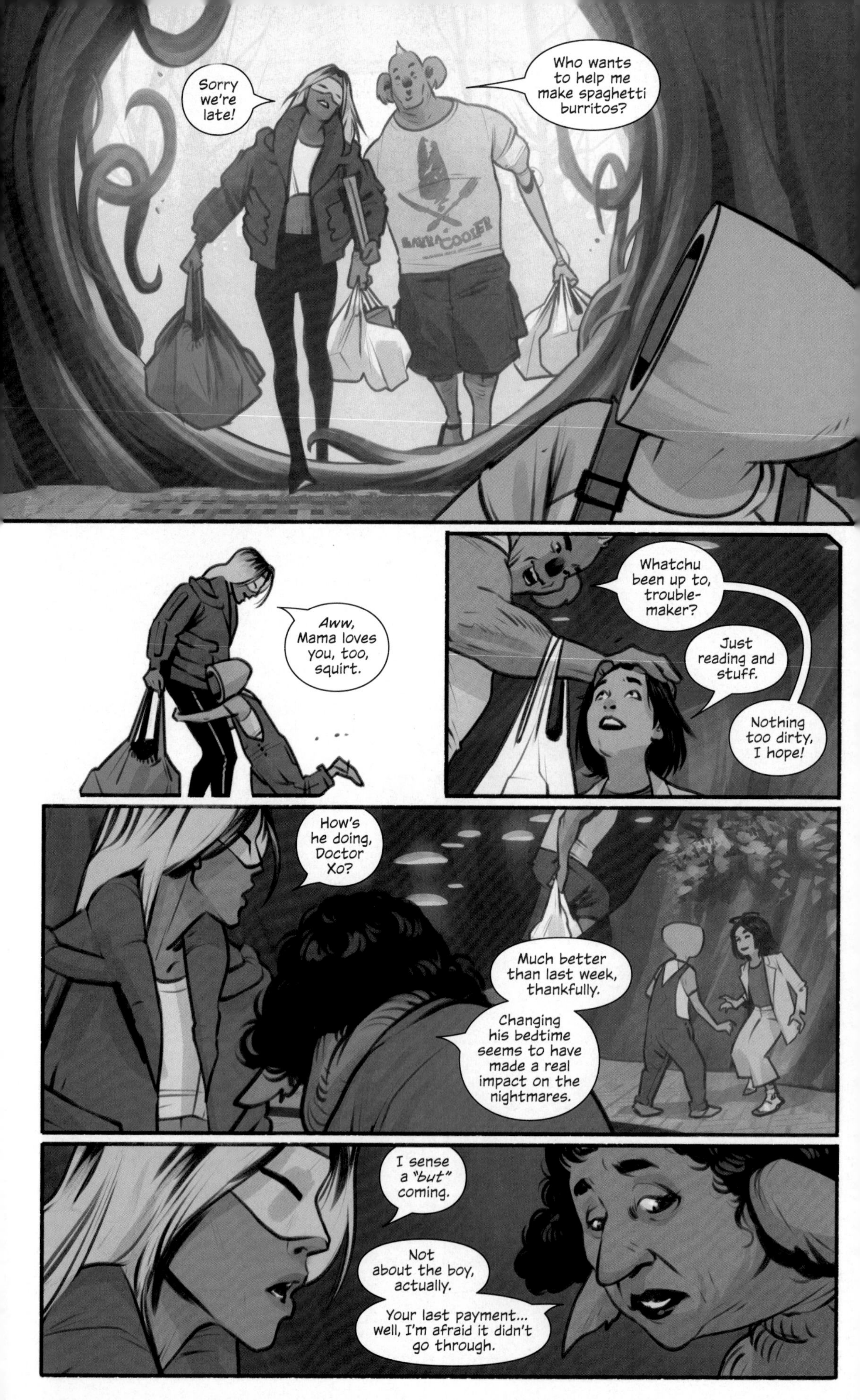
Sorry we're late!
Who wants to help me make spaghetti burritos?
Aww, Mama loves you, too, squirt.
Whatchu been up to, trouble-maker?
Just reading and stuff.
Nothing too dirty, I hope!
How's he doing, Doctor Xo?
Much better than last week, thankfully.
Changing his bedtime seems to have made a real impact on the nightmares.
I sense a *"but"* coming.
Not about the boy, actually.
Your last payment... well, I'm afraid it didn't go through.

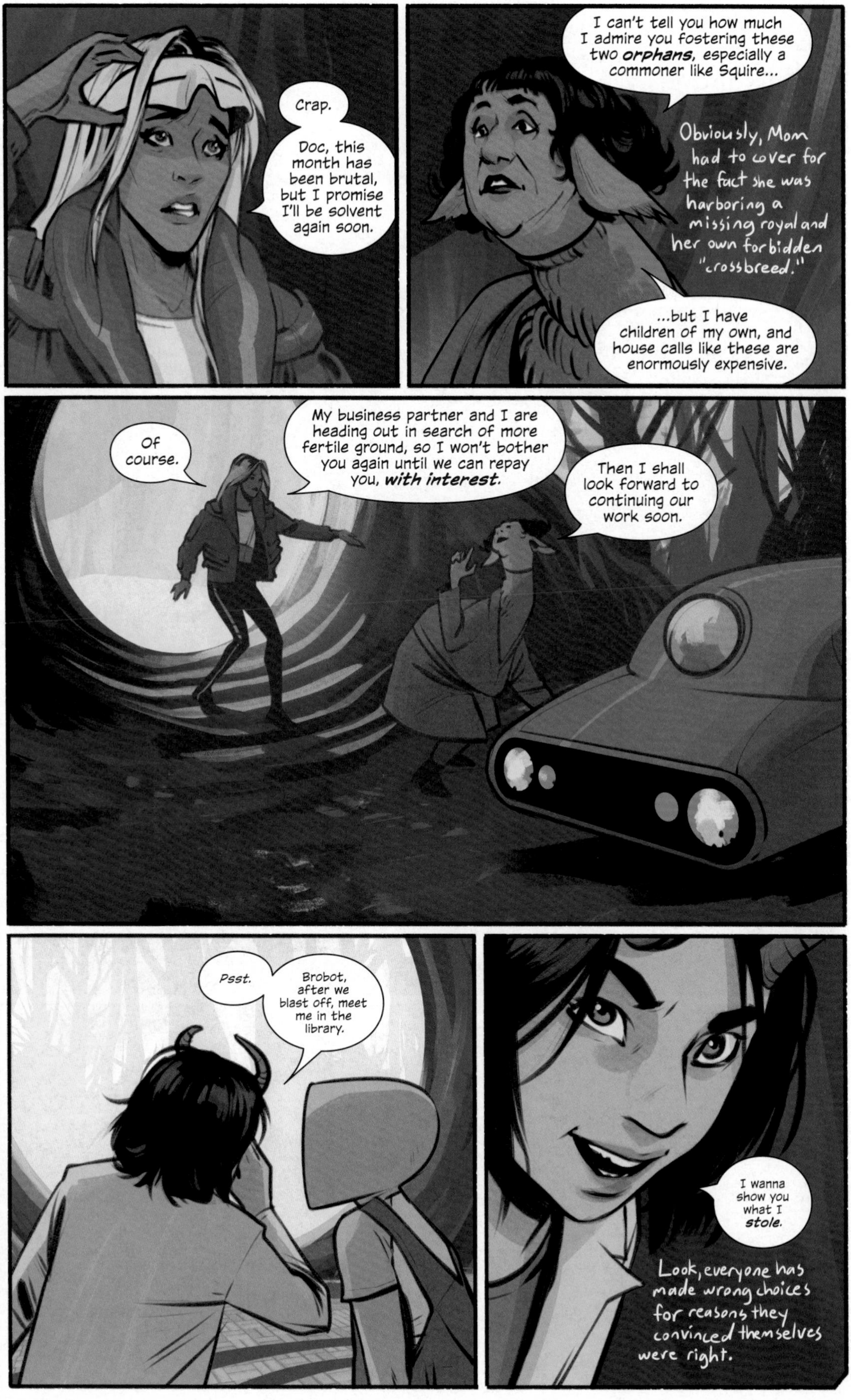

Crap.
Doc, this month has been brutal, but I promise I'll be solvent again soon.
I can't tell you how much I admire you fostering these two **orphans**, especially a commoner like Squire...
Obviously, Mom had to cover for the fact she was harboring a missing royal and her own forbidden "crossbreed."
...but I have children of my own, and house calls like these are enormously expensive.
Of course.
My business partner and I are heading out in search of more fertile ground, so I won't bother you again until we can repay you, **with interest**.
Then I shall look forward to continuing our work soon.
Psst.
Brobot, after we blast off, meet me in the library.
I wanna show you what I **stole**.
Look, everyone has made wrong choices for reasons they convinced themselves were right.

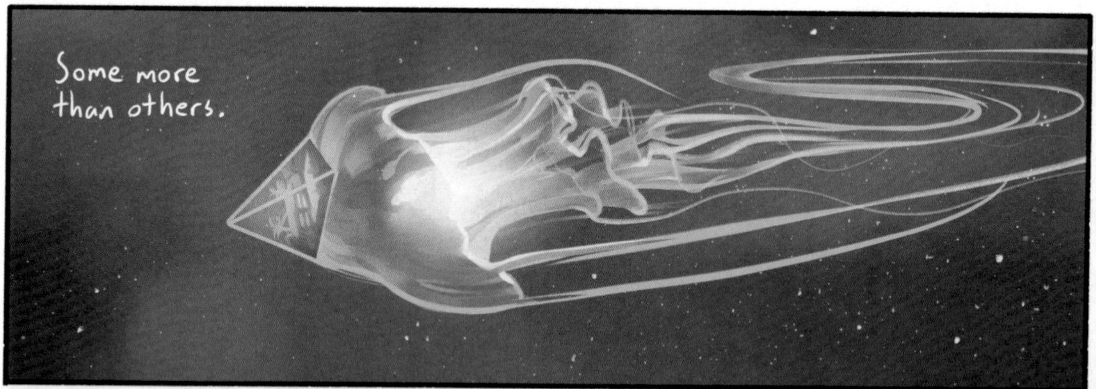
Some more
than others.

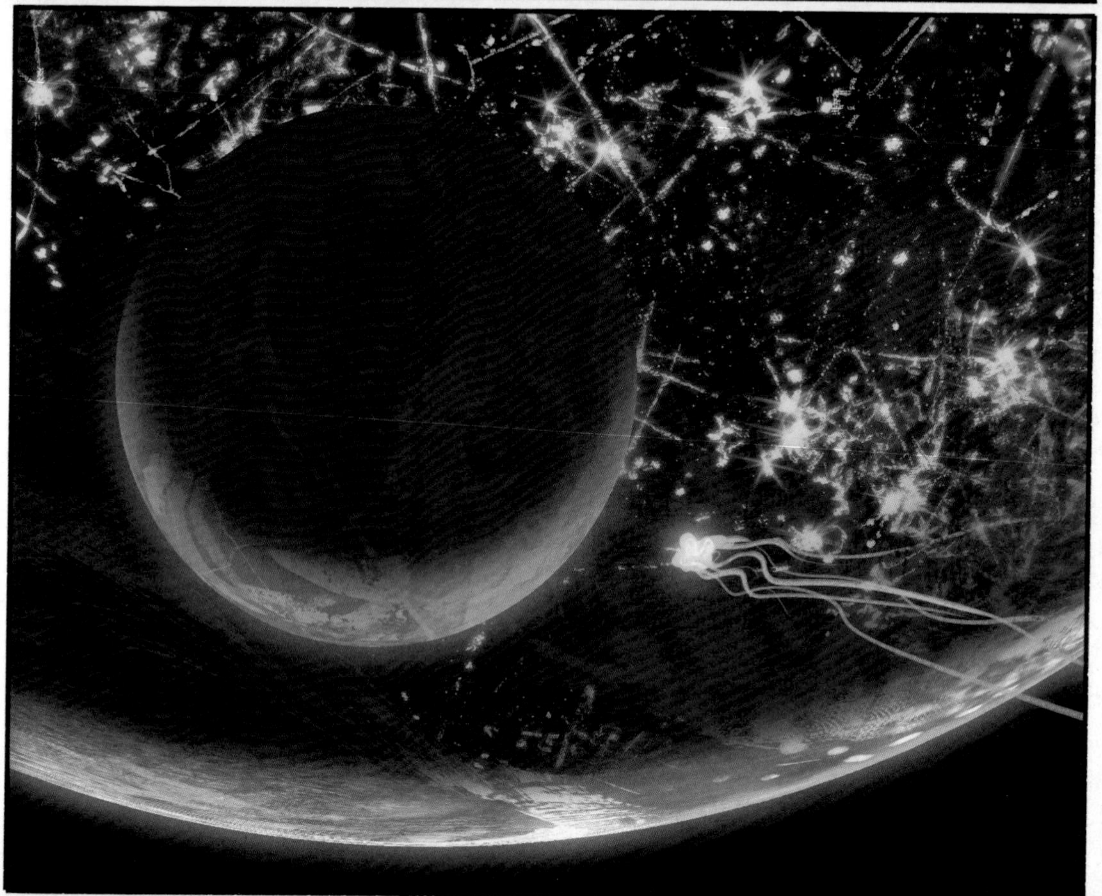

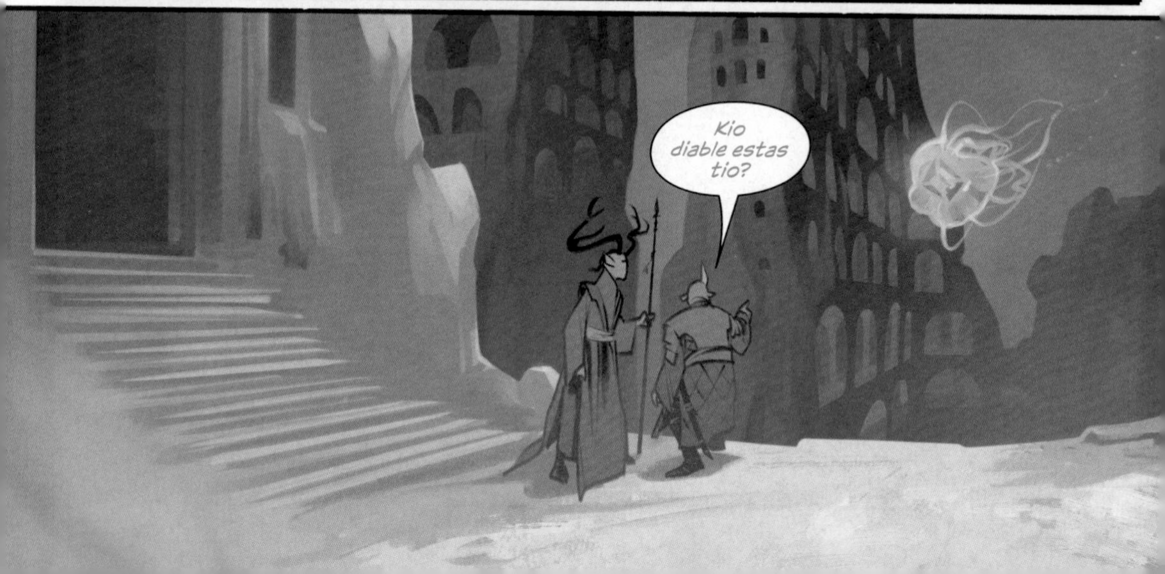
Kio diable estas tio?

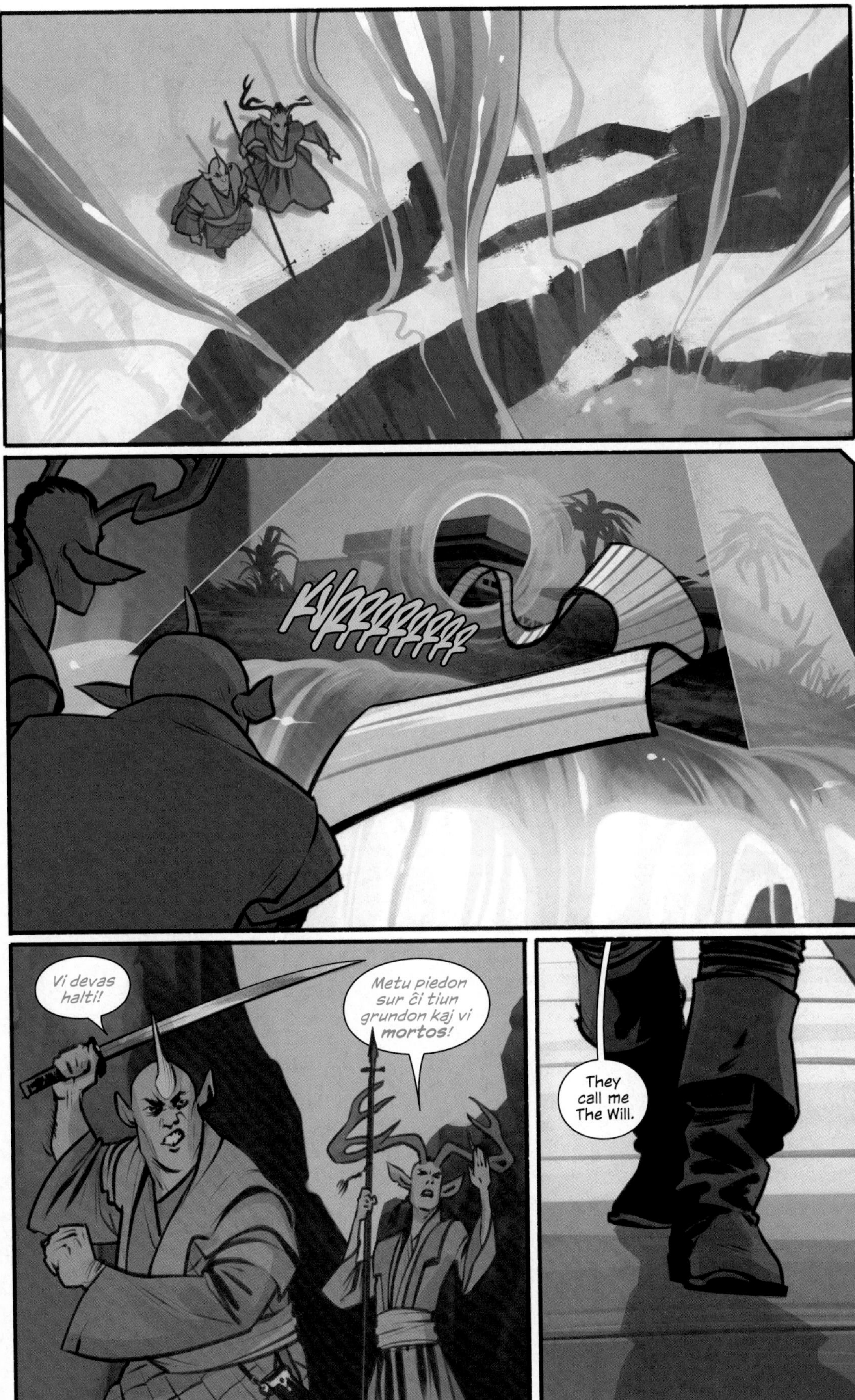
KVRRRRRRRR
Vi devas halti!
Metu piedon sur ĉi tiun grundon kaj vi mortos!
They call me The Will.

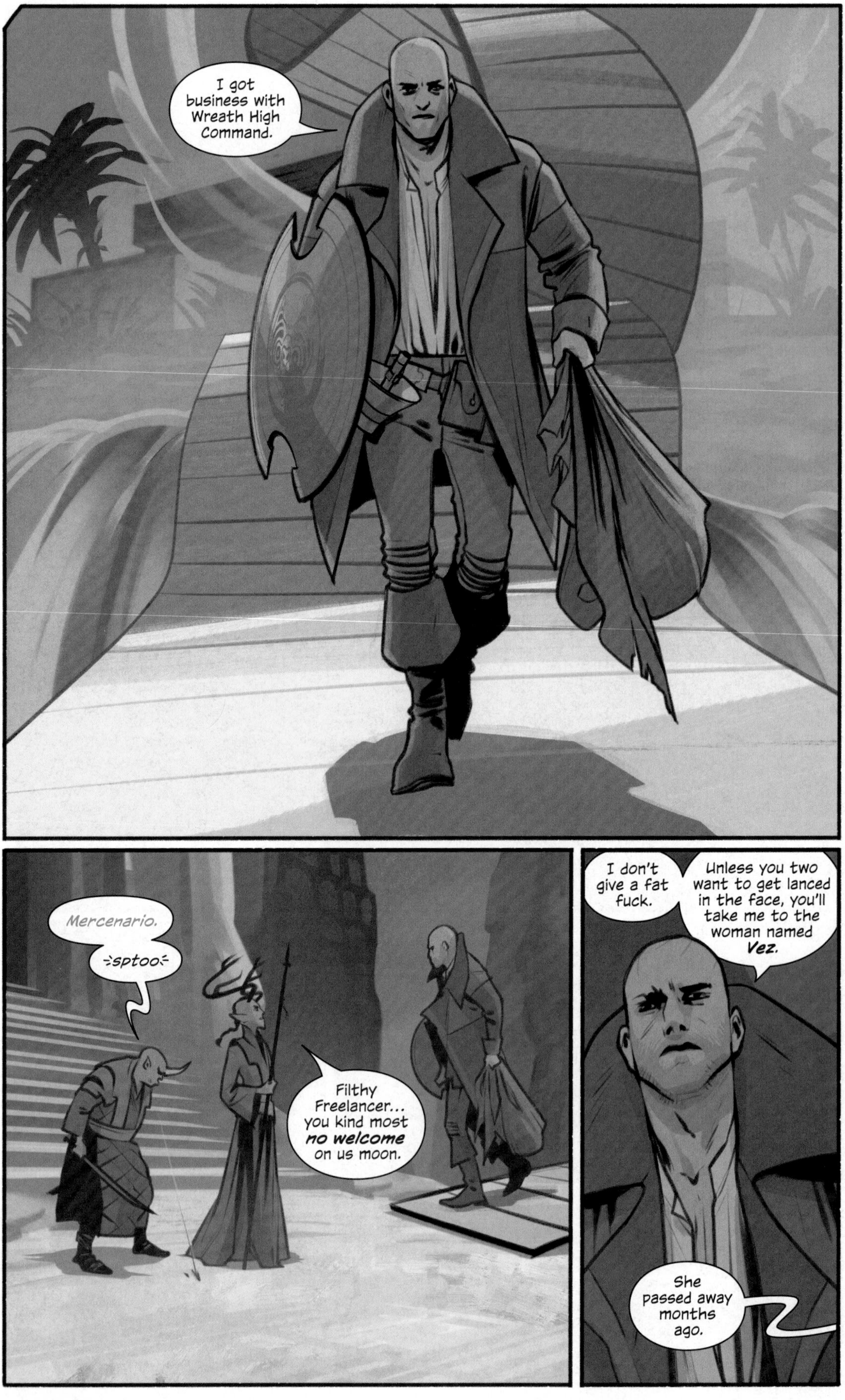
I got business with Wreath High Command.
Mercenario.
-sptoo-
Filthy Freelancer... you kind most **no welcome** on us moon.
I don't give a fat fuck.
Unless you two want to get lanced in the face, you'll take me to the woman named **Vez**.
She passed away months ago.

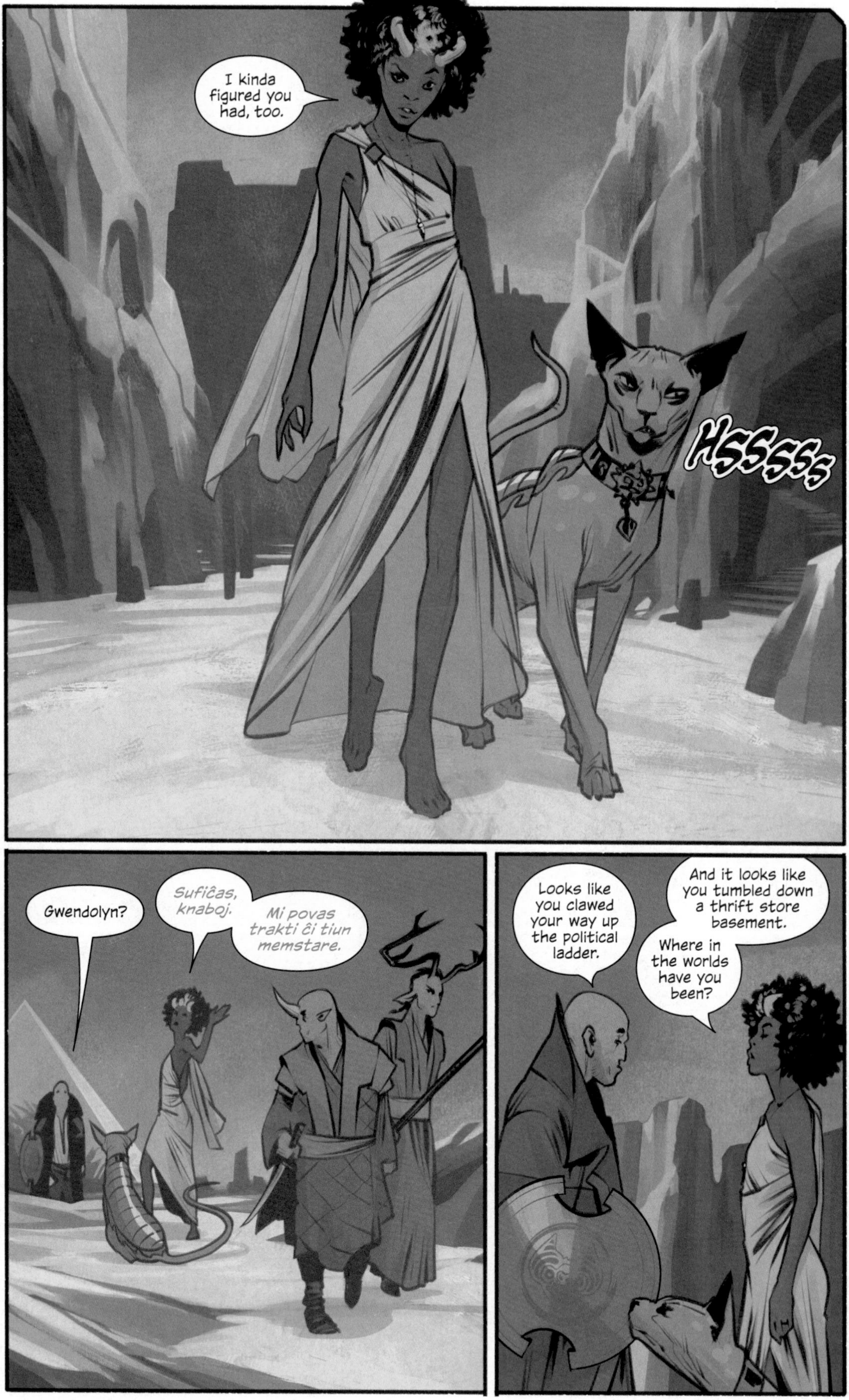
I kinda figured you had, too.
HSSSSS
Gwendolyn?
Suficâs, knaboj.
Mi povas trakti ĉi tiun memstare.
Looks like you clawed your way up the political ladder.
And it looks like you tumbled down a thrift store basement.
Where in the worlds have you been?

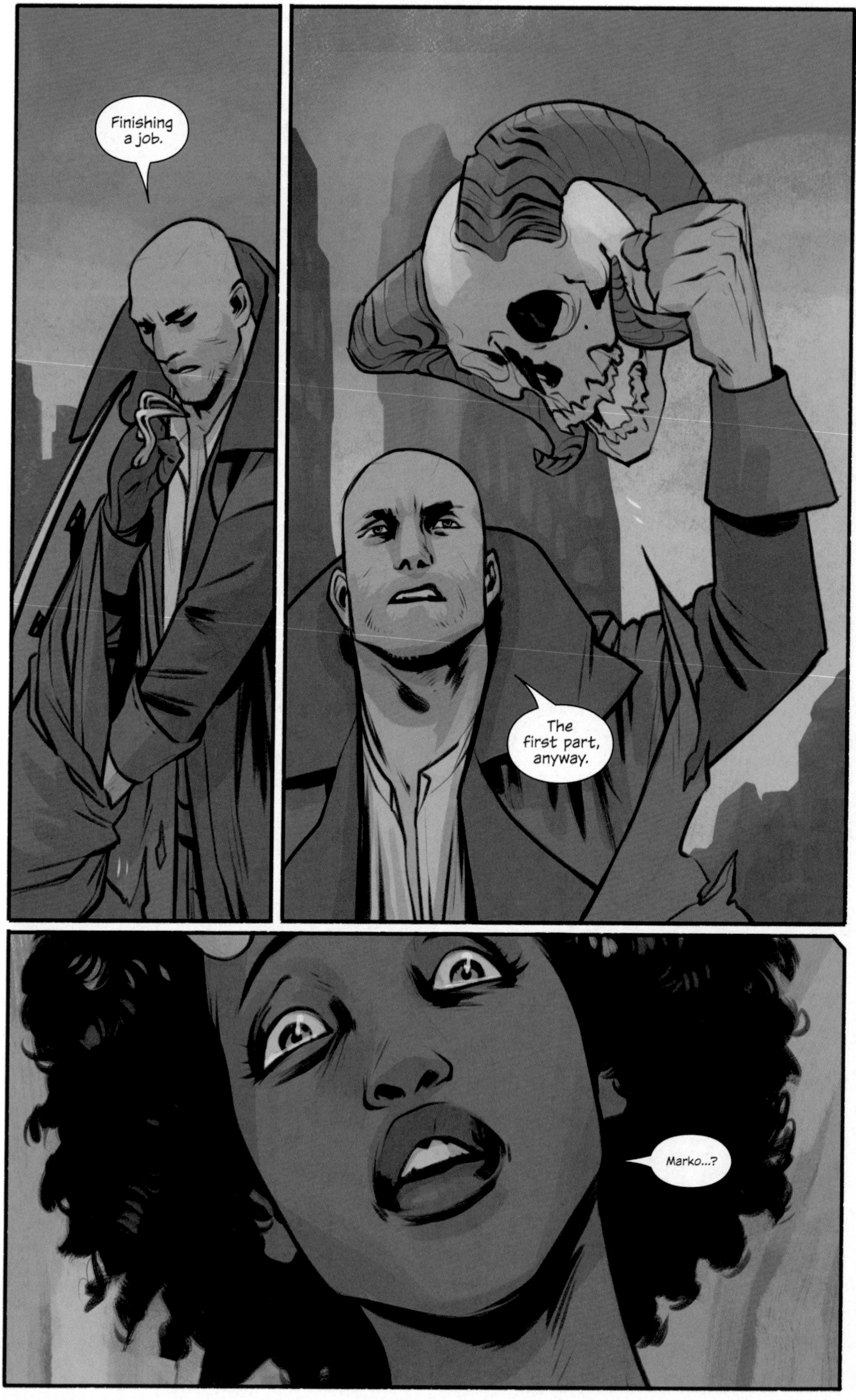
Finishing a job.
The first part, anyway.
Marko...?

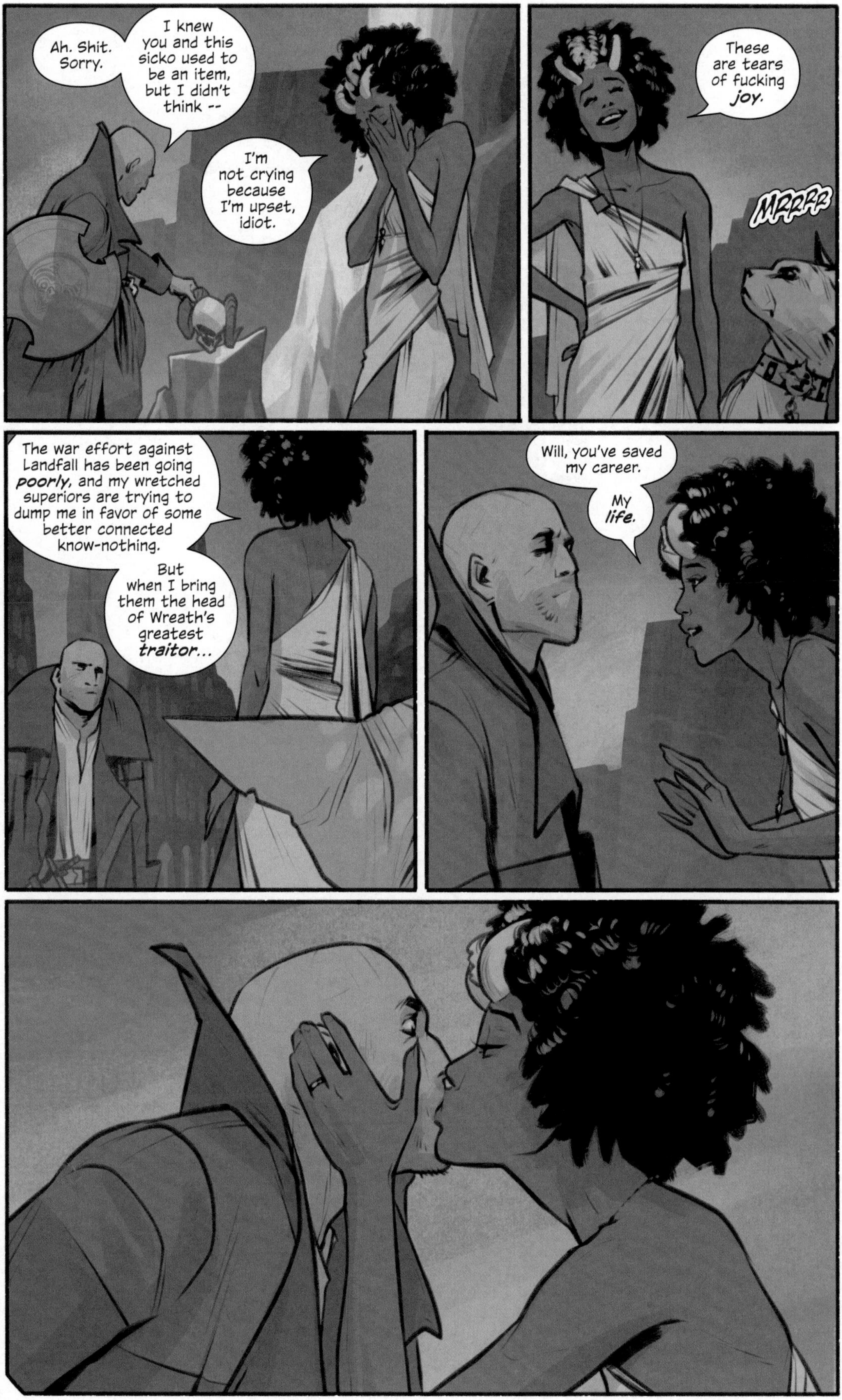
Ah. Shit. Sorry.
I knew you and this sicko used to be an item, but I didn't think --
I'm not crying because I'm upset, idiot.
These are tears of fucking *joy*.
MRRRR
The war effort against Landfall has been going *poorly*, and my wretched superiors are trying to dump me in favor of some better connected know-nothing.
But when I bring them the head of Wreath's greatest *traitor*...
Will, you've saved my career.
My *life*.

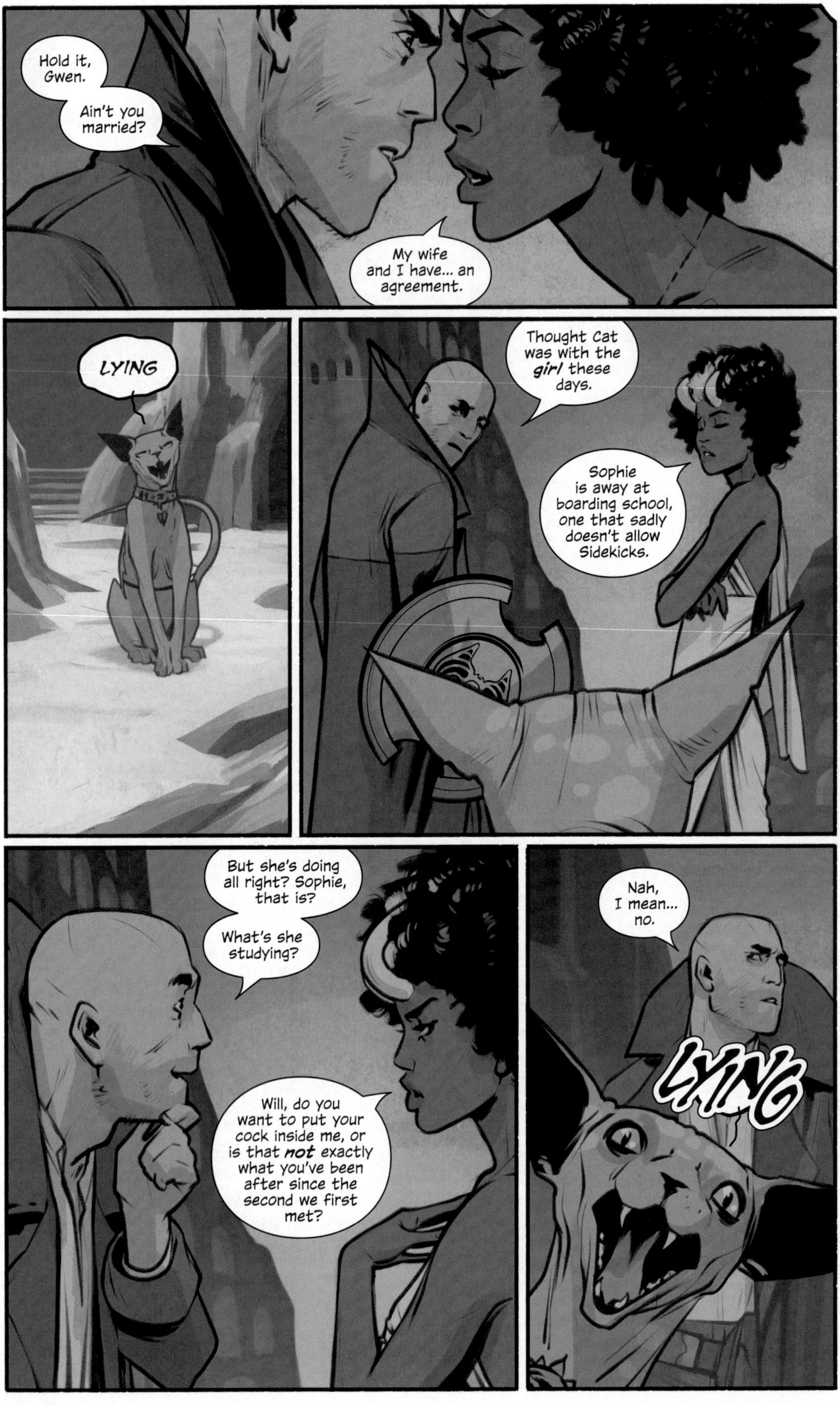

Hold it, Gwen.
Ain't you married?
My wife and I have... an agreement.
LYING
Thought Cat was with the *girl* these days.
Sophie is away at boarding school, one that sadly doesn't allow Sidekicks.
But she's doing all right? Sophie, that is?
What's she studying?
Will, do you want to put your cock inside me, or is that *not* exactly what you've been after since the second we first met?
Nah, I mean... no.
LYING

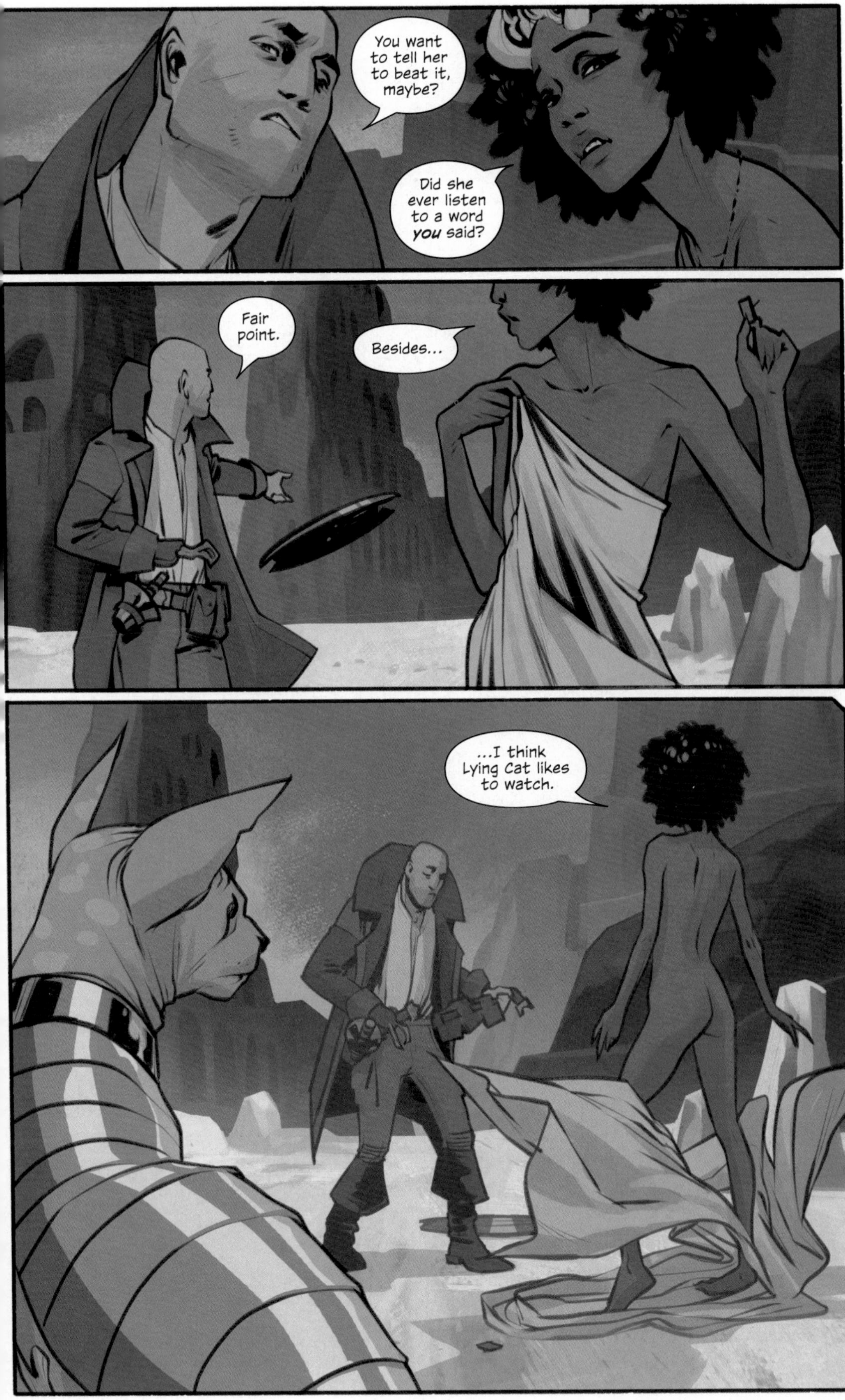
You want to tell her to beat it, maybe?
Did she ever listen to a word *you* said?
Fair point.
Besides...
...I think Lying Cat likes to watch.

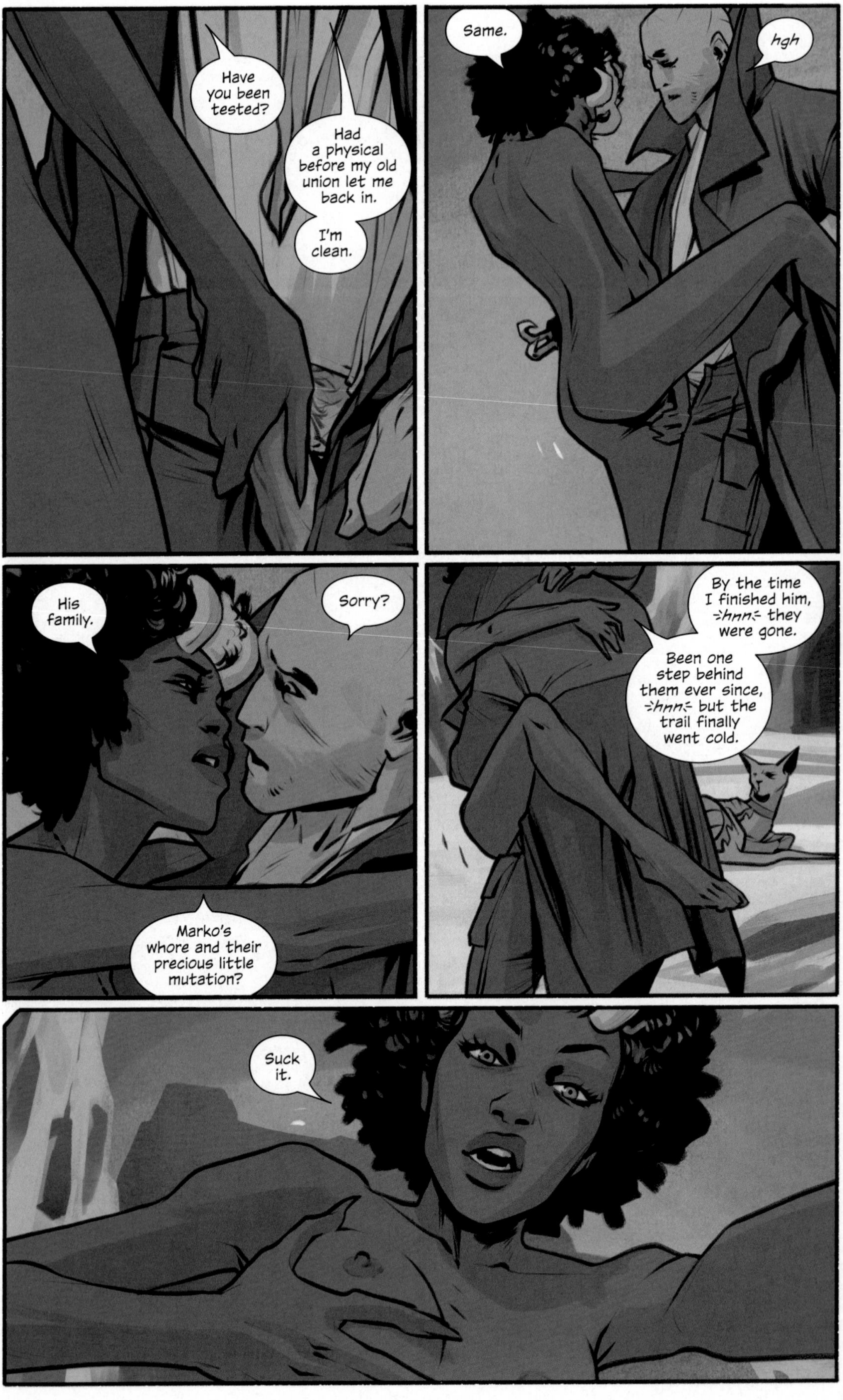
Have you been tested?
Had a physical before my old union let me back in.
I'm clean.
Same.
hgh
His family.
Sorry?
Marko's whore and their precious little mutation?
By the time I finished him, hnn they were gone.
Been one step behind them ever since, hnn but the trail finally went cold.
Suck it.

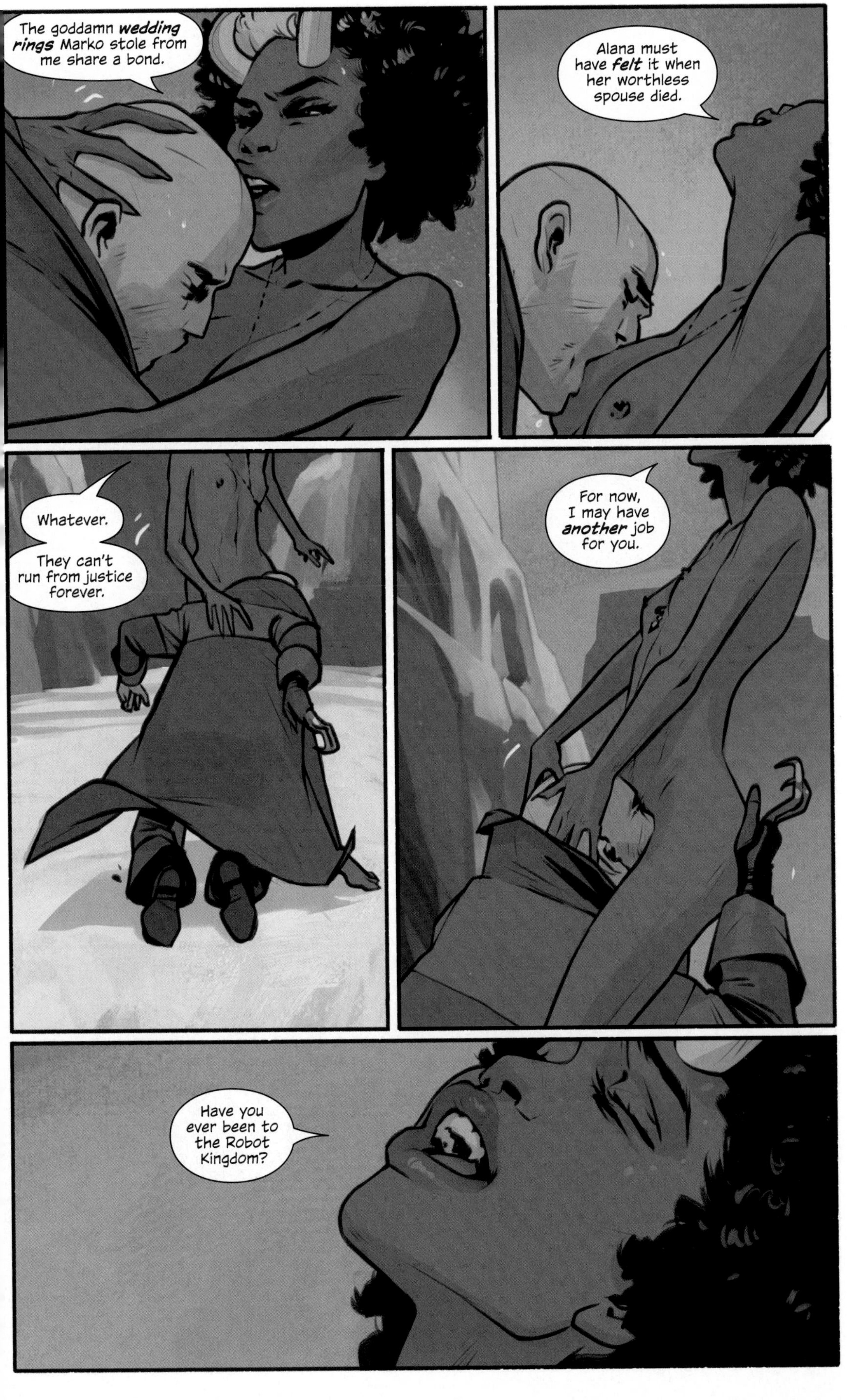
The goddamn *wedding rings* Marko stole from me share a bond.
Alana must have *felt* it when her worthless spouse died.
Whatever.
They can't run from justice forever.
For now, I may have *another* job for you.
Have you ever been to the Robot Kingdom?

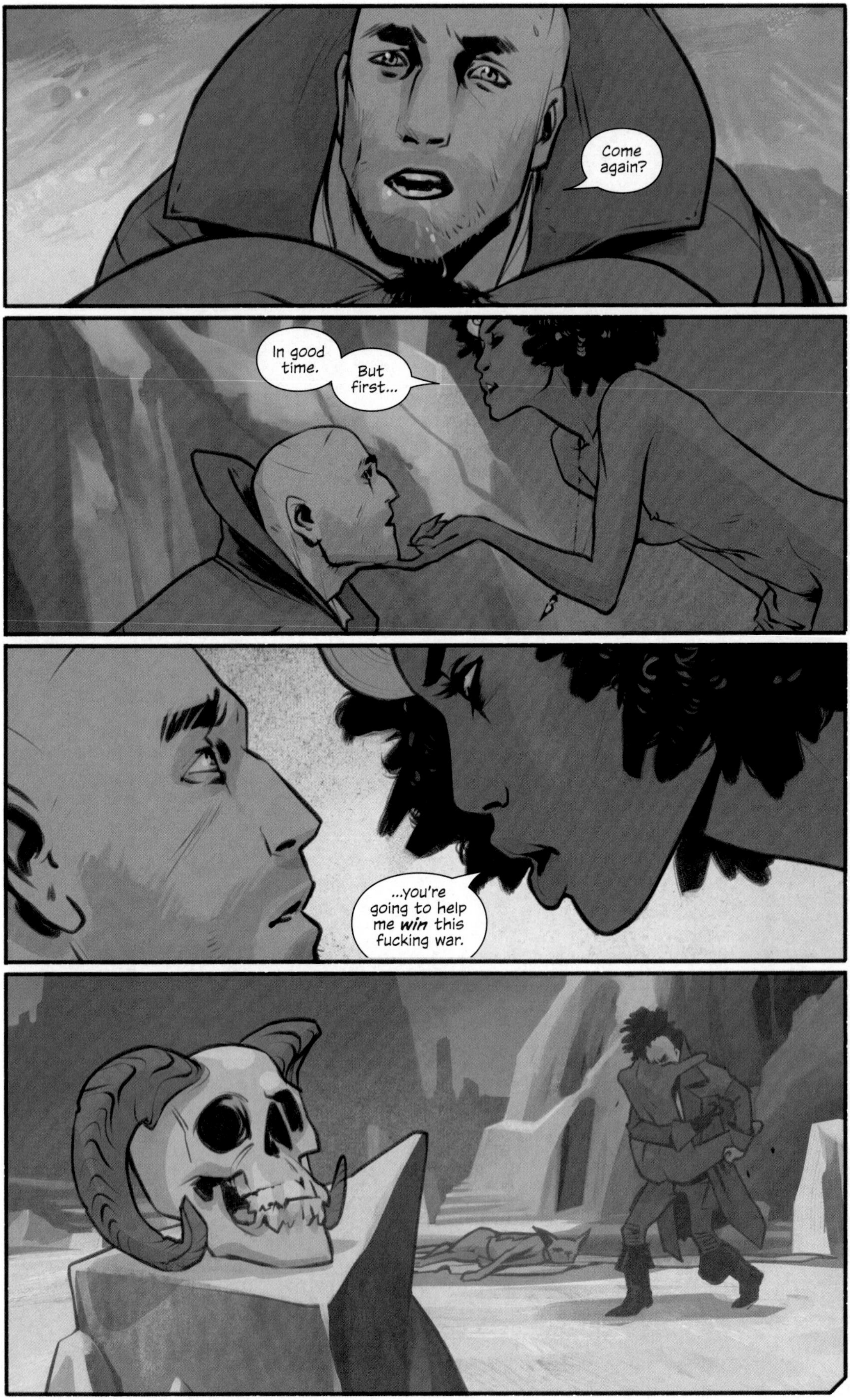

Come again?
In good time.
But first...
...you're going to help me **win** this fucking war.

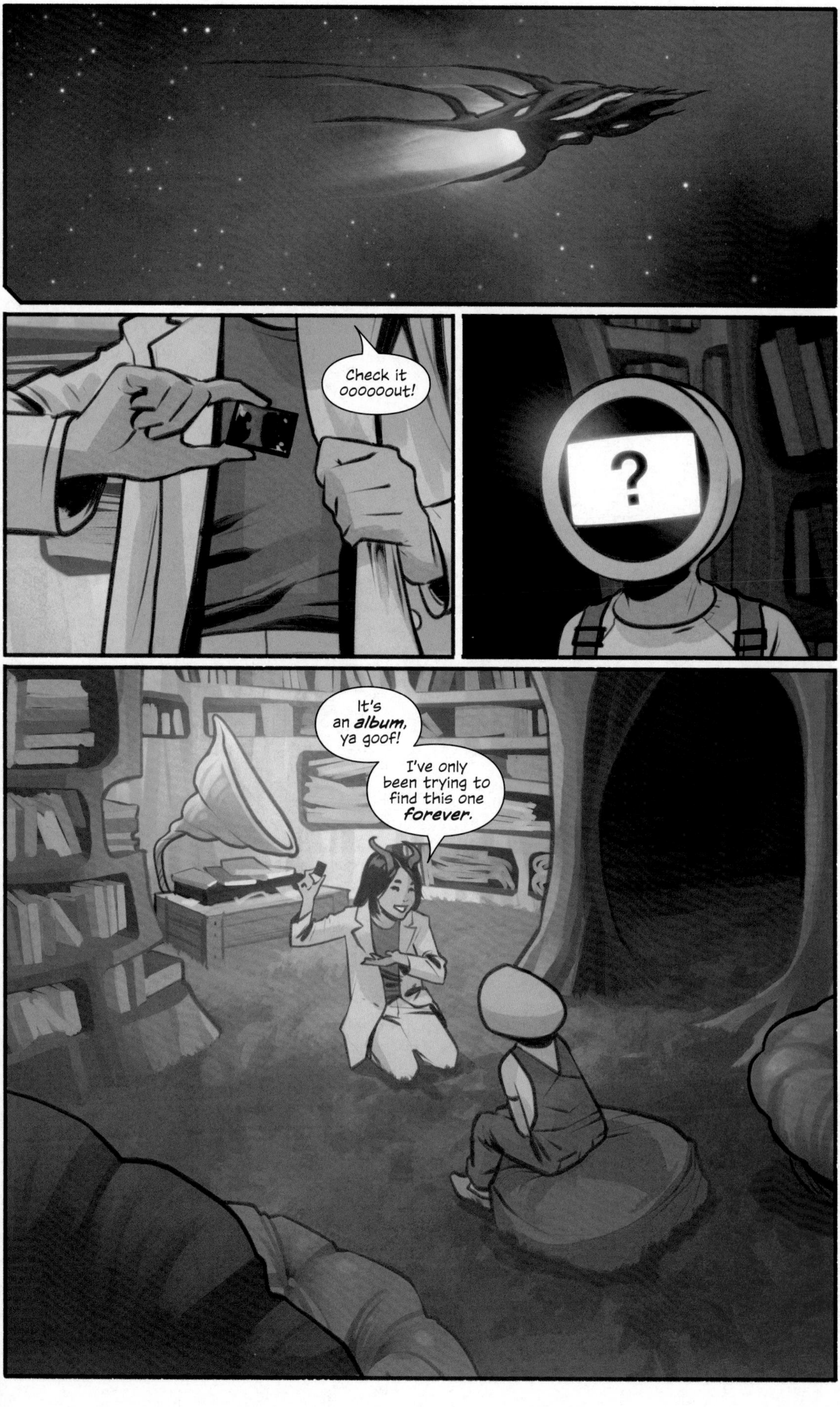
Check it oooooout!
?
It's an *album*, ya goof!
I've only been trying to find this one *forever*.

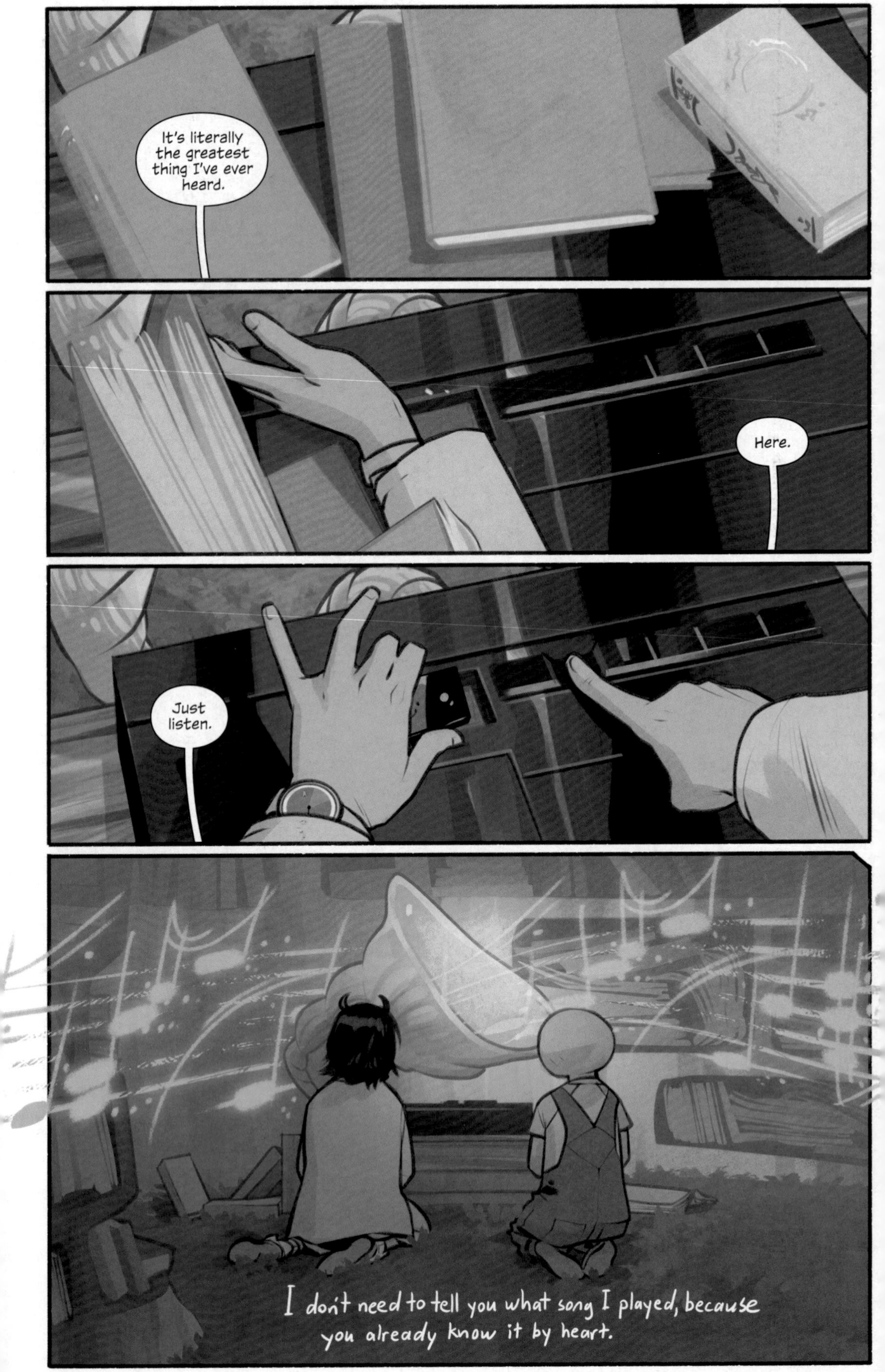

It's literally the greatest thing I've ever heard.
Here.
Just listen.
I don't need to tell you what song I played, because you already know it by heart.

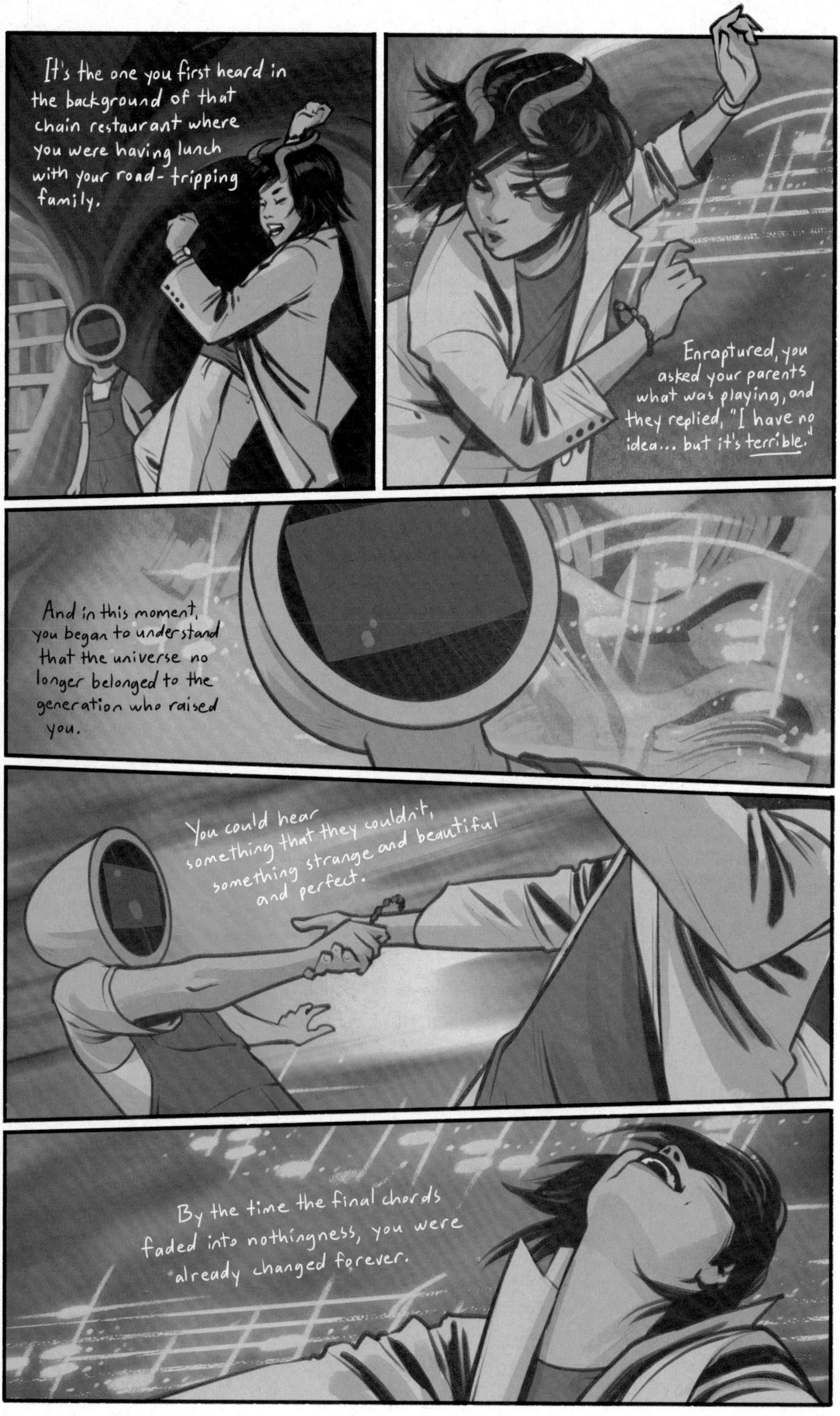
It's the one you first heard in the background of that chain restaurant where you were having lunch with your road-tripping family.
Enraptured, you asked your parents what was playing, and they replied, "I have no idea... but it's terrible."
And in this moment, you began to understand that the universe no longer belonged to the generation who raised you.
You could hear something that they couldn't, something strange and beautiful, something strange and perfect.
By the time the final chords faded into nothingness, you were already changed forever.

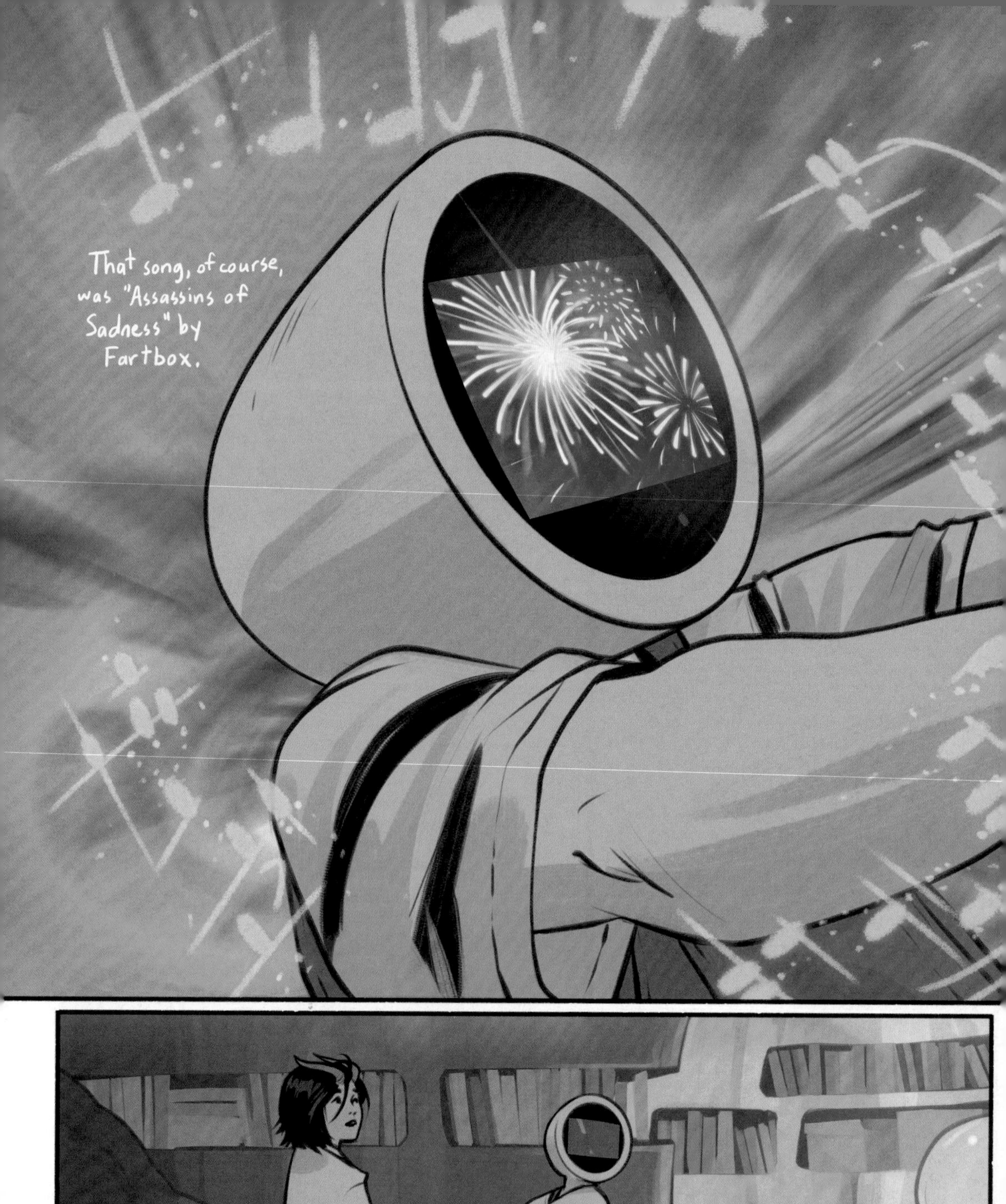
That song, of course, was "Assassins of Sadness" by Fartbox.

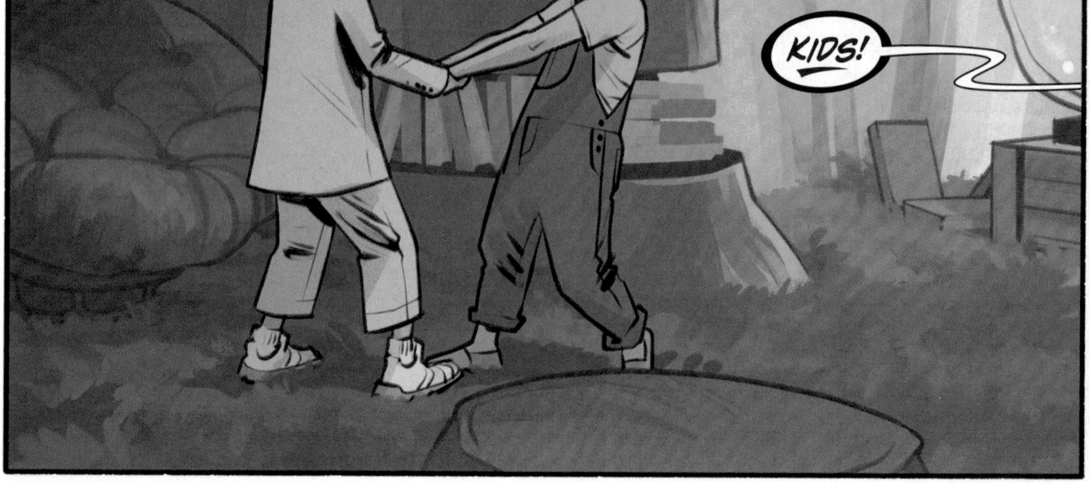
KIDS!

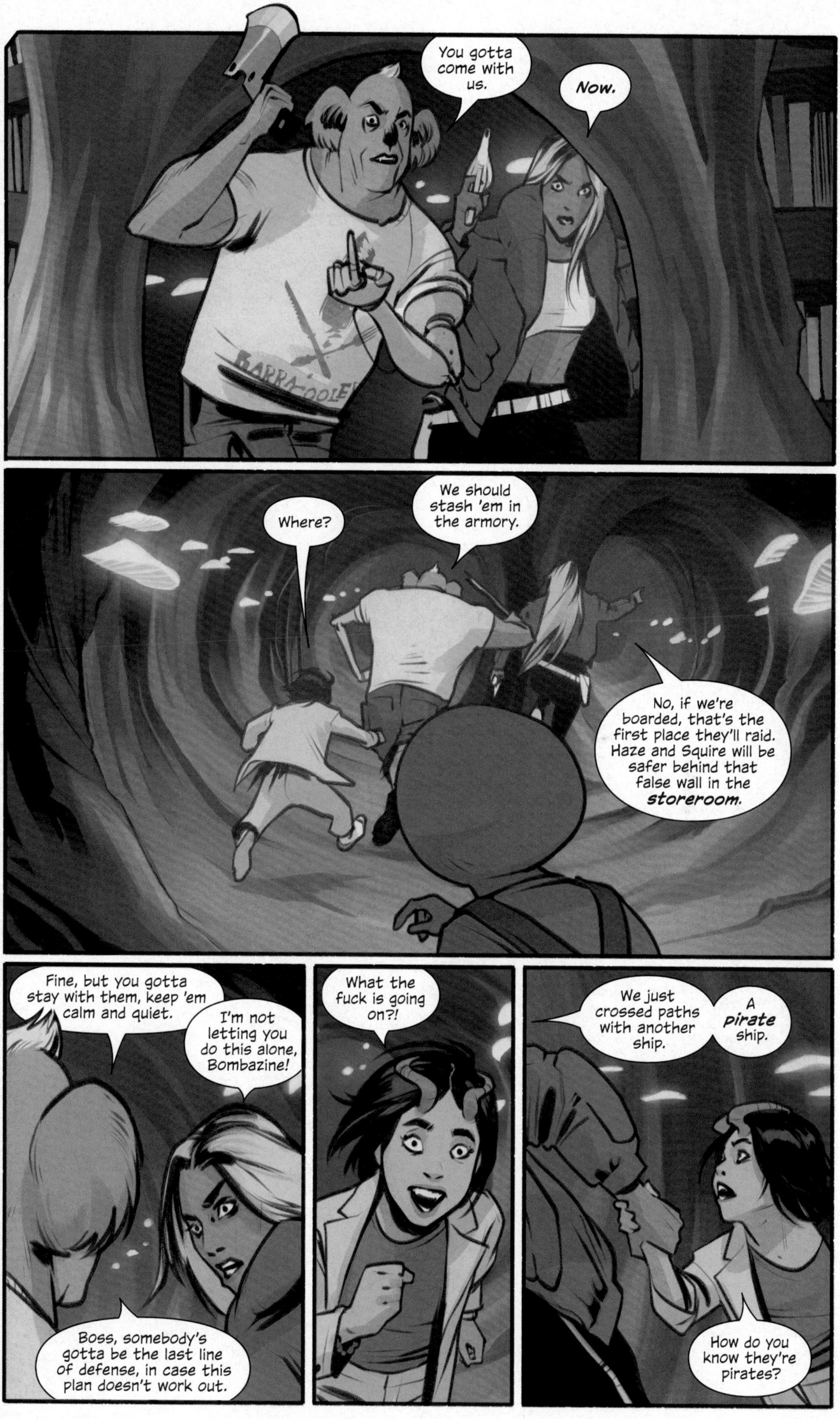
You gotta come with us.
Now.
Where?
We should stash 'em in the armory.
No, if we're boarded, that's the first place they'll raid. Haze and Squire will be safer behind that false wall in the storeroom.
Fine, but you gotta stay with them, keep 'em calm and quiet.
I'm not letting you do this alone, Bombazine!
Boss, somebody's gotta be the last line of defense, in case this plan doesn't work out.
What the fuck is going on?!
We just crossed paths with another ship.
A pirate ship.
How do you know they're pirates?

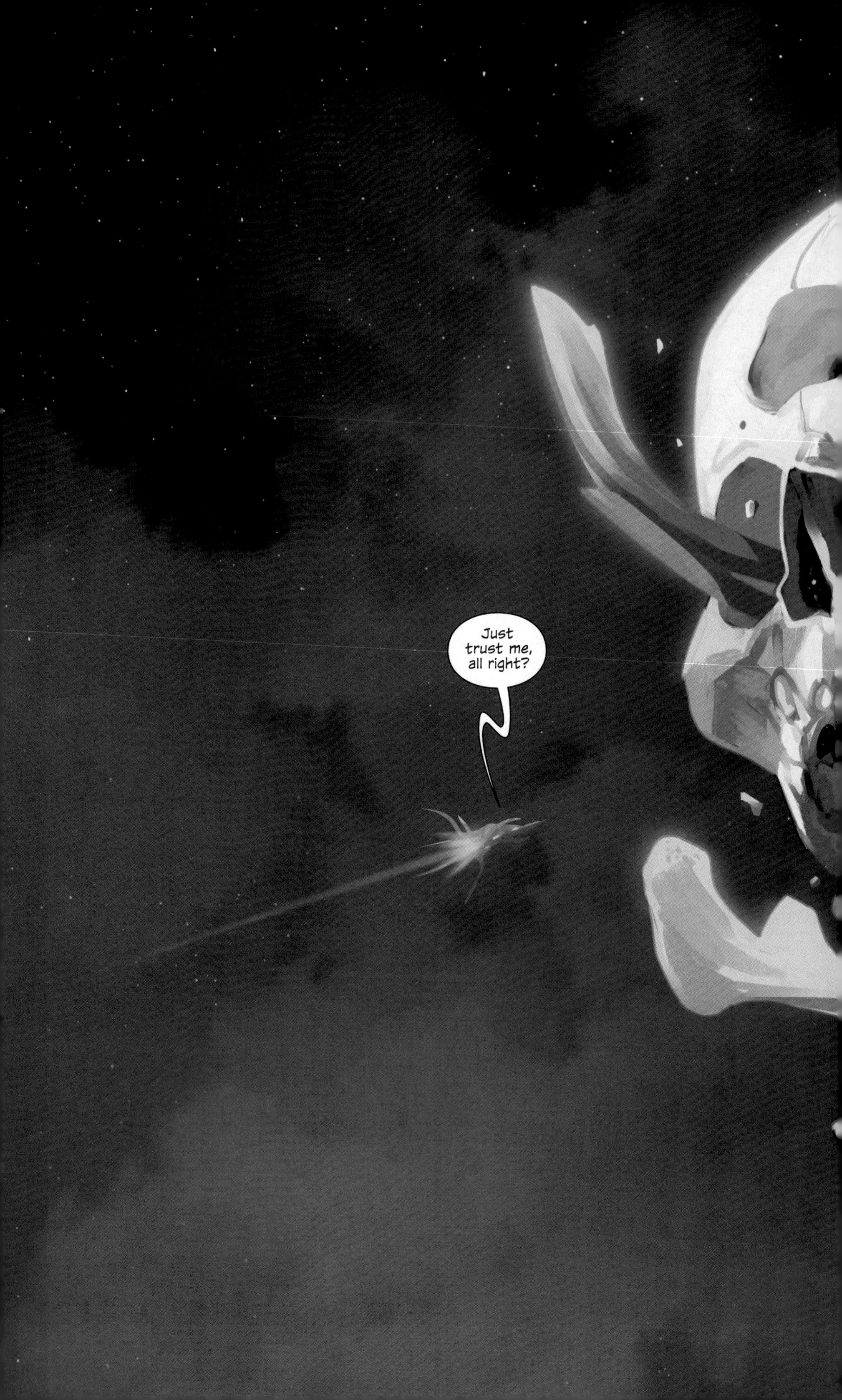
Just trust me, all right?

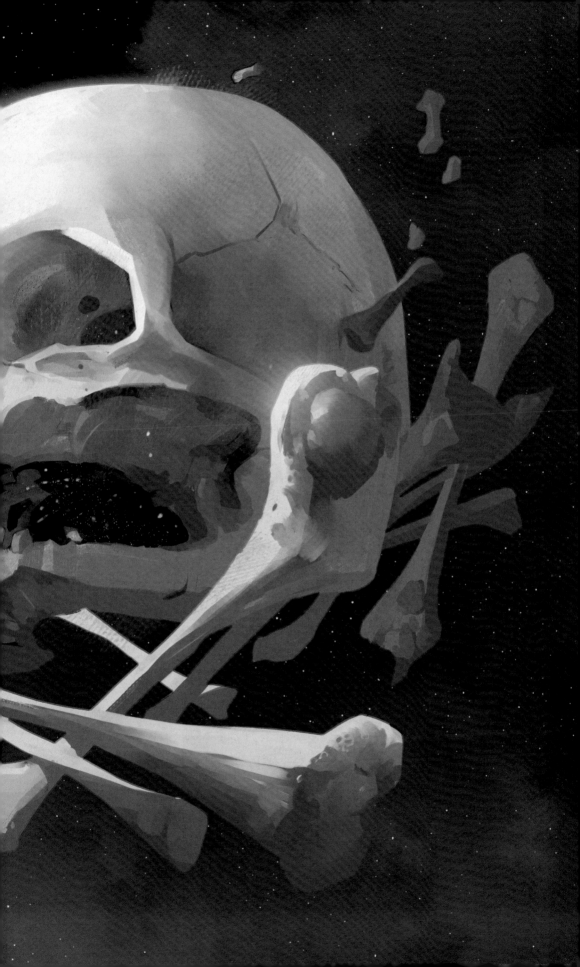

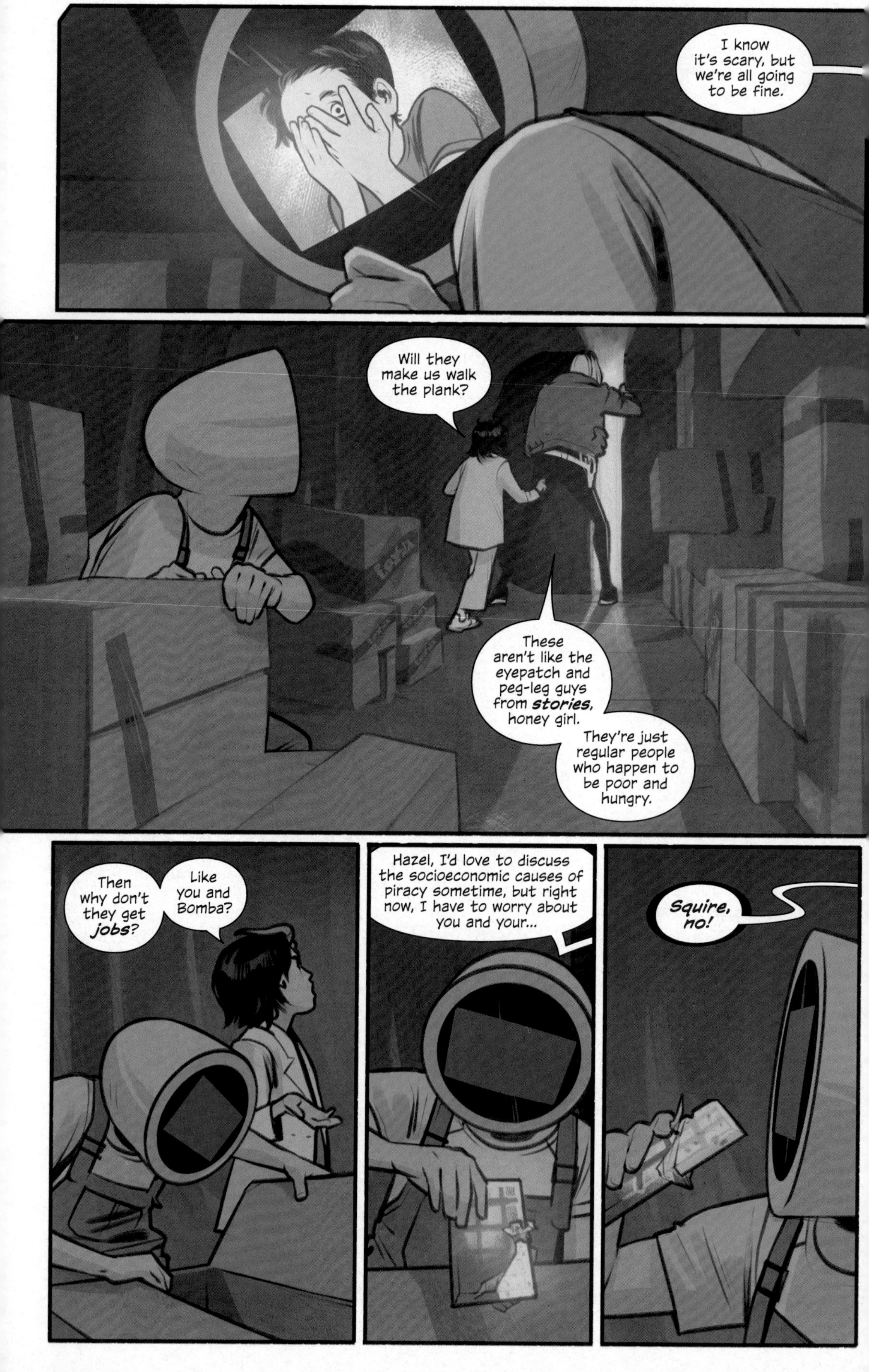
I know it's scary, but we're all going to be fine.
Will they make us walk the plank?
These aren't like the eyepatch and peg-leg guys from **stories**, honey girl.
They're just regular people who happen to be poor and hungry.
Then why don't they get **jobs**?
Like you and Bomba?
Hazel, I'd love to discuss the socioeconomic causes of piracy sometime, but right now, I have to worry about you and your...
Squire, no!

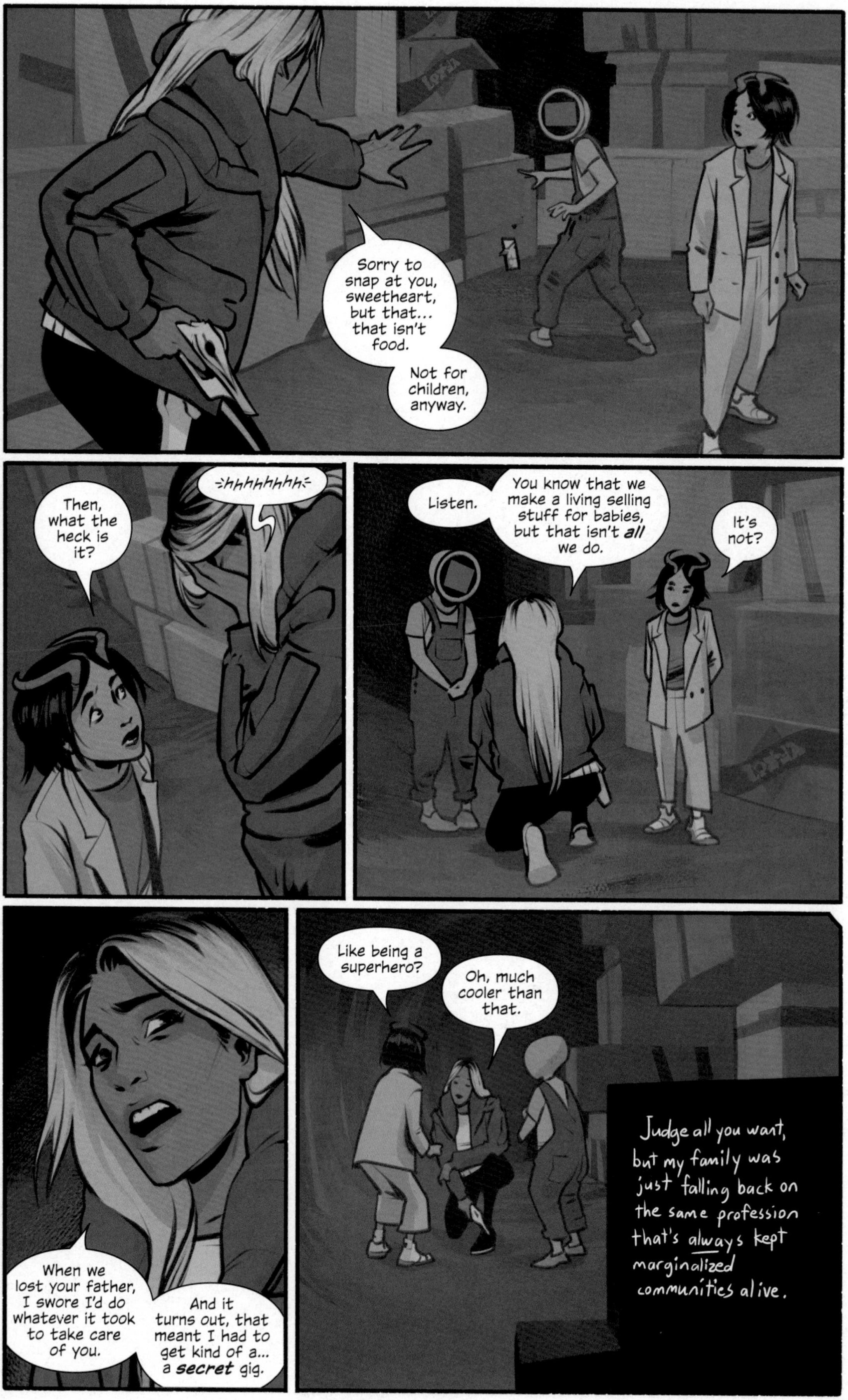
Sorry to snap at you, sweetheart, but that... that isn't food.
Not for children, anyway.
Then, what the heck is it?
hhhhhhhh
Listen.
You know that we make a living selling stuff for babies, but that isn't *all* we do.
It's not?
When we lost your father, I swore I'd do whatever it took to take care of you.
And it turns out, that meant I had to get kind of a... a **secret** gig.
Like being a superhero?
Oh, much cooler than that.
Judge all you want, but my family was just falling back on the same profession that's always kept marginalized communities alive.

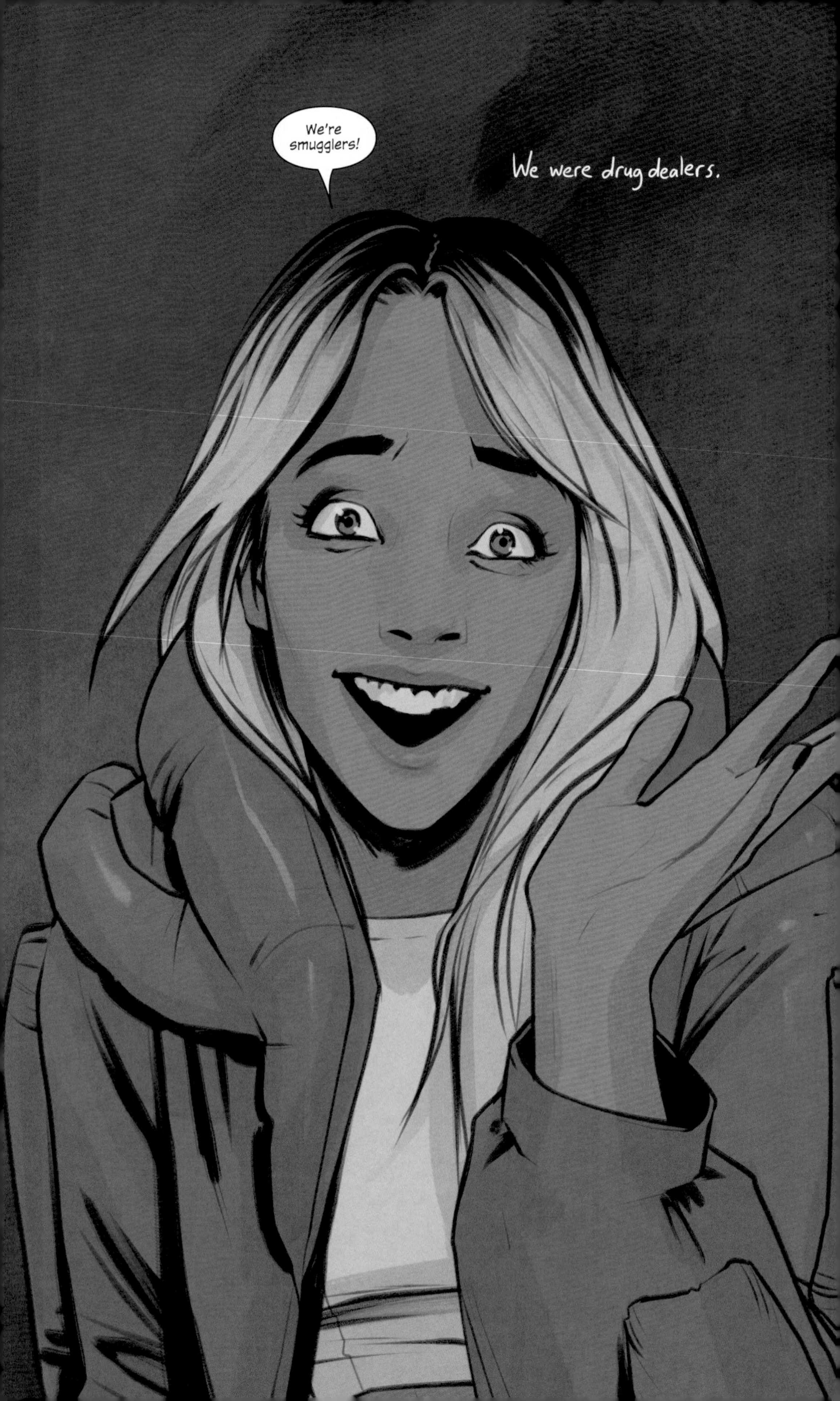
We're smugglers!
We were drug dealers.

end chapter fifty-five

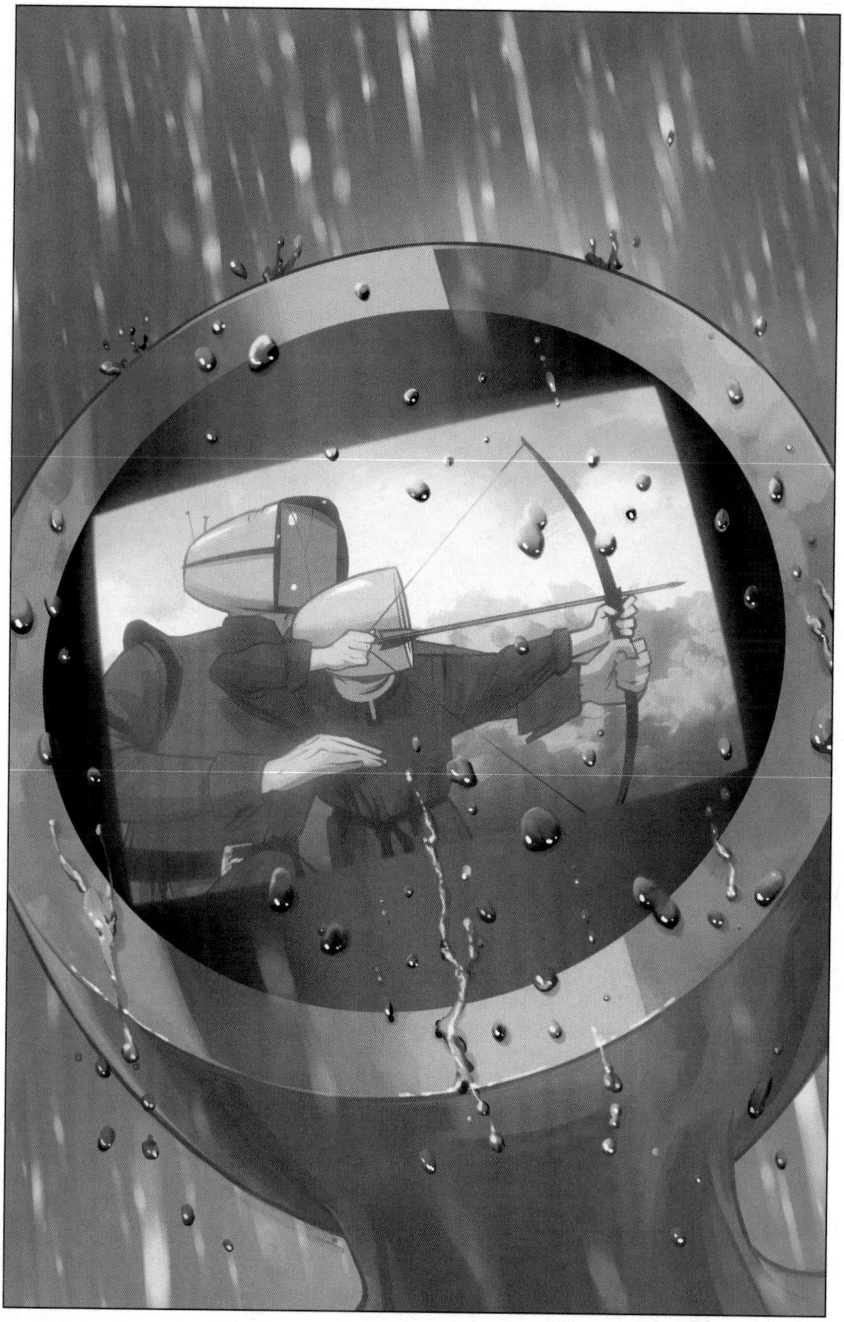

CHAPTER
FIFTY-SIX

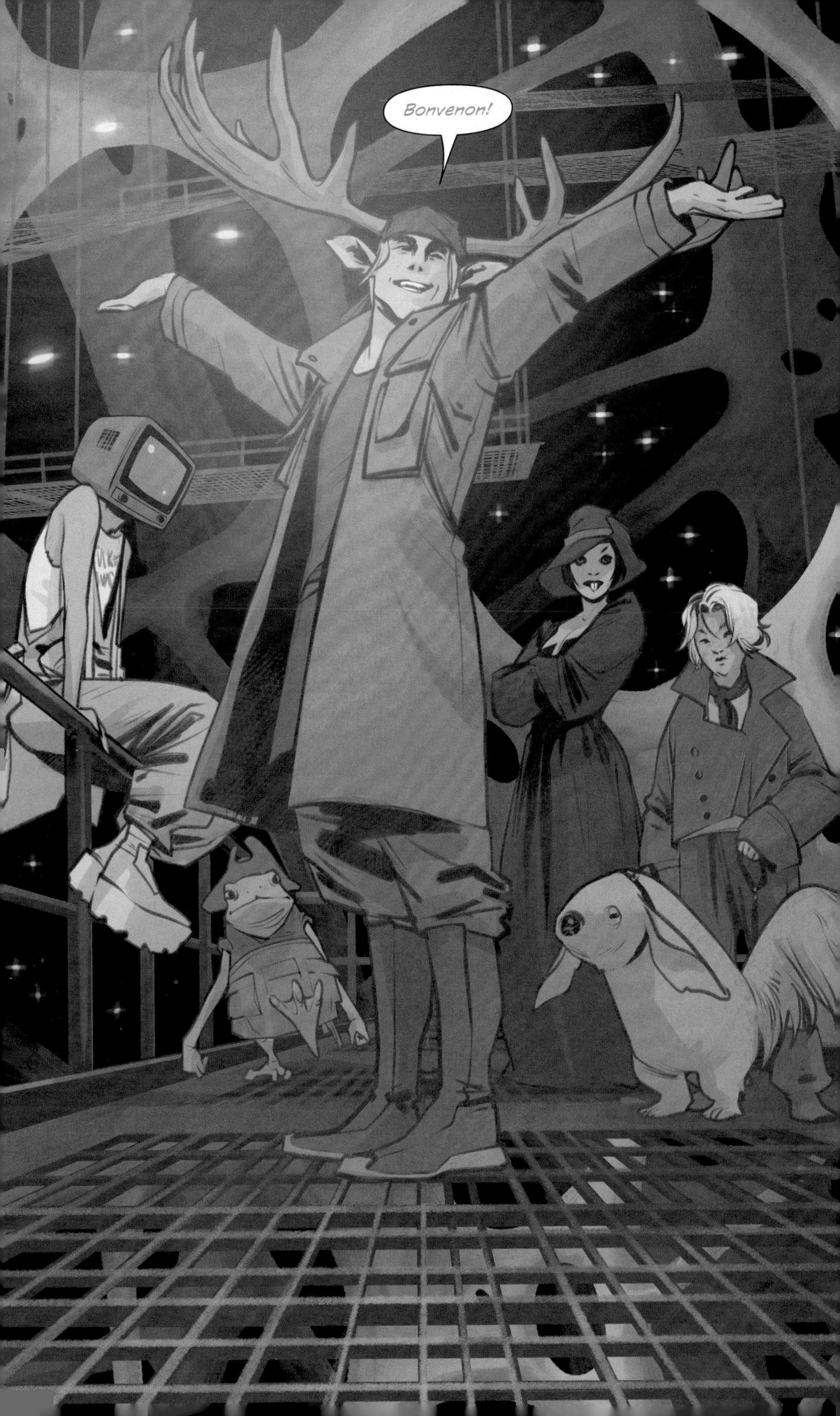
Bonvenon!

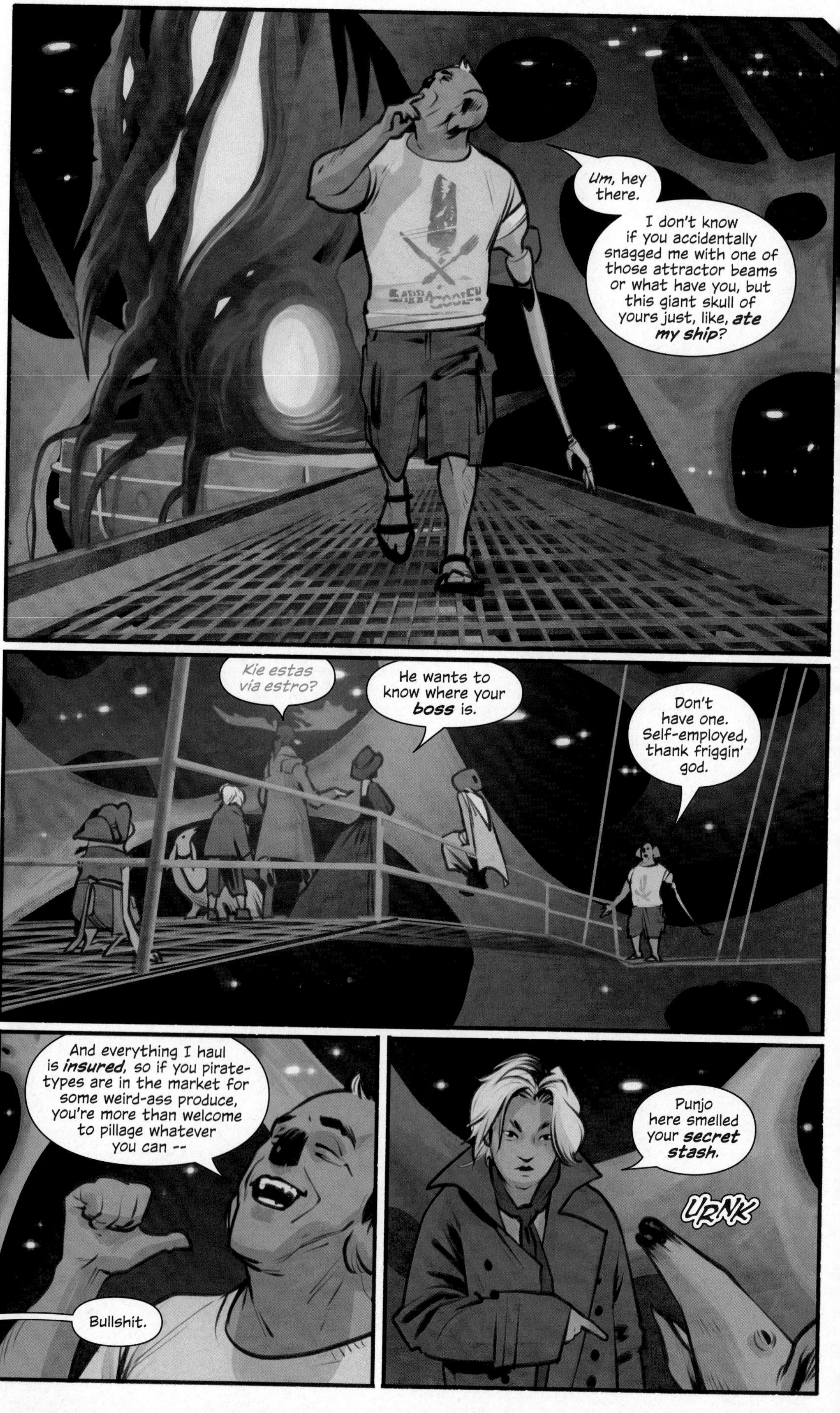

Um, hey there.
I don't know if you accidentally snagged me with one of those attractor beams or what have you, but this giant skull of yours just, like, ate my ship?
Kie estas via estro?
He wants to know where your boss is.
Don't have one. Self-employed, thank friggin' god.
And everything I haul is insured, so if you pirate-types are in the market for some weird-ass produce, you're more than welcome to pillage whatever you can --
Bullshit.
Punjo here smelled your secret stash.
URNK

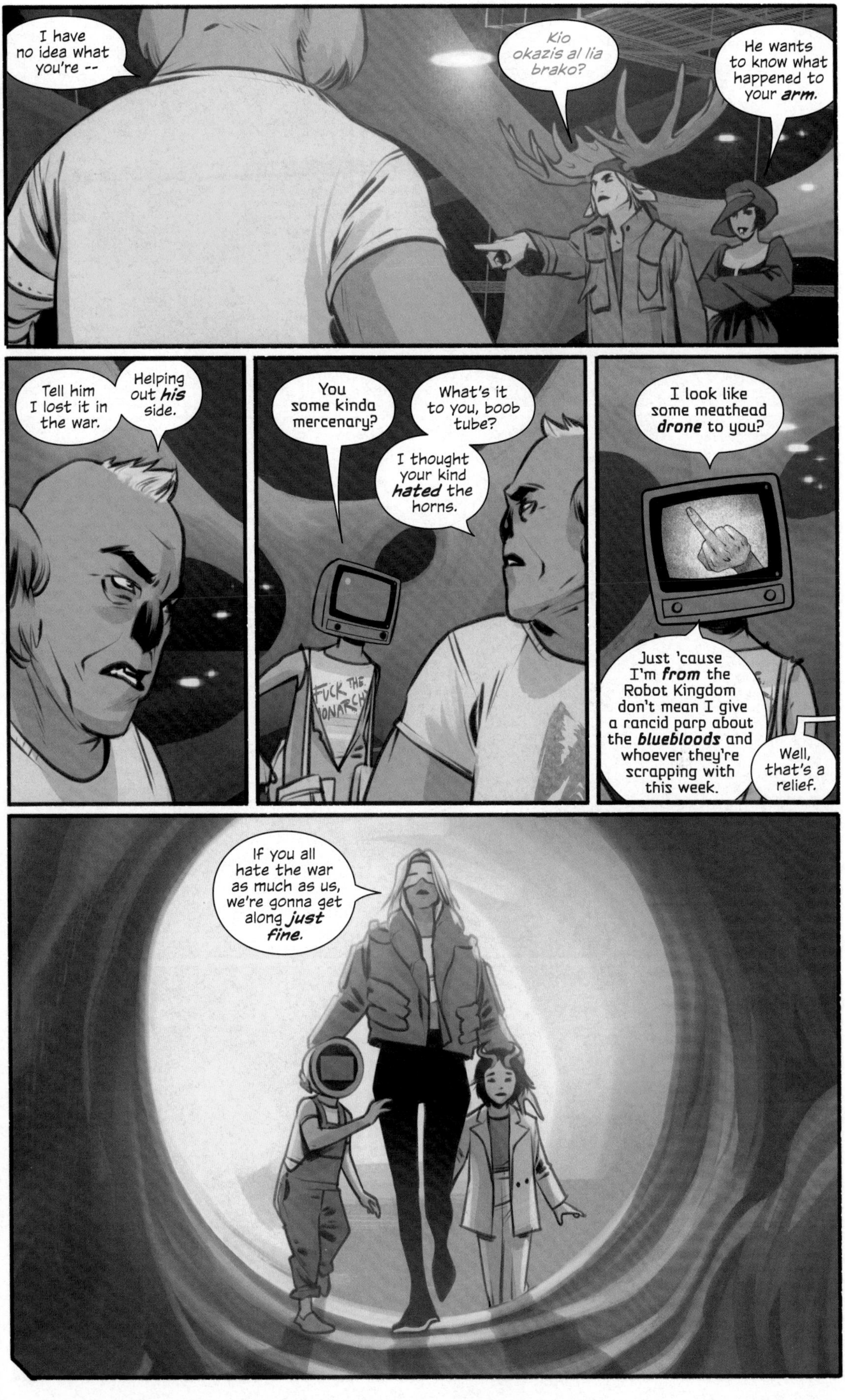
I have no idea what you're --
Kio okazis al lia brako?
He wants to know what happened to your *arm.*
Tell him I lost it in the war.
Helping out *his* side.
You some kinda mercenary?
What's it to you, boob tube?
I thought your kind *hated* the horns.
FUCK THE MONARCHY
I look like some meathead *drone* to you?
Just 'cause I'm *from* the Robot Kingdom don't mean I give a rancid parp about the *bluebloods* and whoever they're scrapping with this week.
Well, that's a relief.
If you all hate the war as much as us, we're gonna get along *just fine.*

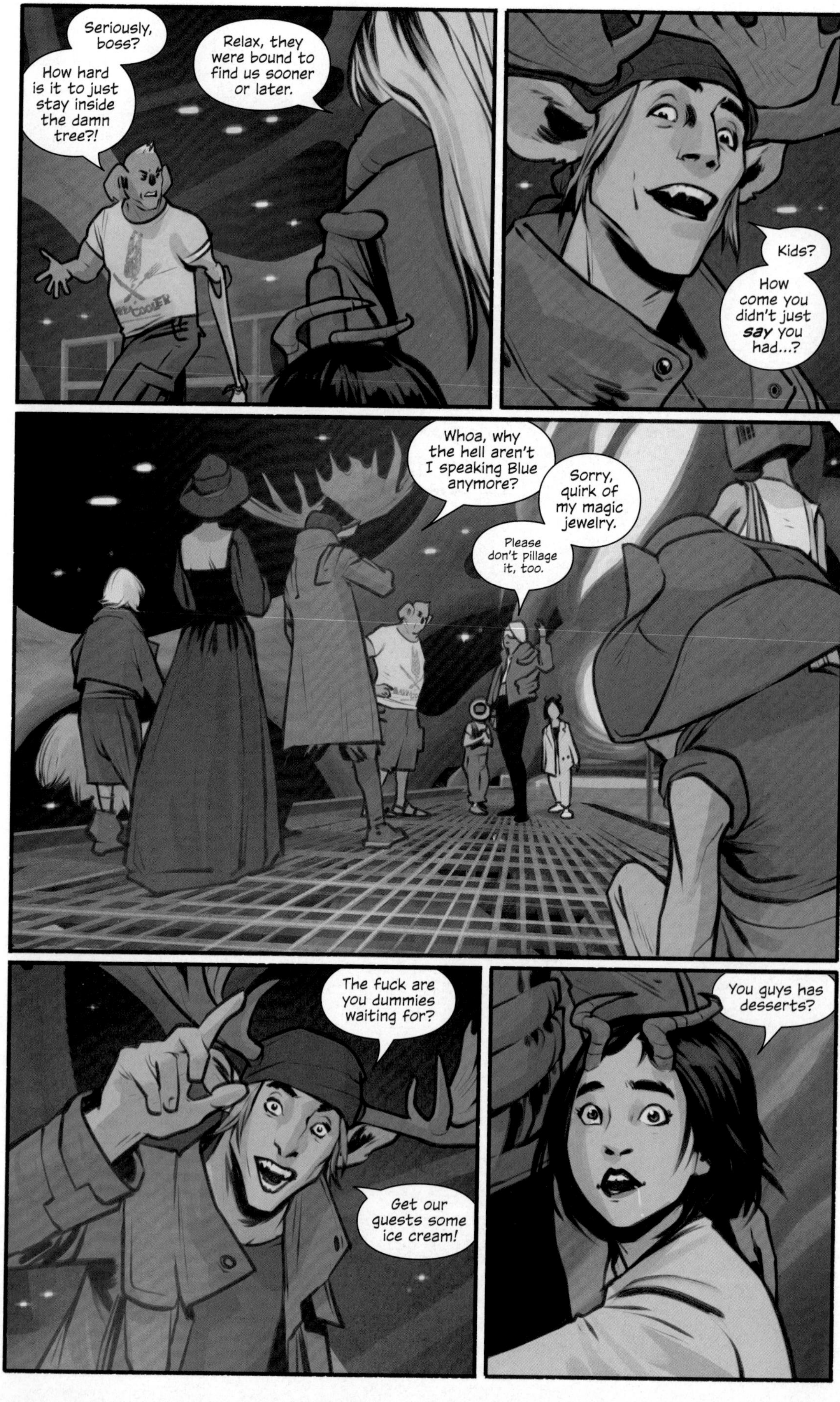

Seriously, boss?
How hard is it to just stay inside the damn tree?!
Relax, they were bound to find us sooner or later.
Kids?
How come you didn't just *say* you had...?
Whoa, why the hell aren't I speaking Blue anymore?
Sorry, quirk of my magic jewelry.
Please don't pillage it, too.
The fuck are you dummies waiting for?
Get our guests some ice cream!
You guys has desserts?

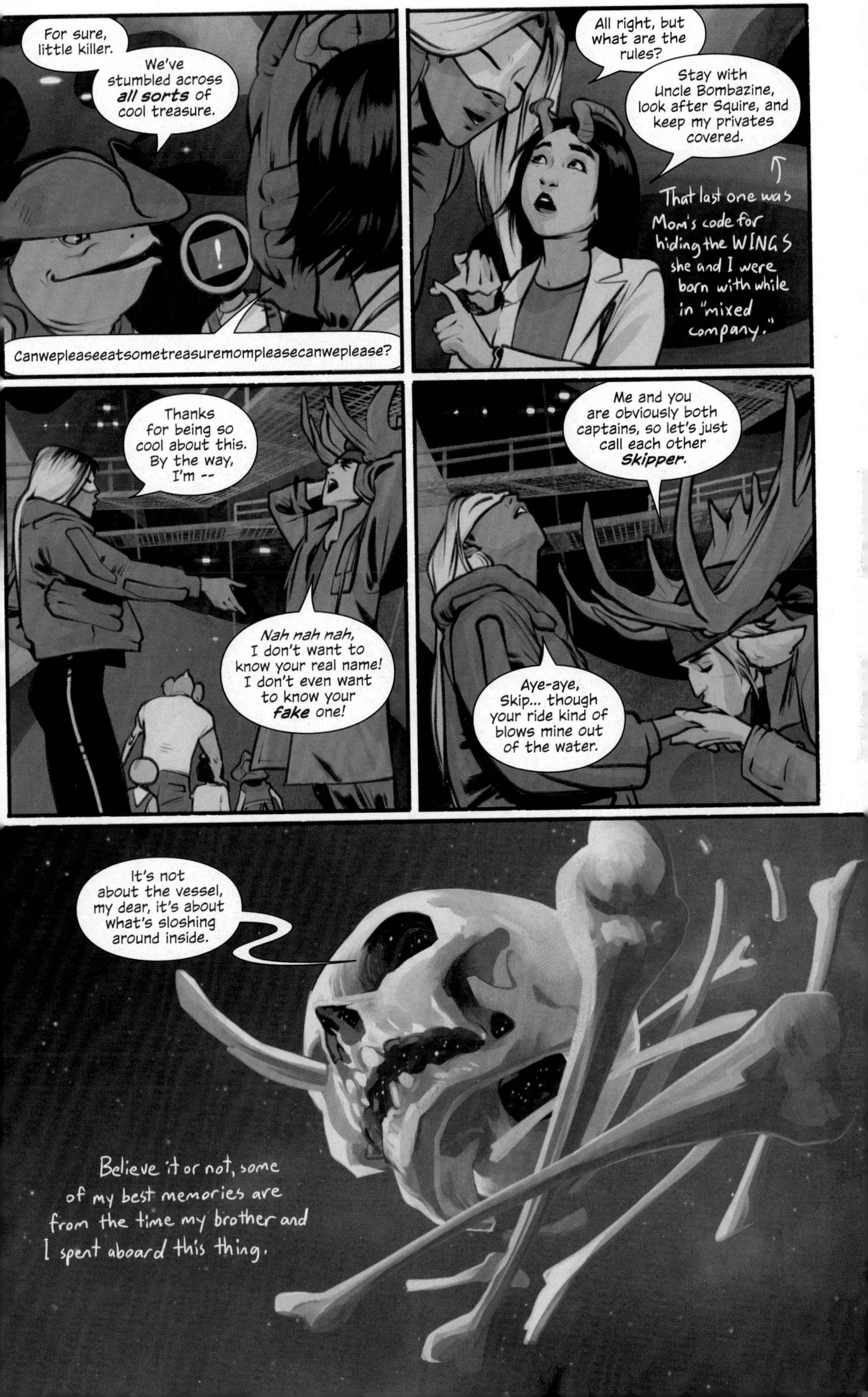
For sure, little killer.
We've stumbled across **all sorts** of cool treasure.
Canwepleaseeatsometreasuremompleasecanweplease?
All right, but what are the rules?
Stay with Uncle Bombazine, look after Squire, and keep my privates covered.
That last one was Mom's code for hiding the WINGS she and I were born with while in "mixed company."
Thanks for being so cool about this. By the way, I'm --
Nah nah nah, I don't want to know your real name! I don't even want to know your ***fake*** one!
Me and you are obviously both captains, so let's just call each other ***Skipper***.
Aye-aye, Skip... though your ride kind of blows mine out of the water.
It's not about the vessel, my dear, it's about what's sloshing around inside.
Believe it or not, some of my best memories are from the time my brother and I spent aboard this thing.

Squire and I desperately needed a break from the endless misery that was still engulfing the rest of the universe.

We both knew all too well that death would never be far away, but at least for a little while...

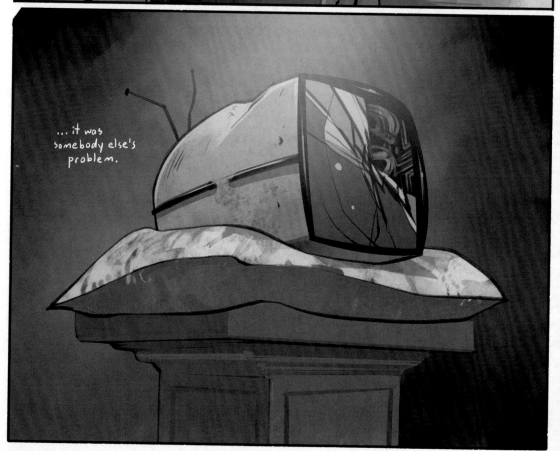

...it was somebody else's problem.

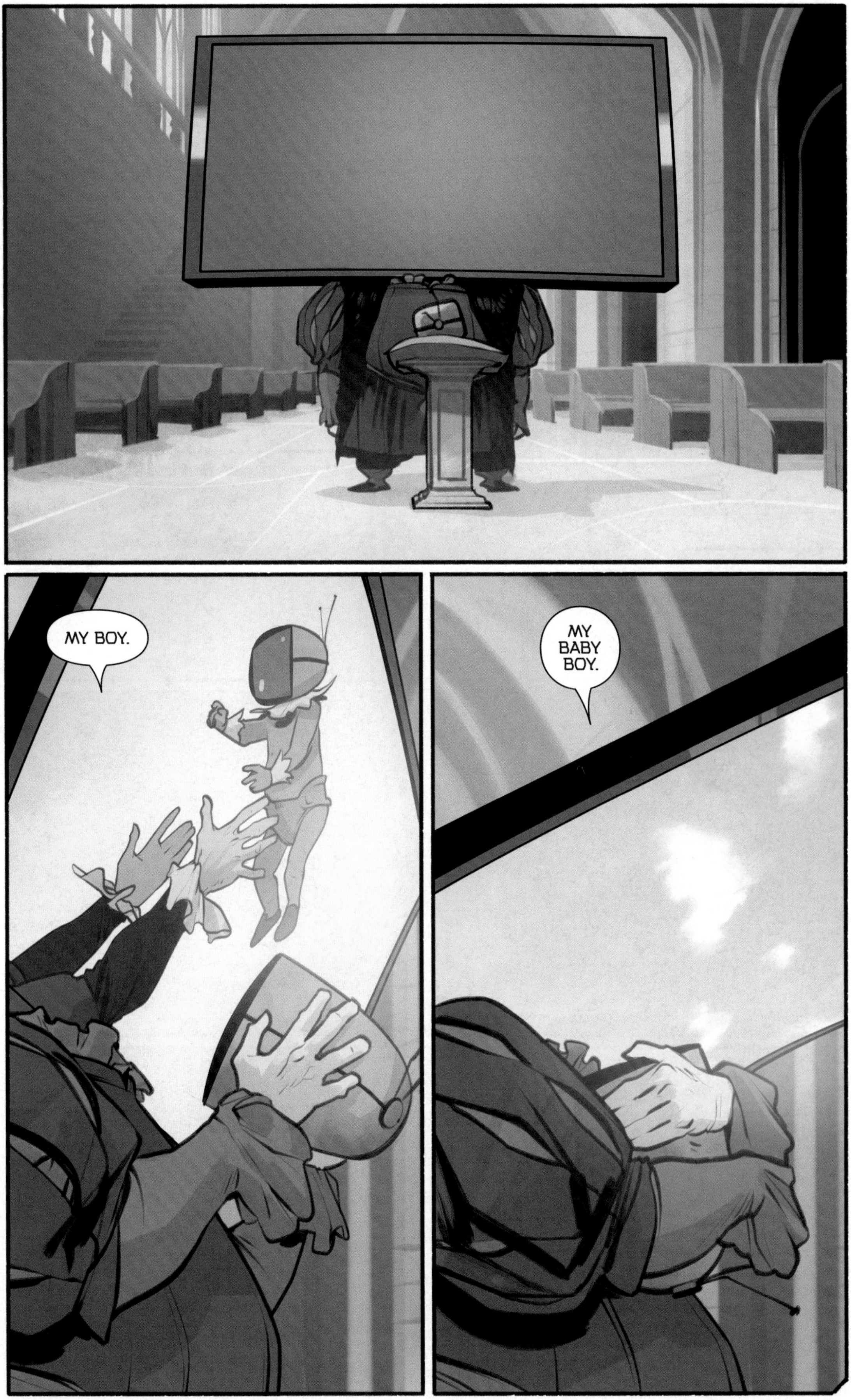
MY BOY.
MY BABY BOY.

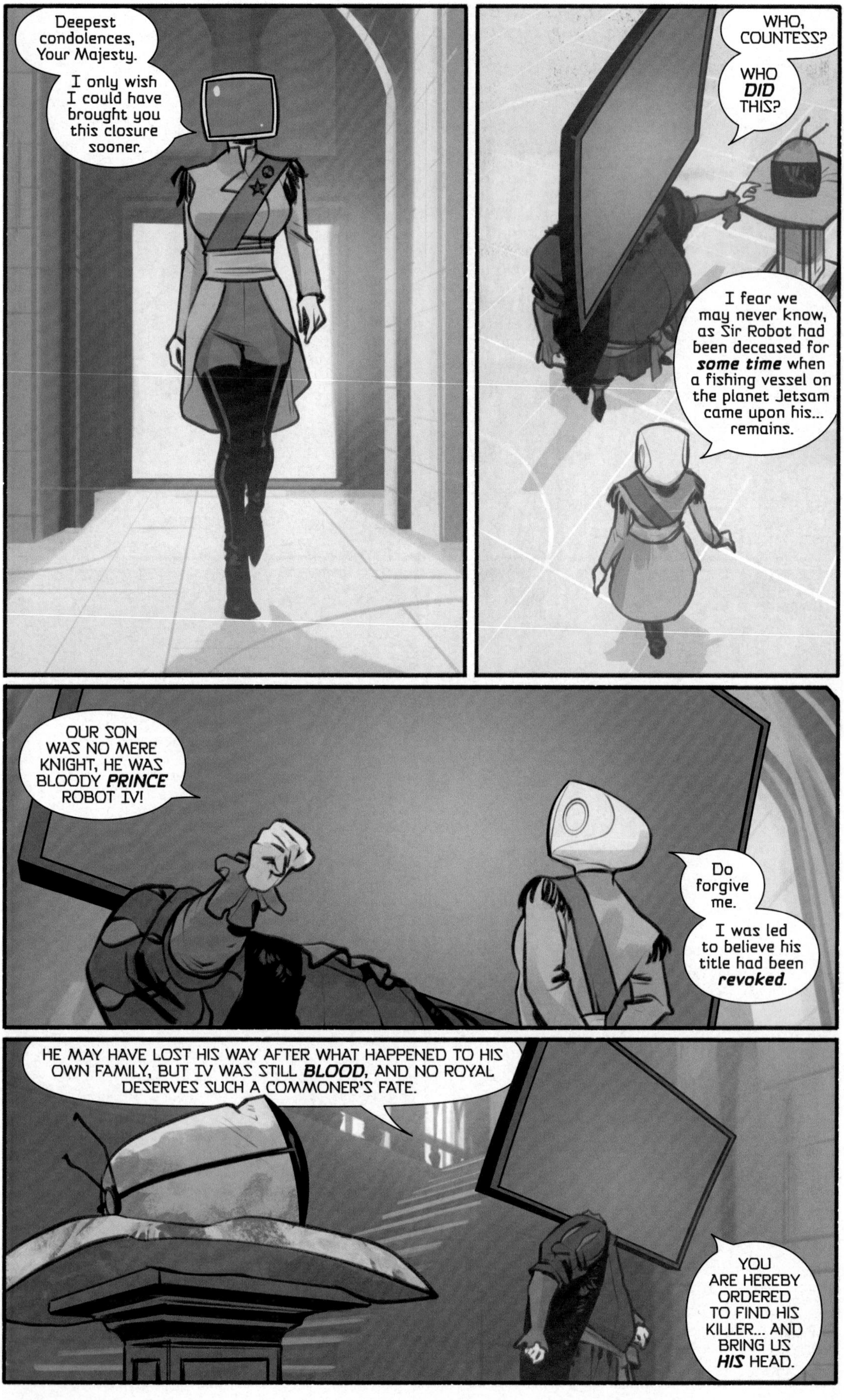
Deepest condolences, Your Majesty.
I only wish I could have brought you this closure sooner.
WHO, COUNTESS?
WHO *DID* THIS?
I fear we may never know, as Sir Robot had been deceased for ***some time*** when a fishing vessel on the planet Jetsam came upon his... remains.
OUR SON WAS NO MERE KNIGHT, HE WAS BLOODY ***PRINCE*** ROBOT IV!
Do forgive me.
I was led to believe his title had been ***revoked***.
HE MAY HAVE LOST HIS WAY AFTER WHAT HAPPENED TO HIS OWN FAMILY, BUT IV WAS STILL ***BLOOD***, AND NO ROYAL DESERVES SUCH A COMMONER'S FATE.
YOU ARE HEREBY ORDERED TO FIND HIS KILLER... AND BRING US ***HIS*** HEAD.

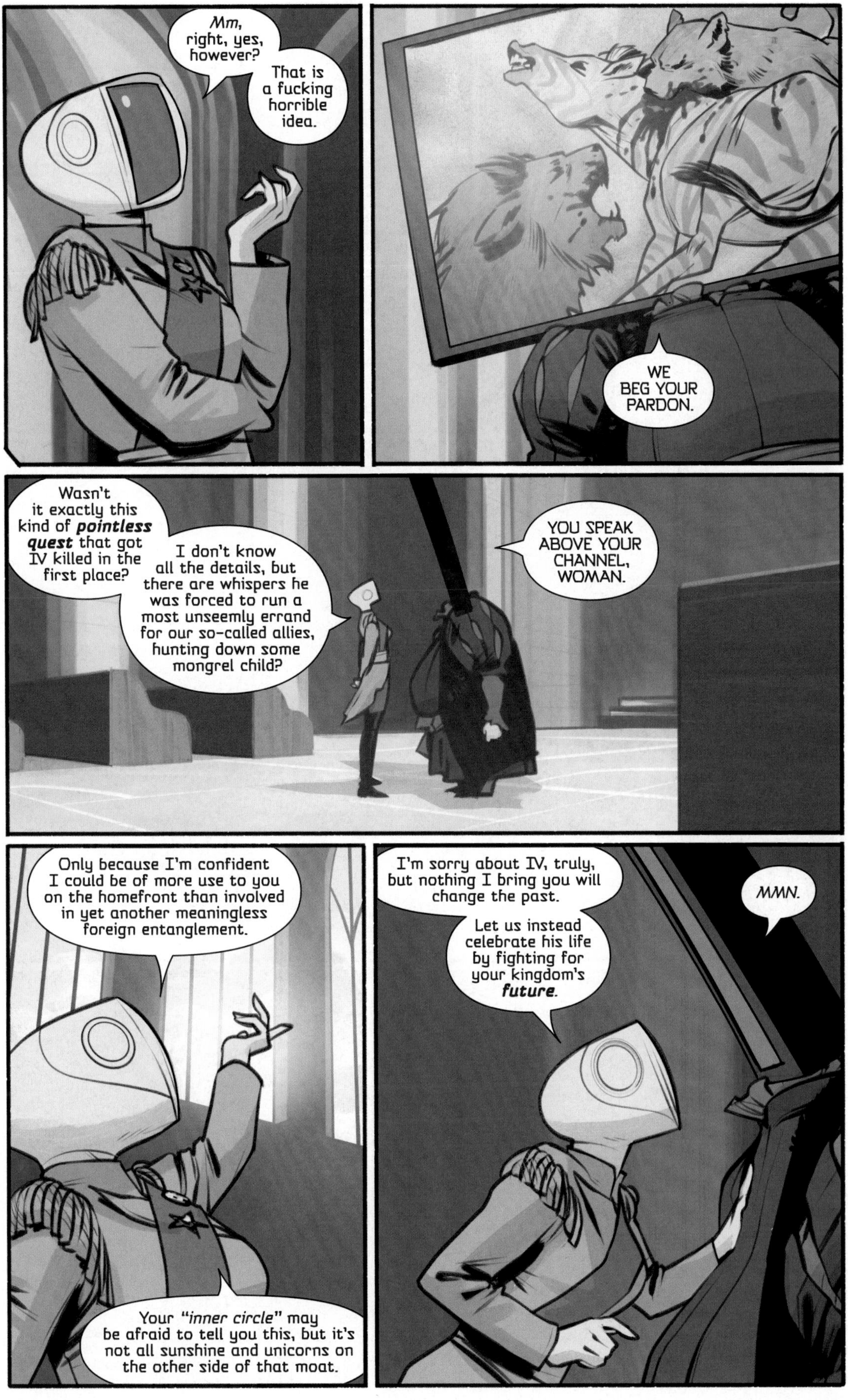

Mm, right, yes, however?
That is a fucking horrible idea.
WE BEG YOUR PARDON.
Wasn't it exactly this kind of ***pointless quest*** that got IV killed in the first place?
I don't know all the details, but there are whispers he was forced to run a most unseemly errand for our so-called allies, hunting down some mongrel child?
YOU SPEAK ABOVE YOUR CHANNEL, WOMAN.
Only because I'm confident I could be of more use to you on the homefront than involved in yet another meaningless foreign entanglement.
Your "*inner circle*" may be afraid to tell you this, but it's not all sunshine and unicorns on the other side of that moat.
I'm sorry about IV, truly, but nothing I bring you will change the past.
Let us instead celebrate his life by fighting for your kingdom's ***future***.
MMN.

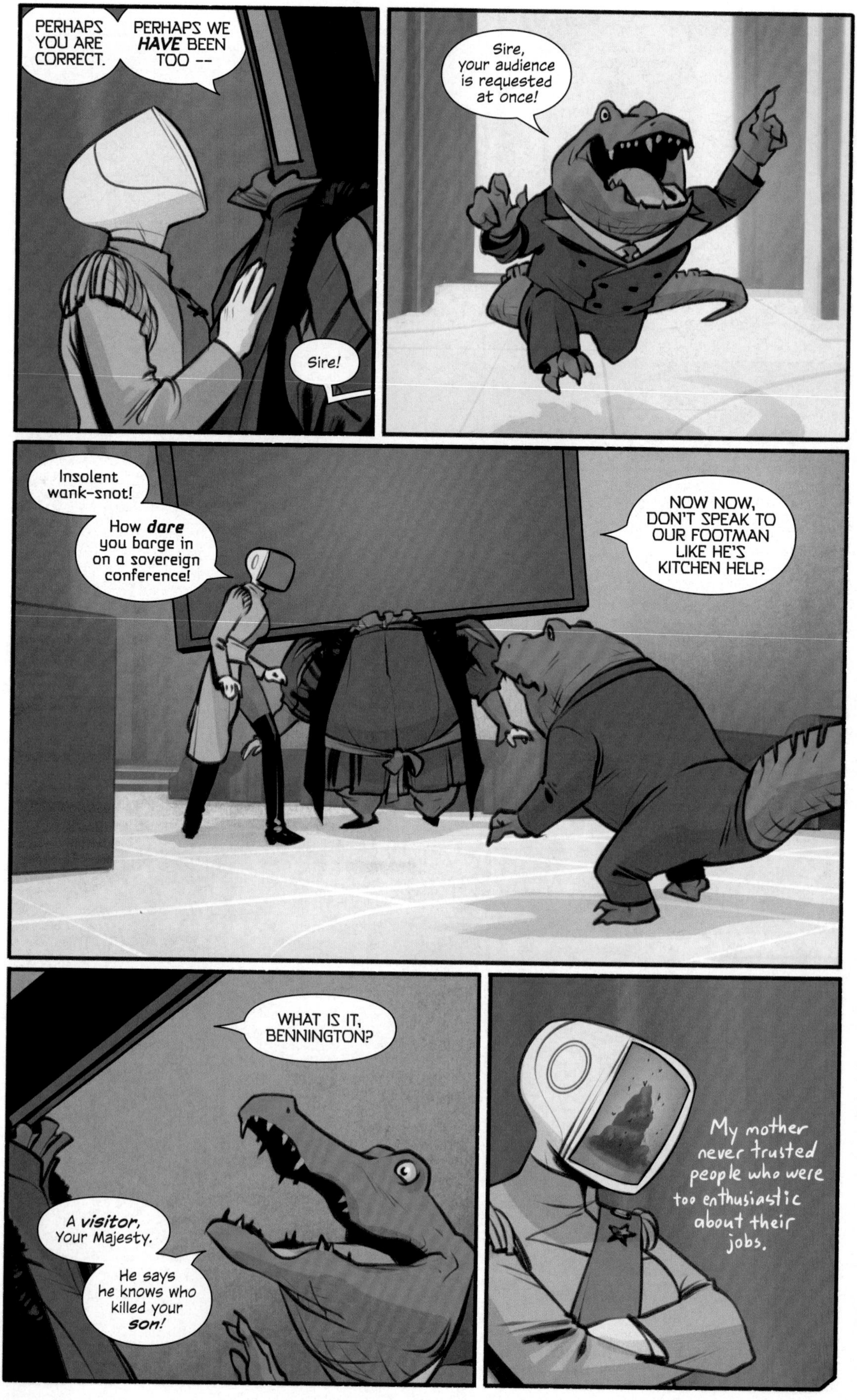
PERHAPS YOU ARE CORRECT.
PERHAPS WE HAVE BEEN TOO --
Sire!
Sire, your audience is requested at once!
Insolent wank-snot!
How dare you barge in on a sovereign conference!
NOW NOW, DON'T SPEAK TO OUR FOOTMAN LIKE HE'S KITCHEN HELP.
WHAT IS IT, BENNINGTON?
A visitor, Your Majesty.
He says he knows who killed your son!
My mother never trusted people who were too enthusiastic about their jobs.

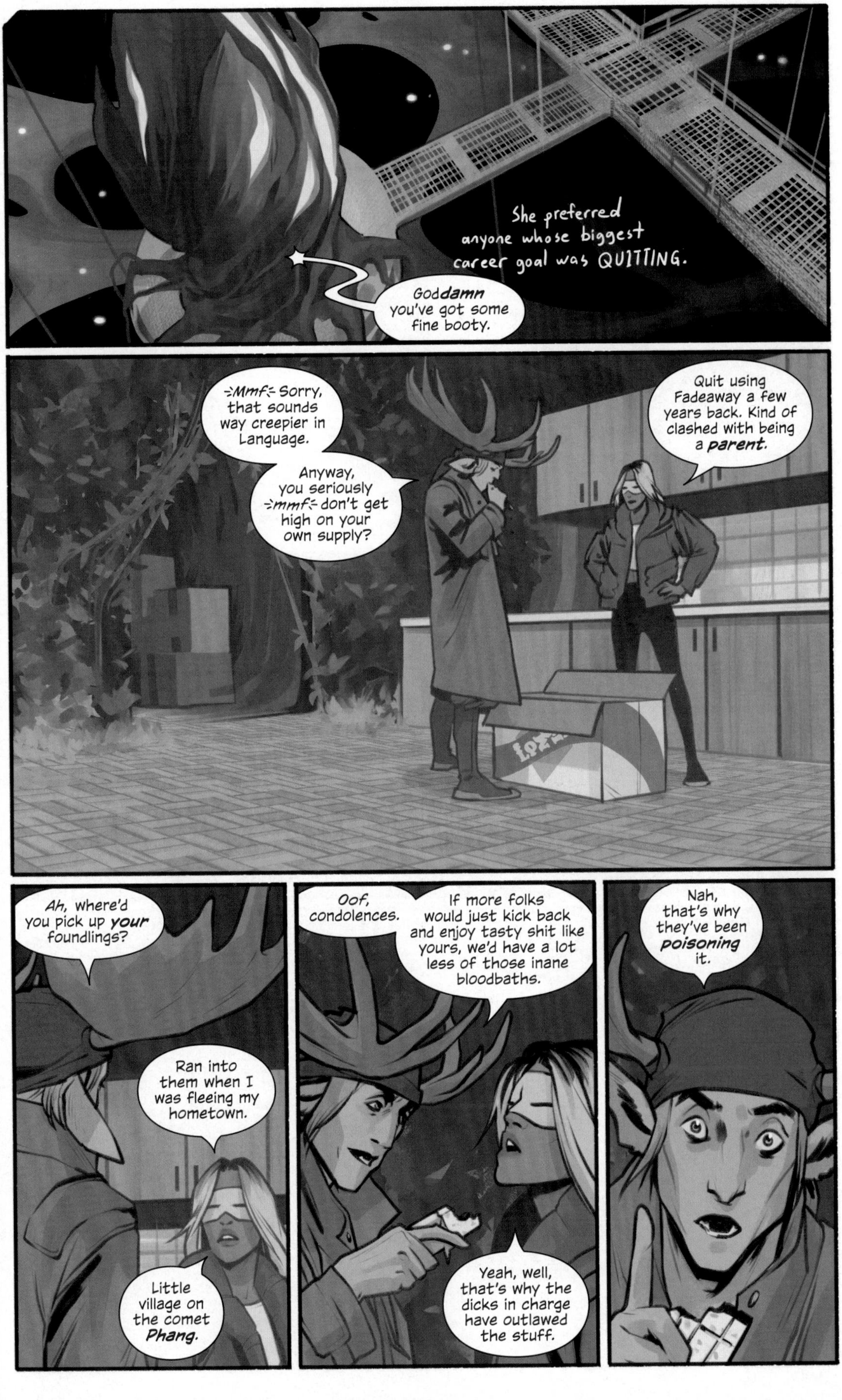
She preferred anyone whose biggest career goal was QUITTING.
Goddamn you've got some fine booty.
=Mmf= Sorry, that sounds way creepier in Language.
Anyway, you seriously =mmf= don't get high on your own supply?
Quit using Fadeaway a few years back. Kind of clashed with being a parent.
Ah, where'd you pick up your foundlings?
Ran into them when I was fleeing my hometown.
Little village on the comet Phang.
Oof, condolences.
If more folks would just kick back and enjoy tasty shit like yours, we'd have a lot less of those inane bloodbaths.
Yeah, well, that's why the dicks in charge have outlawed the stuff.
Nah, that's why they've been poisoning it.

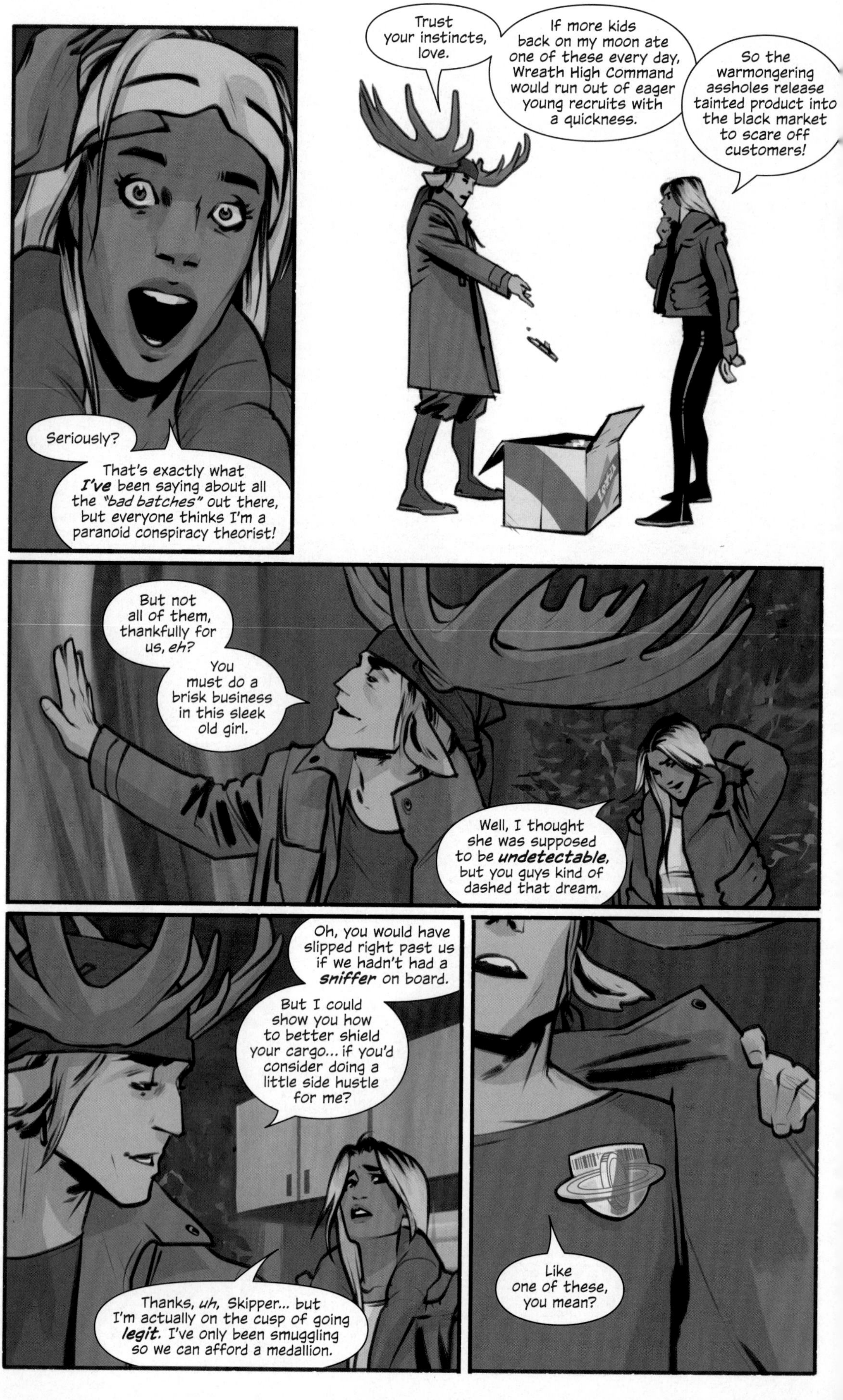
Seriously?
That's exactly what *I've* been saying about all the *"bad batches"* out there, but everyone thinks I'm a paranoid conspiracy theorist!
Trust your instincts, love.
If more kids back on my moon ate one of these every day, Wreath High Command would run out of eager young recruits with a quickness.
So the warmongering assholes release tainted product into the black market to scare off customers!
But not all of them, thankfully for us, *eh?*
You must do a brisk business in this sleek old girl.
Well, I thought she was supposed to be ***undetectable***, but you guys kind of dashed that dream.
Oh, you would have slipped right past us if we hadn't had a ***sniffer*** on board.
But I could show you how to better shield your cargo... if you'd consider doing a little side hustle for me?
Thanks, *uh*, Skipper... but I'm actually on the cusp of going ***legit***. I've only been smuggling so we can afford a medallion.
Like one of these, you mean?

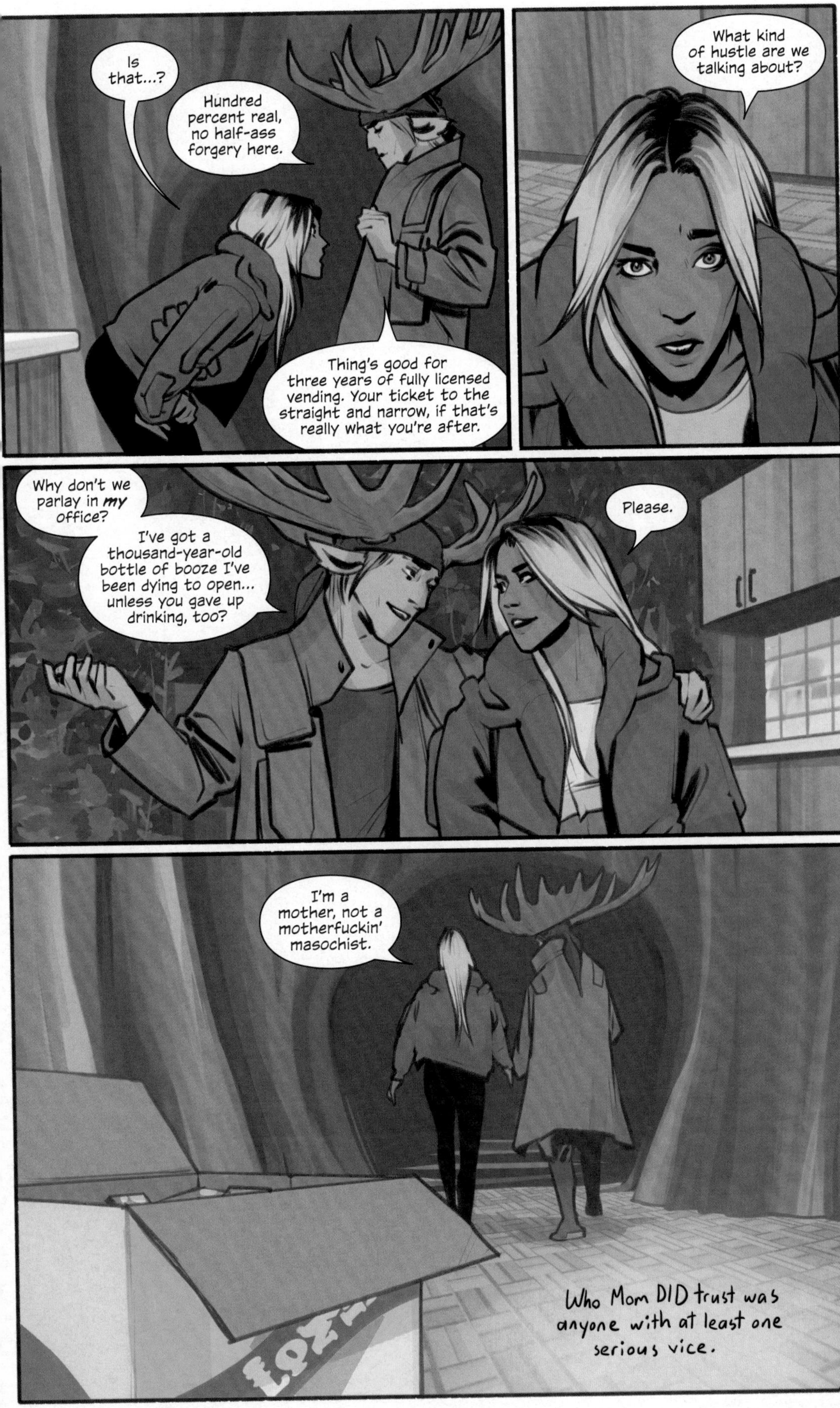
Is that...?
Hundred percent real, no half-ass forgery here.
Thing's good for three years of fully licensed vending. Your ticket to the straight and narrow, if that's really what you're after.
What kind of hustle are we talking about?
Why don't we parlay in *my* office?
I've got a thousand-year-old bottle of booze I've been dying to open... unless you gave up drinking, too?
Please.
I'm a mother, not a motherfuckin' masochist.
Who Mom DID trust was anyone with at least one serious vice.

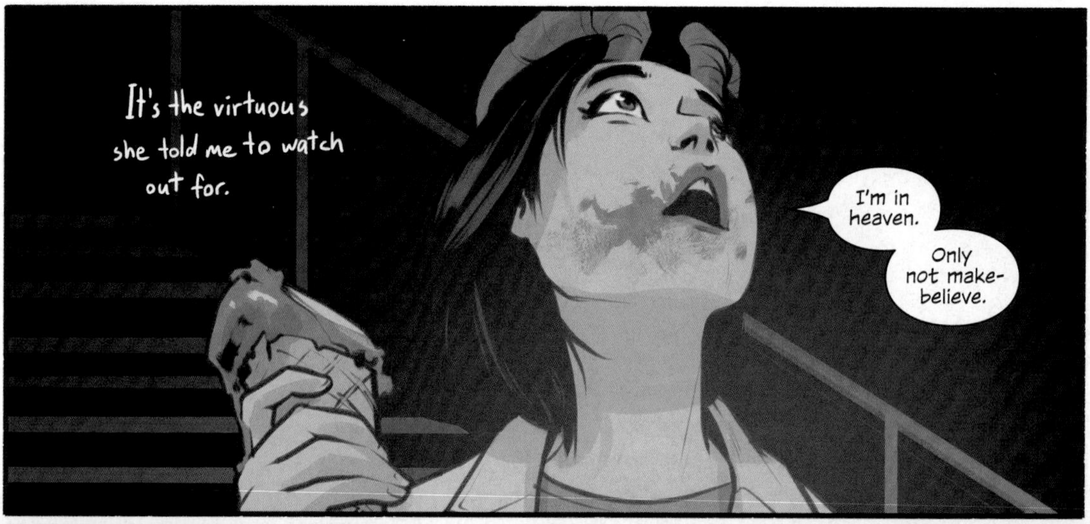
It's the virtuous she told me to watch out for.
I'm in heaven.
Only not make-believe.

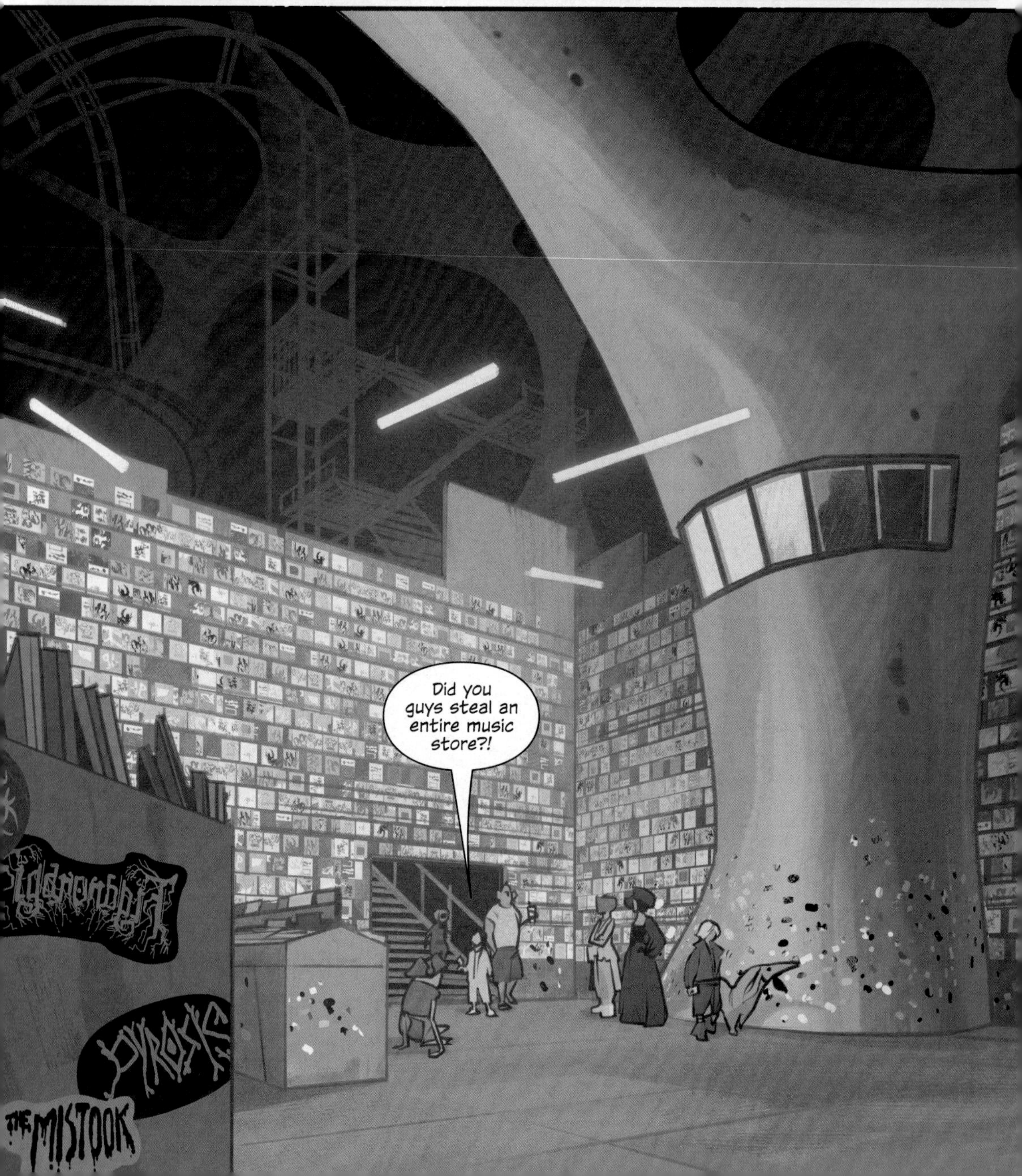
Did you guys steal an entire music store?!
THE MISTOOK

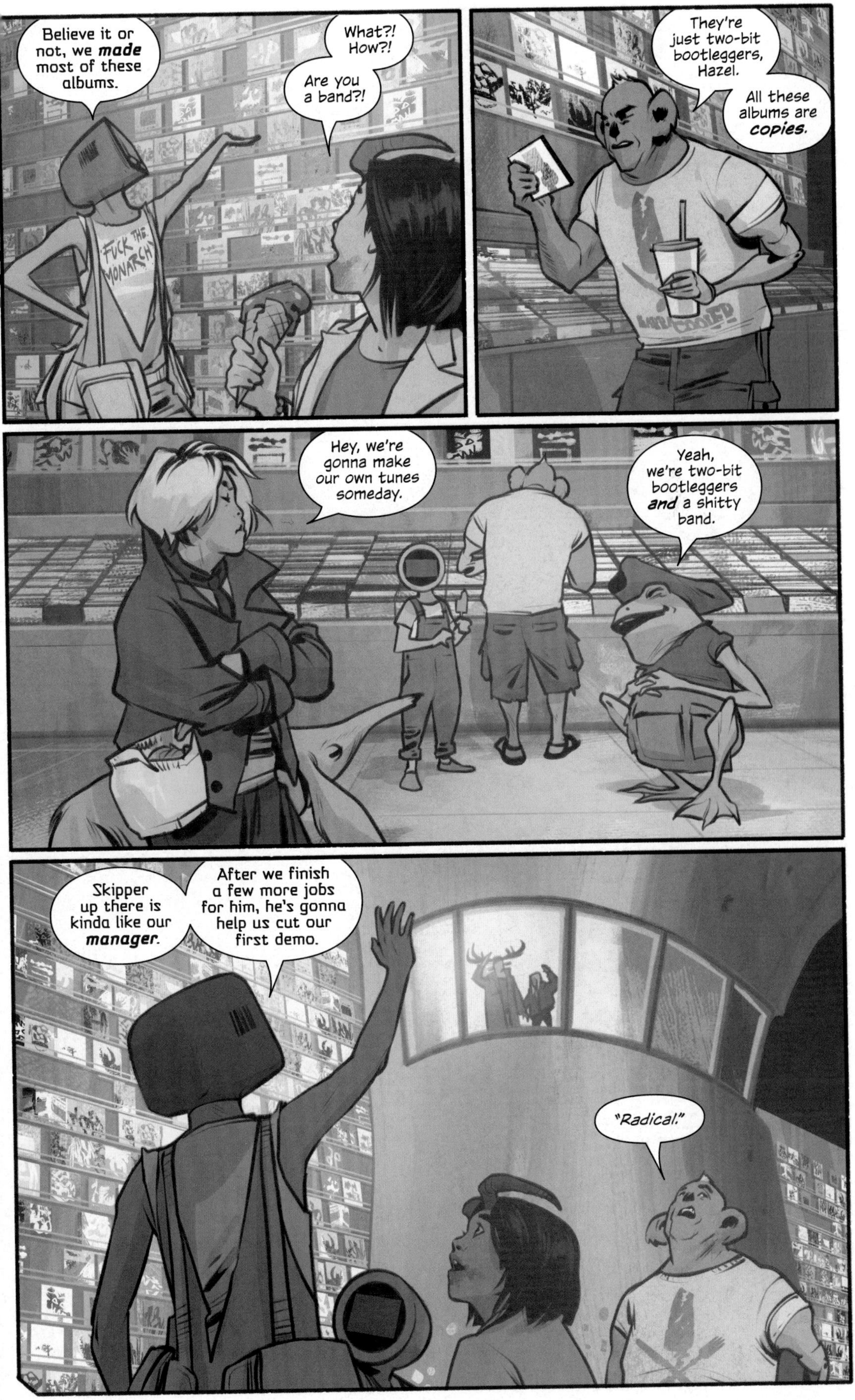
Believe it or not, we *made* most of these albums.
What?! How?!
Are you a band?!
They're just two-bit bootleggers, Hazel.
All these albums are *copies*.
FUCK THE MONARCHY
Hey, we're gonna make our own tunes someday.
Yeah, we're two-bit bootleggers *and* a shitty band.
Skipper up there is kinda like our *manager*.
After we finish a few more jobs for him, he's gonna help us cut our first demo.
"Radical."

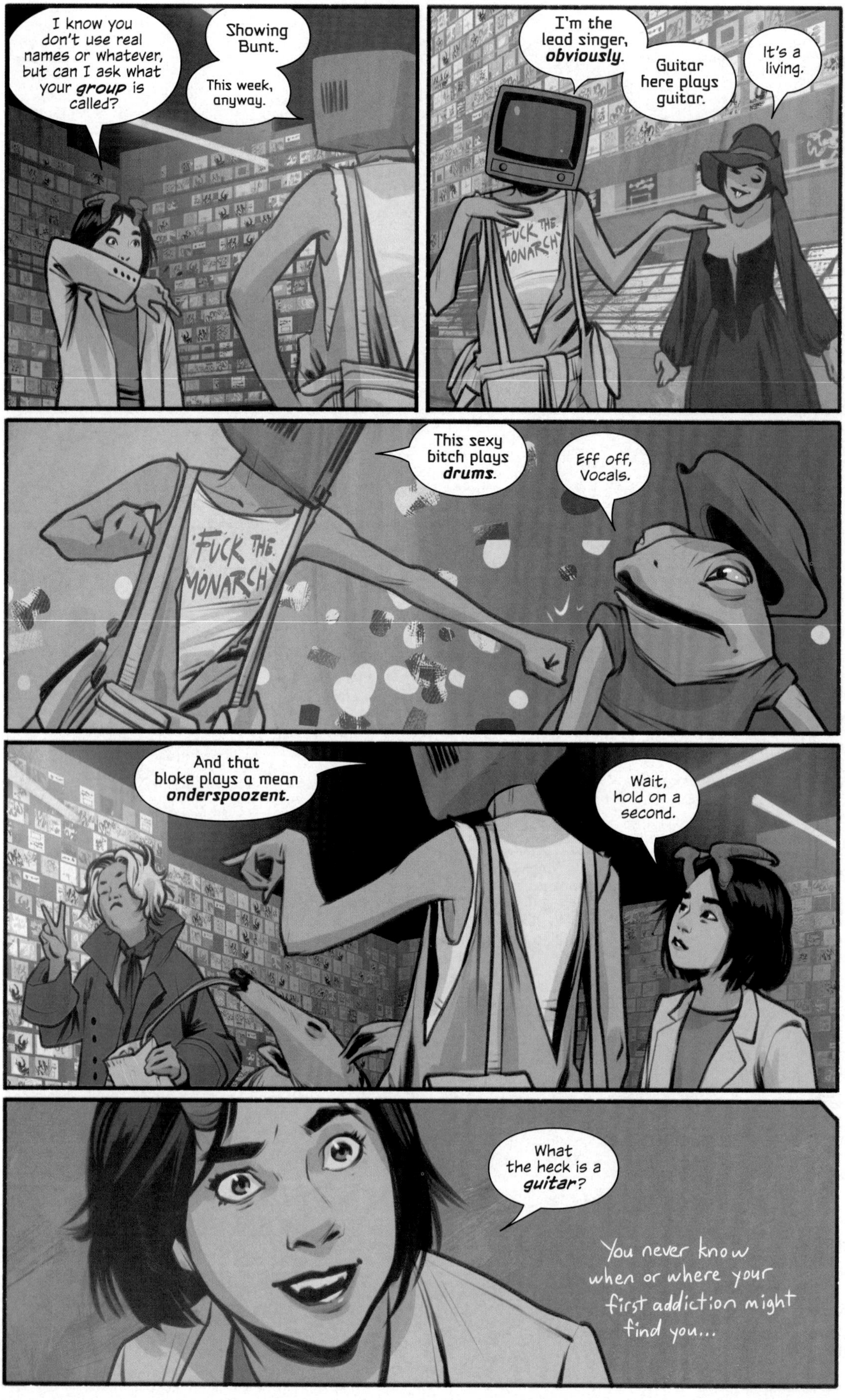
I know you don't use real names or whatever, but can I ask what your *group* is called?
Showing Bunt.
This week, anyway.
I'm the lead singer, *obviously*.
Guitar here plays guitar.
It's a living.
FUCK THE MONARCHY
This sexy bitch plays *drums*.
Eff off, Vocals.
FUCK THE MONARCHY
And that bloke plays a mean *onderspoozent*.
Wait, hold on a second.
What the heck is a *guitar*?
You never know when or where your first addiction might find you...

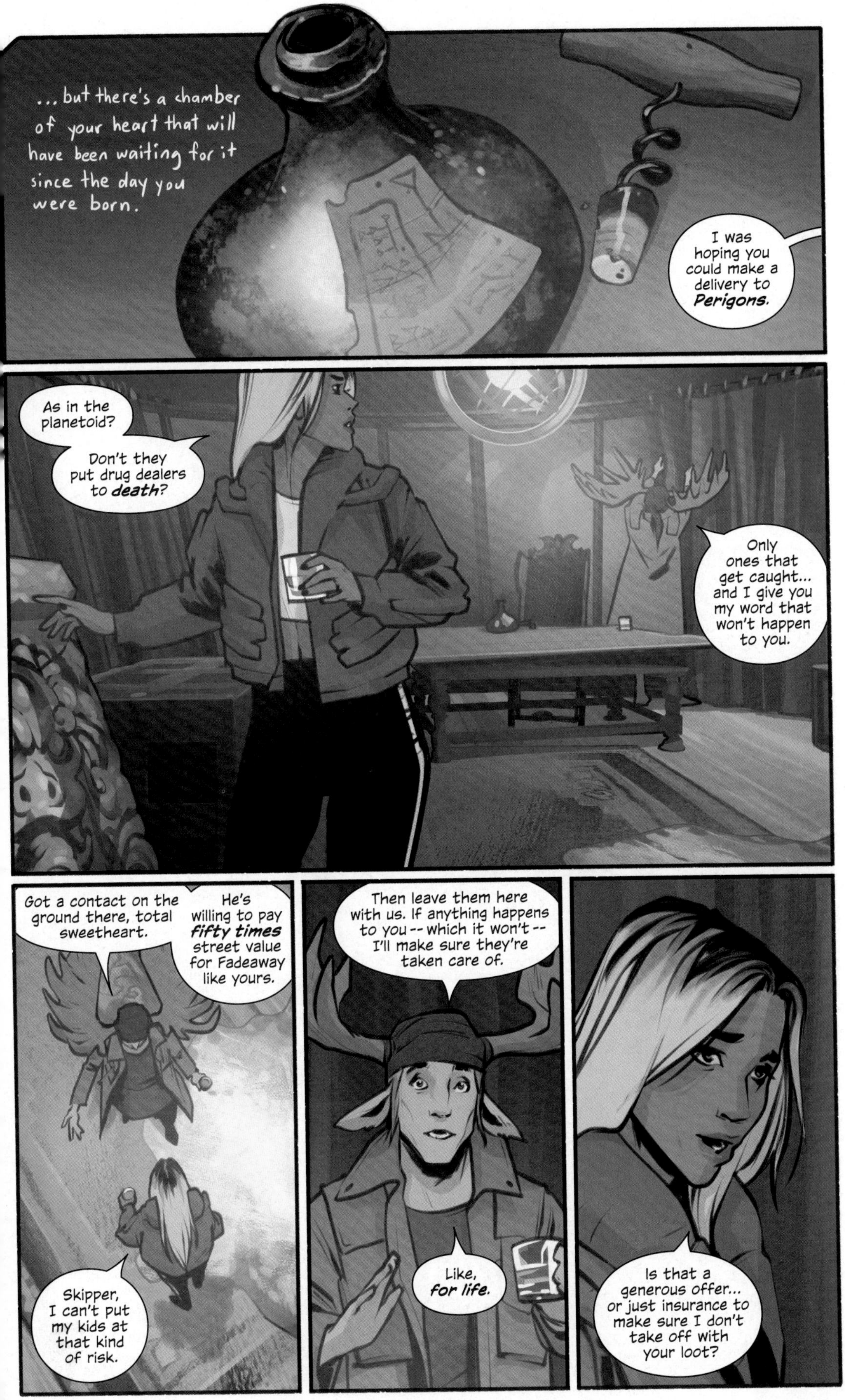

...but there's a chamber of your heart that will have been waiting for it since the day you were born.
I was hoping you could make a delivery to ***Perigons.***
As in the planetoid?
Don't they put drug dealers to ***death***?
Only ones that get caught... and I give you my word that won't happen to you.
Got a contact on the ground there, total sweetheart.
He's willing to pay ***fifty times*** street value for Fadeaway like yours.
Skipper, I can't put my kids at that kind of risk.
Then leave them here with us. If anything happens to you -- which it won't -- I'll make sure they're taken care of.
Like, ***for life.***
Is that a generous offer... or just insurance to make sure I don't take off with your loot?

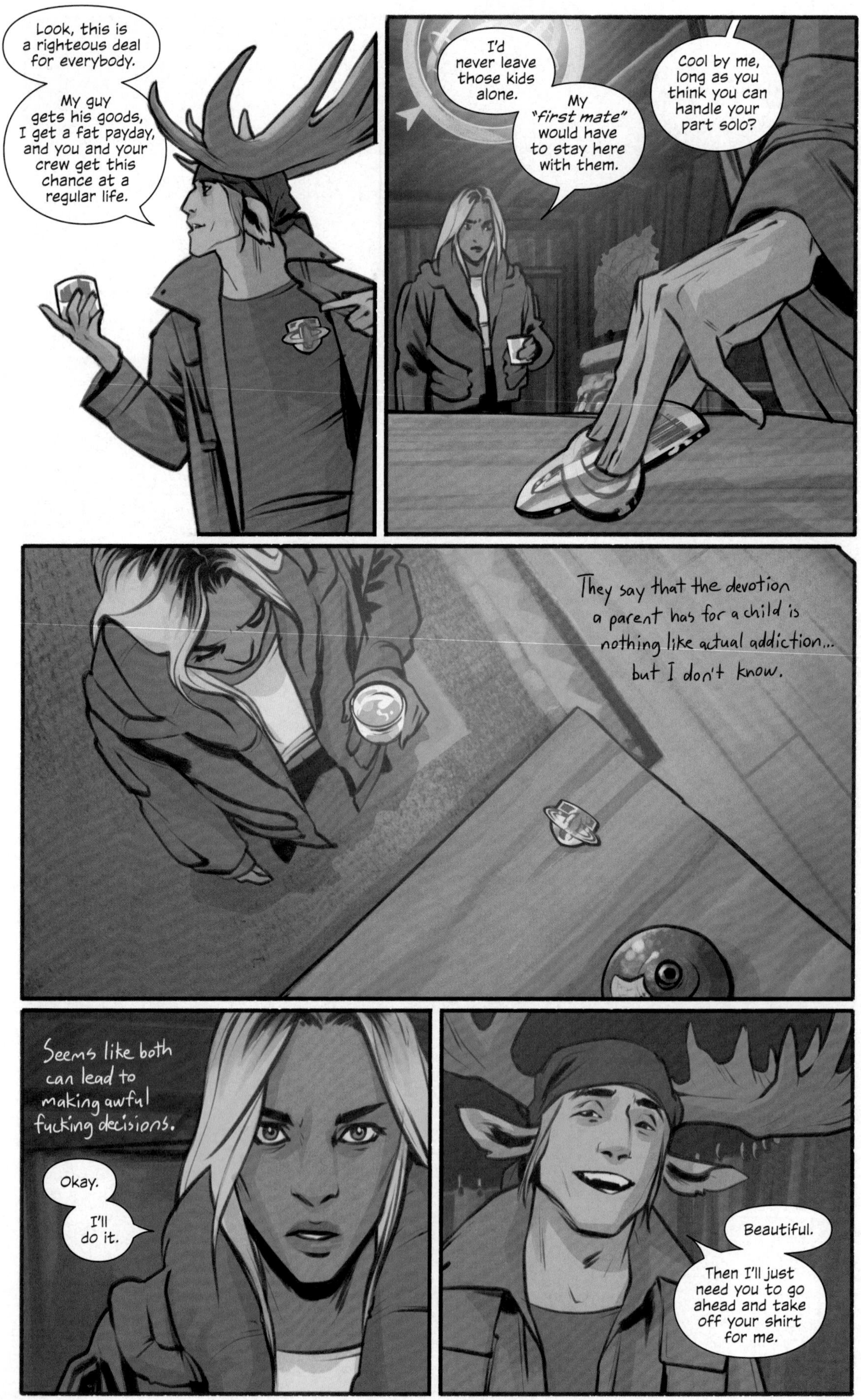
Look, this is a righteous deal for everybody.
My guy gets his goods, I get a fat payday, and you and your crew get this chance at a regular life.
I'd never leave those kids alone.
My "first mate" would have to stay here with them.
Cool by me, long as you think you can handle your part solo?
They say that the devotion a parent has for a child is nothing like actual addiction... but I don't know.
Seems like both can lead to making awful fucking decisions.
Okay.
I'll do it.
Beautiful.
Then I'll just need you to go ahead and take off your shirt for me.

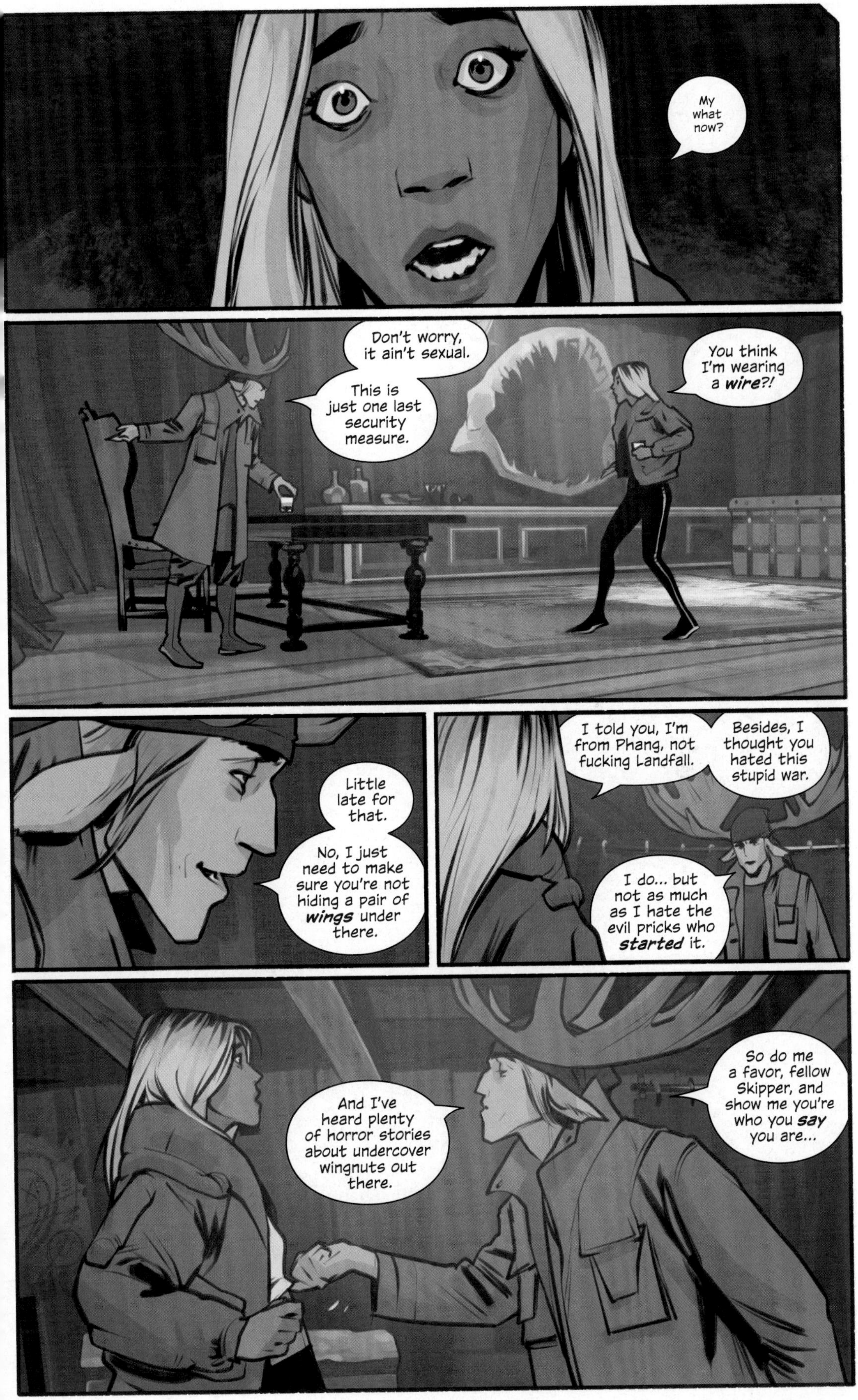
My what now?
Don't worry, it ain't sexual.
This is just one last security measure.
You think I'm wearing a ***wire?!***
Little late for that.
No, I just need to make sure you're not hiding a pair of ***wings*** under there.
I told you, I'm from Phang, not fucking Landfall.
Besides, I thought you hated this stupid war.
I do... but not as much as I hate the evil pricks who ***started*** it.
And I've heard plenty of horror stories about undercover wingnuts out there.
So do me a favor, fellow Skipper, and show me you're who you ***say*** you are...

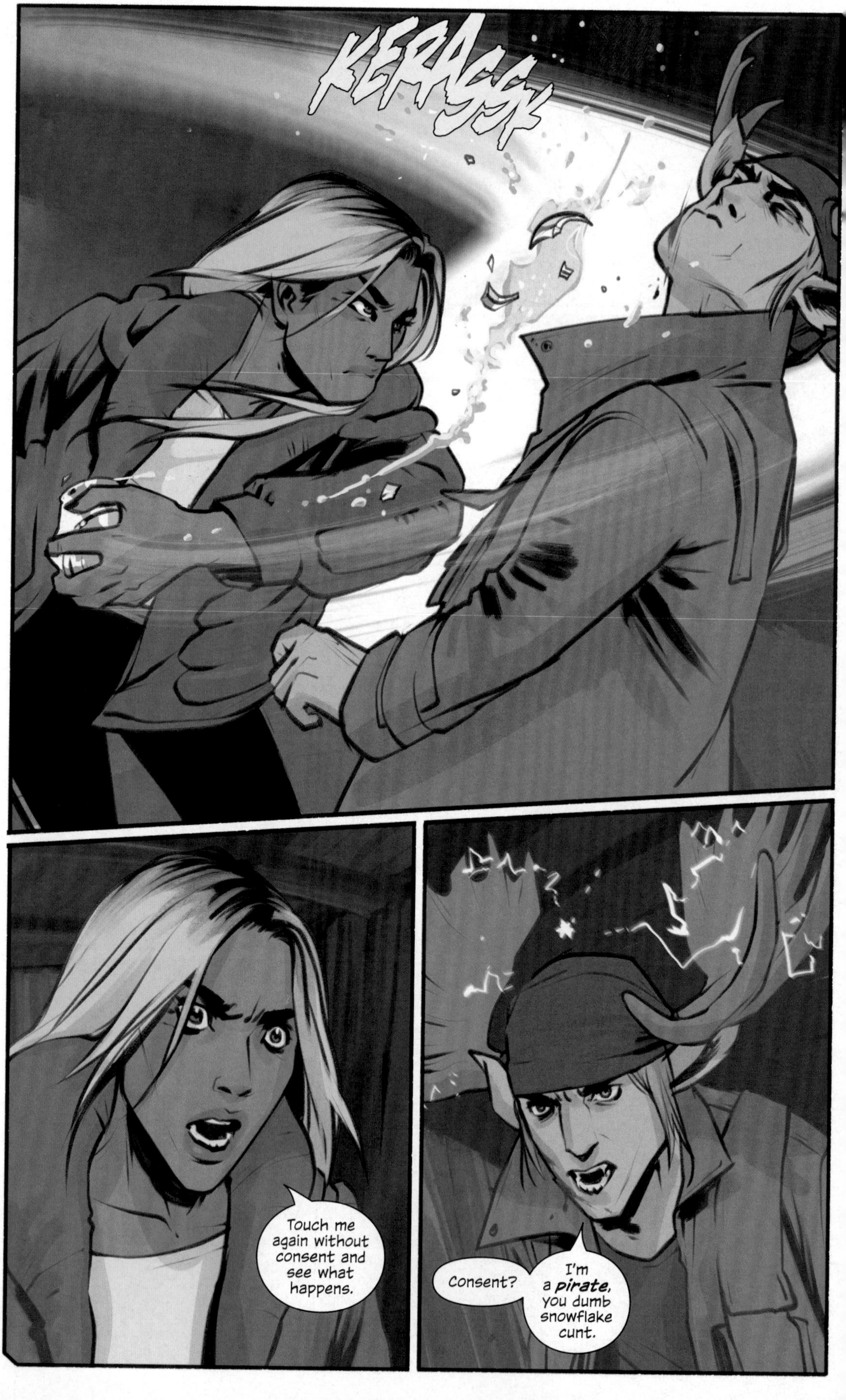
KERASSK
Touch me again without consent and see what happens.
Consent?
I'm a ***pirate,*** you dumb snowflake cunt.

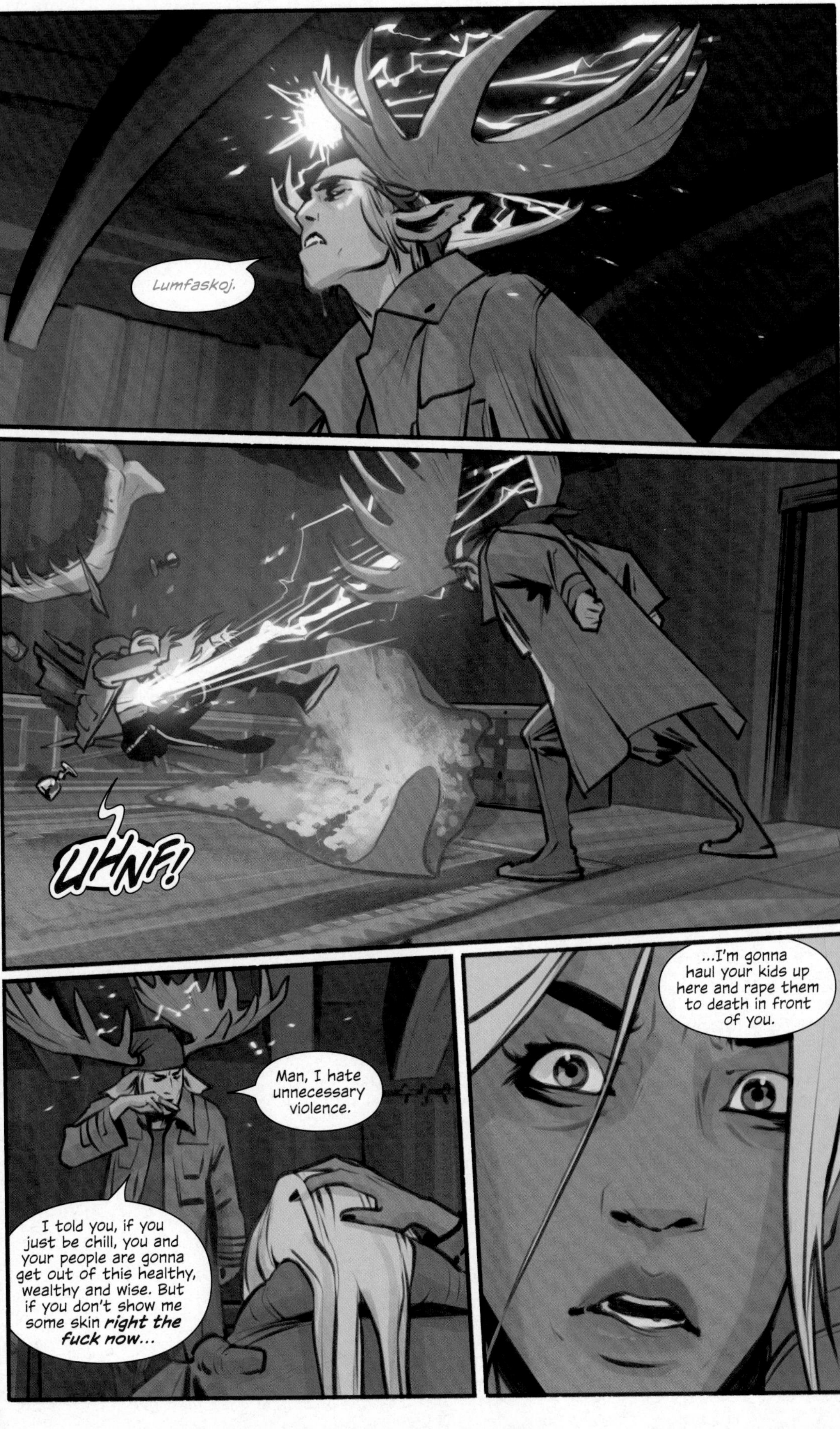

Lumfaskoj.
UHNF!
Man, I hate unnecessary violence.
I told you, if you just be chill, you and your people are gonna get out of this healthy, wealthy and wise. But if you don't show me some skin ***right the fuck now...***
...I'm gonna haul your kids up here and rape them to death in front of you.

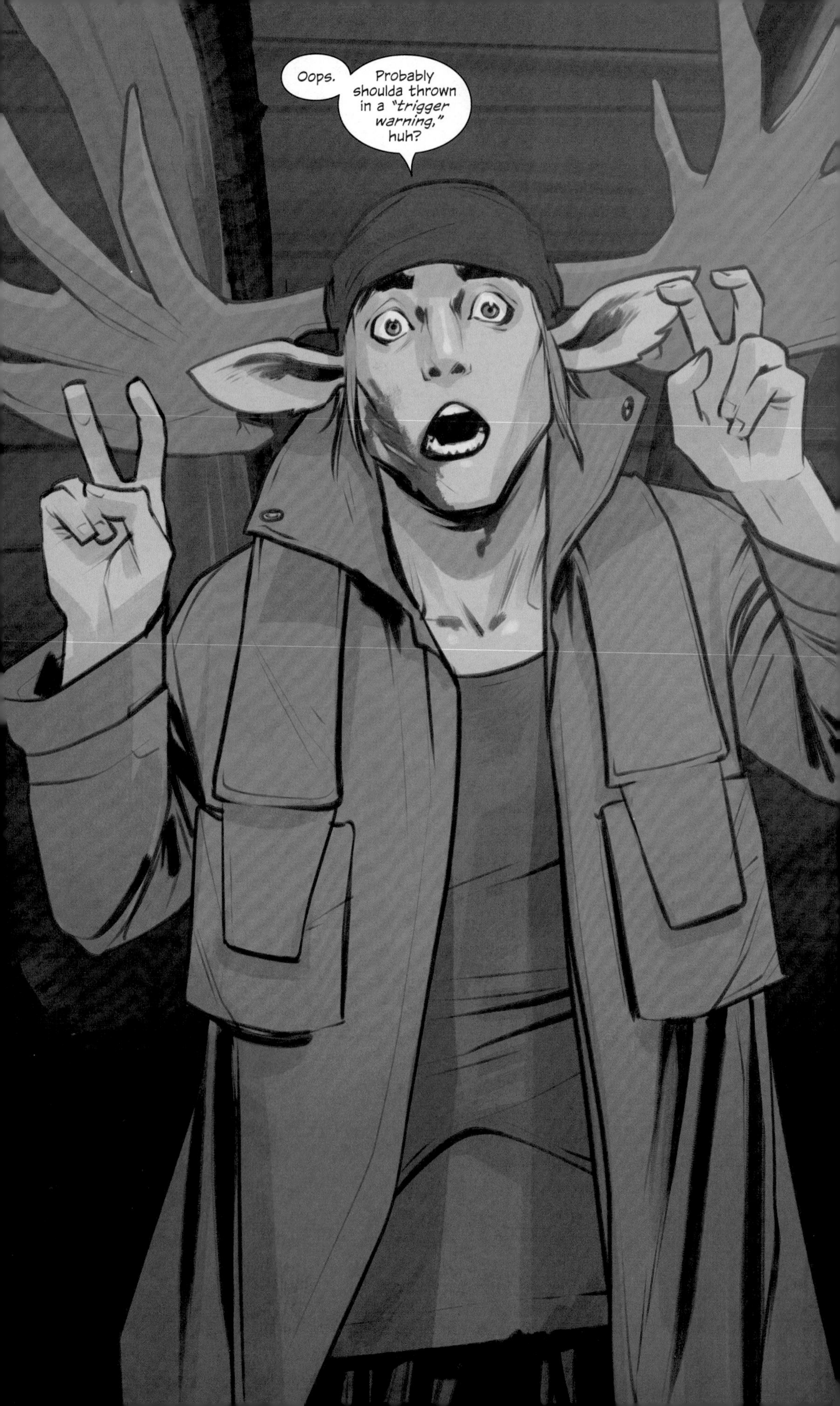
Oops.
Probably shoulda thrown in a *"trigger warning,"* huh?

end chapter fifty-six

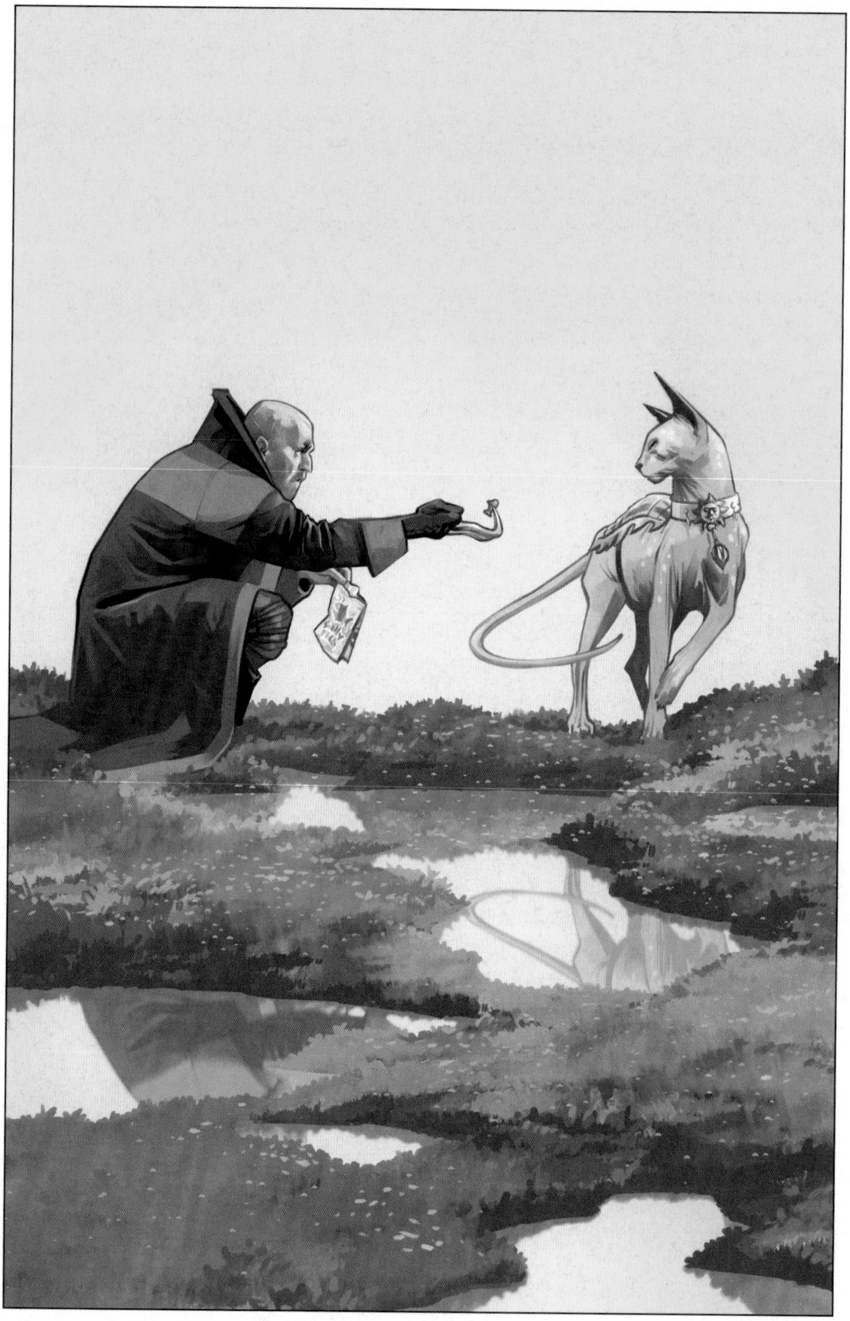

CHAPTER
FIFTY-SEVEN

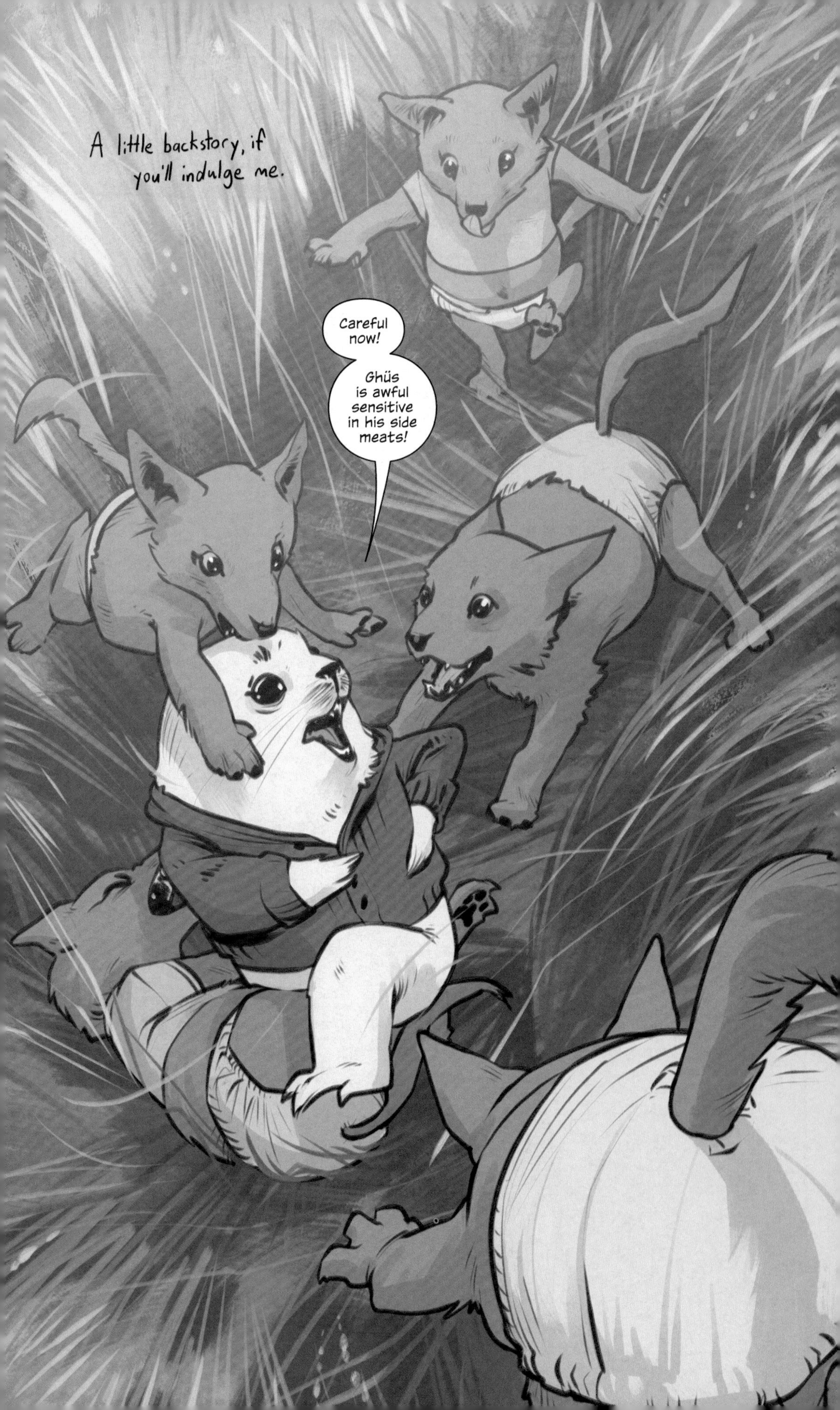
A little backstory, if you'll indulge me.
Careful now!
Ghüs is awful sensitive in his side meats!

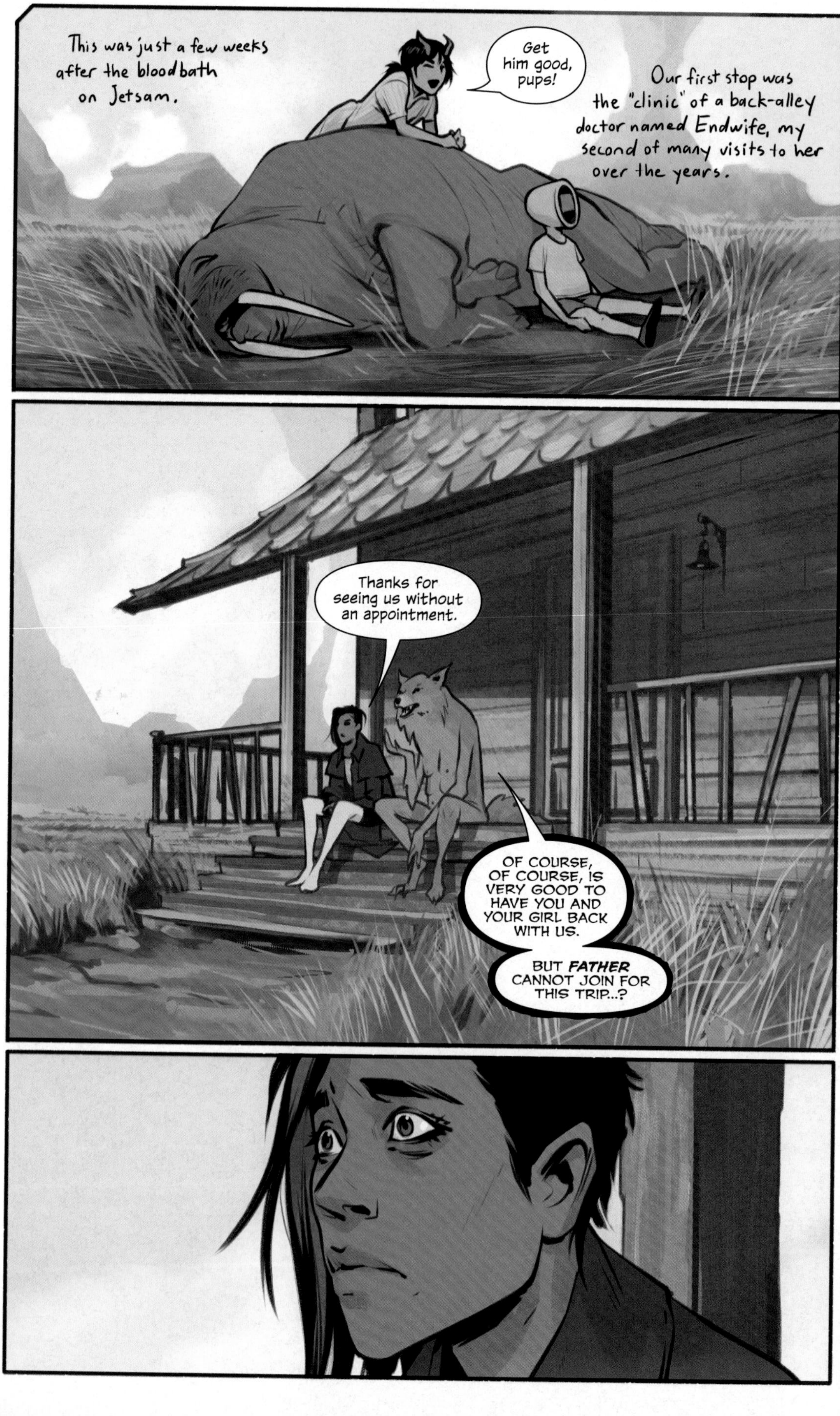
This was just a few weeks after the bloodbath on Jetsam.
Get him good, pups!
Our first stop was the "clinic" of a back-alley doctor named Endwife, my second of many visits to her over the years.
Thanks for seeing us without an appointment.
OF COURSE, OF COURSE, IS VERY GOOD TO HAVE YOU AND YOUR GIRL BACK WITH US.
BUT FATHER CANNOT JOIN FOR THIS TRIP...?

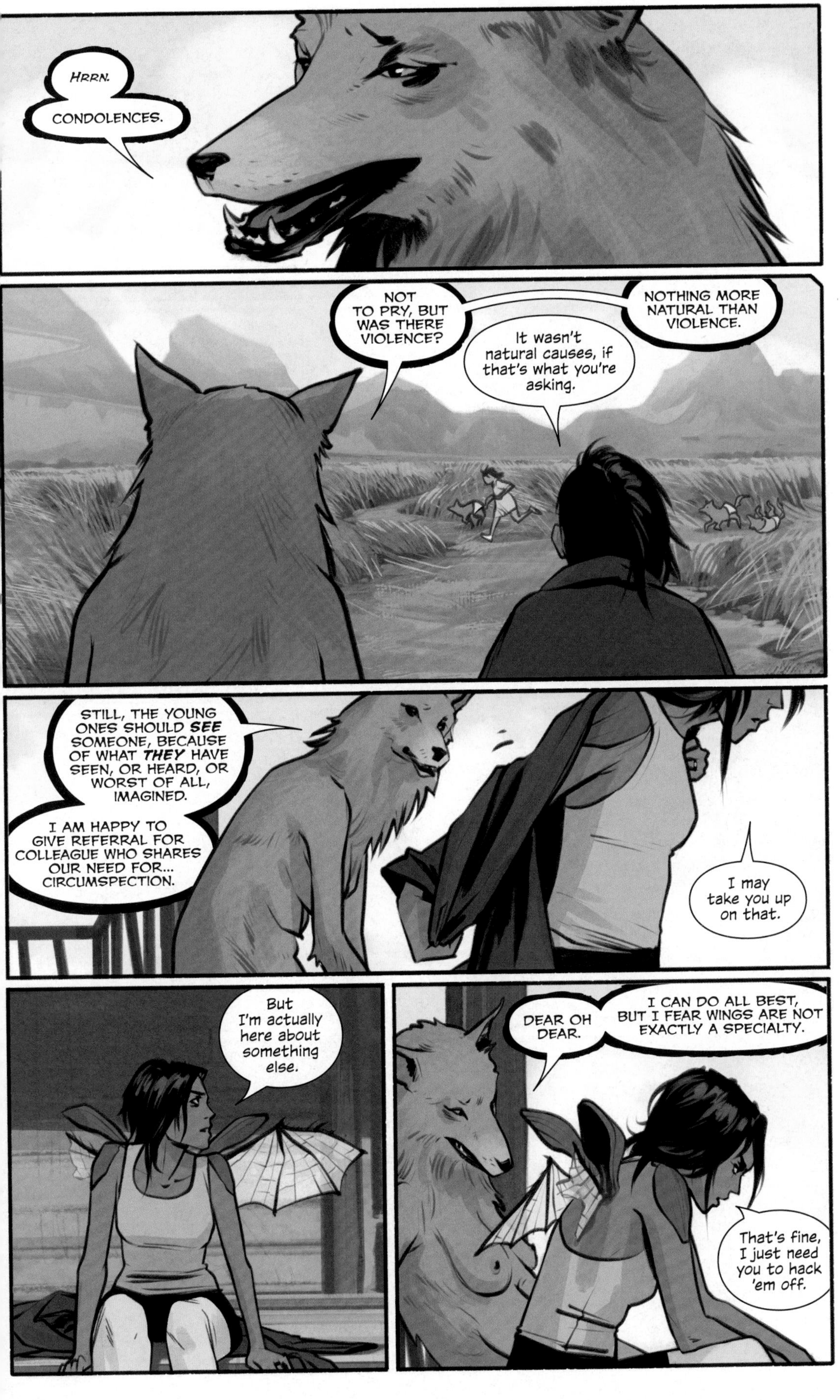
HRRN.
CONDOLENCES.
NOT TO PRY, BUT WAS THERE VIOLENCE?
It wasn't natural causes, if that's what you're asking.
NOTHING MORE NATURAL THAN VIOLENCE.
STILL, THE YOUNG ONES SHOULD SEE SOMEONE, BECAUSE OF WHAT THEY HAVE SEEN, OR HEARD, OR WORST OF ALL, IMAGINED.
I AM HAPPY TO GIVE REFERRAL FOR COLLEAGUE WHO SHARES OUR NEED FOR... CIRCUMSPECTION.
I may take you up on that.
But I'm actually here about something else.
DEAR OH DEAR.
I CAN DO ALL BEST, BUT I FEAR WINGS ARE NOT EXACTLY A SPECIALTY.
That's fine, I just need you to hack 'em off.

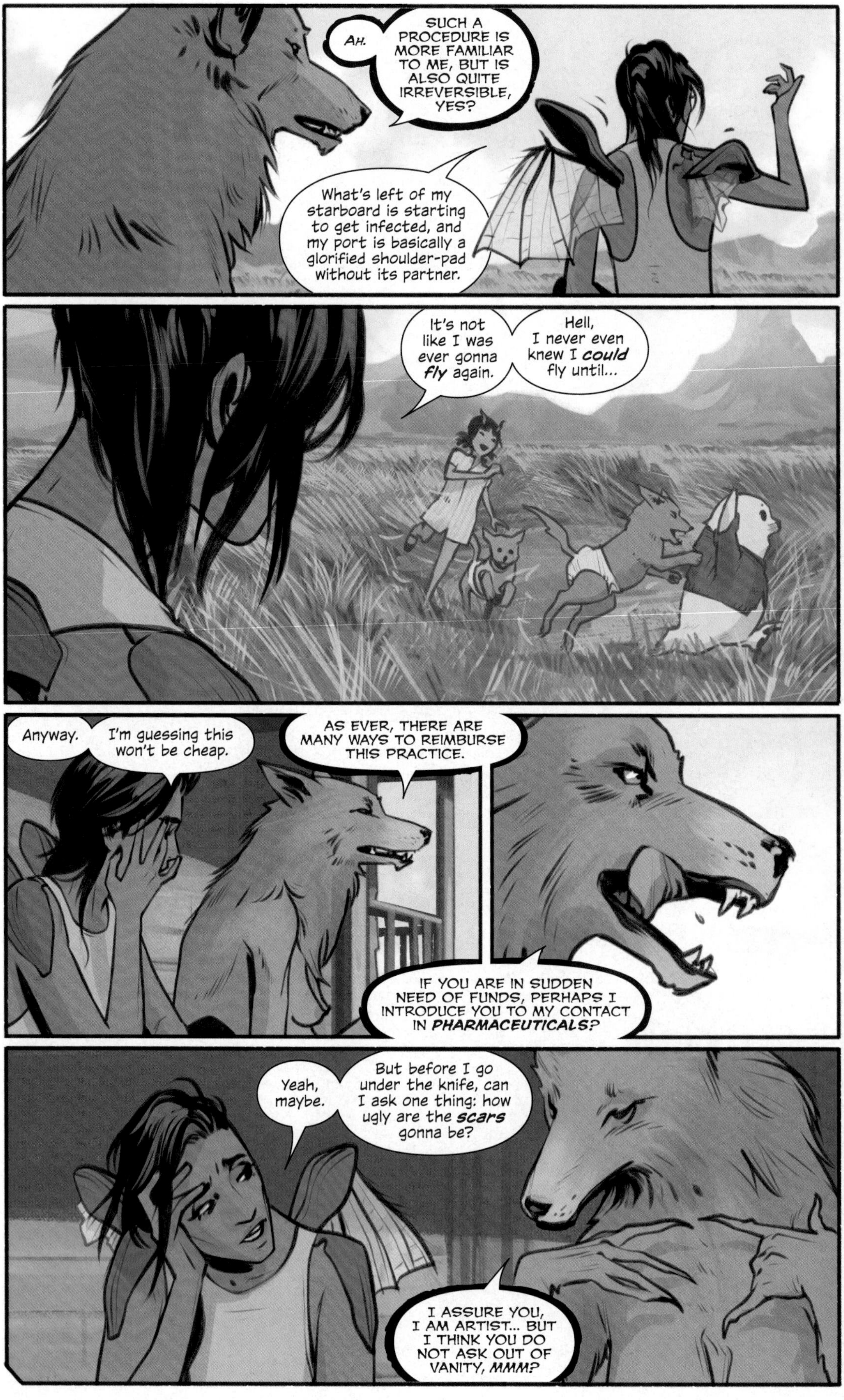
AH.
SUCH A PROCEDURE IS MORE FAMILIAR TO ME, BUT IS ALSO QUITE IRREVERSIBLE, YES?
What's left of my starboard is starting to get infected, and my port is basically a glorified shoulder-pad without its partner.
It's not like I was ever gonna *fly* again.
Hell, I never even knew I *could* fly until...
Anyway.
I'm guessing this won't be cheap.
AS EVER, THERE ARE MANY WAYS TO REIMBURSE THIS PRACTICE.
IF YOU ARE IN SUDDEN NEED OF FUNDS, PERHAPS I INTRODUCE YOU TO MY CONTACT IN *PHARMACEUTICALS?*
Yeah, maybe.
But before I go under the knife, can I ask one thing: how ugly are the *scars* gonna be?
I ASSURE YOU, I AM ARTIST... BUT I THINK YOU DO NOT ASK OUT OF VANITY, *MMM?*

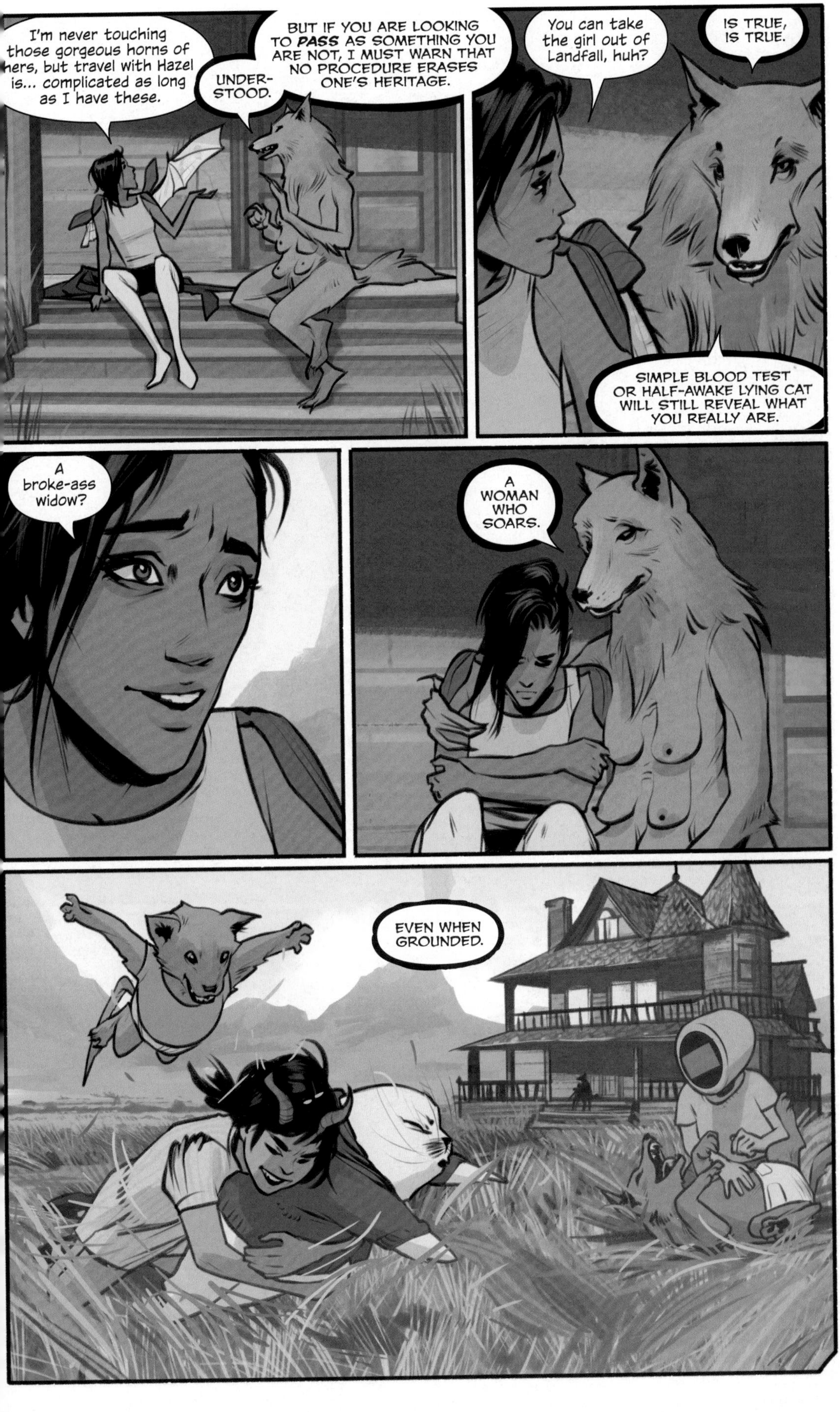
I'm never touching those gorgeous horns of hers, but travel with Hazel is... complicated as long as I have these.
UNDER-STOOD.
BUT IF YOU ARE LOOKING TO *PASS* AS SOMETHING YOU ARE NOT, I MUST WARN THAT NO PROCEDURE ERASES ONE'S HERITAGE.
You can take the girl out of Landfall, huh?
IS TRUE, IS TRUE.
SIMPLE BLOOD TEST OR HALF-AWAKE LYING CAT WILL STILL REVEAL WHAT YOU REALLY ARE.
A broke-ass widow?
A WOMAN WHO SOARS.
EVEN WHEN GROUNDED.

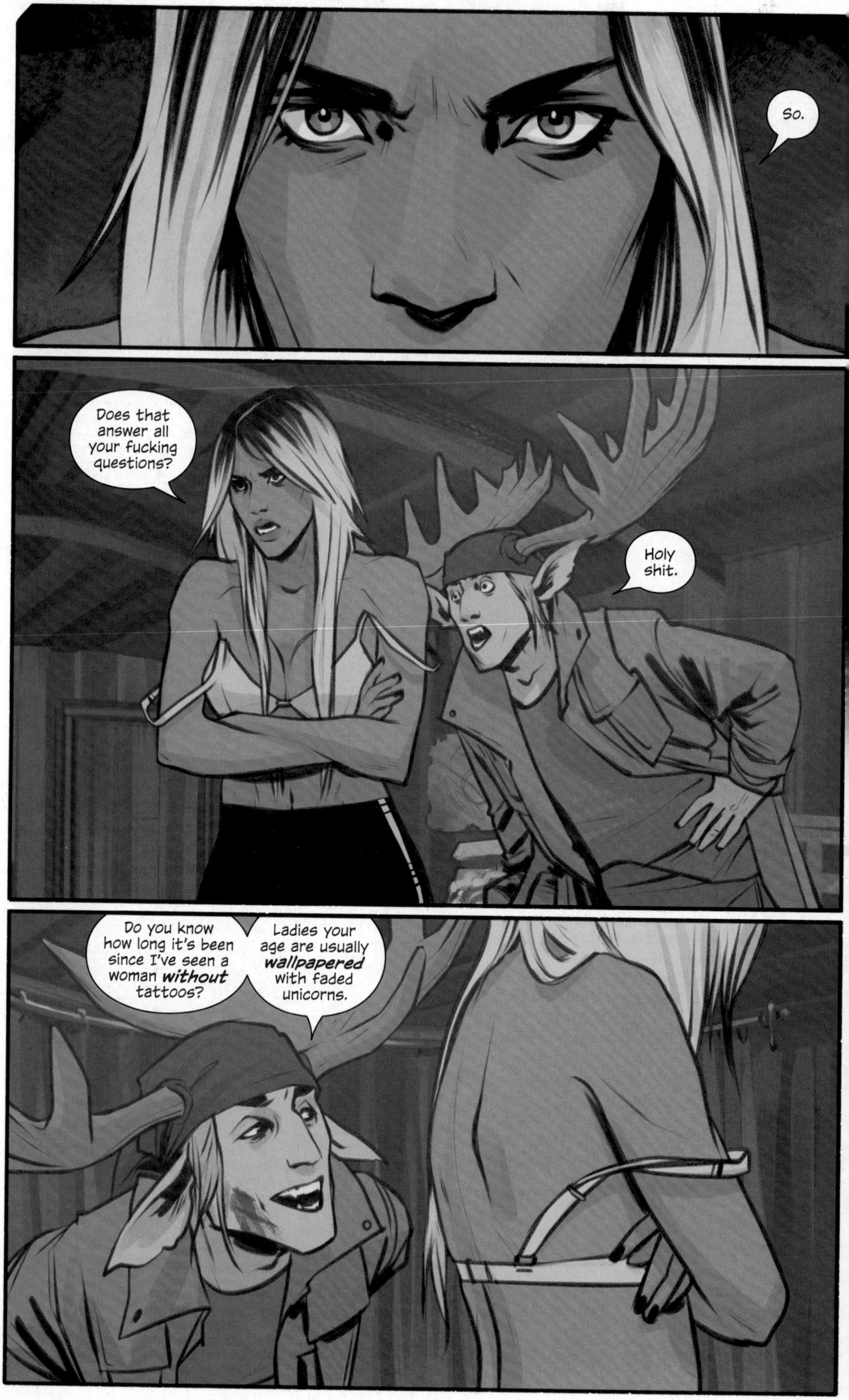
So.
Does that answer all your fucking questions?
Holy shit.
Do you know how long it's been since I've seen a woman **without** tattoos?
Ladies your age are usually **wallpapered** with faded unicorns.

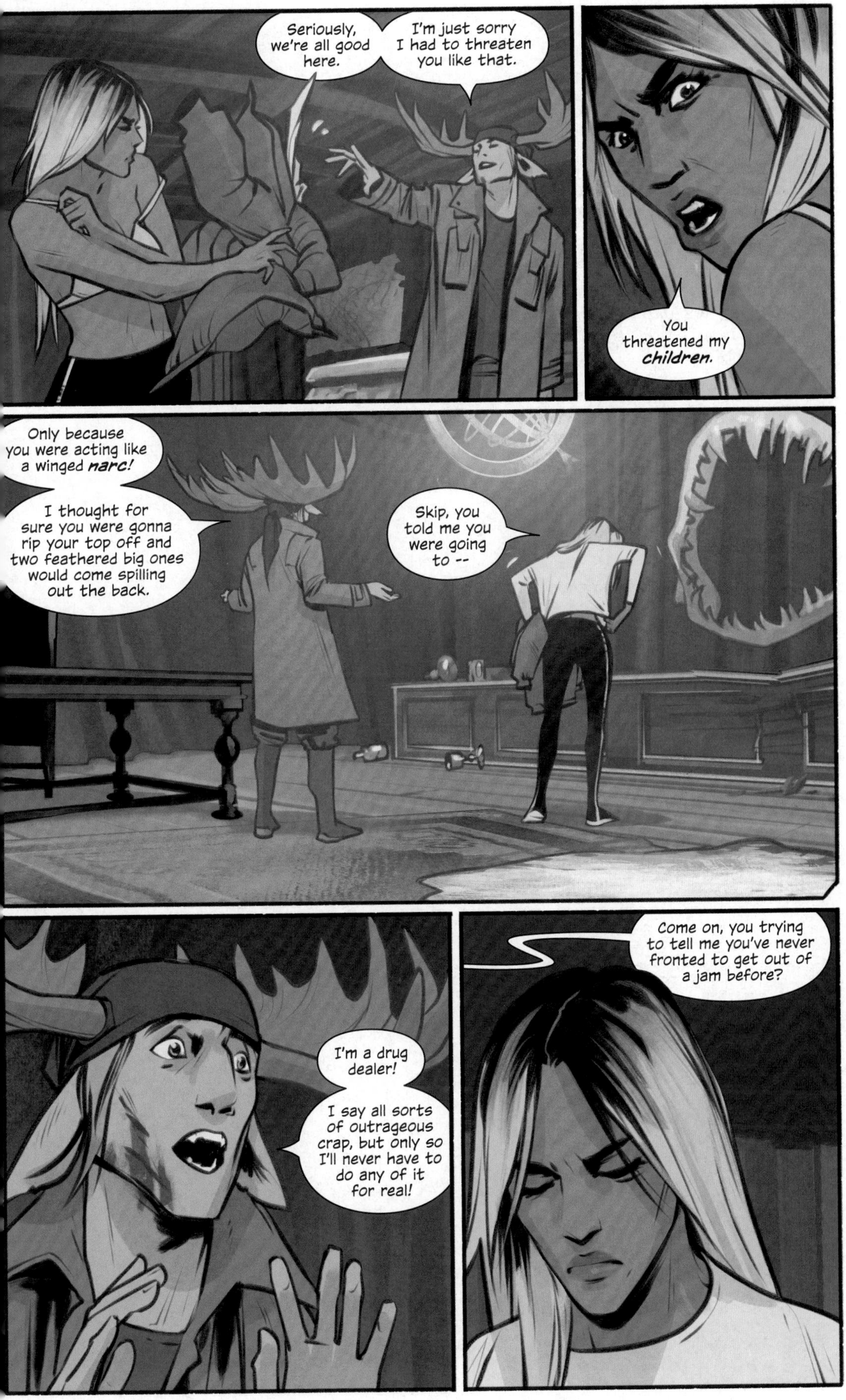
Seriously, we're all good here.
I'm just sorry I had to threaten you like that.
You threatened my *children*.
Only because you were acting like a winged *narc!*
I thought for sure you were gonna rip your top off and two feathered big ones would come spilling out the back.
Skip, you told me you were going to --
Come on, you trying to tell me you've never fronted to get out of a jam before?
I'm a drug dealer!
I say all sorts of outrageous crap, but only so I'll never have to do any of it for real!

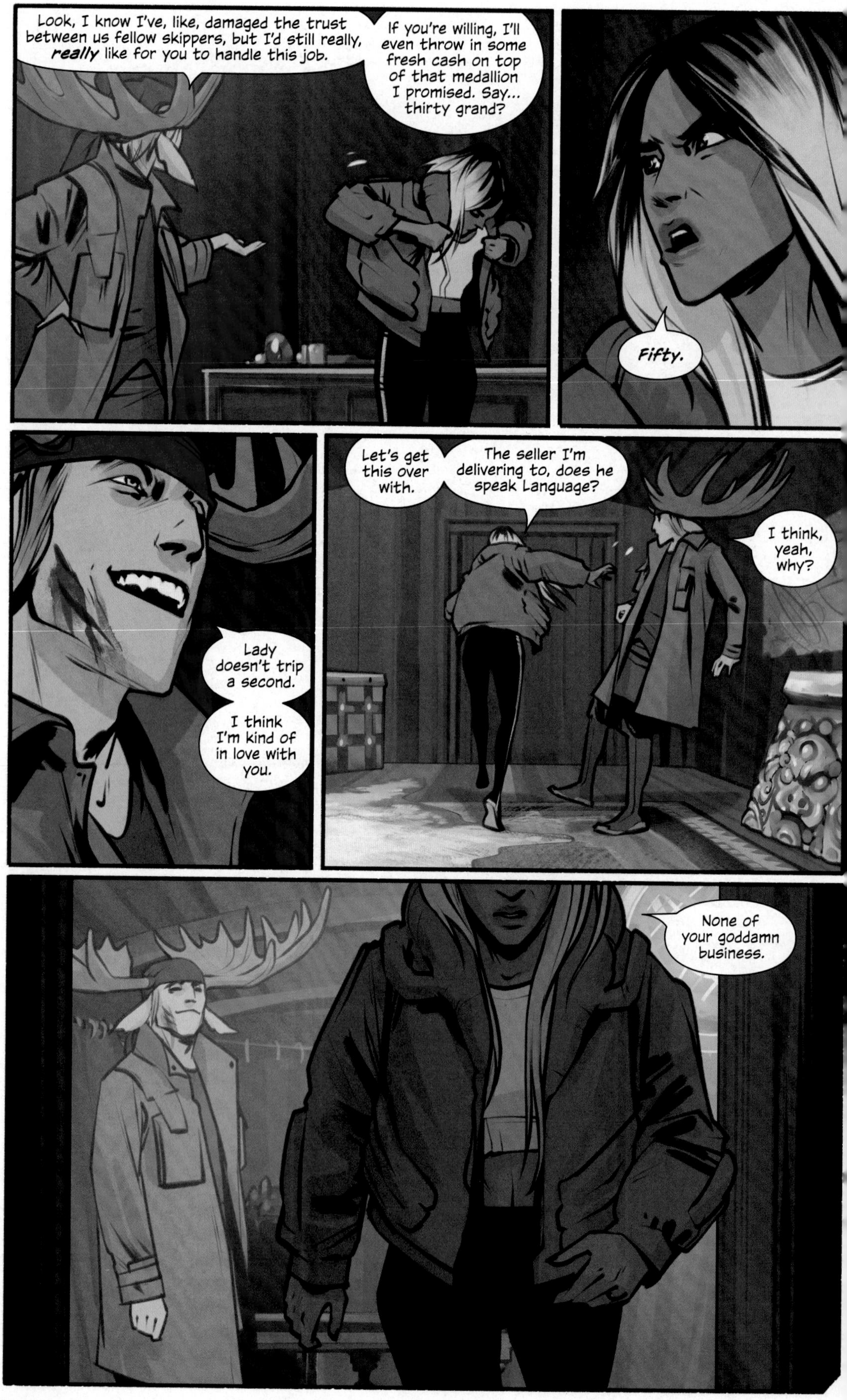

Look, I know I've, like, damaged the trust between us fellow skippers, but I'd still really, *really* like for you to handle this job.
If you're willing, I'll even throw in some fresh cash on top of that medallion I promised. Say... thirty grand?
Fifty.
Lady doesn't trip a second.
I think I'm kind of in love with you.
Let's get this over with.
The seller I'm delivering to, does he speak Language?
I think, yeah, why?
None of your goddamn business.

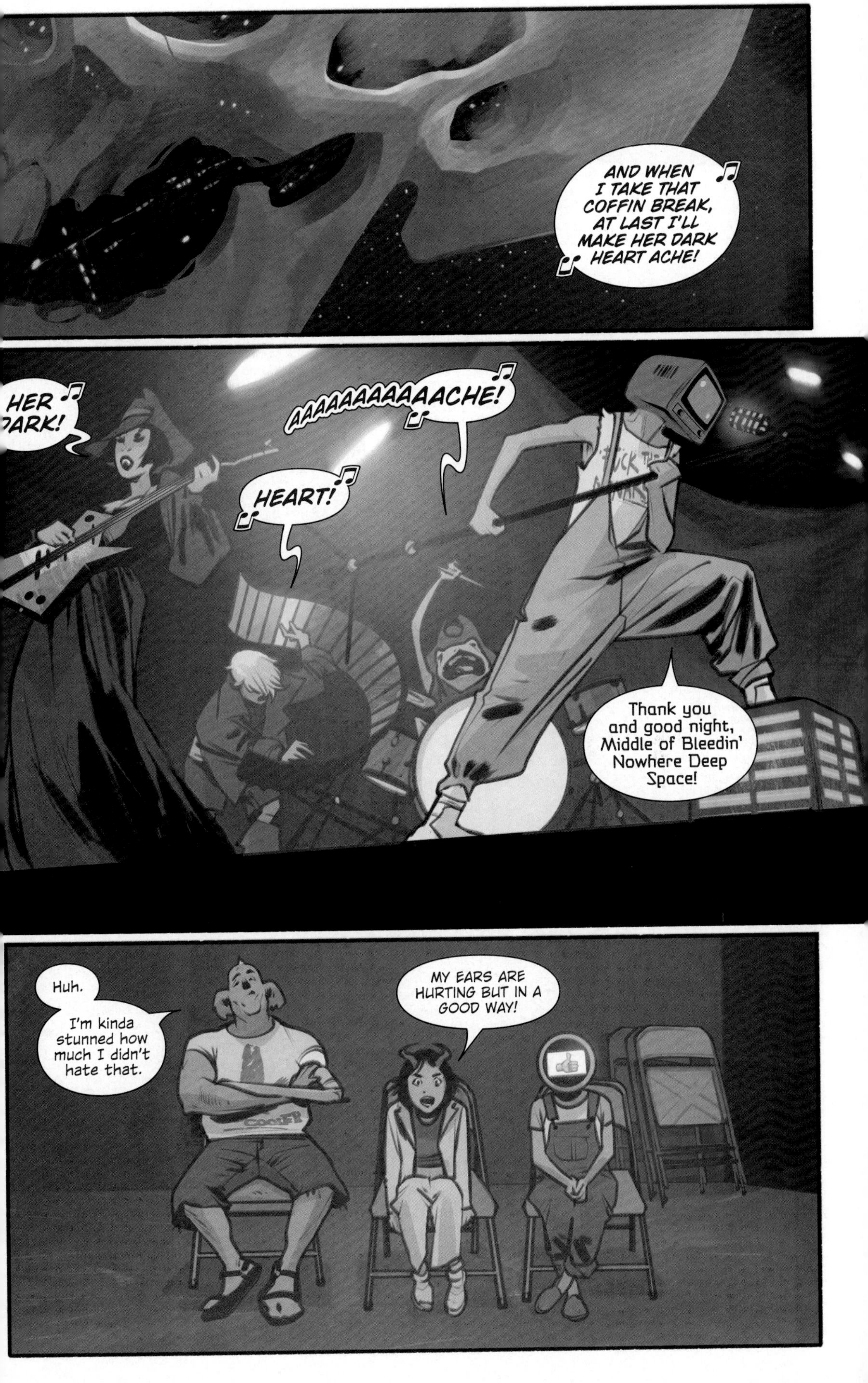
AND WHEN I TAKE THAT COFFIN BREAK, AT LAST I'LL MAKE HER DARK HEART ACHE!
HER DARK!
HEART!
AAAAAAAAAAACHE!
Thank you and good night, Middle of Bleedin' Nowhere Deep Space!
Huh.
I'm kinda stunned how much I didn't hate that.
MY EARS ARE HURTING BUT IN A GOOD WAY!

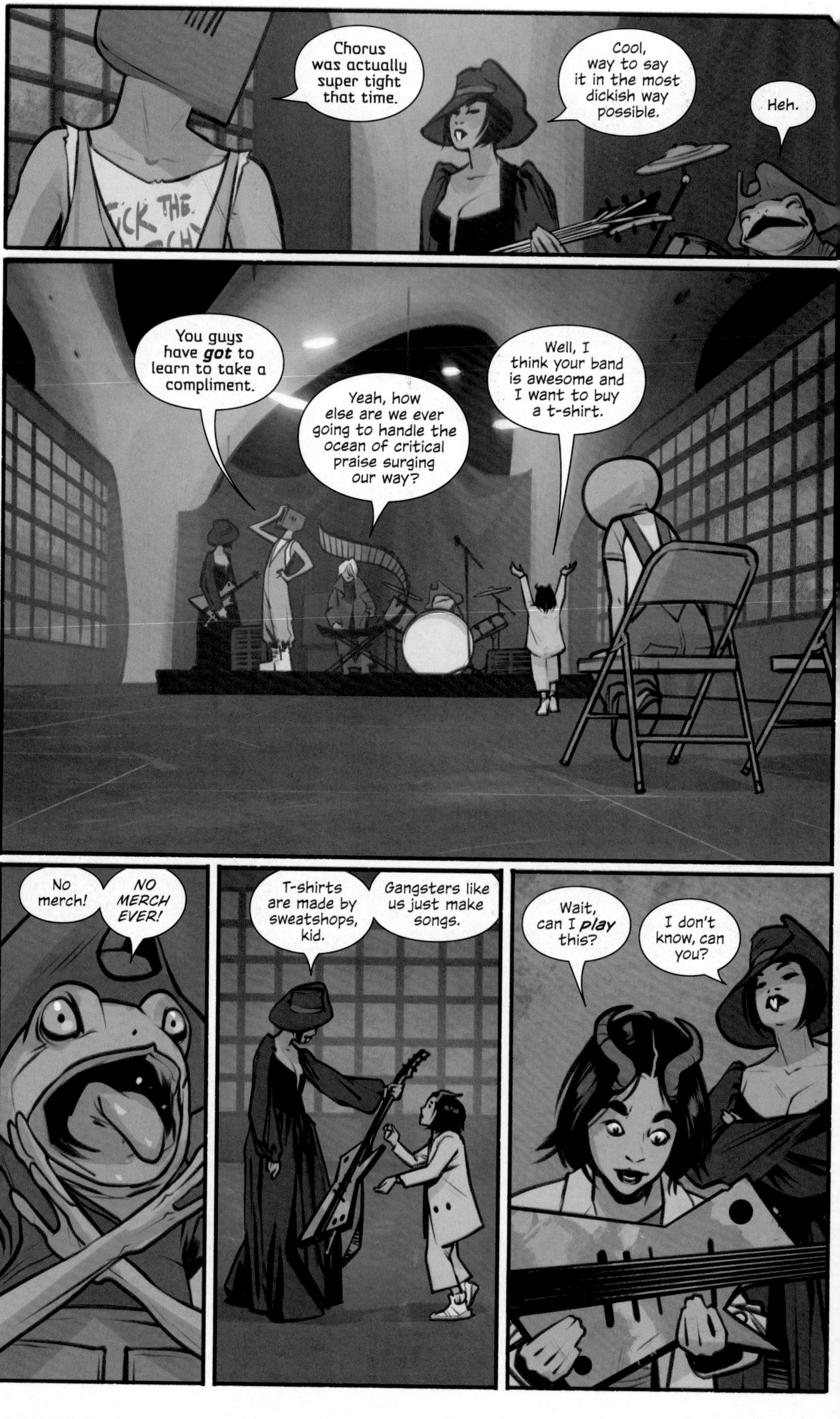
Chorus was actually super tight that time.
Cool, way to say it in the most dickish way possible.
Heh.
You guys have **got** to learn to take a compliment.
Yeah, how else are we ever going to handle the ocean of critical praise surging our way?
Well, I think your band is awesome and I want to buy a t-shirt.
No merch!
NO MERCH EVER!
T-shirts are made by sweatshops, kid.
Gangsters like us just make songs.
Wait, can I *play* this?
I don't know, can you?

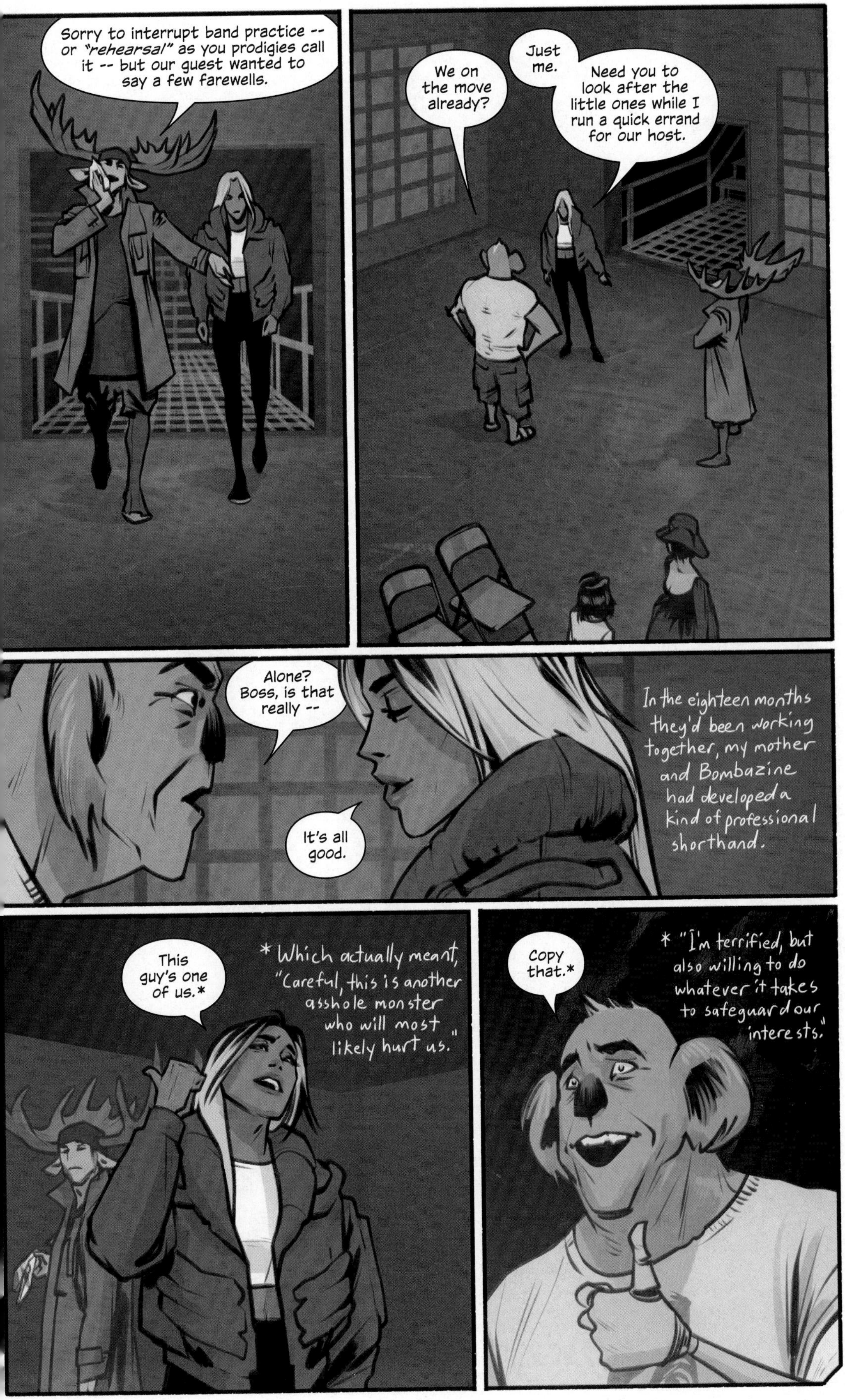
Sorry to interrupt band practice -- or "rehearsal" as you prodigies call it -- but our guest wanted to say a few farewells.
We on the move already?
Just me.
Need you to look after the little ones while I run a quick errand for our host.
Alone? Boss, is that really --
It's all good.
In the eighteen months they'd been working together, my mother and Bombazine had developed a kind of professional shorthand.
This guy's one of us.*
* Which actually meant, "Careful, this is another asshole monster who will most likely hurt us."
Copy that.*
* "I'm terrified, but also willing to do whatever it takes to safeguard our interests."

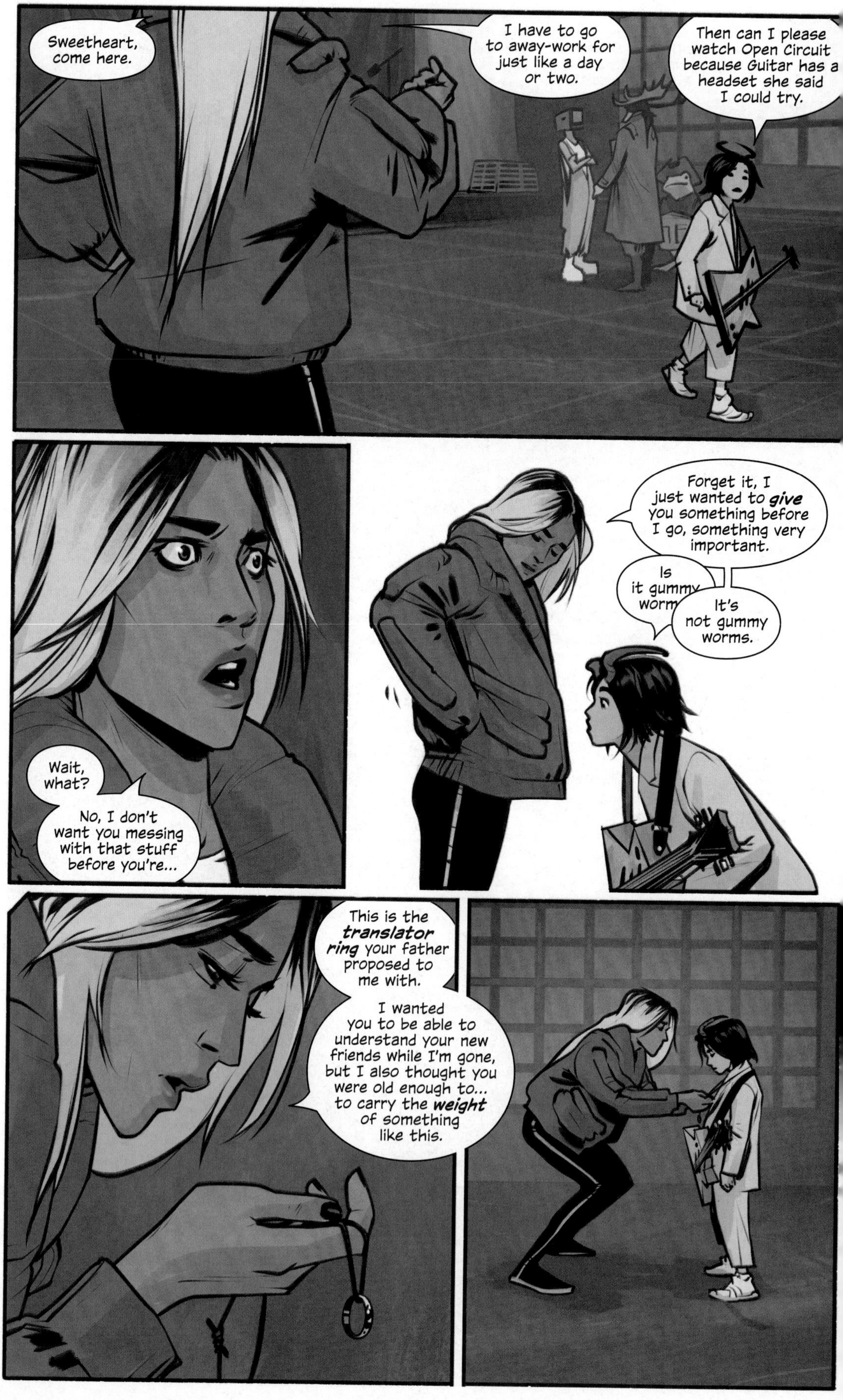
Sweetheart, come here.
I have to go to away-work for just like a day or two.
Then can I please watch Open Circuit because Guitar has a headset she said I could try.
Wait, what?
No, I don't want you messing with that stuff before you're...
Forget it, I just wanted to *give* you something before I go, something very important.
Is it gummy worms?
It's not gummy worms.
This is the *translator ring* your father proposed to me with.
I wanted you to be able to understand your new friends while I'm gone, but I also thought you were old enough to... to carry the *weight* of something like this.

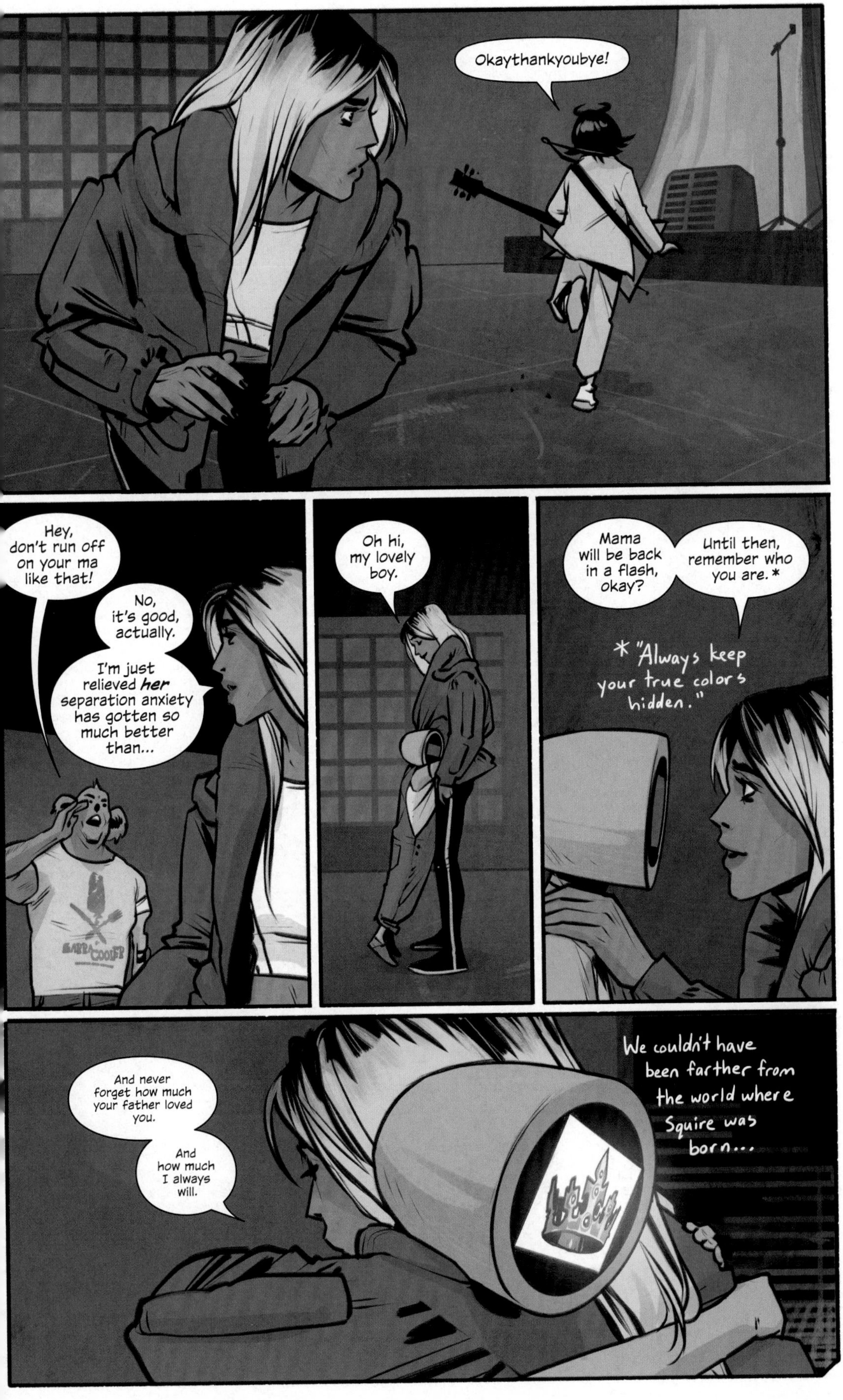

Okaythankyoubye!
Hey, don't run off on your ma like that!
No, it's good, actually.
I'm just relieved **her** separation anxiety has gotten so much better than...
Oh hi, my lovely boy.
Mama will be back in a flash, okay?
Until then, remember who you are.*
*"Always keep your true colors hidden."
And never forget how much your father loved you.
And how much I always will.
We couldn't have been farther from the world where Squire was born...

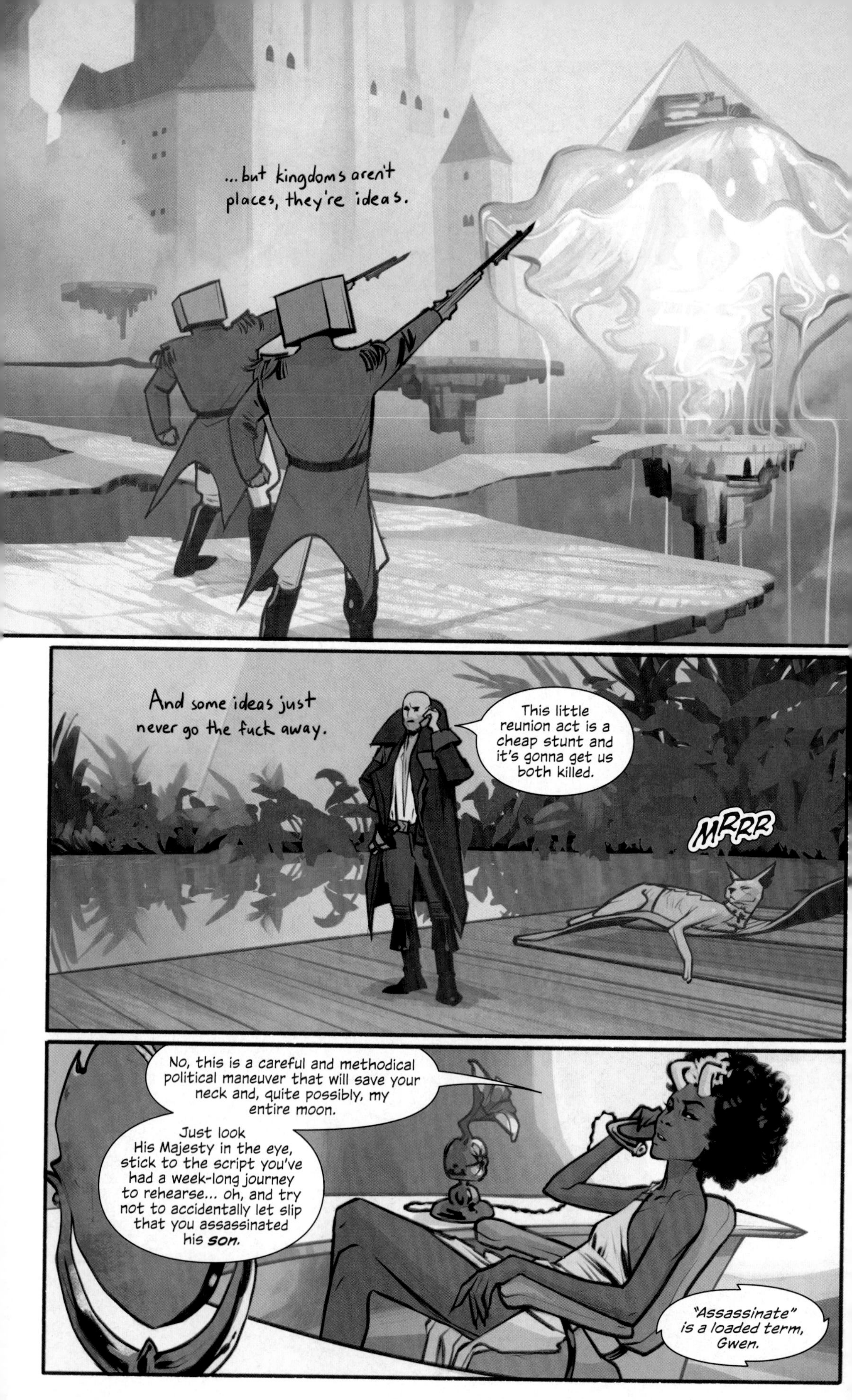
...but kingdoms aren't places, they're ideas.
And some ideas just never go the fuck away.
This little reunion act is a cheap stunt and it's gonna get us both killed.
MRRR
No, this is a careful and methodical political maneuver that will save your neck and, quite possibly, my entire moon.
Just look His Majesty in the eye, stick to the script you've had a week-long journey to rehearse... oh, and try not to accidentally let slip that you assassinated his *son*.
"Assassinate" is a loaded term, Gwen.

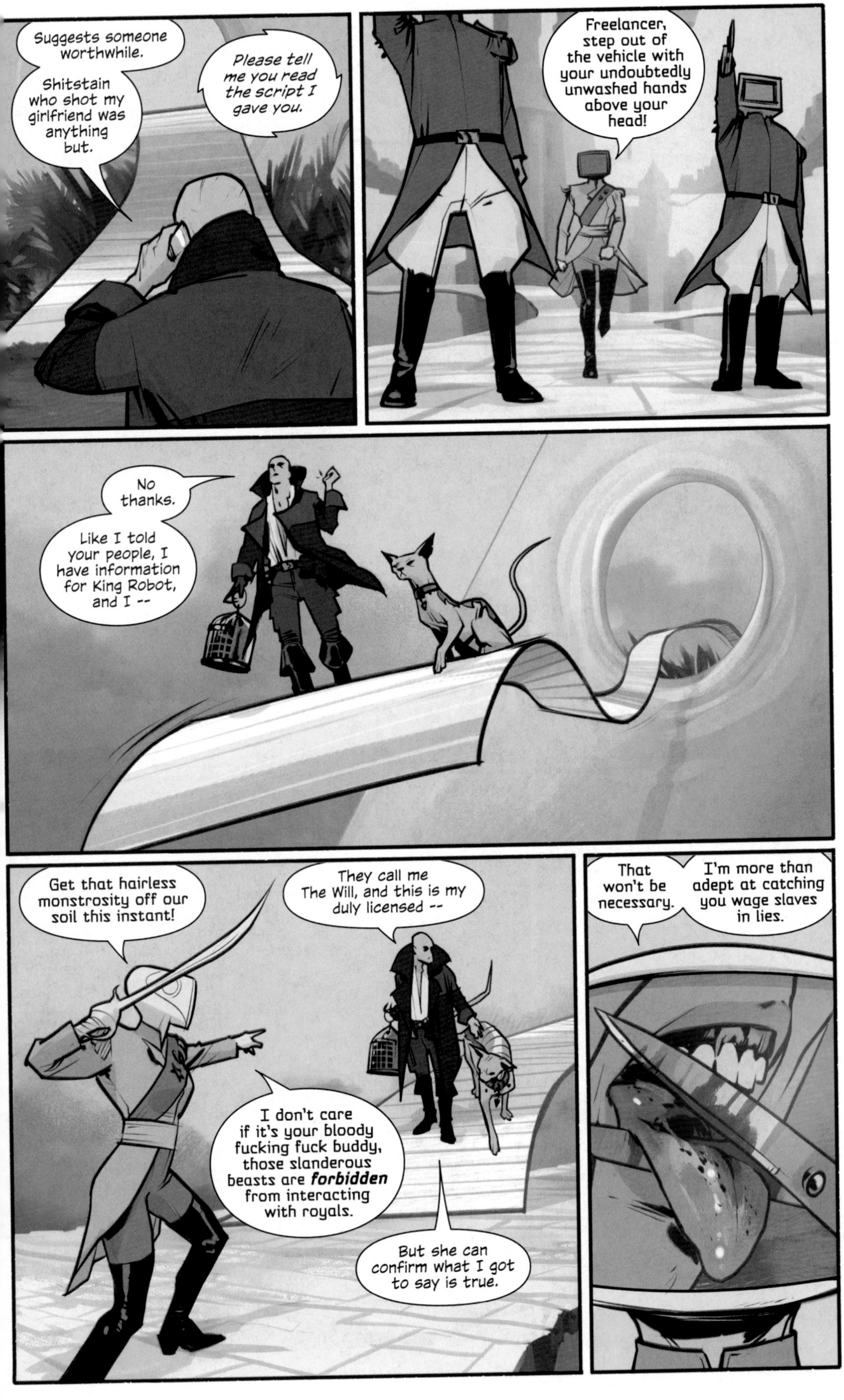
Suggests someone worthwhile.
Shitstain who shot my girlfriend was anything but.
Please tell me you read the script I gave you.
Freelancer, step out of the vehicle with your undoubtedly unwashed hands above your head!
No thanks.
Like I told your people, I have information for King Robot, and I --
Get that hairless monstrosity off our soil this instant!
They call me The Will, and this is my duly licensed --
I don't care if it's your bloody fucking fuck buddy, those slanderous beasts are ***forbidden*** from interacting with royals.
But she can confirm what I got to say is true.
That won't be necessary.
I'm more than adept at catching you wage slaves in lies.

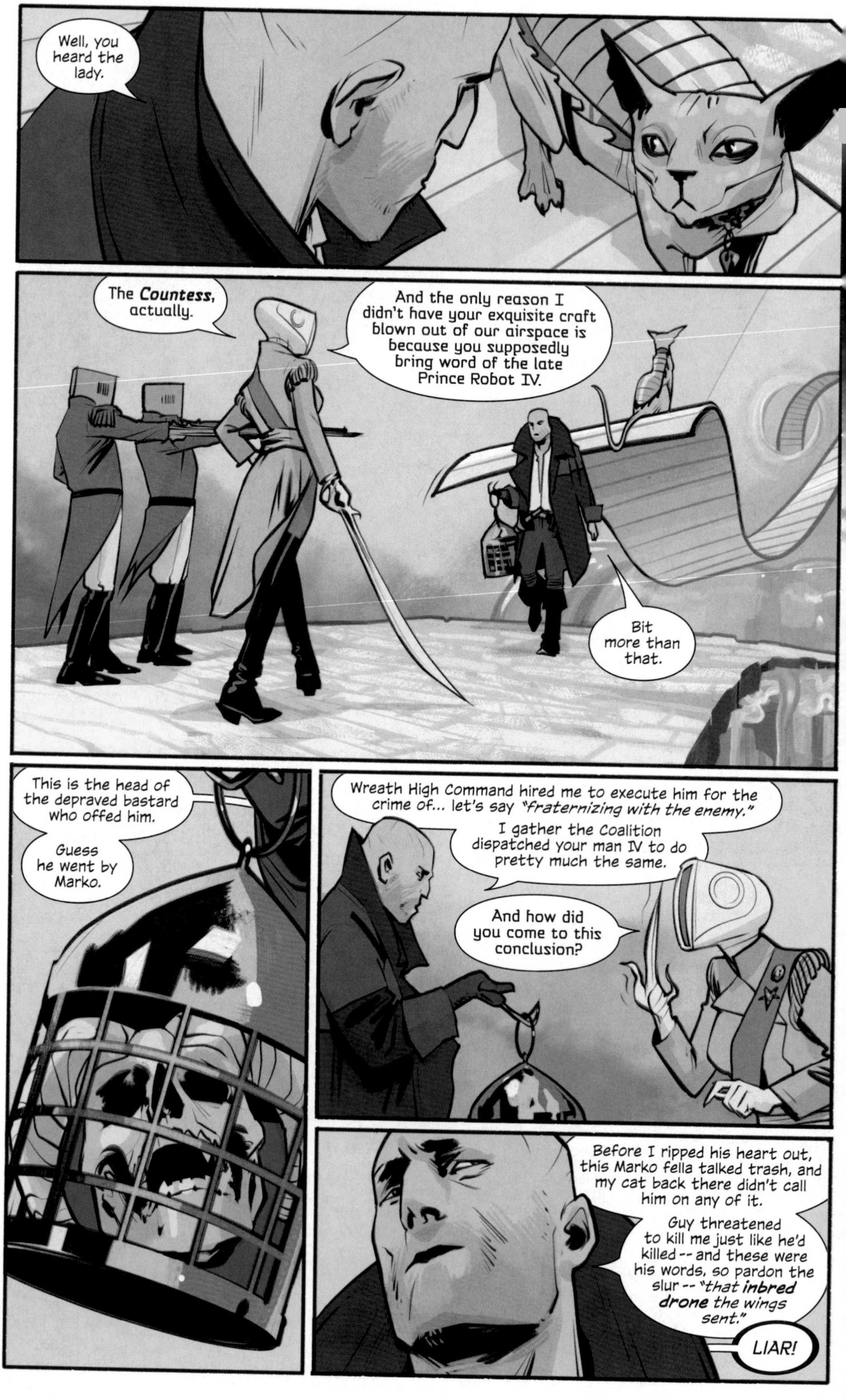
Well, you heard the lady.
The *Countess*, actually.
And the only reason I didn't have your exquisite craft blown out of our airspace is because you supposedly bring word of the late Prince Robot IV.
Bit more than that.
This is the head of the depraved bastard who offed him.
Guess he went by Marko.
Wreath High Command hired me to execute him for the crime of... let's say *"fraternizing with the enemy."*
I gather the Coalition dispatched your man IV to do pretty much the same.
And how did you come to this conclusion?
Before I ripped his heart out, this Marko fella talked trash, and my cat back there didn't call him on any of it.
Guy threatened to kill me just like he'd killed -- and these were his words, so pardon the slur -- *"that **inbred drone** the wings sent."*
LIAR!

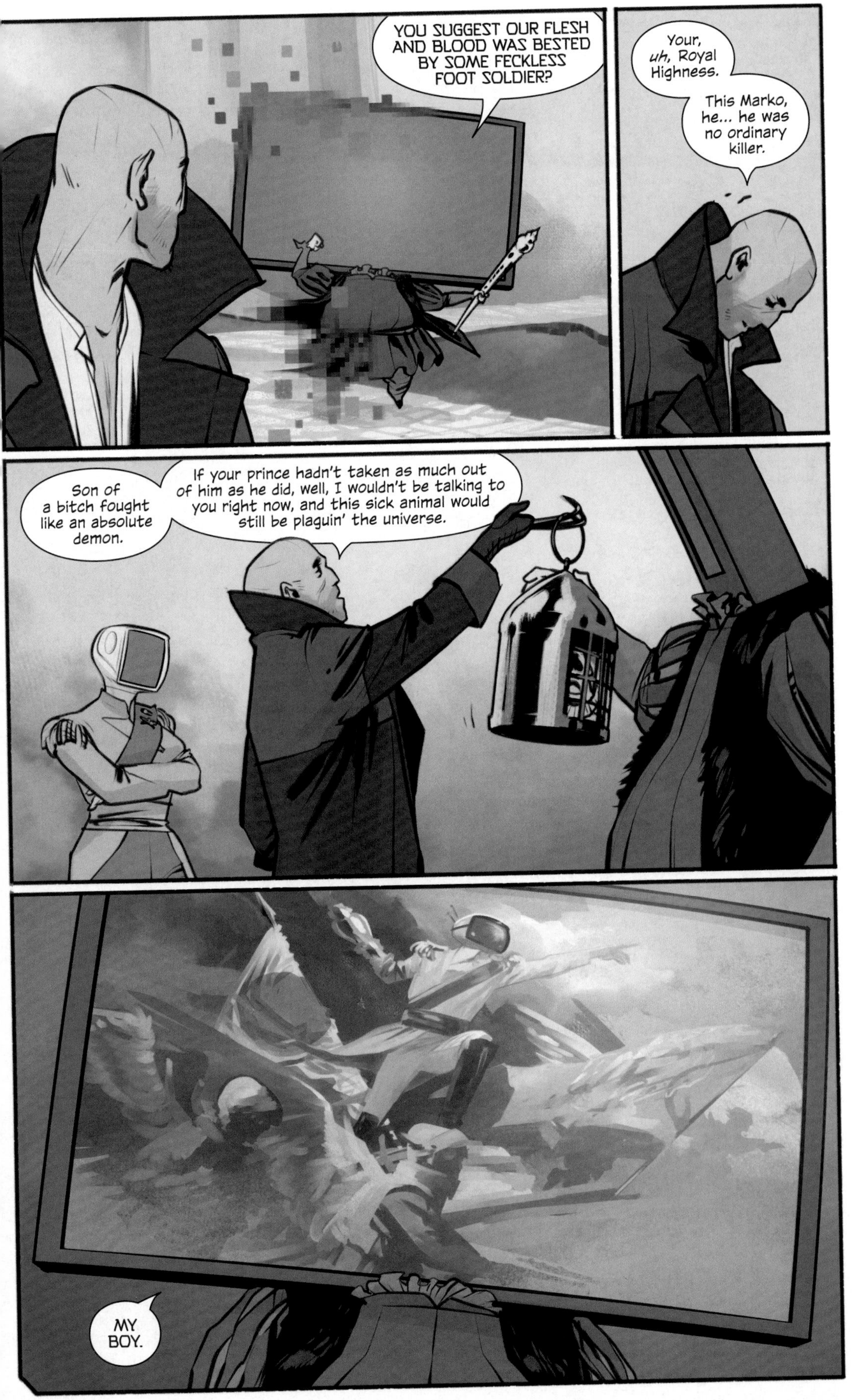
YOU SUGGEST OUR FLESH AND BLOOD WAS BESTED BY SOME FECKLESS FOOT SOLDIER?
Your, *uh*, Royal Highness.
This Marko, he... he was no ordinary killer.
Son of a bitch fought like an absolute demon.
If your prince hadn't taken as much out of him as he did, well, I wouldn't be talking to you right now, and this sick animal would still be plaguin' the universe.
MY BOY.

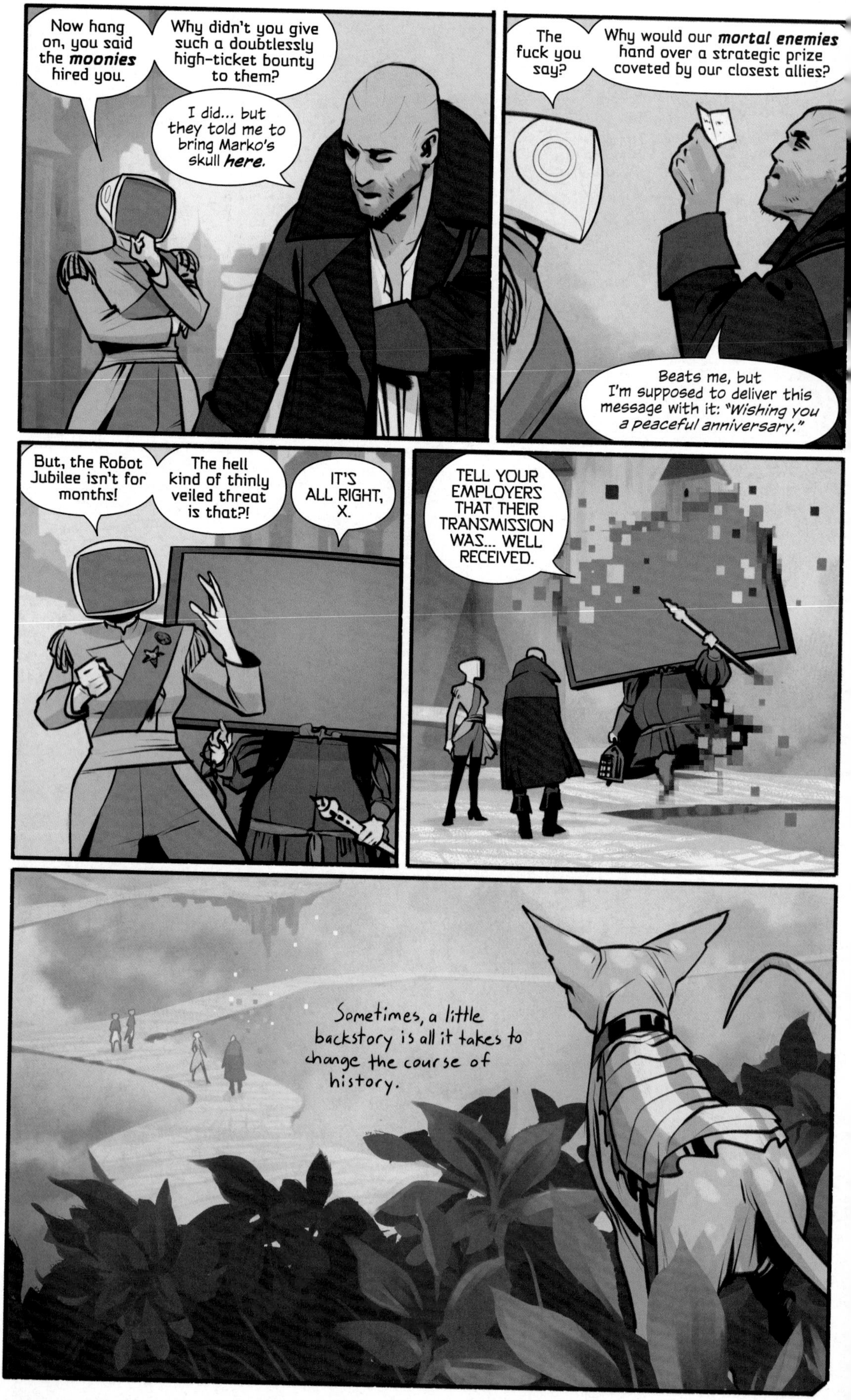

Now hang on, you said the ***moonies*** hired you.
Why didn't you give such a doubtlessly high-ticket bounty to them?
I did... but they told me to bring Marko's skull ***here.***
The fuck you say?
Why would our ***mortal enemies*** hand over a strategic prize coveted by our closest allies?
Beats me, but I'm supposed to deliver this message with it: *"Wishing you a peaceful anniversary."*
But, the Robot Jubilee isn't for months!
The hell kind of thinly veiled threat is that?!
IT'S ALL RIGHT, X.
TELL YOUR EMPLOYERS THAT THEIR TRANSMISSION WAS... WELL RECEIVED.
Sometimes, a little backstory is all it takes to change the course of history.

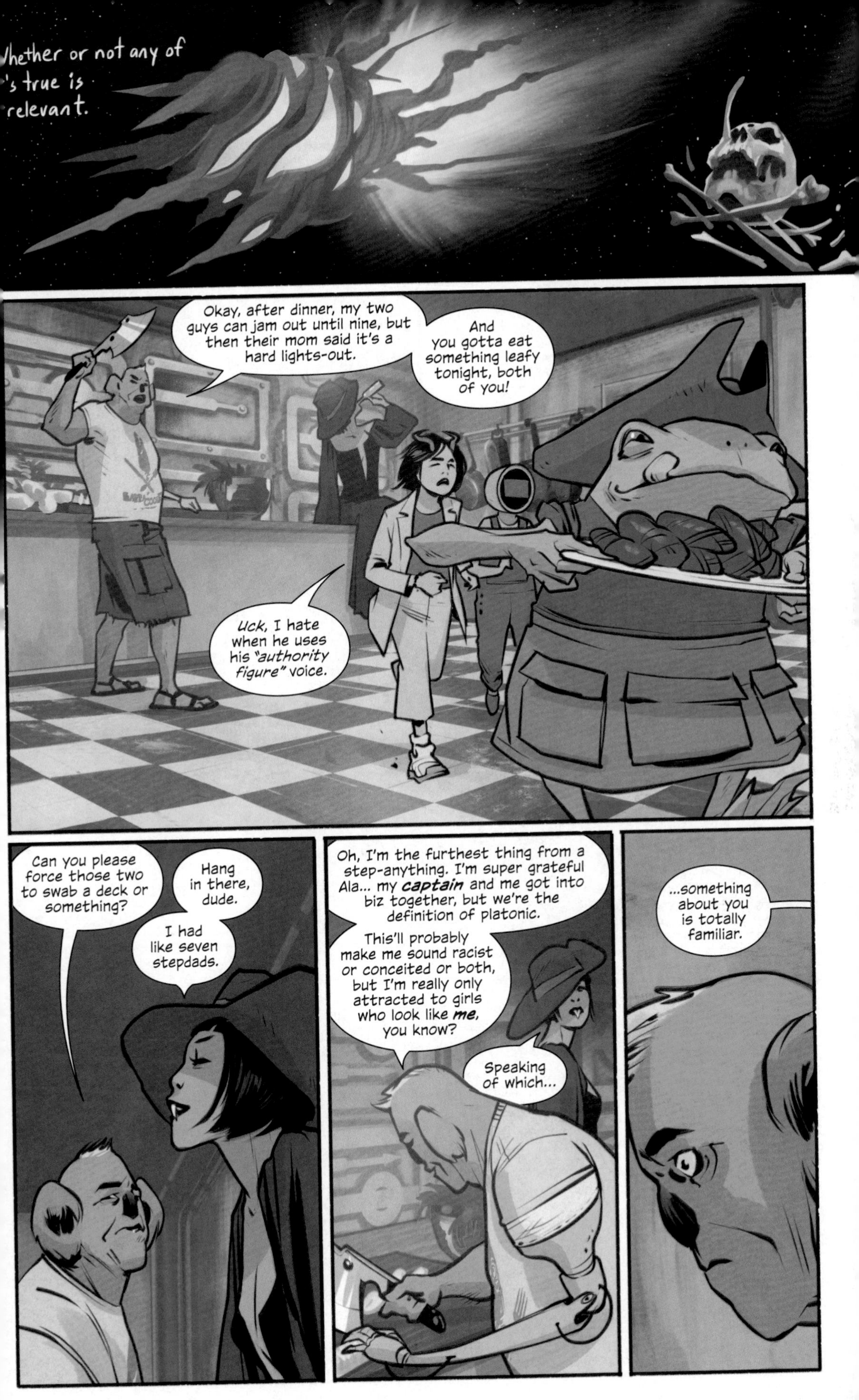

Whether or not any of
's true is
relevant.
Okay, after dinner, my two guys can jam out until nine, but then their mom said it's a hard lights-out.
And you gotta eat something leafy tonight, both of you!
Uck, I hate when he uses his *"authority figure"* voice.
Can you please force those two to swab a deck or something?
Hang in there, dude.
I had like seven stepdads.
Oh, I'm the furthest thing from a step-anything. I'm super grateful Ala... my ***captain*** and me got into biz together, but we're the definition of platonic.
This'll probably make me sound racist or conceited or both, but I'm really only attracted to girls who look like ***me,*** you know?
Speaking of which...
...something about you is totally familiar.

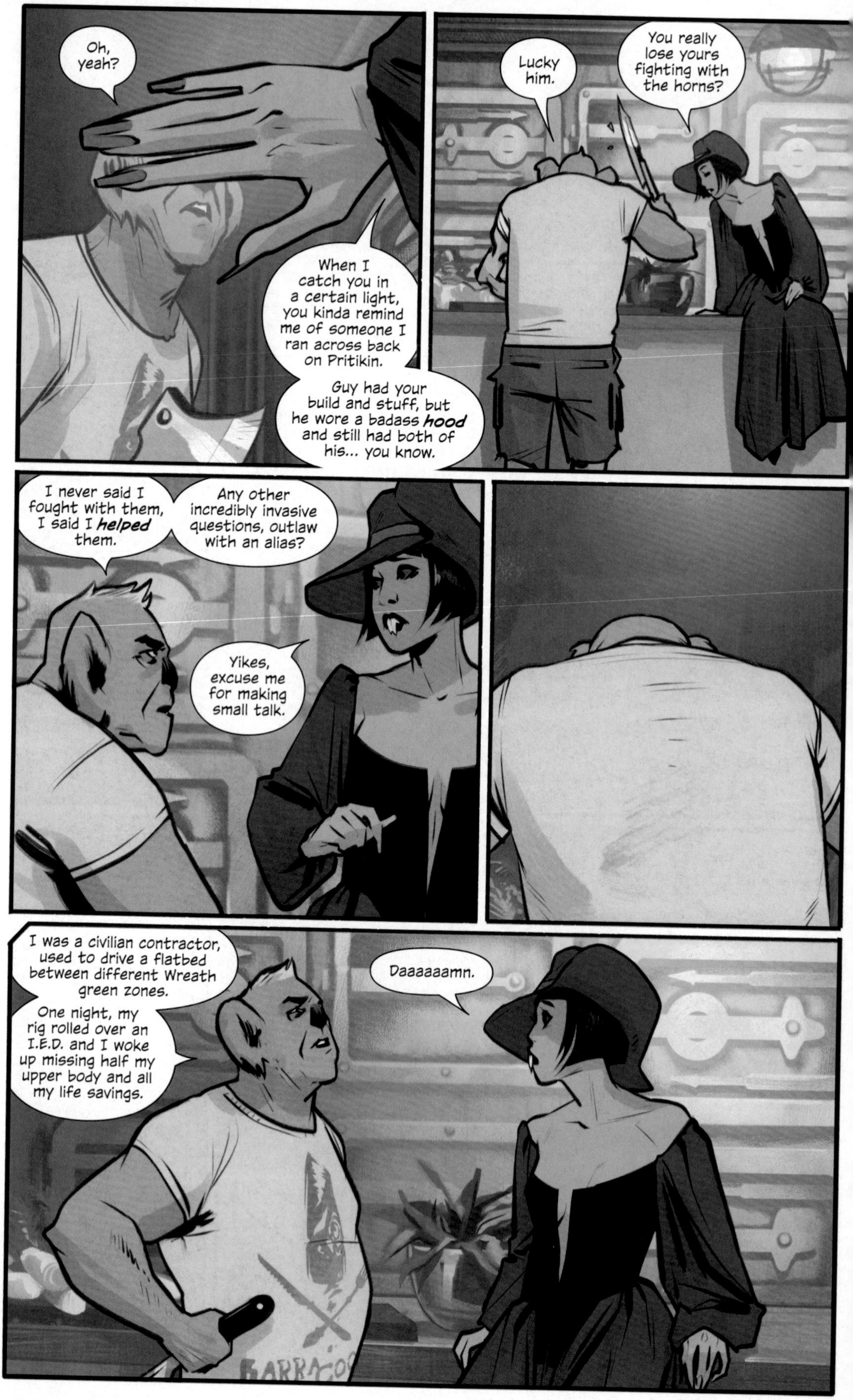
Oh, yeah?
Lucky him.
You really lose yours fighting with the horns?
When I catch you in a certain light, you kinda remind me of someone I ran across back on Pritikin.
Guy had your build and stuff, but he wore a badass ***hood*** and still had both of his... you know.
I never said I fought with them, I said I ***helped*** them.
Any other incredibly invasive questions, outlaw with an alias?
Yikes, excuse me for making small talk.
I was a civilian contractor, used to drive a flatbed between different Wreath green zones.
One night, my rig rolled over an I.E.D. and I woke up missing half my upper body and all my life savings.
Daaaaaamn.

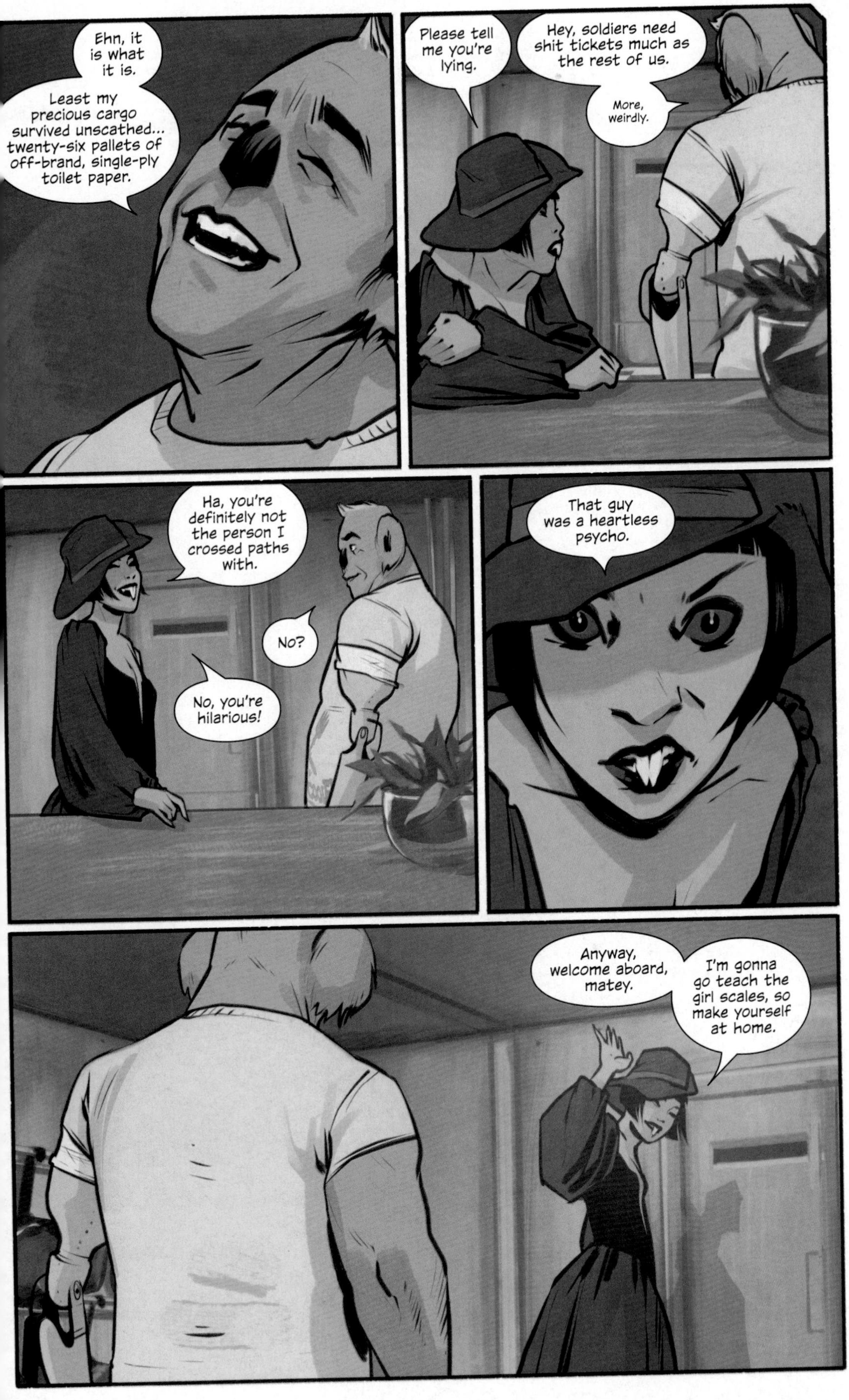
Ehn, it is what it is.
Least my precious cargo survived unscathed... twenty-six pallets of off-brand, single-ply toilet paper.
Please tell me you're lying.
Hey, soldiers need shit tickets much as the rest of us.
More, weirdly.
Ha, you're definitely not the person I crossed paths with.
No?
No, you're hilarious!
That guy was a heartless psycho.
Anyway, welcome aboard, matey.
I'm gonna go teach the girl scales, so make yourself at home.

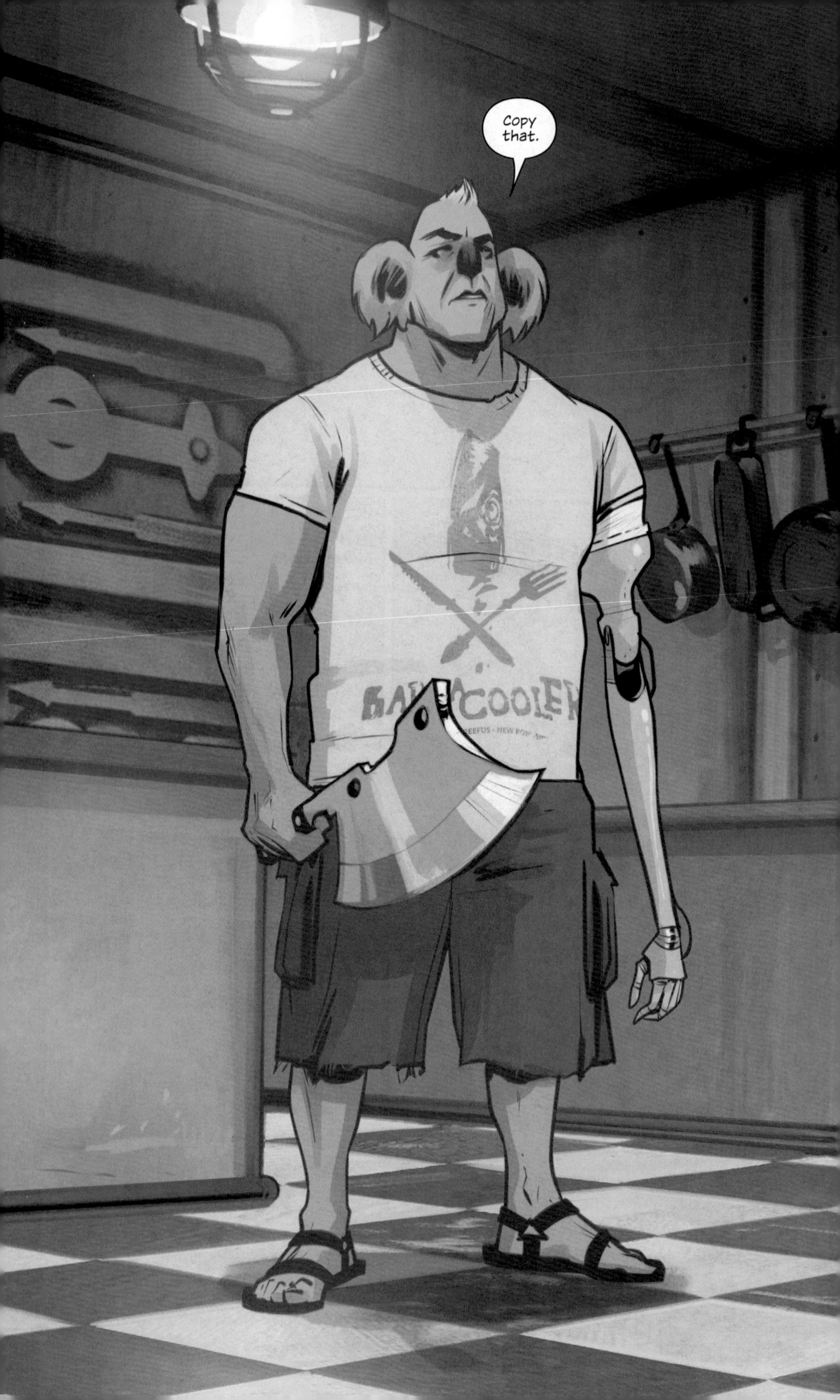
Copy that.

end chapter fifty-seven

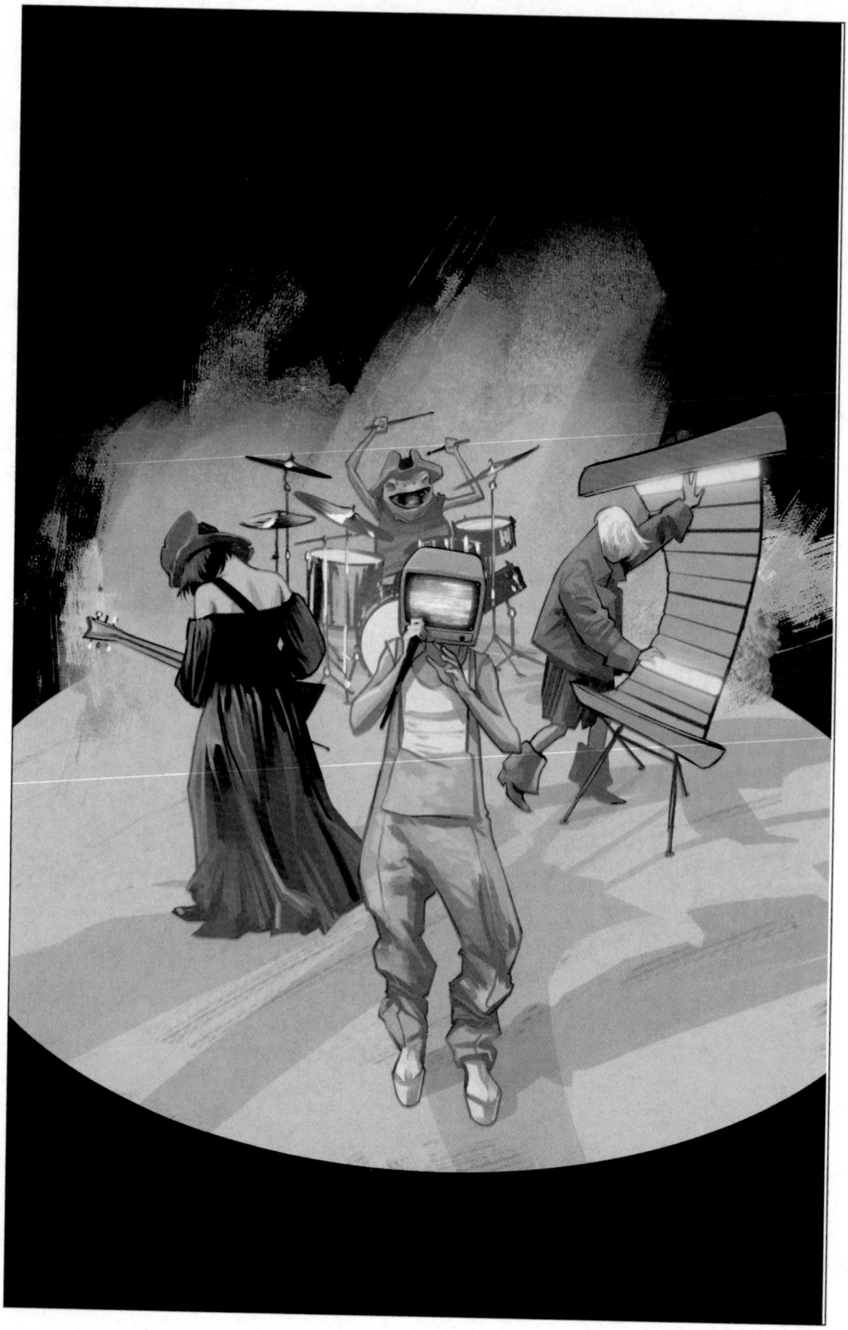

CHAPTER
FIFTY-EIGHT

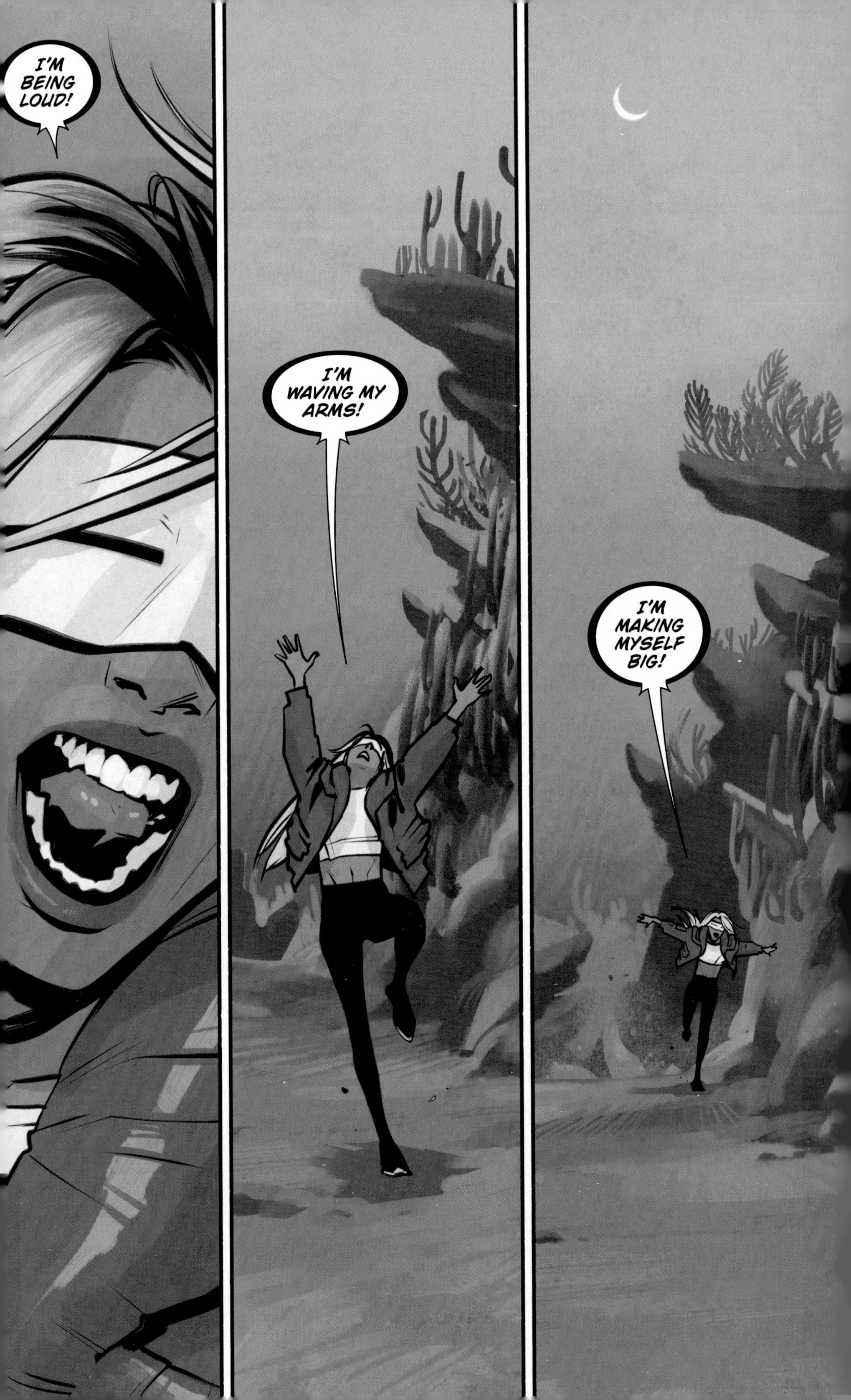
I'M BEING LOUD!
I'M WAVING MY ARMS!
I'M MAKING MYSELF BIG!

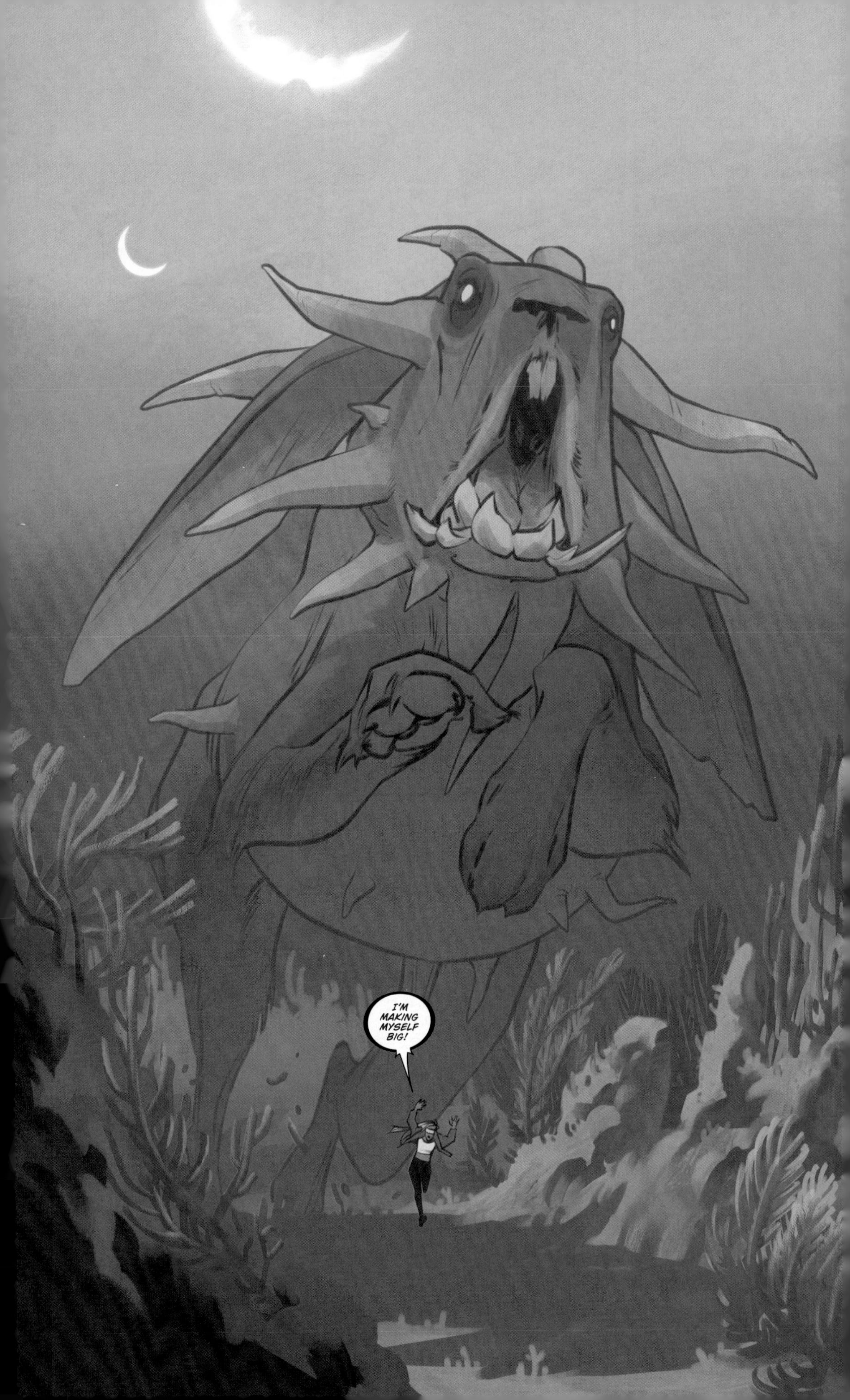
I'M MAKING MYSELF BIG!

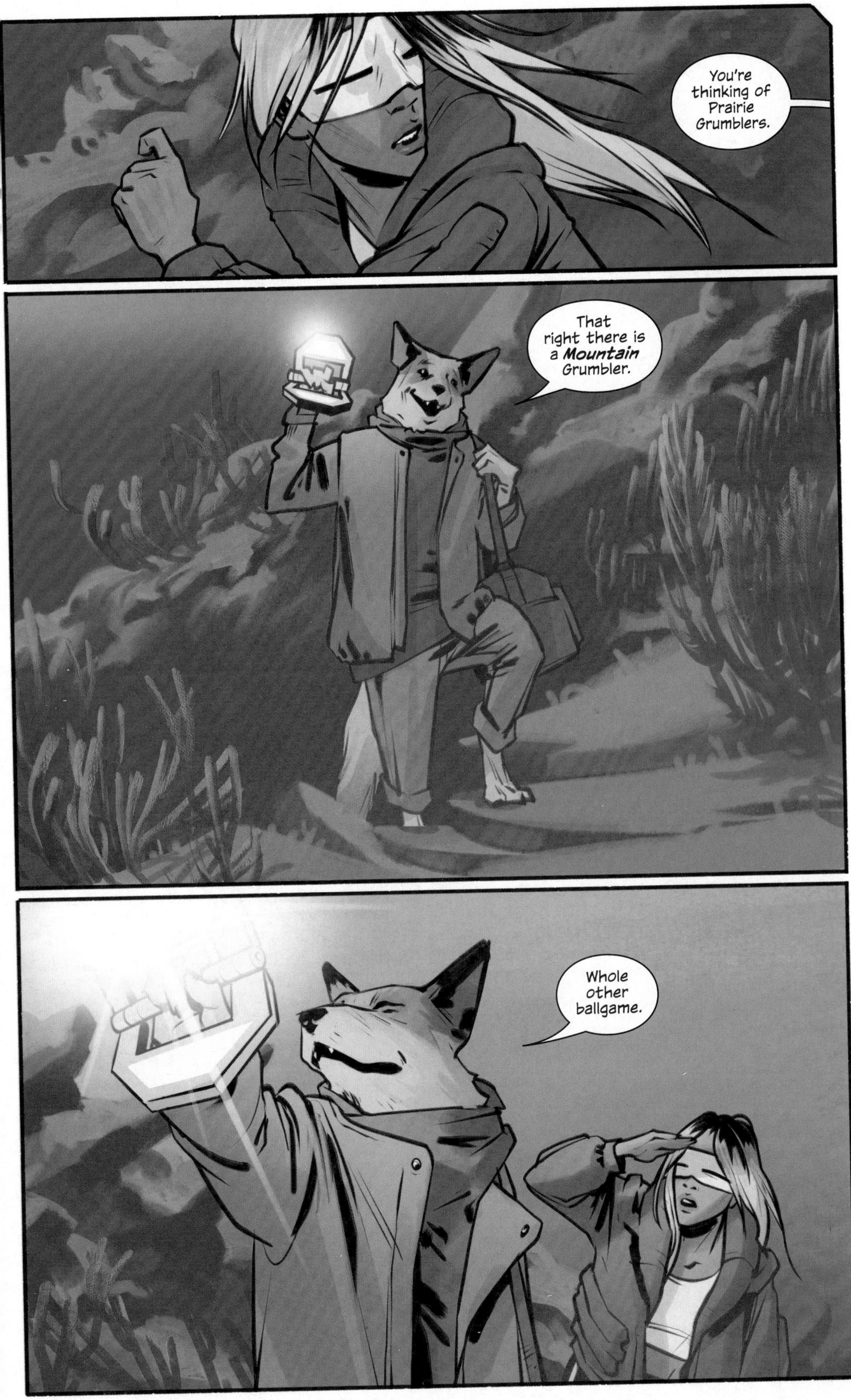
You're thinking of Prairie Grumblers.
That right there is a *Mountain* Grumbler.
Whole other ballgame.

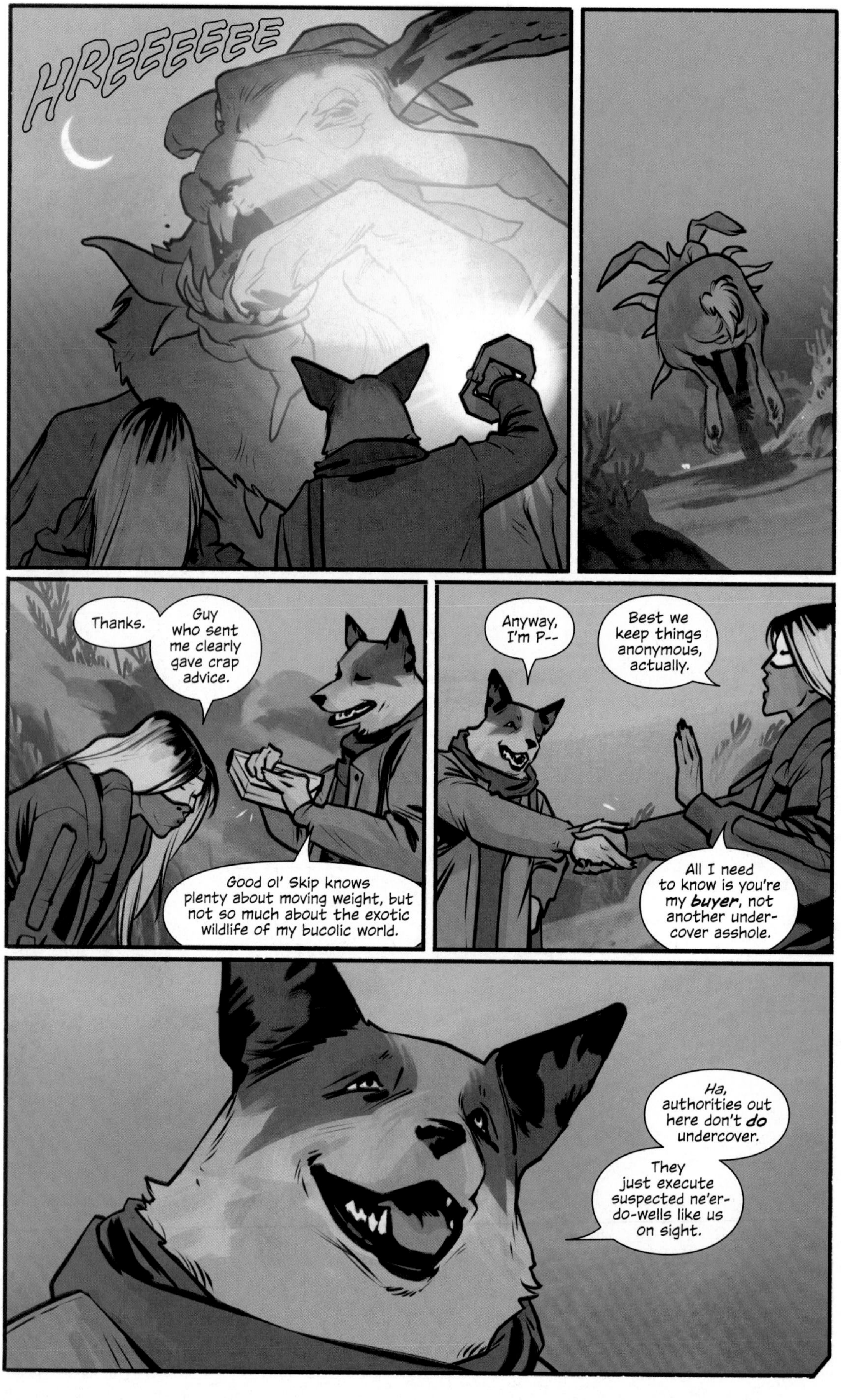
HREEEEEEE
Thanks.
Guy who sent me clearly gave crap advice.
Good ol' Skip knows plenty about moving weight, but not so much about the exotic wildlife of my bucolic world.
Anyway, I'm P--
Best we keep things anonymous, actually.
All I need to know is you're my *buyer*, not another under-cover asshole.
Ha, authorities out here don't ***do*** undercover.
They just execute suspected ne'er-do-wells like us on sight.

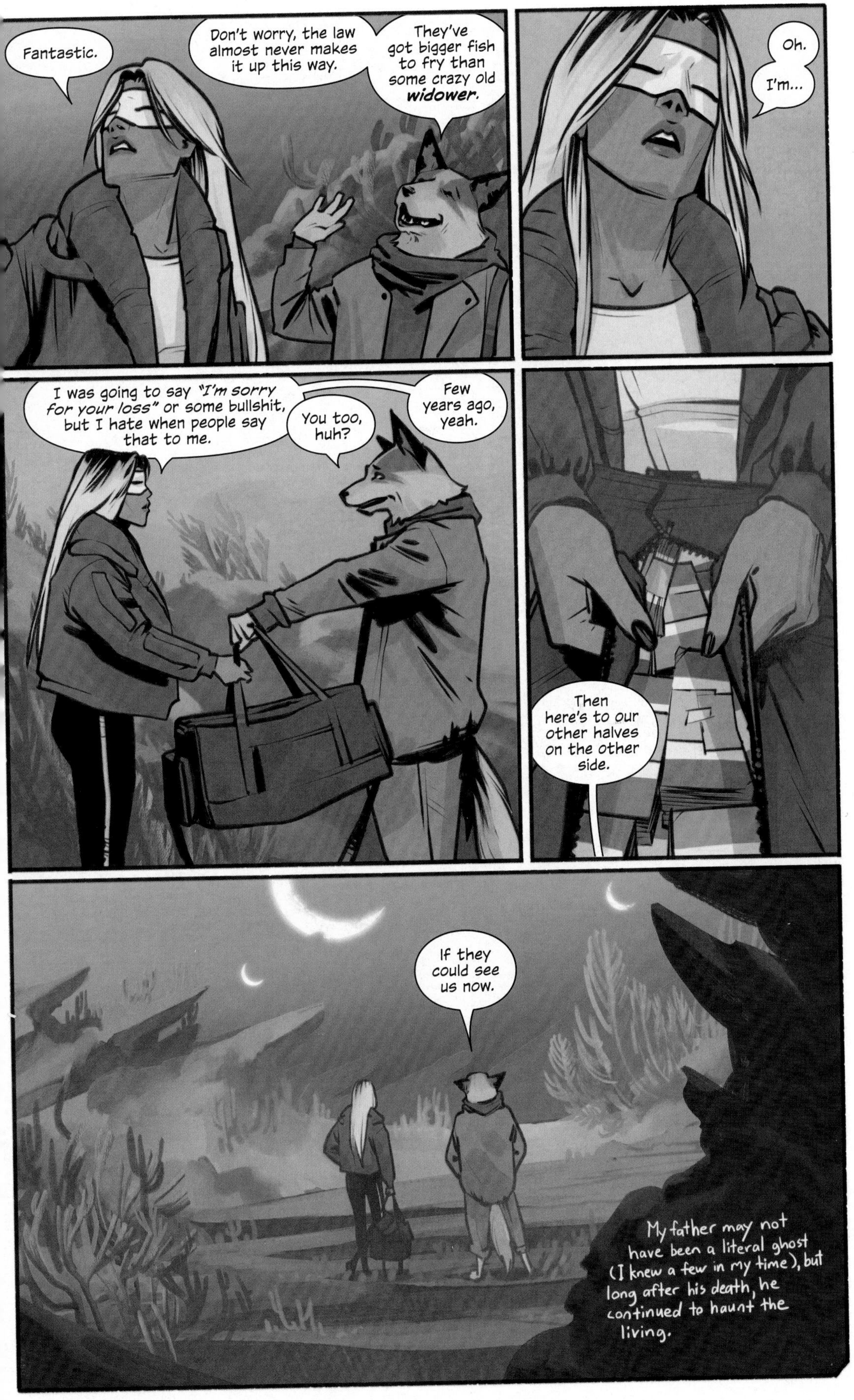

Fantastic.
Don't worry, the law almost never makes it up this way.
They've got bigger fish to fry than some crazy old **widower**.
Oh.
I'm...
I was going to say *"I'm sorry for your loss"* or some bullshit, but I hate when people say that to me.
You too, huh?
Few years ago, yeah.
Then here's to our other halves on the other side.
If they could see us now.
My father may not have been a literal ghost (I knew a few in my time), but long after his death, he continued to haunt the living.

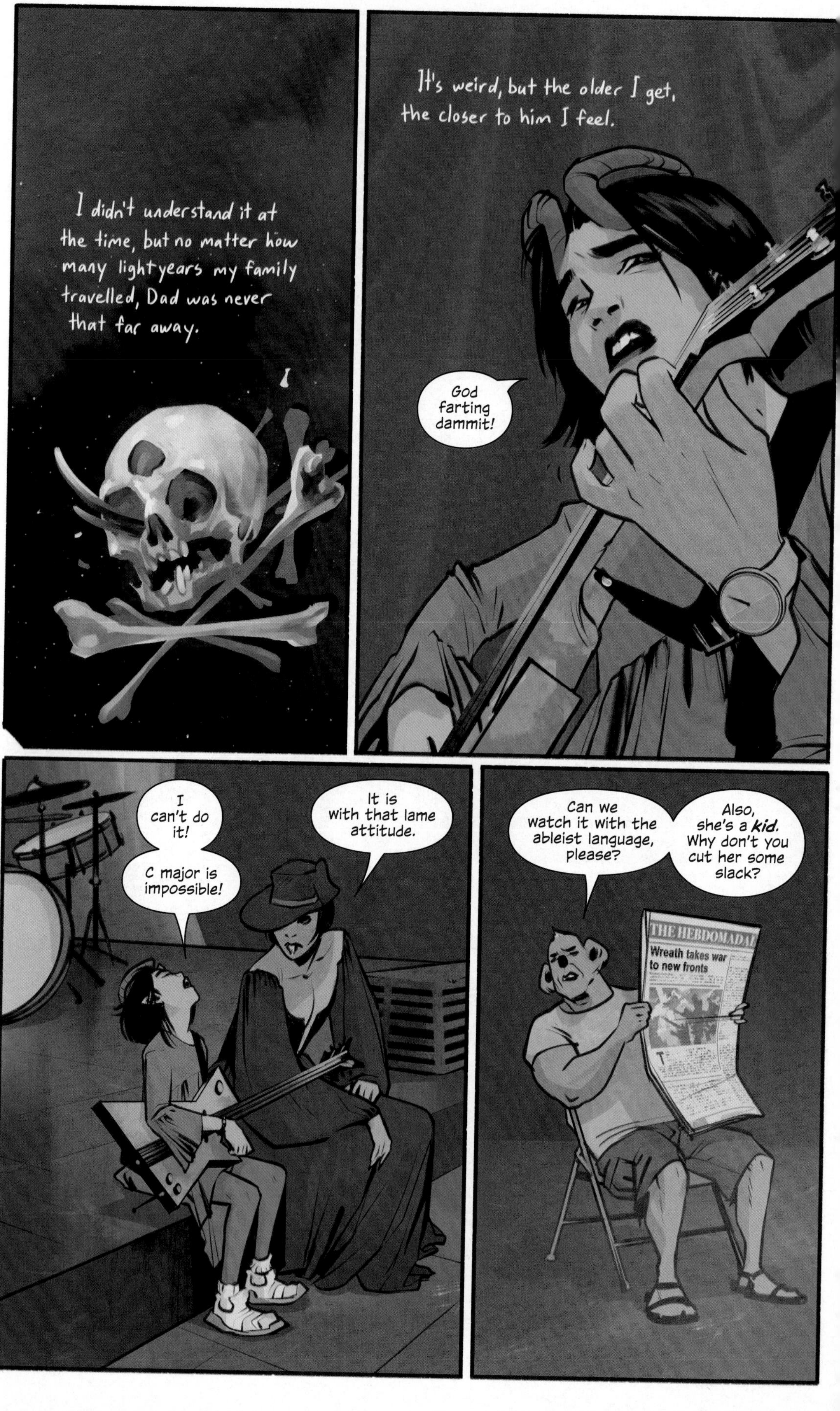
I didn't understand it at the time, but no matter how many lightyears my family travelled, Dad was never that far away.
It's weird, but the older I get, the closer to him I feel.
God farting dammit!
I can't do it!
C major is impossible!
It is with that lame attitude.
Can we watch it with the ableist language, please?
Also, she's a *kid*. Why don't you cut her some slack?
THE HEBDOMADAL
Wreath takes war to new fronts

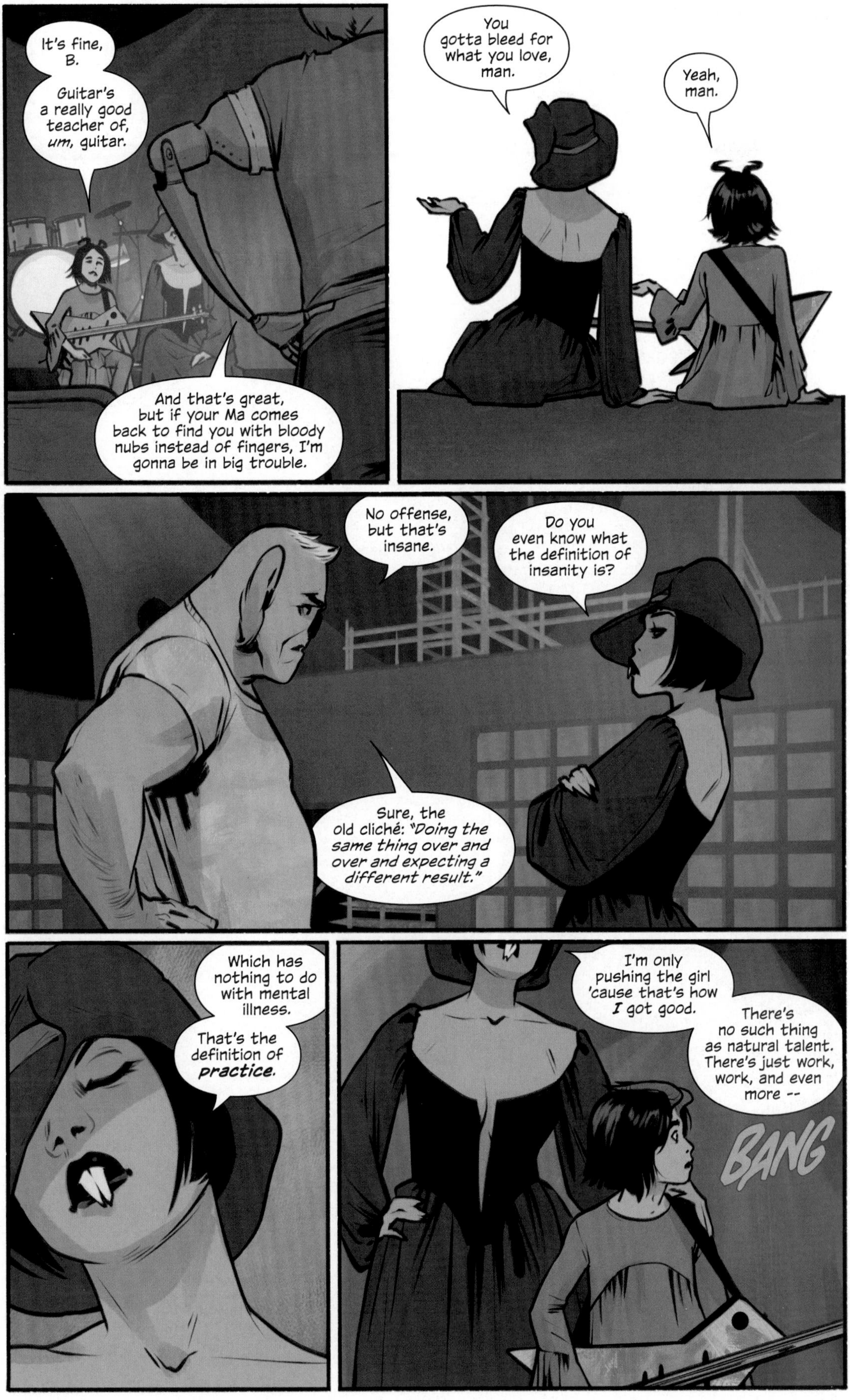
It's fine, B.
Guitar's a really good teacher of, *um*, guitar.
And that's great, but if your Ma comes back to find you with bloody nubs instead of fingers, I'm gonna be in big trouble.
You gotta bleed for what you love, man.
Yeah, man.
No offense, but that's insane.
Do you even know what the definition of insanity is?
Sure, the old cliché: *"Doing the same thing over and over and expecting a different result."*
Which has nothing to do with mental illness.
That's the definition of ***practice***.
I'm only pushing the girl 'cause that's how ***I*** got good.
There's no such thing as natural talent. There's just work, work, and even more --
BANG

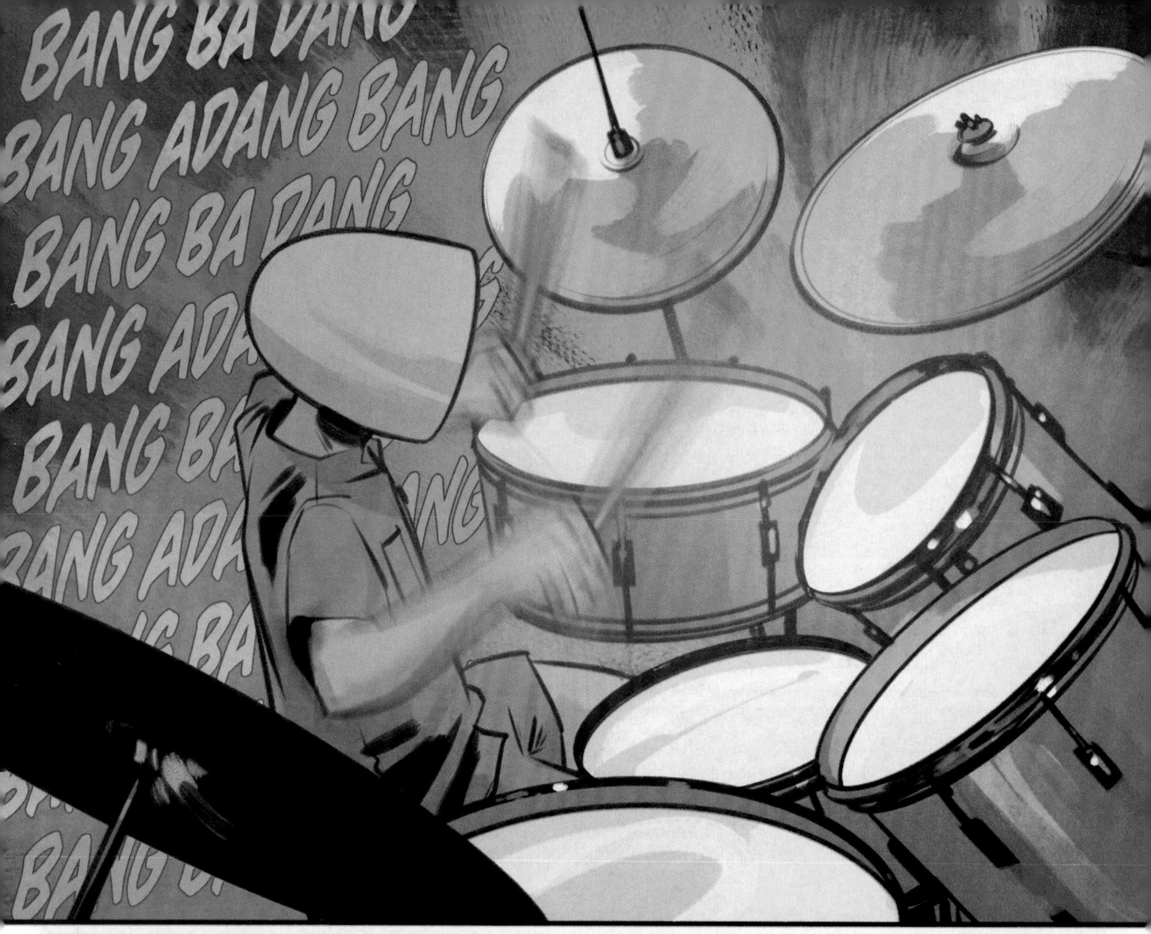
BANG BA DANG
BANG ADANG BANG
BANG BA DANG
BANG ADA
BANG BA
BANG ADA
BANG

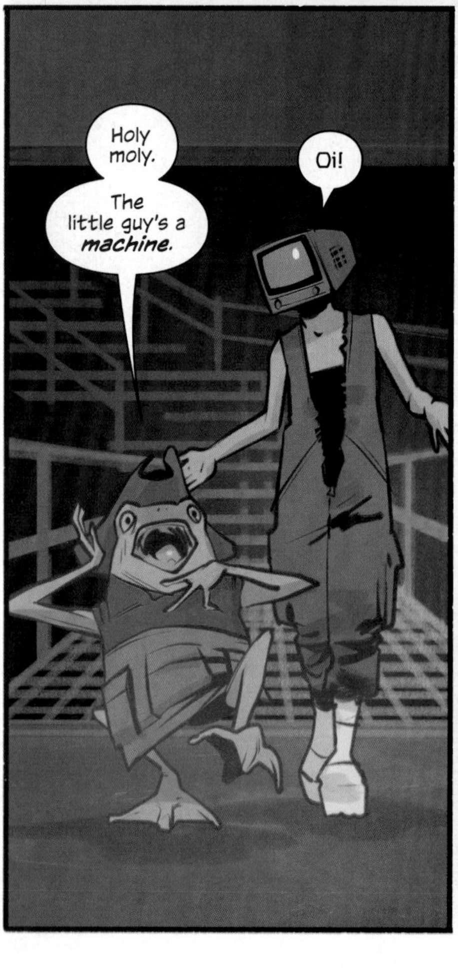
Holy moly.
The little guy's a ***machine***.
Oi!

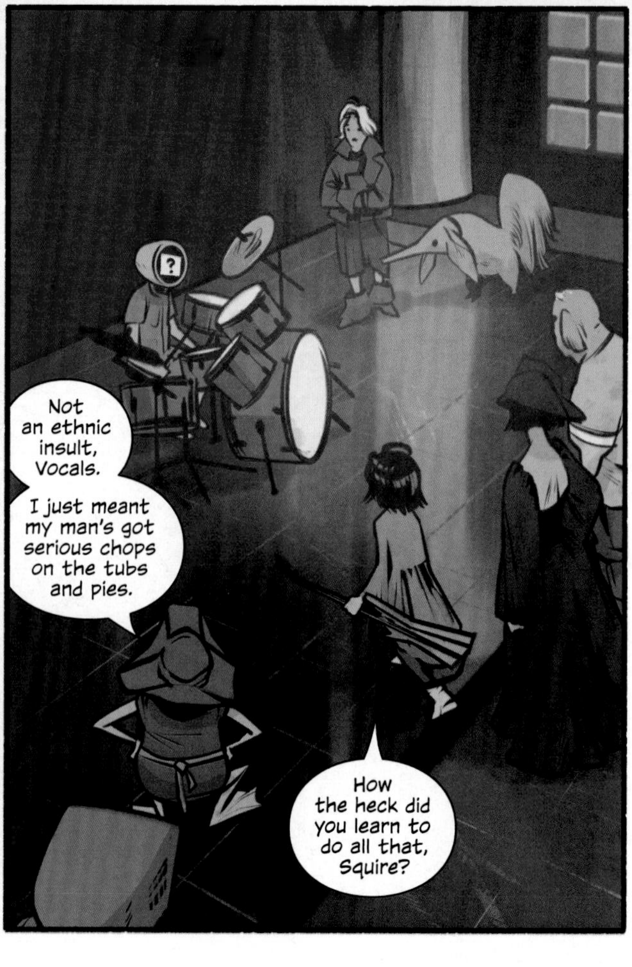
Not an ethnic insult, Vocals.
I just meant my man's got serious chops on the tubs and pies.
How the heck did you learn to do all that, Squire?

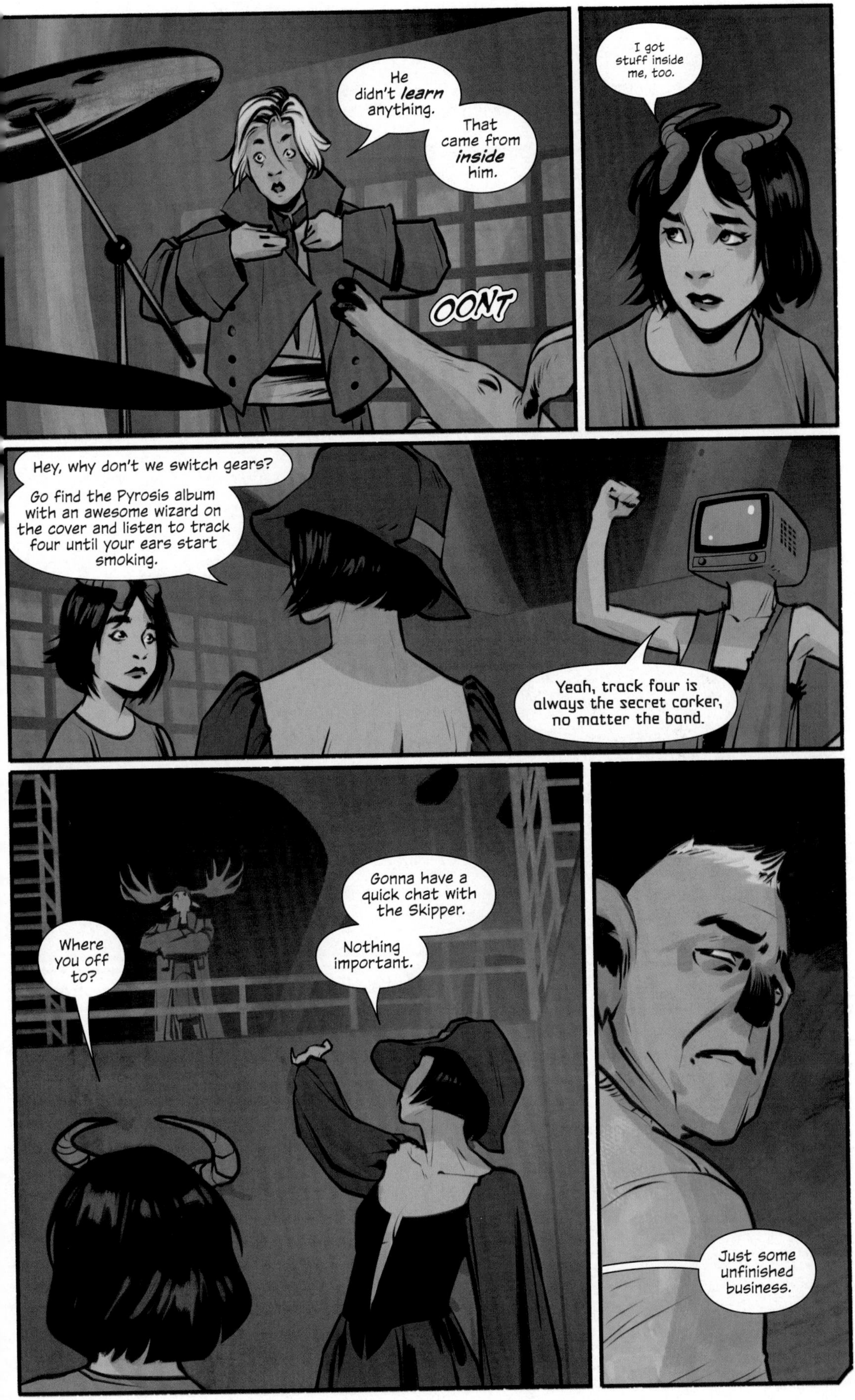
He didn't *learn* anything.
That came from *inside* him.
OONT
I got stuff inside me, too.
Hey, why don't we switch gears?
Go find the Pyrosis album with an awesome wizard on the cover and listen to track four until your ears start smoking.
Yeah, track four is always the secret corker, no matter the band.
Where you off to?
Gonna have a quick chat with the Skipper.
Nothing important.
Just some unfinished business.

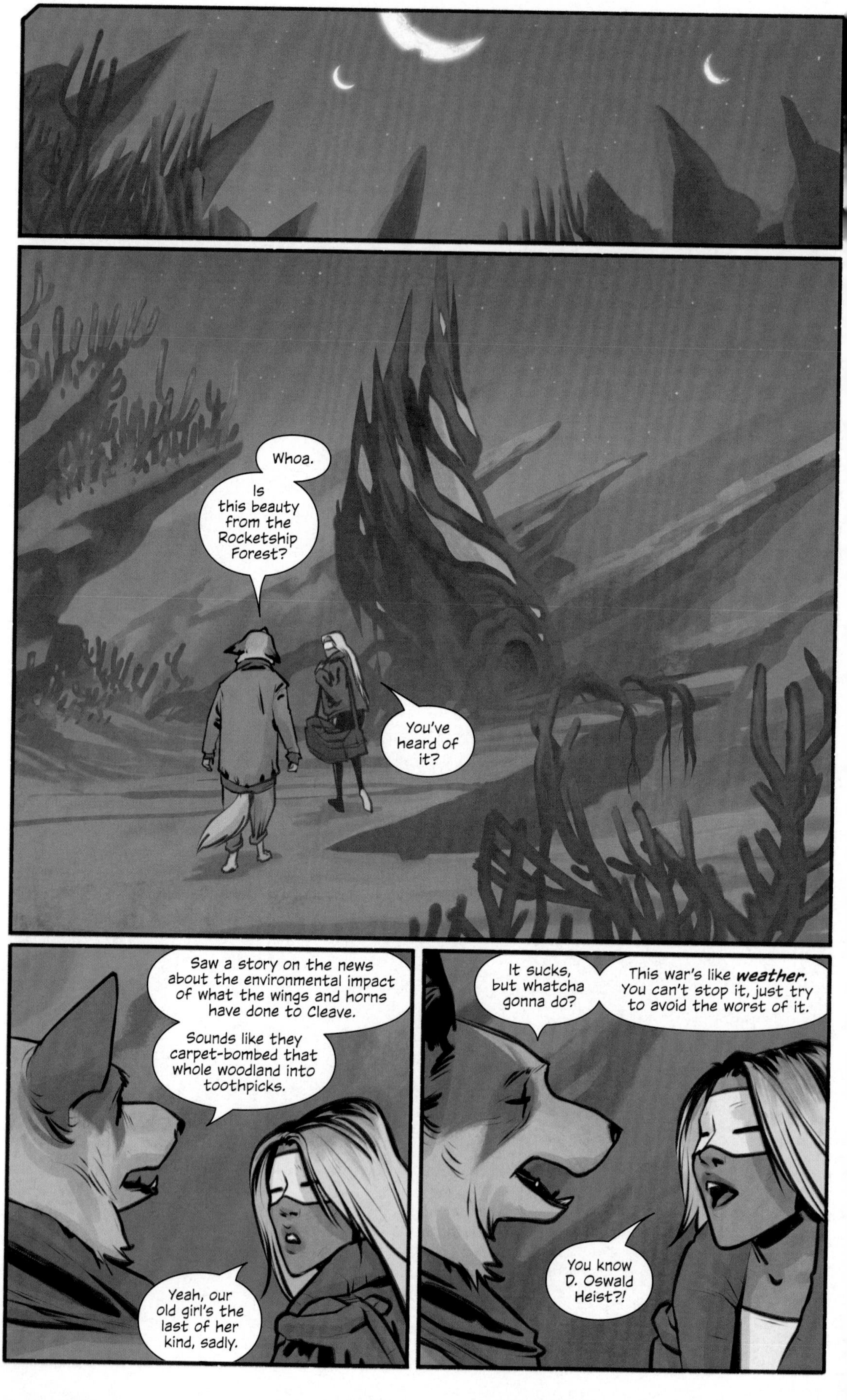

Whoa.
Is this beauty from the Rocketship Forest?
You've heard of it?
Saw a story on the news about the environmental impact of what the wings and horns have done to Cleave.
Sounds like they carpet-bombed that whole woodland into toothpicks.
Yeah, our old girl's the last of her kind, sadly.
It sucks, but whatcha gonna do?
This war's like *weather*. You can't stop it, just try to avoid the worst of it.
You know D. Oswald Heist?!

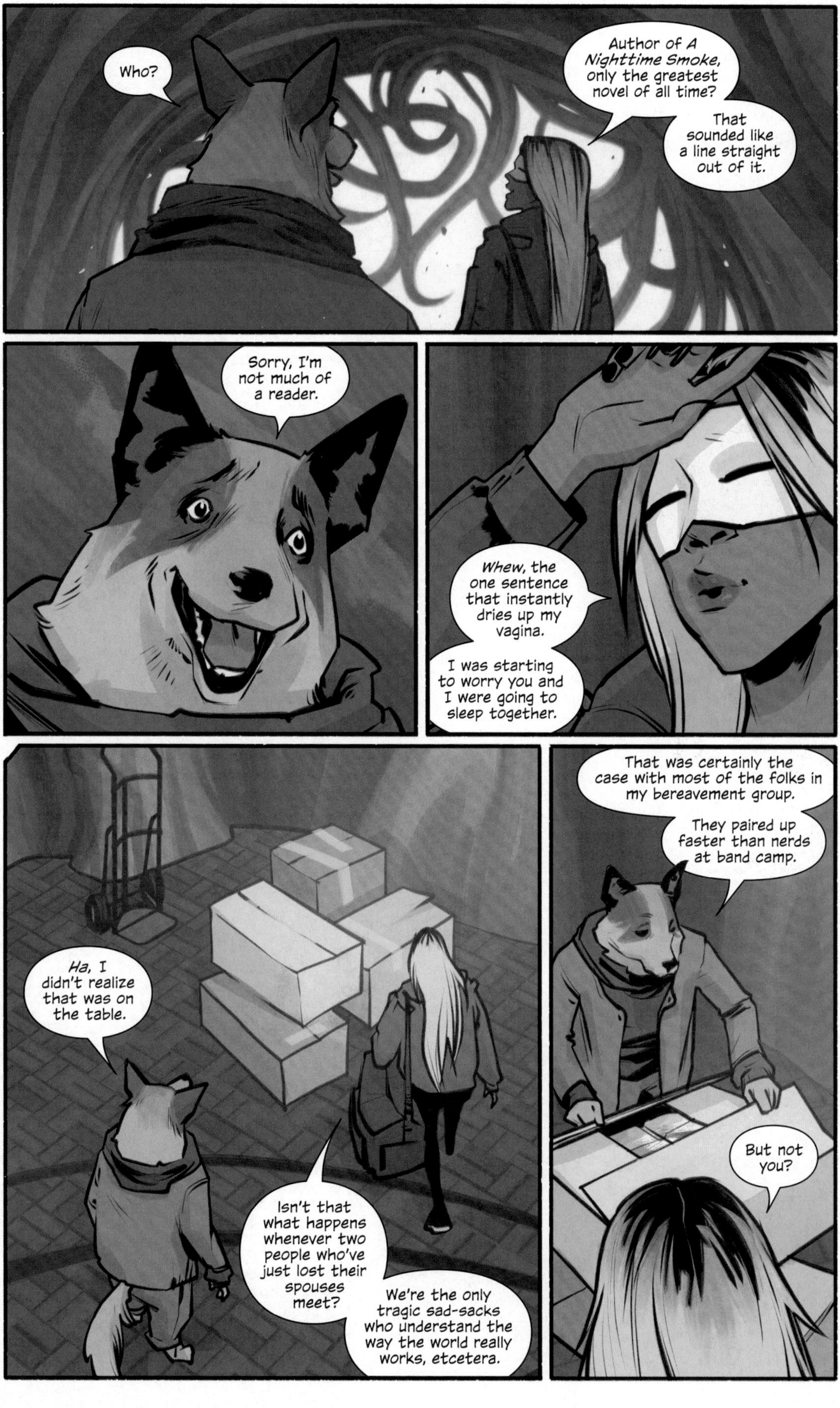
Who?
Author of *A Nighttime Smoke*, only the greatest novel of all time?
That sounded like a line straight out of it.
Sorry, I'm not much of a reader.
Whew, the one sentence that instantly dries up my vagina.
I was starting to worry you and I were going to sleep together.
Ha, I didn't realize that was on the table.
Isn't that what happens whenever two people who've just lost their spouses meet?
We're the only tragic sad-sacks who understand the way the world really works, etcetera.
That was certainly the case with most of the folks in my bereavement group.
They paired up faster than nerds at band camp.
But not you?

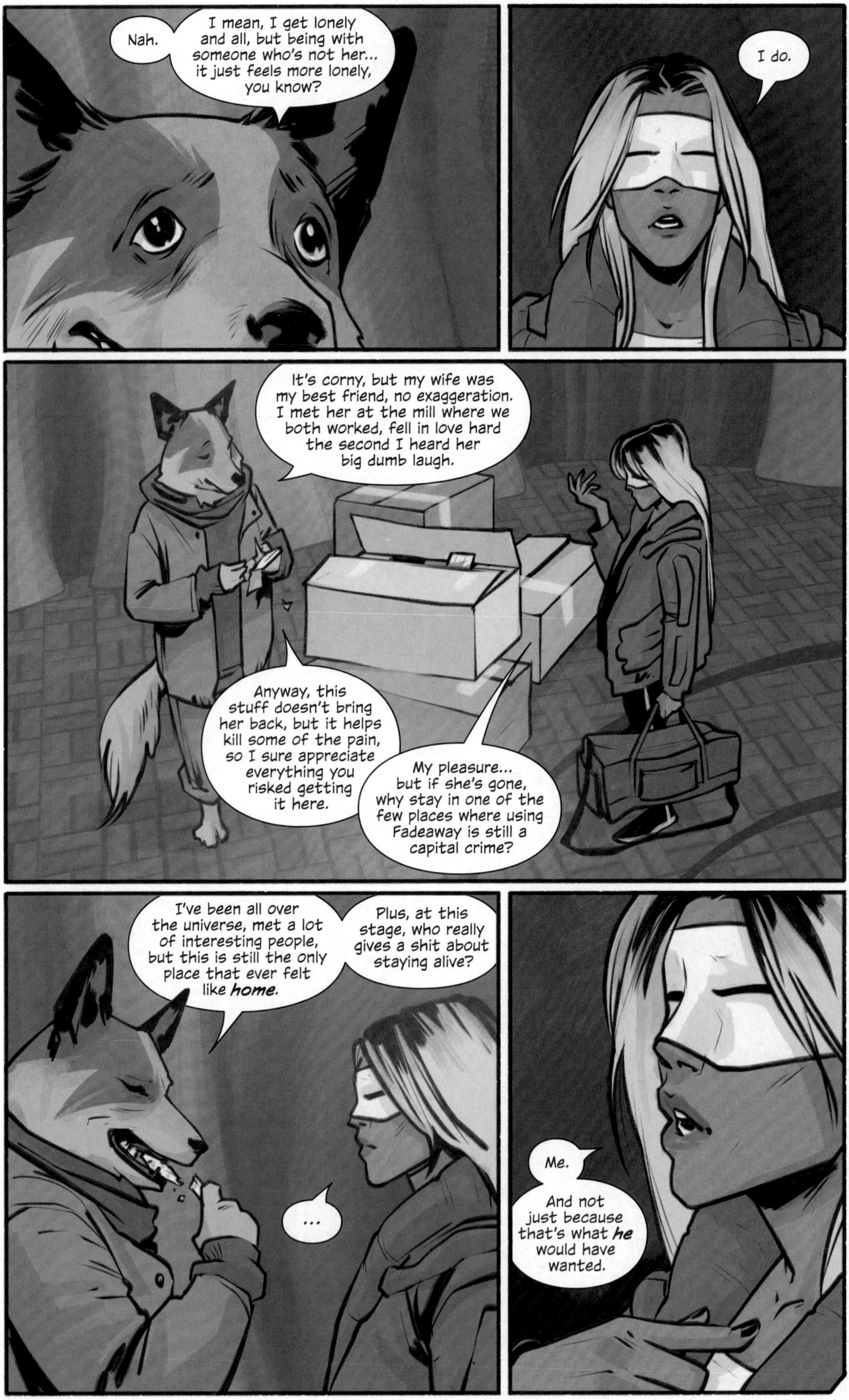

Nah.
I mean, I get lonely and all, but being with someone who's not her... it just feels more lonely, you know?
I do.
It's corny, but my wife was my best friend, no exaggeration. I met her at the mill where we both worked, fell in love hard the second I heard her big dumb laugh.
Anyway, this stuff doesn't bring her back, but it helps kill some of the pain, so I sure appreciate everything you risked getting it here.
My pleasure... but if she's gone, why stay in one of the few places where using Fadeaway is still a capital crime?
I've been all over the universe, met a lot of interesting people, but this is still the only place that ever felt like *home*.
Plus, at this stage, who really gives a shit about staying alive?
...
Me.
And not just because that's what *he* would have wanted.

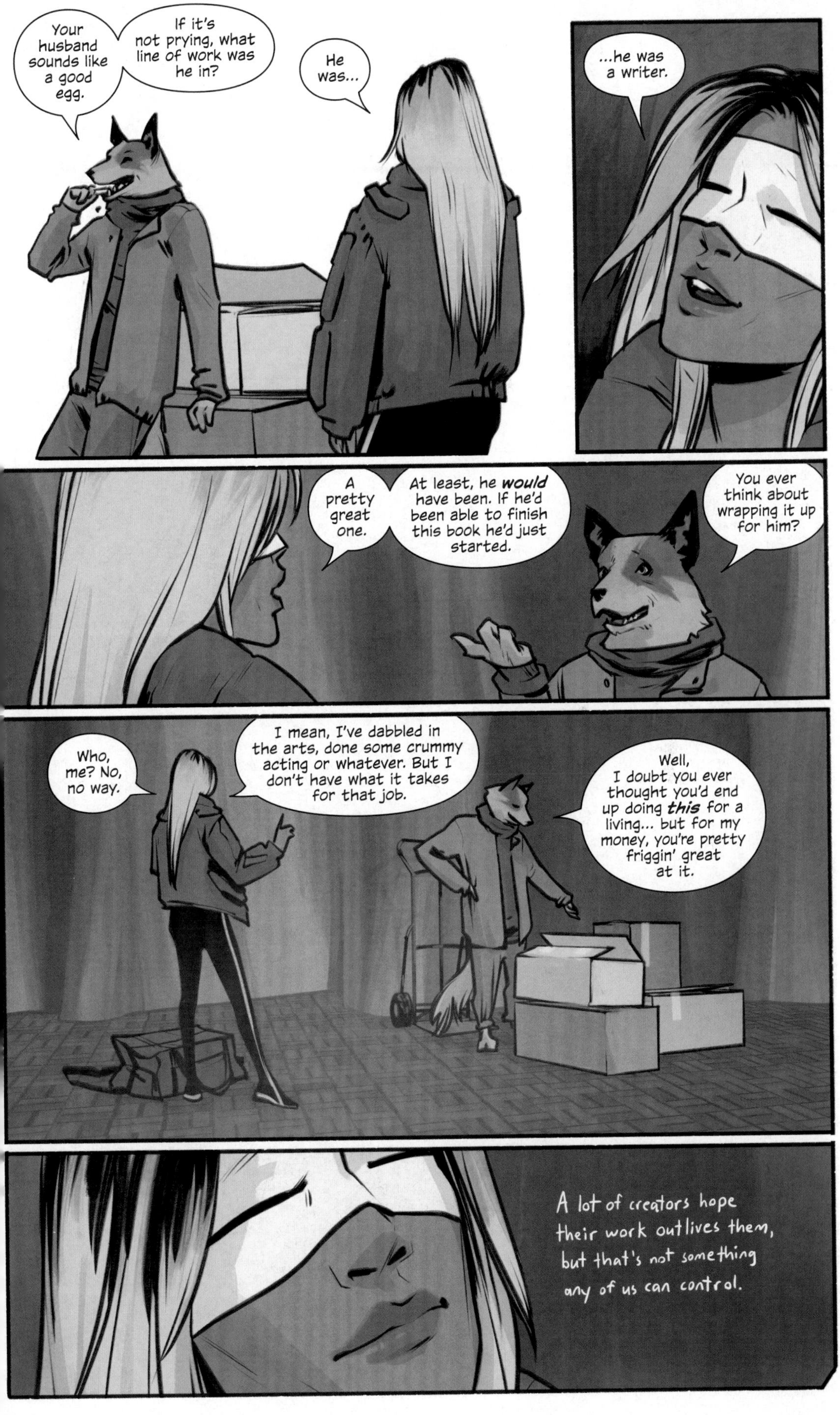

Your husband sounds like a good egg.
If it's not prying, what line of work was he in?
He was...
...he was a writer.
A pretty great one.
At least, he *would* have been. If he'd been able to finish this book he'd just started.
You ever think about wrapping it up for him?
Who, me? No, no way.
I mean, I've dabbled in the arts, done some crummy acting or whatever. But I don't have what it takes for that job.
Well, I doubt you ever thought you'd end up doing *this* for a living... but for my money, you're pretty friggin' great at it.
A lot of creators hope their work outlives them, but that's not something any of us can control.

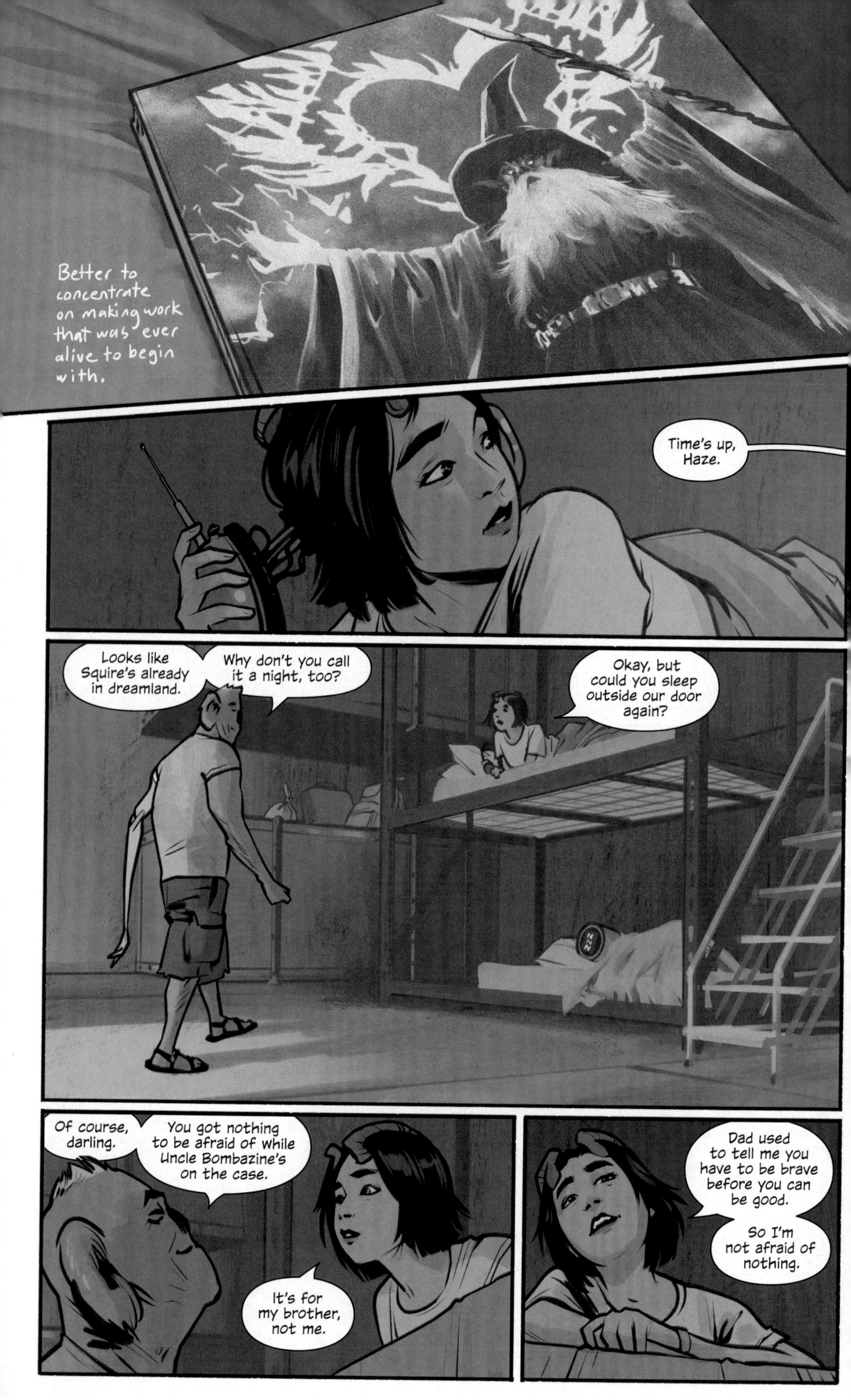

Better to concentrate on making work that was ever alive to begin with.
Time's up, Haze.
Looks like Squire's already in dreamland.
Why don't you call it a night, too?
Okay, but could you sleep outside our door again?
Of course, darling.
You got nothing to be afraid of while Uncle Bombazine's on the case.
It's for my brother, not me.
Dad used to tell me you have to be brave before you can be good.
So I'm not afraid of nothing.

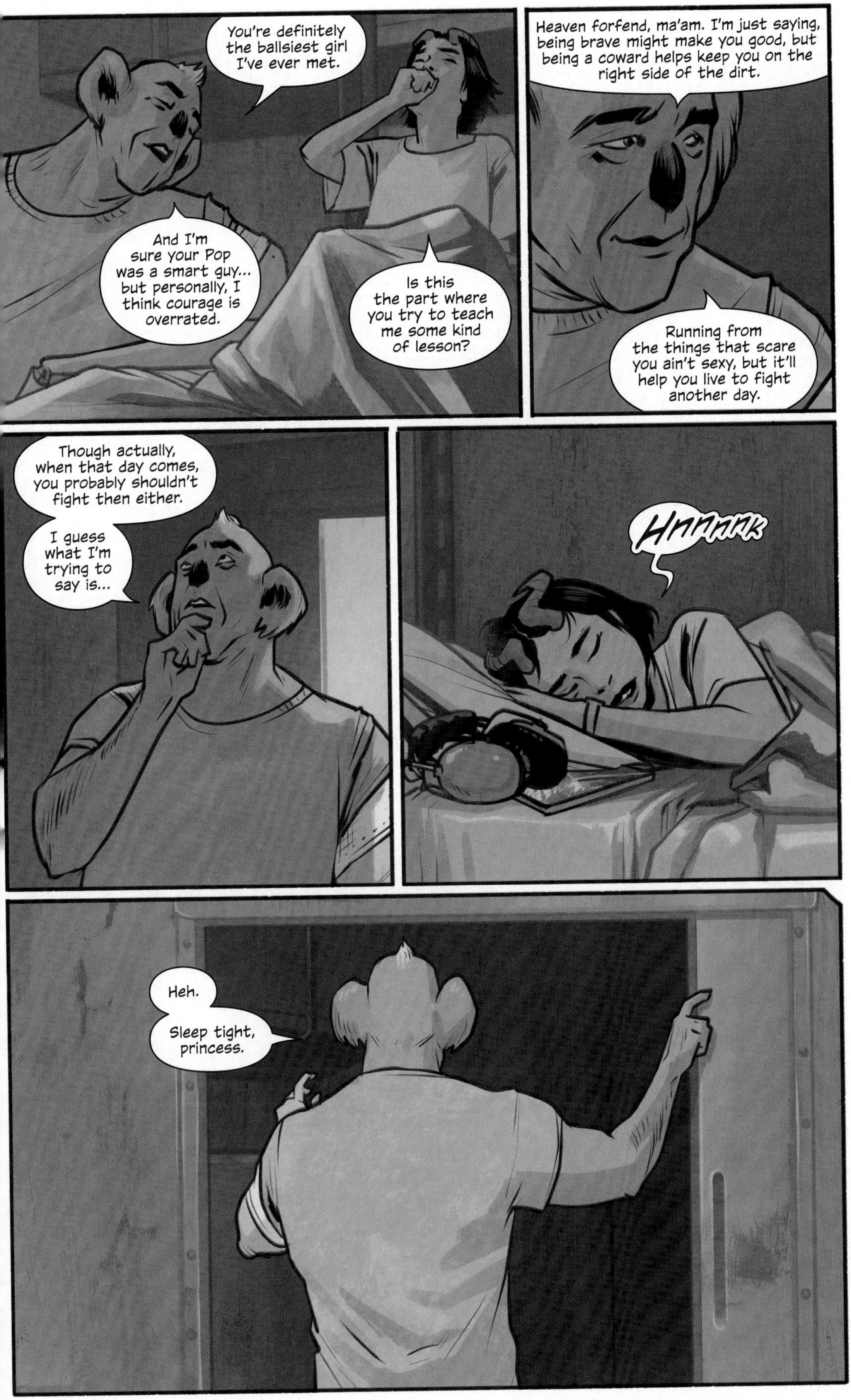

You're definitely the ballsiest girl I've ever met.
And I'm sure your Pop was a smart guy... but personally, I think courage is overrated.
Is this the part where you try to teach me some kind of lesson?
Heaven forfend, ma'am. I'm just saying, being brave might make you good, but being a coward helps keep you on the right side of the dirt.
Running from the things that scare you ain't sexy, but it'll help you live to fight another day.
Though actually, when that day comes, you probably shouldn't fight then either.
I guess what I'm trying to say is...
Hnnnnk
Heh.
Sleep tight, princess.

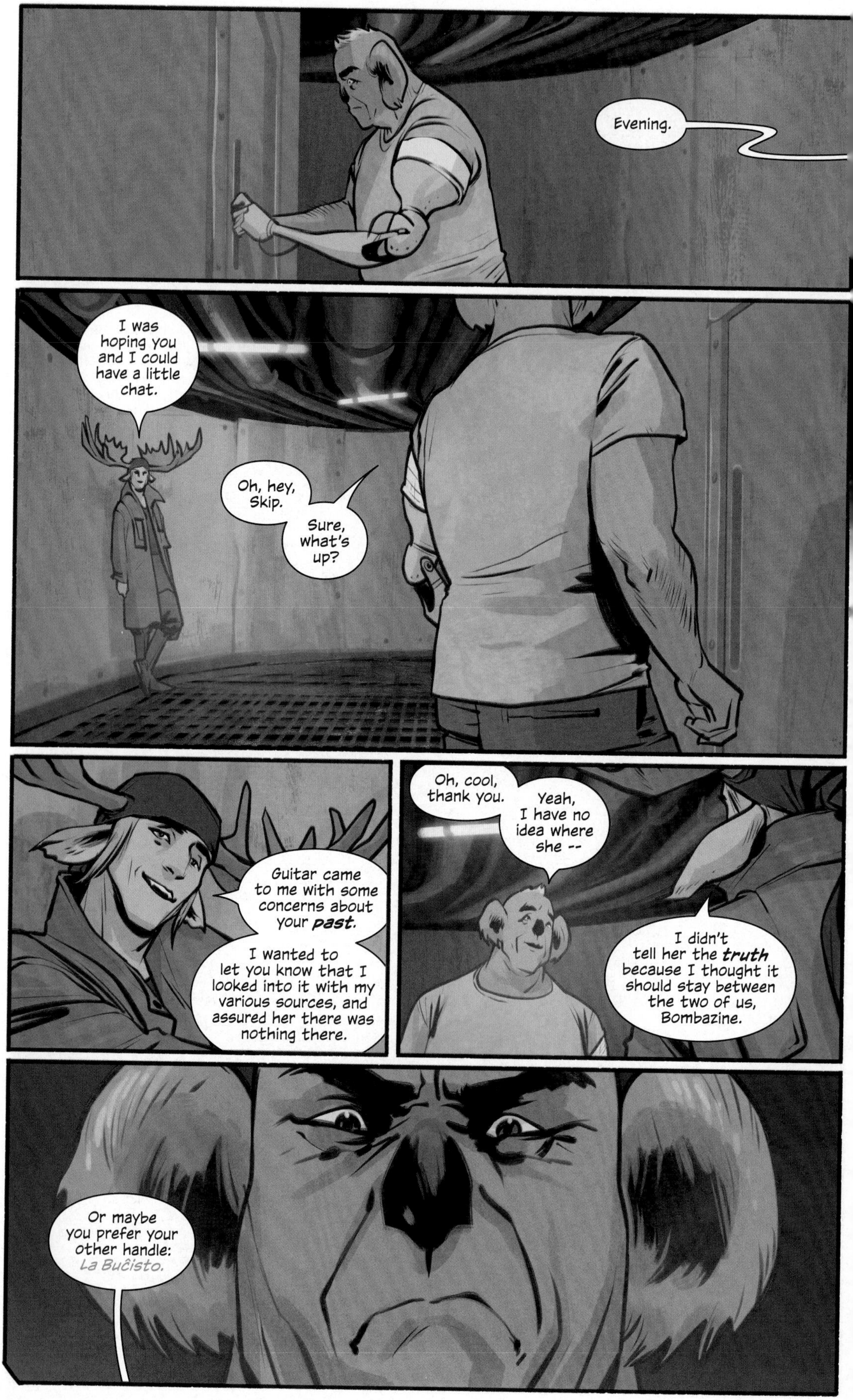
Evening.
I was hoping you and I could have a little chat.
Oh, hey, Skip.
Sure, what's up?
Guitar came to me with some concerns about your **past**.
I wanted to let you know that I looked into it with my various sources, and assured her there was nothing there.
Oh, cool, thank you.
Yeah, I have no idea where she --
I didn't tell her the **truth** because I thought it should stay between the two of us, Bombazine.
Or maybe you prefer your other handle: *La Buĉisto.*

Ah, ah, ah!

I know exactly what you're thinking. Time to poison my food? Or maybe just saw off my head?

But I've taken measures to ensure that everyone in the galaxy will hear about your dirty little secret if anything untoward ever befalls me **or** my crew.

Do what you want, but you can't tell my boss.

She trusted me. With her *children.*

After everything that woman's been through, if she finds out how wrong she was about me...

Friend, you and I are cut from the same cloth. You have absolutely nothing to worry about.

All I ask is one small favor.

Over the years, lots of different men attempted to fill the void left by my father, some good, some less so..

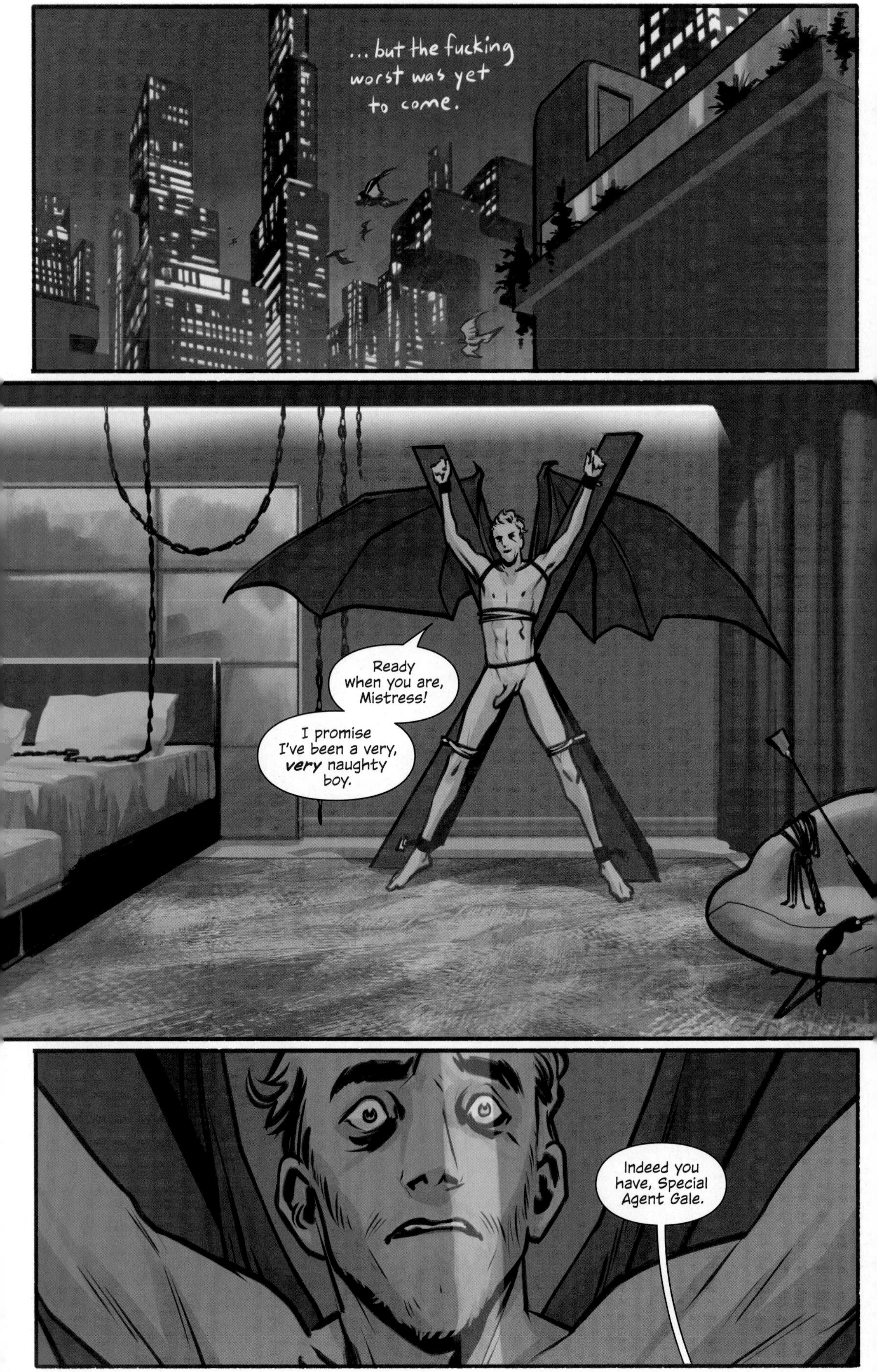
... but the fucking worst was yet to come.
Ready when you are, Mistress!
I promise I've been a very, ***very*** naughty boy.
Indeed you have, Special Agent Gale.

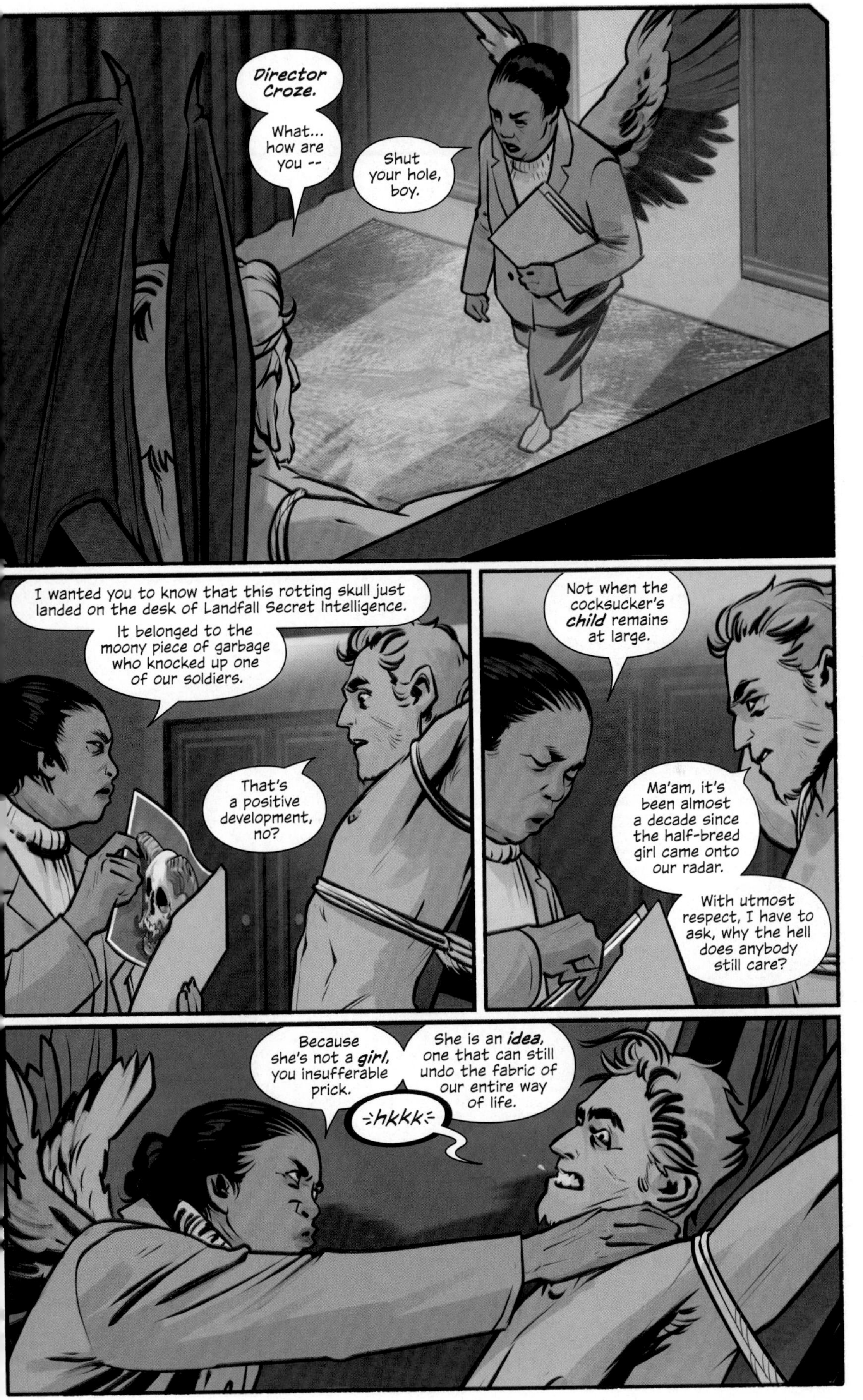
Director Croze.
What... how are you --
Shut your hole, boy.
I wanted you to know that this rotting skull just landed on the desk of Landfall Secret Intelligence.
It belonged to the moony piece of garbage who knocked up one of our soldiers.
That's a positive development, no?
Not when the cocksucker's *child* remains at large.
Ma'am, it's been almost a decade since the half-breed girl came onto our radar.
With utmost respect, I have to ask, why the hell does anybody still care?
Because she's not a *girl*, you insufferable prick.
She is an *idea*, one that can still undo the fabric of our entire way of life.
hkkk

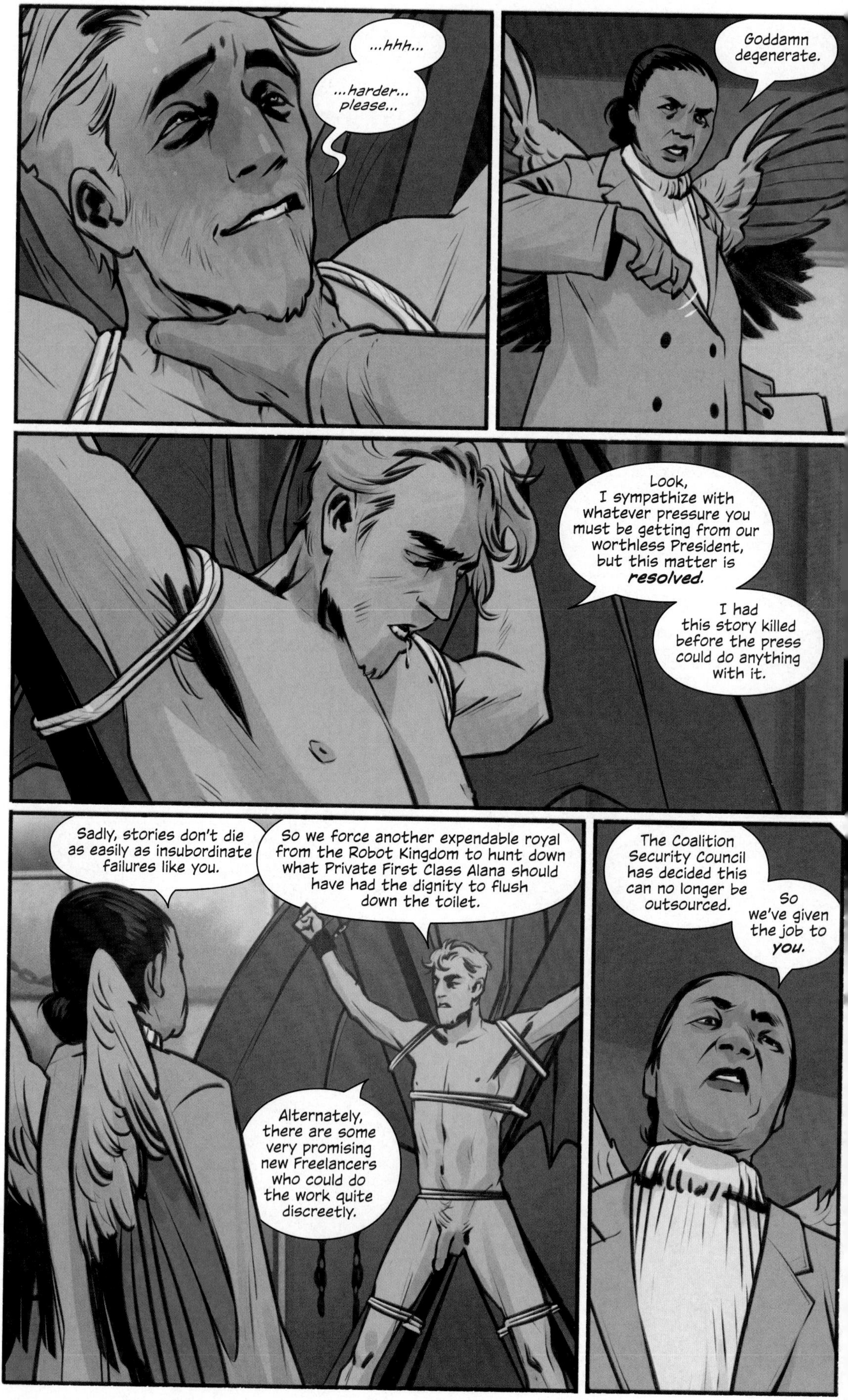

...hhh...
...harder... please...
Goddamn degenerate.
Look, I sympathize with whatever pressure you must be getting from our worthless President, but this matter is ***resolved.***
I had this story killed before the press could do anything with it.
Sadly, stories don't die as easily as insubordinate failures like you.
So we force another expendable royal from the Robot Kingdom to hunt down what Private First Class Alana should have had the dignity to flush down the toilet.
Alternately, there are some very promising new Freelancers who could do the work quite discreetly.
The Coalition Security Council has decided this can no longer be outsourced.
So we've given the job to ***you.***

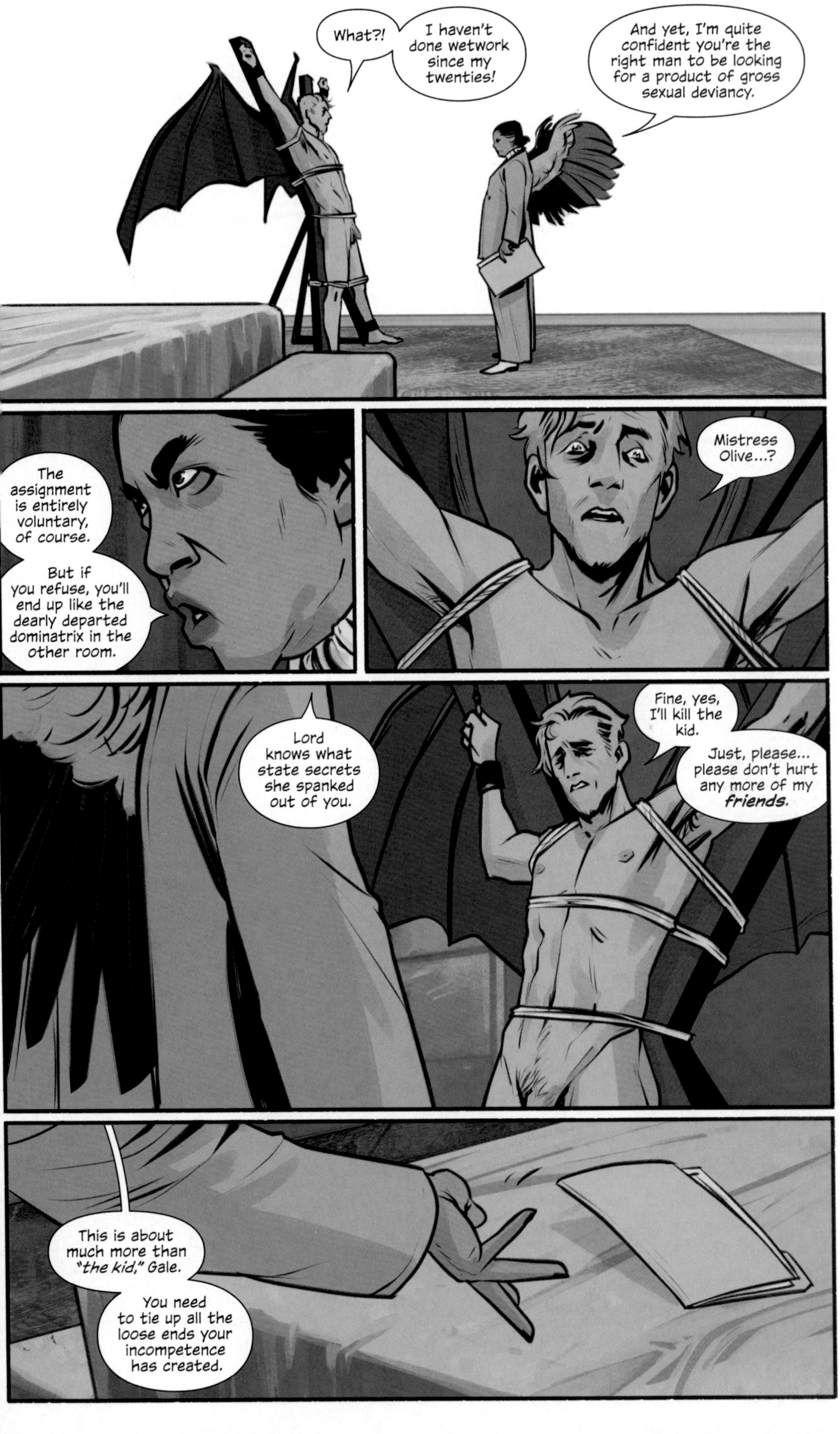
What?!
I haven't done wetwork since my twenties!
And yet, I'm quite confident you're the right man to be looking for a product of gross sexual deviancy.
The assignment is entirely voluntary, of course.
But if you refuse, you'll end up like the dearly departed dominatrix in the other room.
Mistress Olive...?
Lord knows what state secrets she spanked out of you.
Fine, yes, I'll kill the kid.
Just, please... please don't hurt any more of my *friends*.
This is about much more than *"the kid,"* Gale.
You need to tie up all the loose ends your incompetence has created.

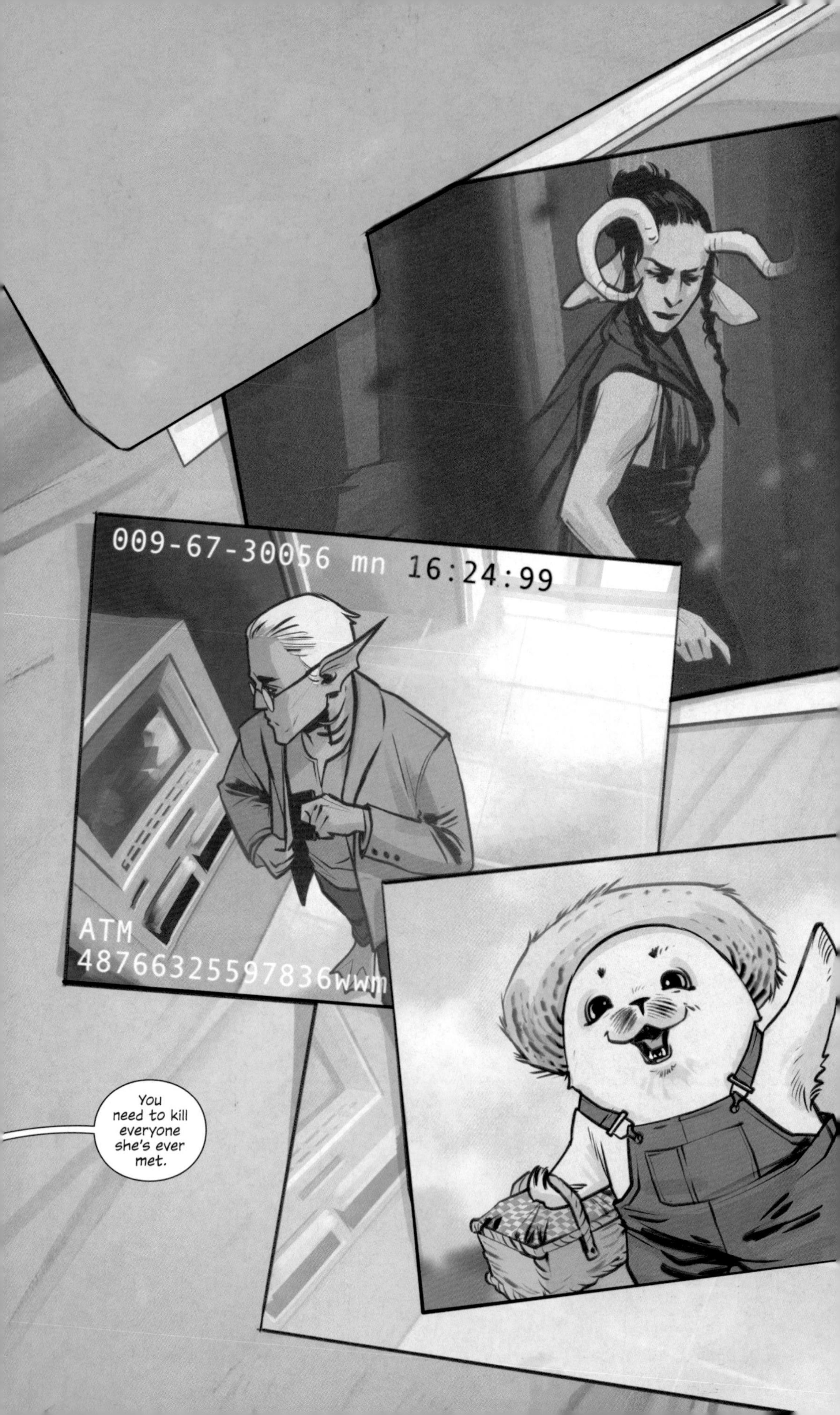
009-67-30056 mn 16:24:99
ATM
48766325597836wwm
You need to kill everyone she's ever met.

end chapter fifty-eight

CHAPTER
FIFTY-NINE

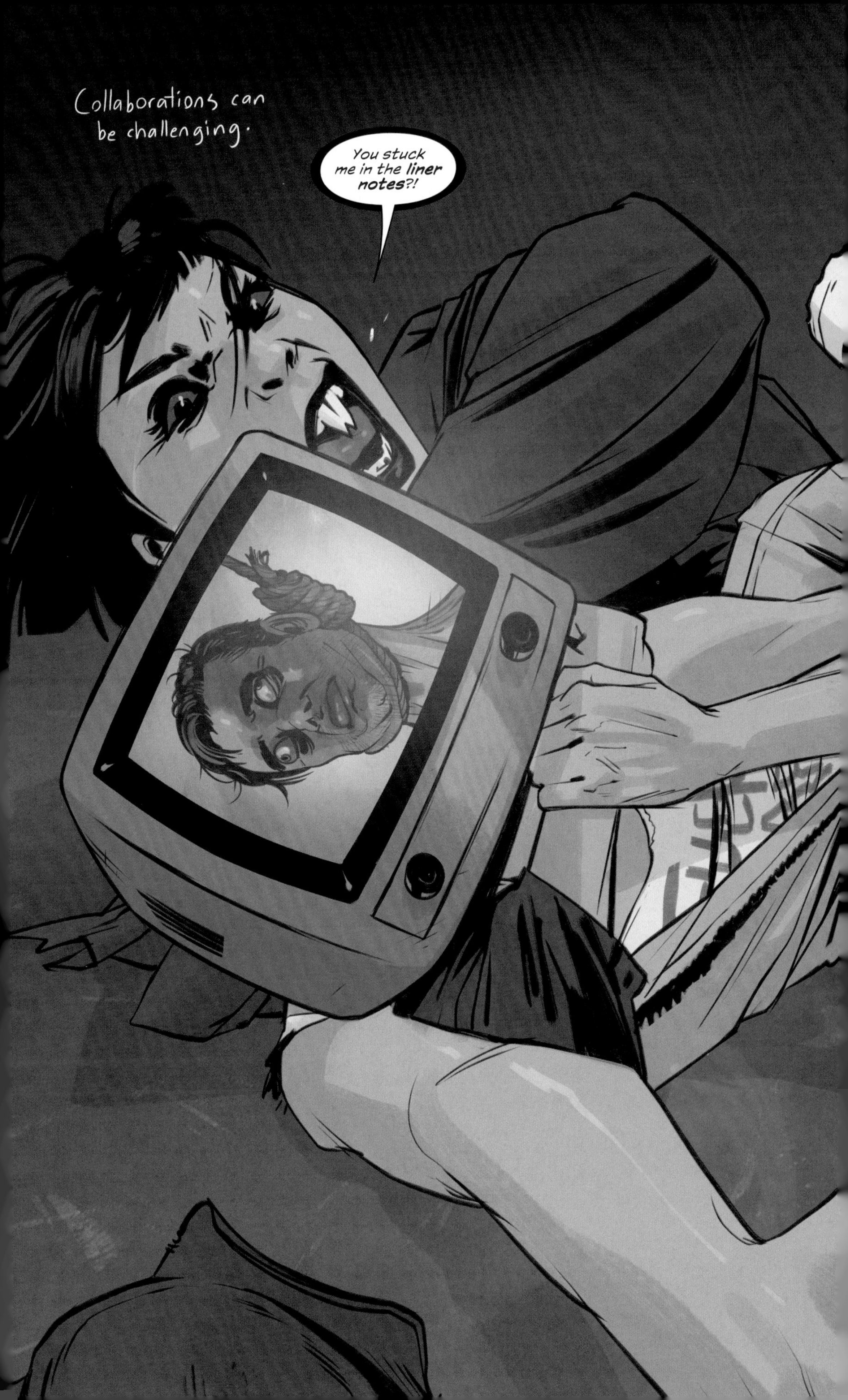
Collaborations can be challenging.
You stuck me in the **liner notes**?!

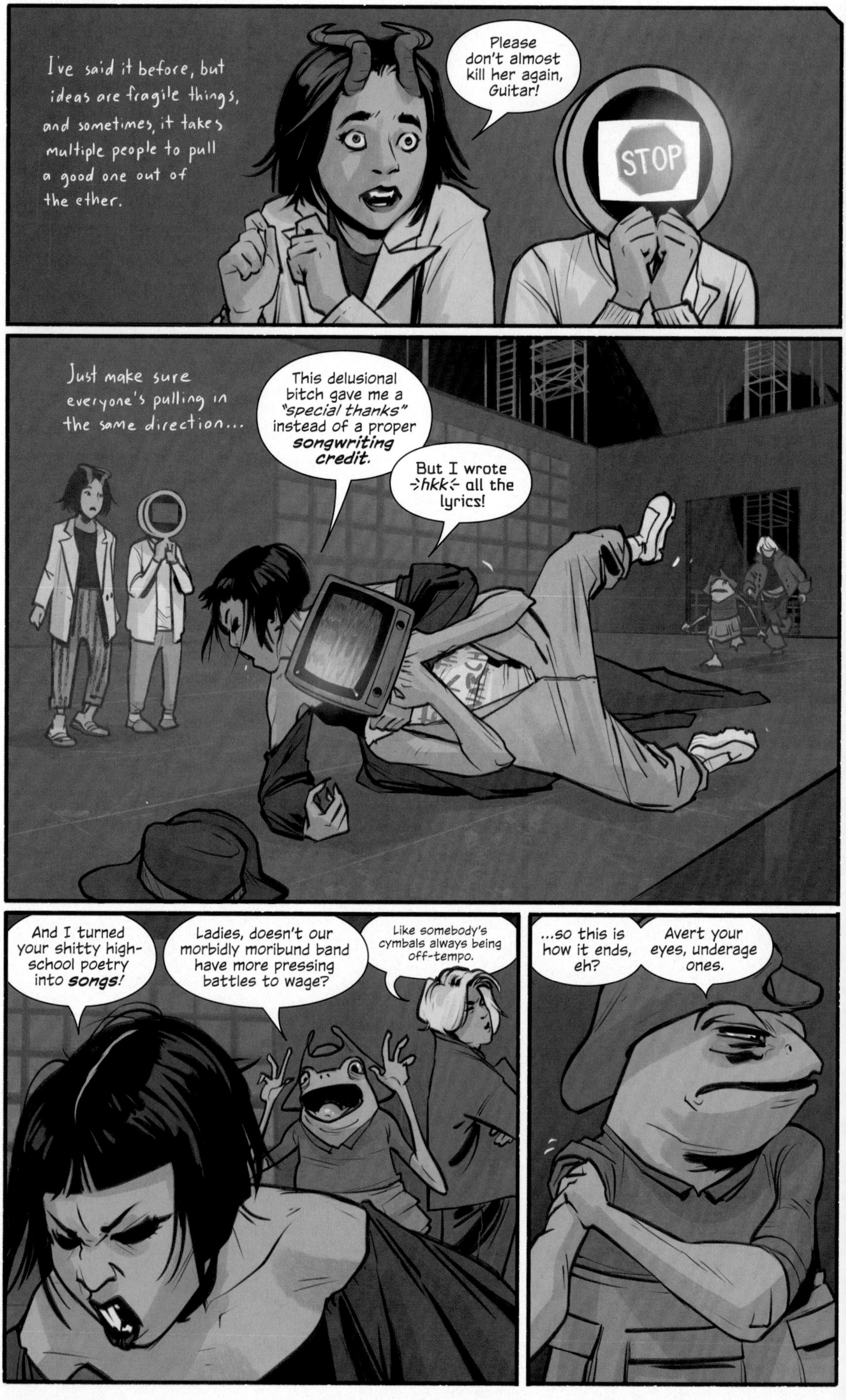
I've said it before, but ideas are fragile things, and sometimes, it takes multiple people to pull a good one out of the ether.
Please don't almost kill her again, Guitar!
STOP
Just make sure everyone's pulling in the same direction...
This delusional bitch gave me a *"special thanks"* instead of a proper ***songwriting credit.***
But I wrote *-hkk-* all the lyrics!
And I turned your shitty high-school poetry into ***songs!***
Ladies, doesn't our morbidly moribund band have more pressing battles to wage?
Like somebody's cymbals always being off-tempo.
...so this is how it ends, eh?
Avert your eyes, underage ones.

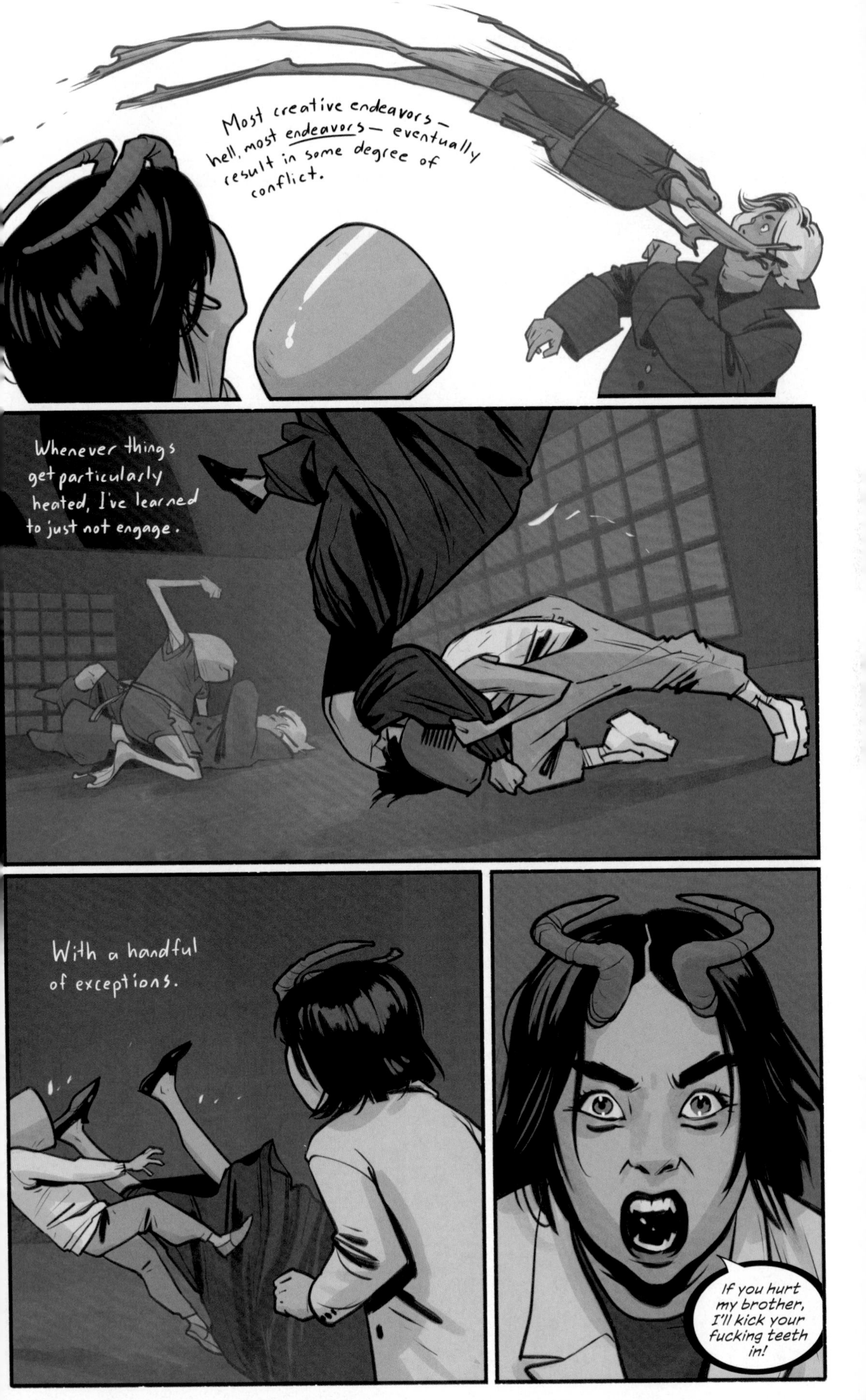
Most creative endeavors— hell, most endeavors— eventually result in some degree of conflict.
Whenever things get particularly heated, I've learned to just not engage.
With a handful of exceptions.
If you hurt my brother, I'll kick your fucking teeth in!

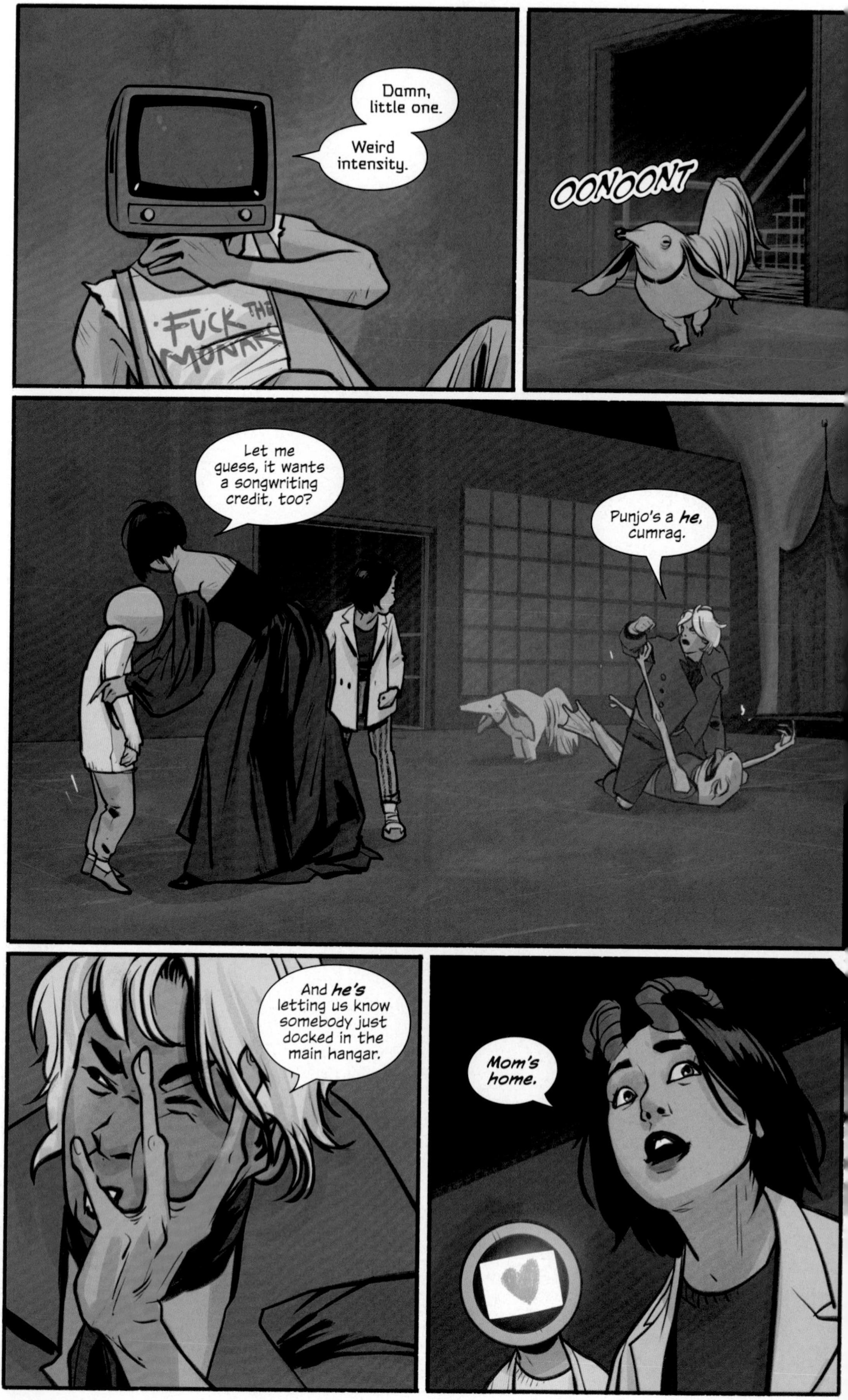
Damn, little one.
Weird intensity.
FUCK THE MONAR
OONOONT
Let me guess, it wants a songwriting credit, too?
Punjo's a ***he***, cumrag.
And ***he's*** letting us know somebody just docked in the main hangar.
Mom's home.

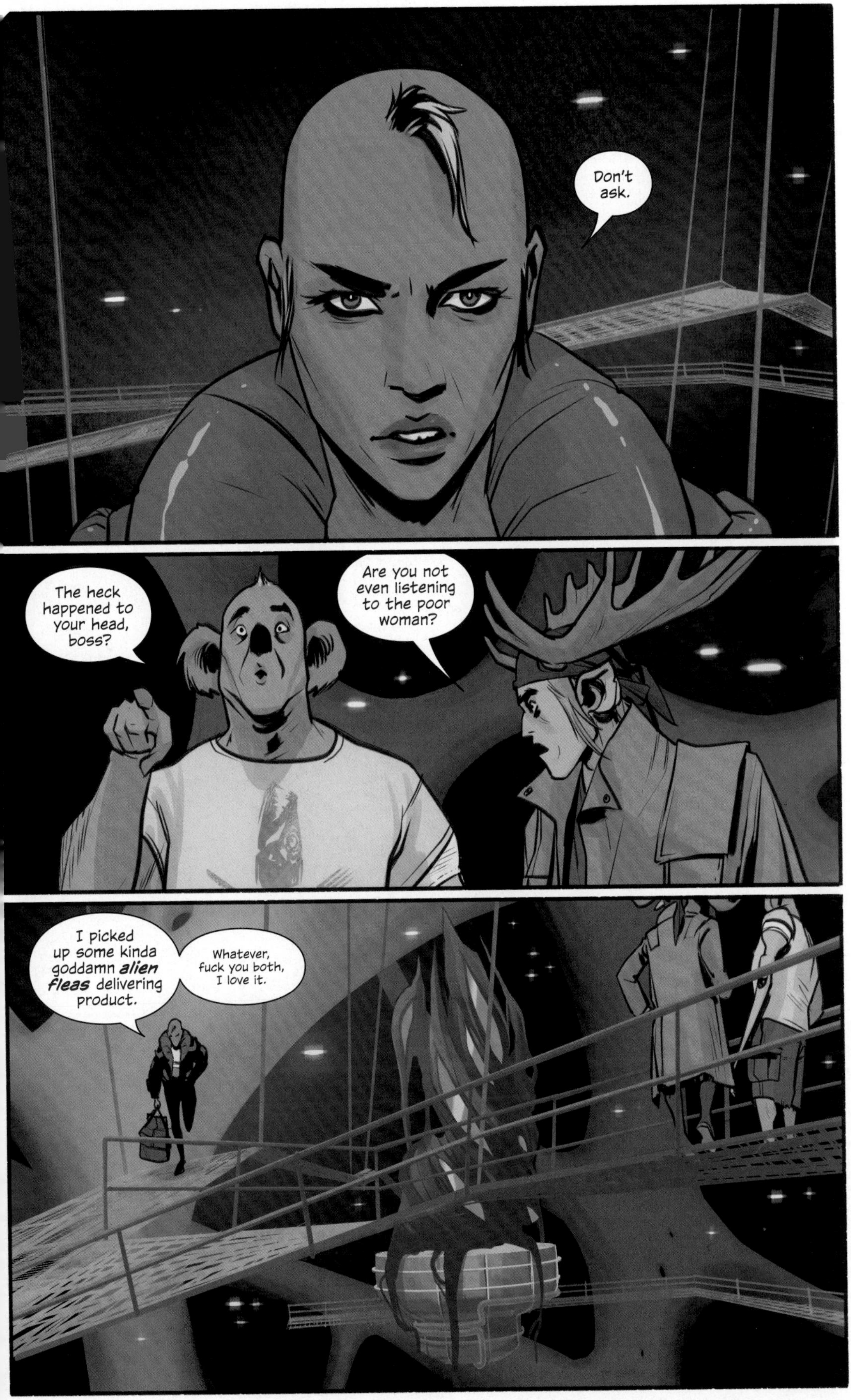

Don't ask.
The heck happened to your head, boss?
Are you not even listening to the poor woman?
I picked up some kinda goddamn *alien fleas* delivering product.
Whatever, fuck you both, I love it.

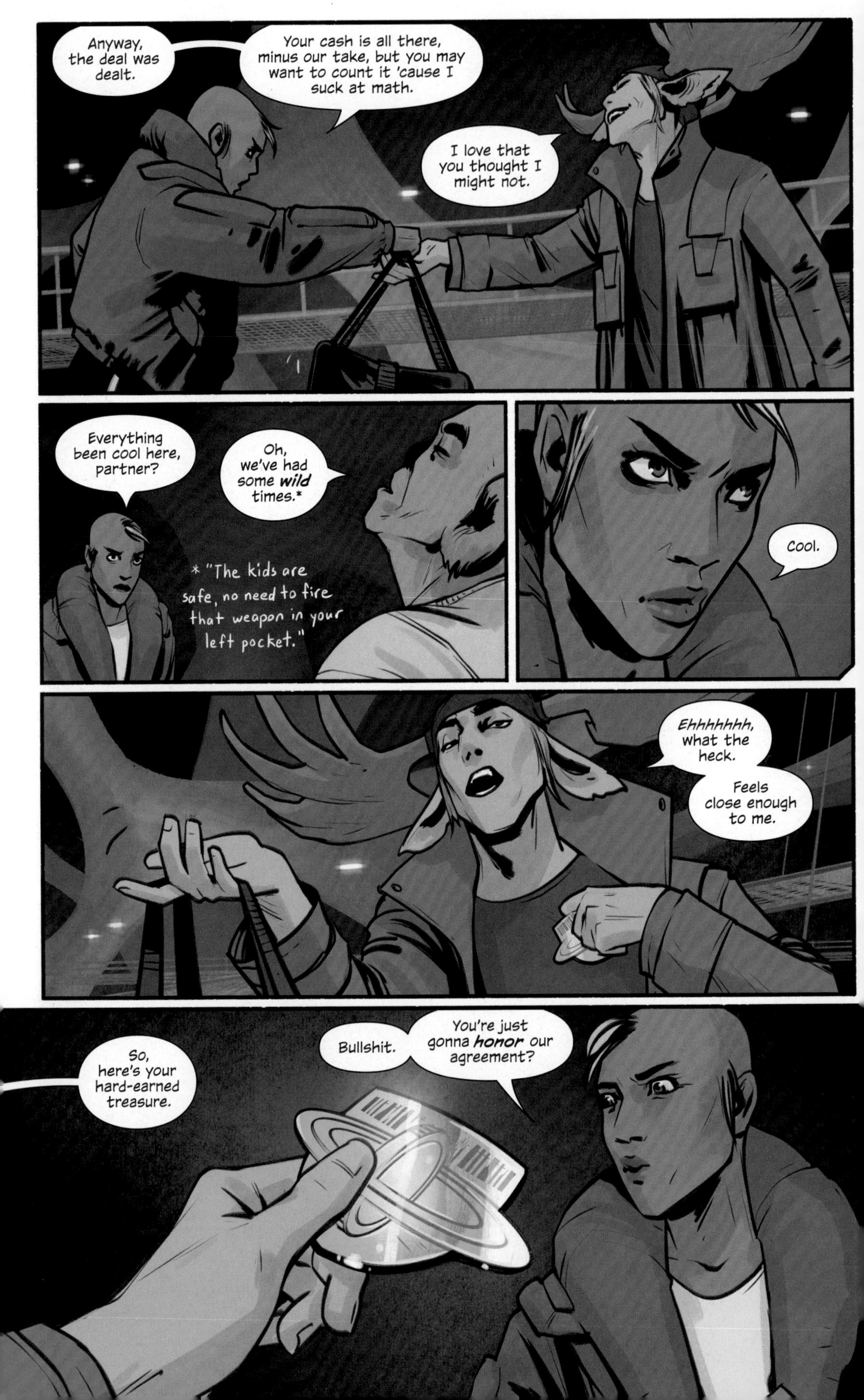
Anyway, the deal was dealt.
Your cash is all there, minus our take, but you may want to count it 'cause I suck at math.
I love that you thought I might not.
Everything been cool here, partner?
Oh, we've had some *wild* times.*
* "The kids are safe, no need to fire that weapon in your left pocket."
Cool.
Ehhhhhhh, what the heck.
Feels close enough to me.
So, here's your hard-earned treasure.
Bullshit.
You're just gonna *honor* our agreement?

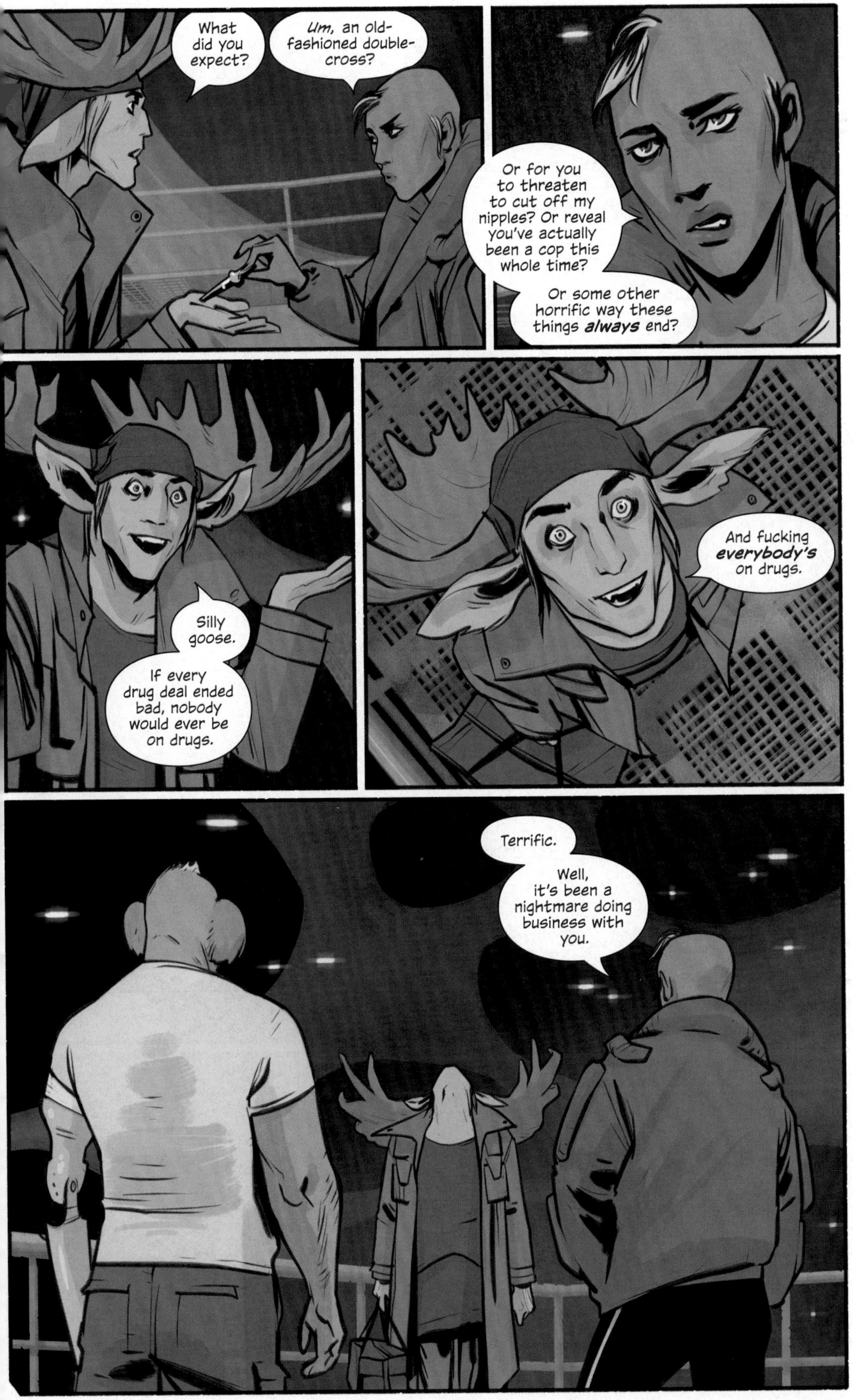
What did you expect?
Um, an old-fashioned double-cross?
Or for you to threaten to cut off my nipples? Or reveal you've actually been a cop this whole time?
Or some other horrific way these things ***always*** end?
Silly goose.
If every drug deal ended bad, nobody would ever be on drugs.
And fucking ***everybody's*** on drugs.
Terrific.
Well, it's been a nightmare doing business with you.

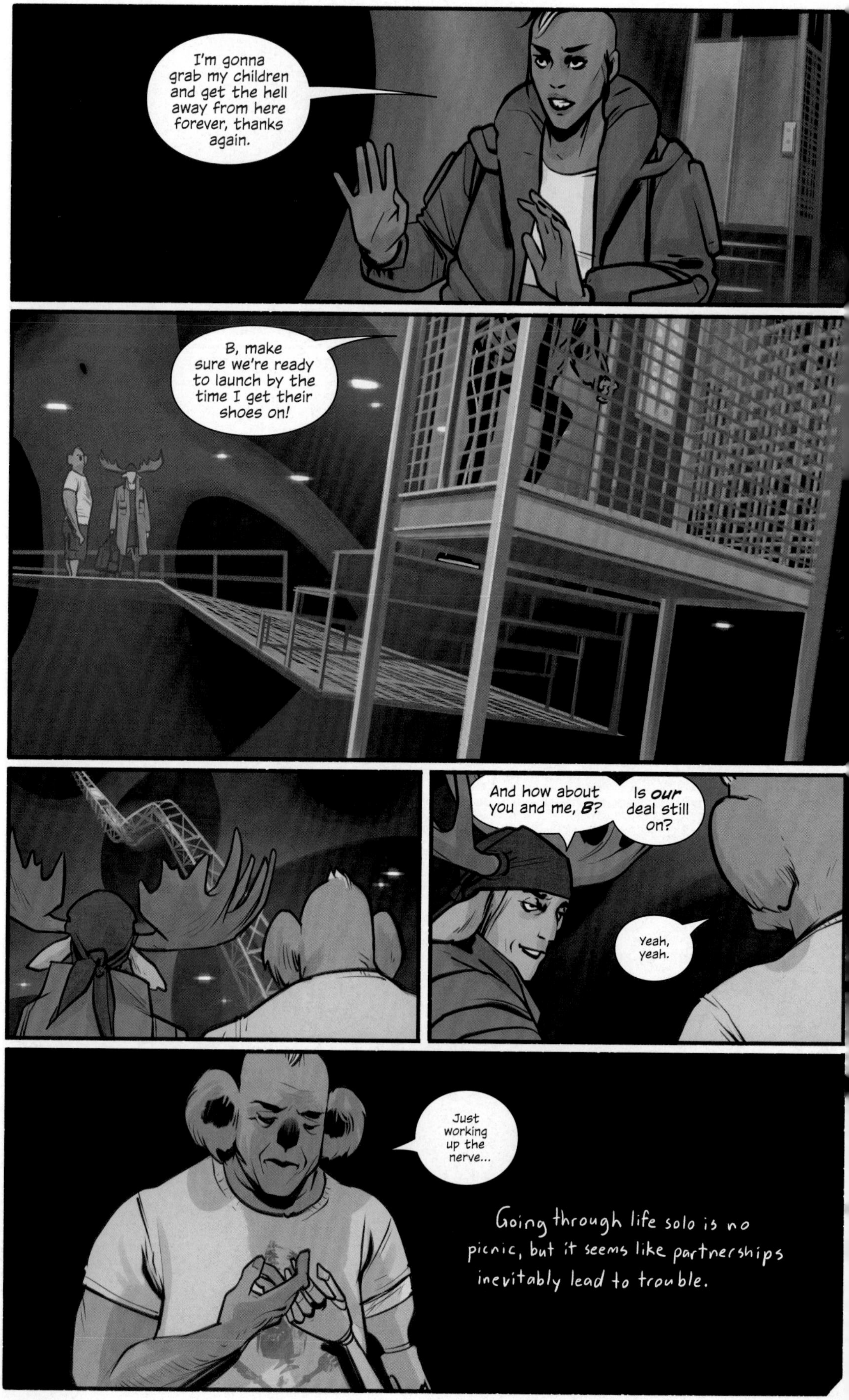
I'm gonna grab my children and get the hell away from here forever, thanks again.
B, make sure we're ready to launch by the time I get their shoes on!
And how about you and me, B?
Is our deal still on?
Yeah, yeah.
Just working up the nerve...
Going through life solo is no picnic, but it seems like partnerships inevitably lead to trouble.

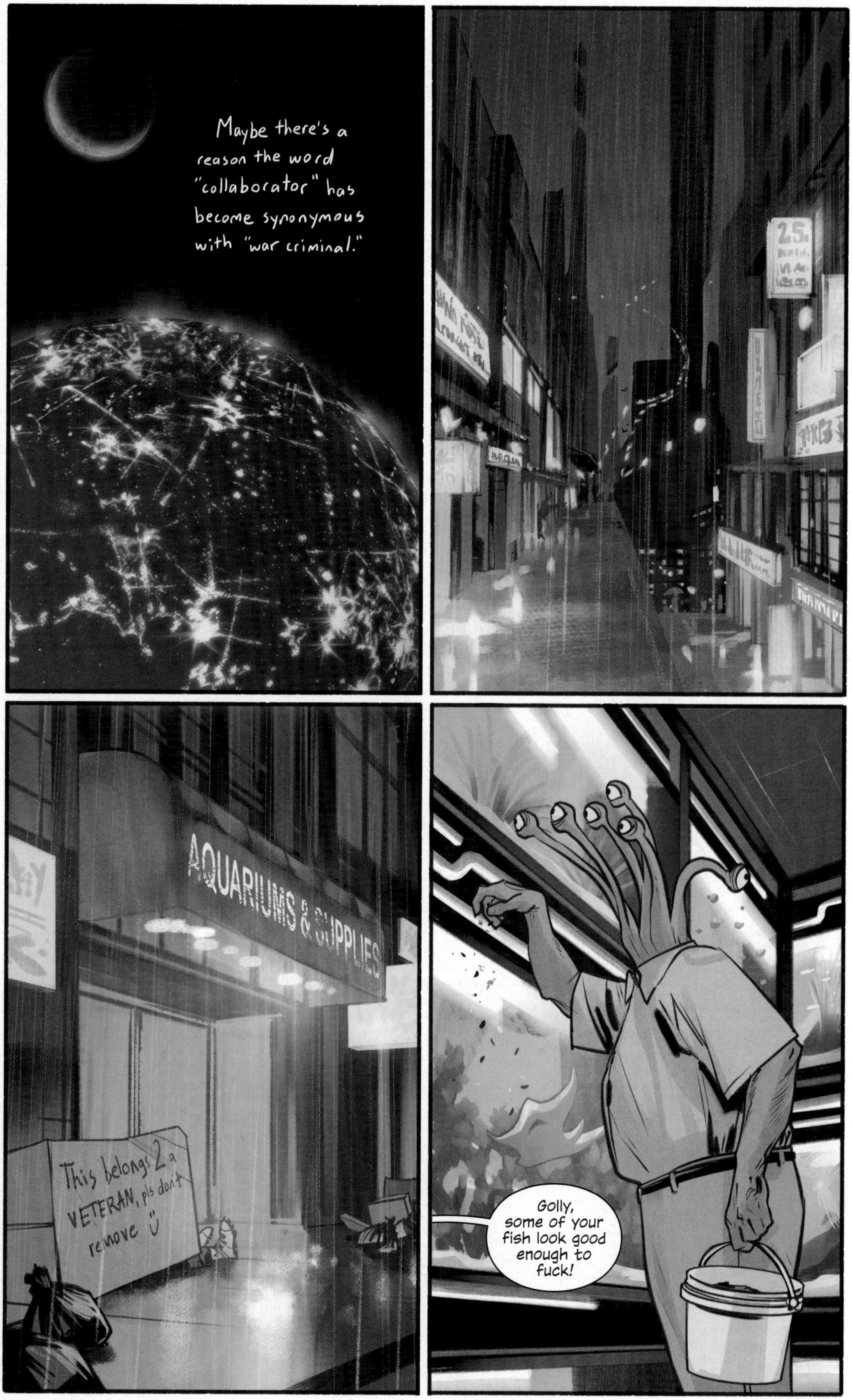
Maybe there's a reason the word "collaborator" has become synonymous with "war criminal."
AQUARIUMS & SUPPLIES
This belongs 2 a VETERAN, pls don't remove :)
Golly, some of your fish look good enough to fuck!

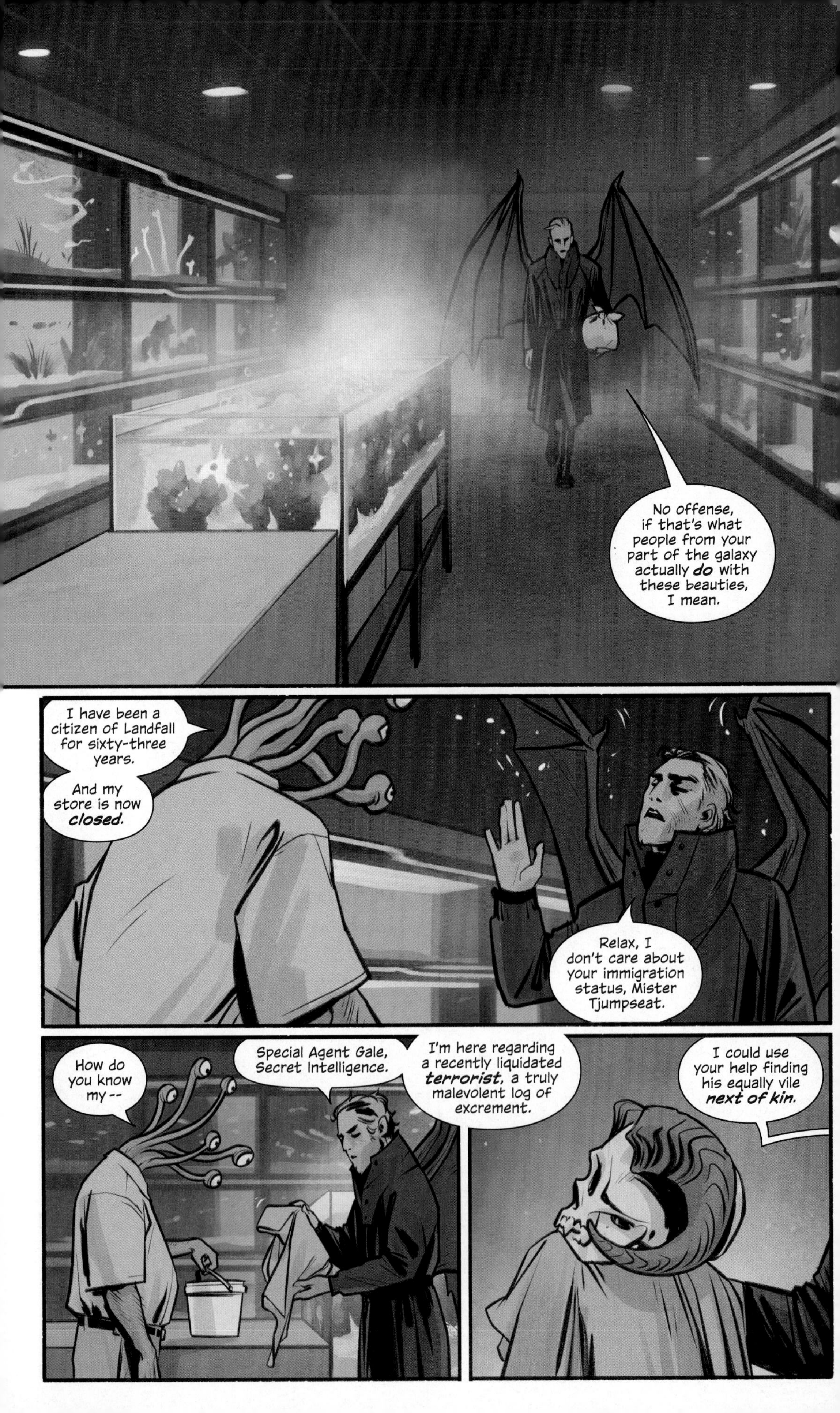
No offense, if that's what people from your part of the galaxy actually *do* with these beauties, I mean.
I have been a citizen of Landfall for sixty-three years.
And my store is now *closed.*
Relax, I don't care about your immigration status, Mister Tjumpseat.
How do you know my --
Special Agent Gale, Secret Intelligence.
I'm here regarding a recently liquidated *terrorist*, a truly malevolent log of excrement.
I could use your help finding his equally vile *next of kin.*

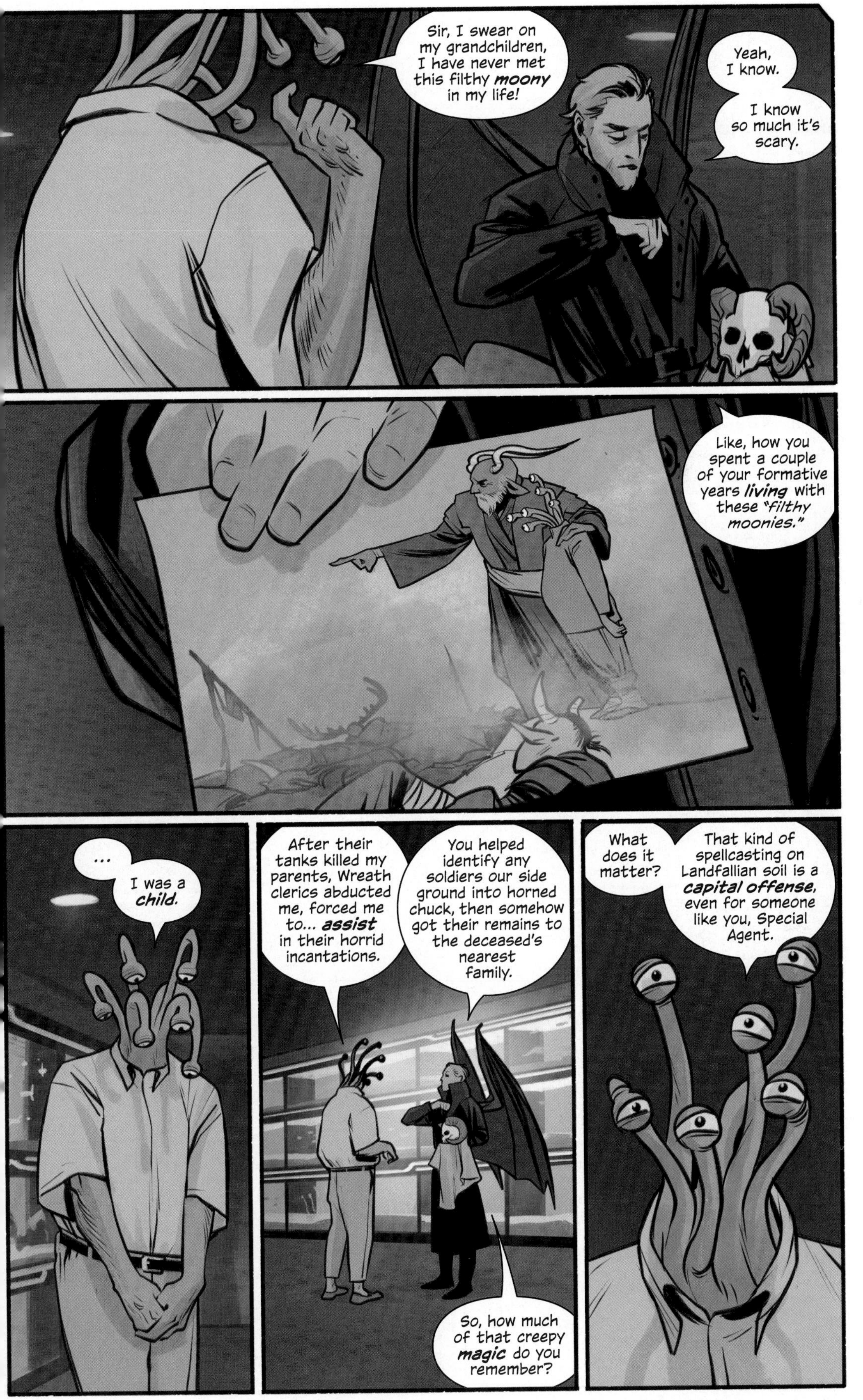

Sir, I swear on my grandchildren, I have never met this filthy **moony** in my life!
Yeah, I know.
I know so much it's scary.
Like, how you spent a couple of your formative years **living** with these *"filthy moonies."*
...
I was a **child**.
After their tanks killed my parents, Wreath clerics abducted me, forced me to... **assist** in their horrid incantations.
You helped identify any soldiers our side ground into horned chuck, then somehow got their remains to the deceased's nearest family.
So, how much of that creepy **magic** do you remember?
What does it matter?
That kind of spellcasting on Landfallian soil is a **capital offense**, even for someone like you, Special Agent.

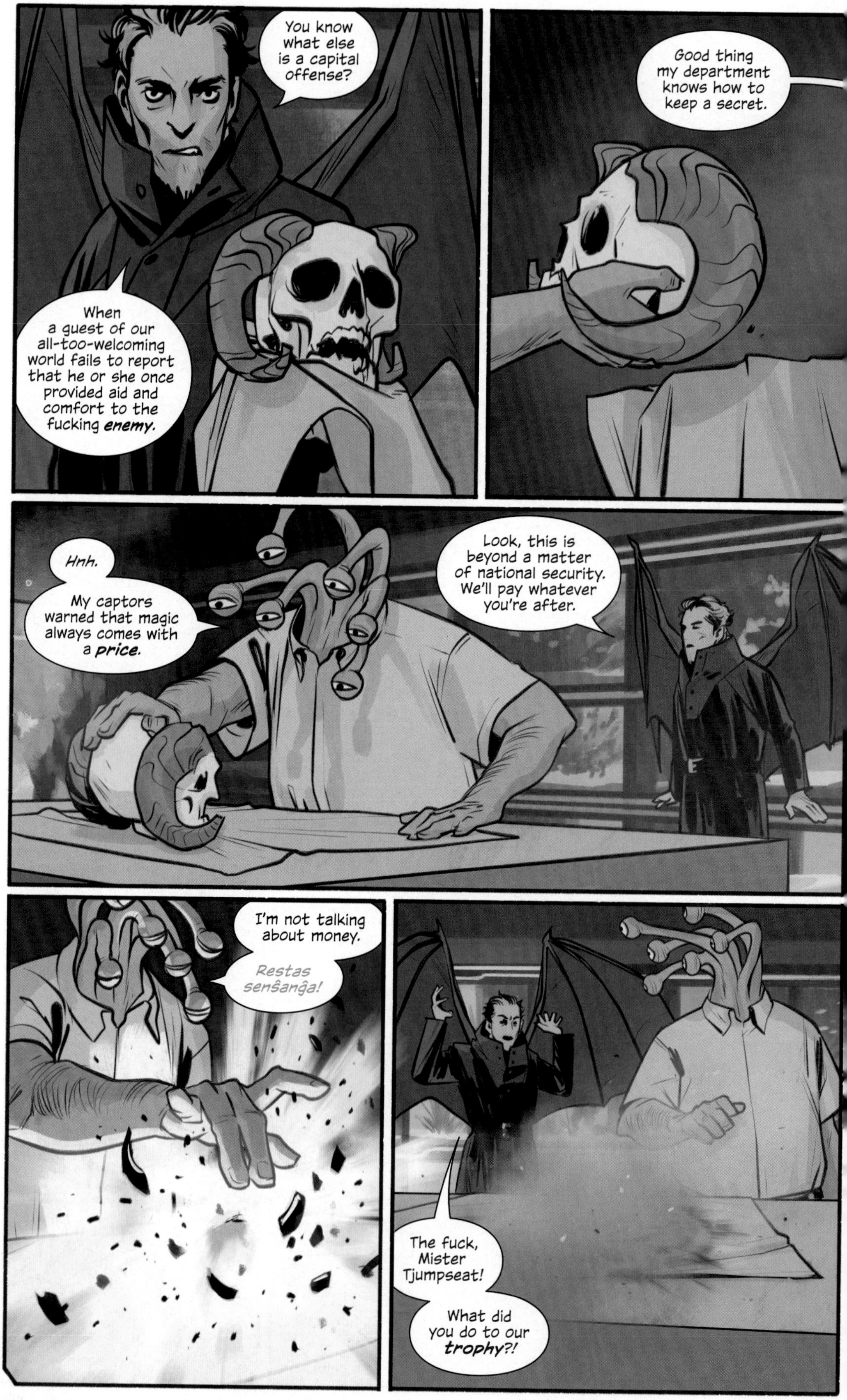

You know what else is a capital offense?
When a guest of our all-too-welcoming world fails to report that he or she once provided aid and comfort to the fucking *enemy.*
Good thing my department knows how to keep a secret.
Hnh.
My captors warned that magic always comes with a ***price.***
Look, this is beyond a matter of national security. We'll pay whatever you're after.
I'm not talking about money.
Restas senŝanĝa!
The fuck, Mister Tjumpseat!
What did you do to our ***trophy****?!*

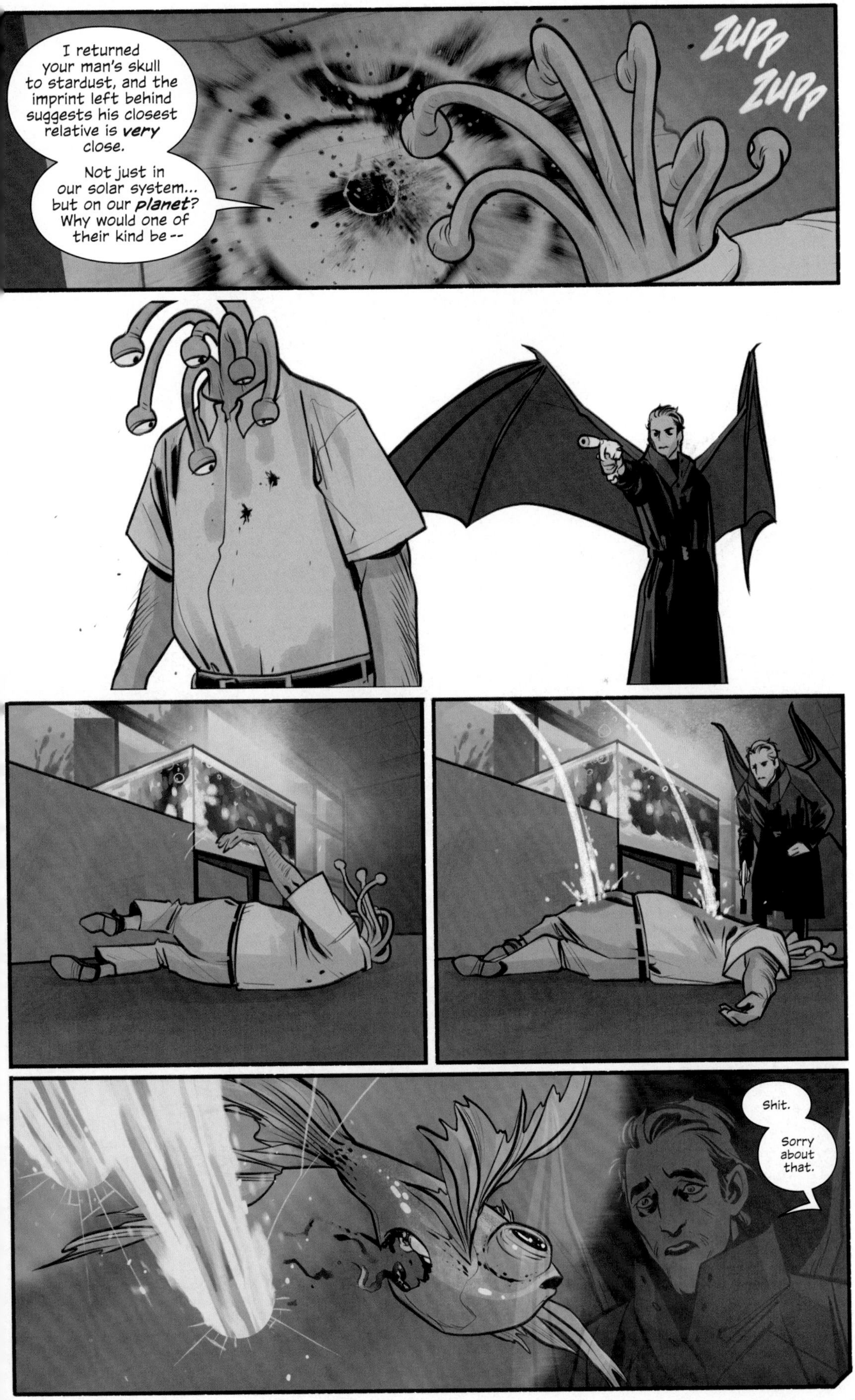

I returned your man's skull to stardust, and the imprint left behind suggests his closest relative is *very* close.
Not just in our solar system... but on our ***planet***? Why would one of their kind be --
ZUPP
ZUPP
Shit.
Sorry about that.

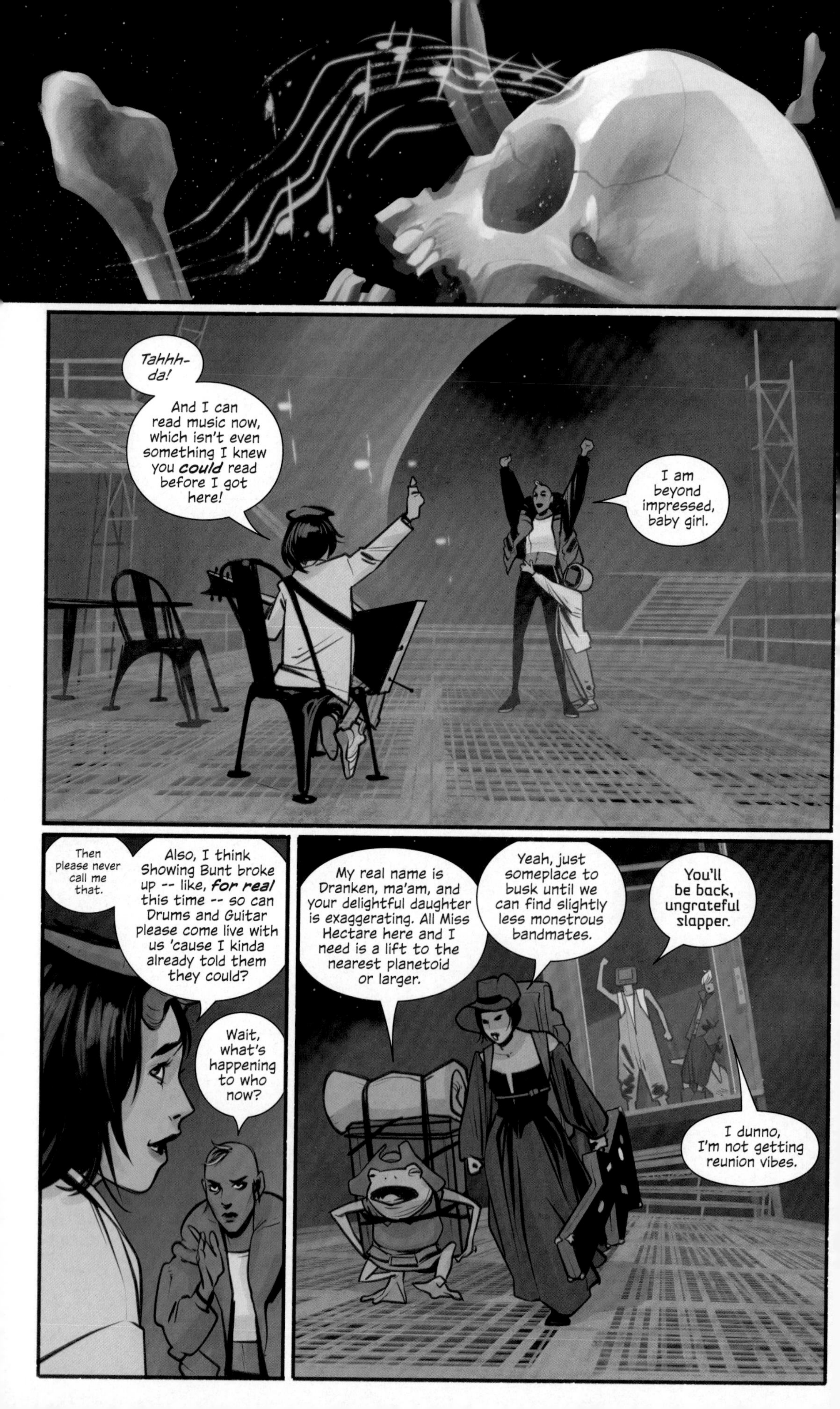
Tahhh-da!
And I can read music now, which isn't even something I knew you *could* read before I got here!
I am beyond impressed, baby girl.
Then please never call me that.
Also, I think Showing Bunt broke up -- like, *for real* this time -- so can Drums and Guitar please come live with us 'cause I kinda already told them they could?
Wait, what's happening to who now?
My real name is Dranken, ma'am, and your delightful daughter is exaggerating. All Miss Hectare here and I need is a lift to the nearest planetoid or larger.
Yeah, just someplace to busk until we can find slightly less monstrous bandmates.
You'll be back, ungrateful slapper.
I dunno, I'm not getting reunion vibes.

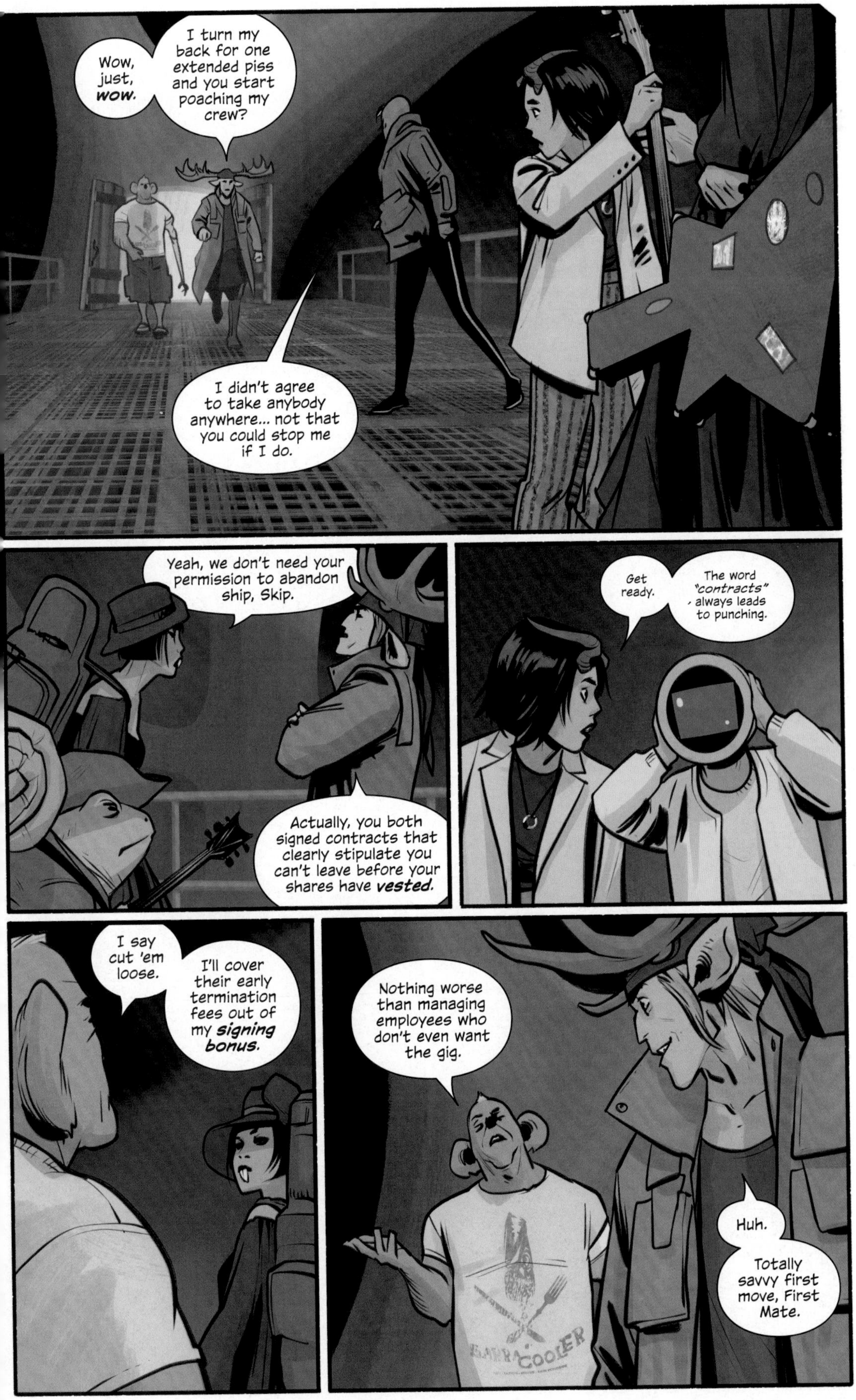
Wow, just, ***wow.***
I turn my back for one extended piss and you start poaching my crew?
I didn't agree to take anybody anywhere... not that you could stop me if I do.
Yeah, we don't need your permission to abandon ship, Skip.
Actually, you both signed contracts that clearly stipulate you can't leave before your shares have ***vested.***
Get ready.
The word *"contracts"* always leads to punching.
I say cut 'em loose.
I'll cover their early termination fees out of my ***signing bonus.***
Nothing worse than managing employees who don't even want the gig.
Huh.
Totally savvy first move, First Mate.

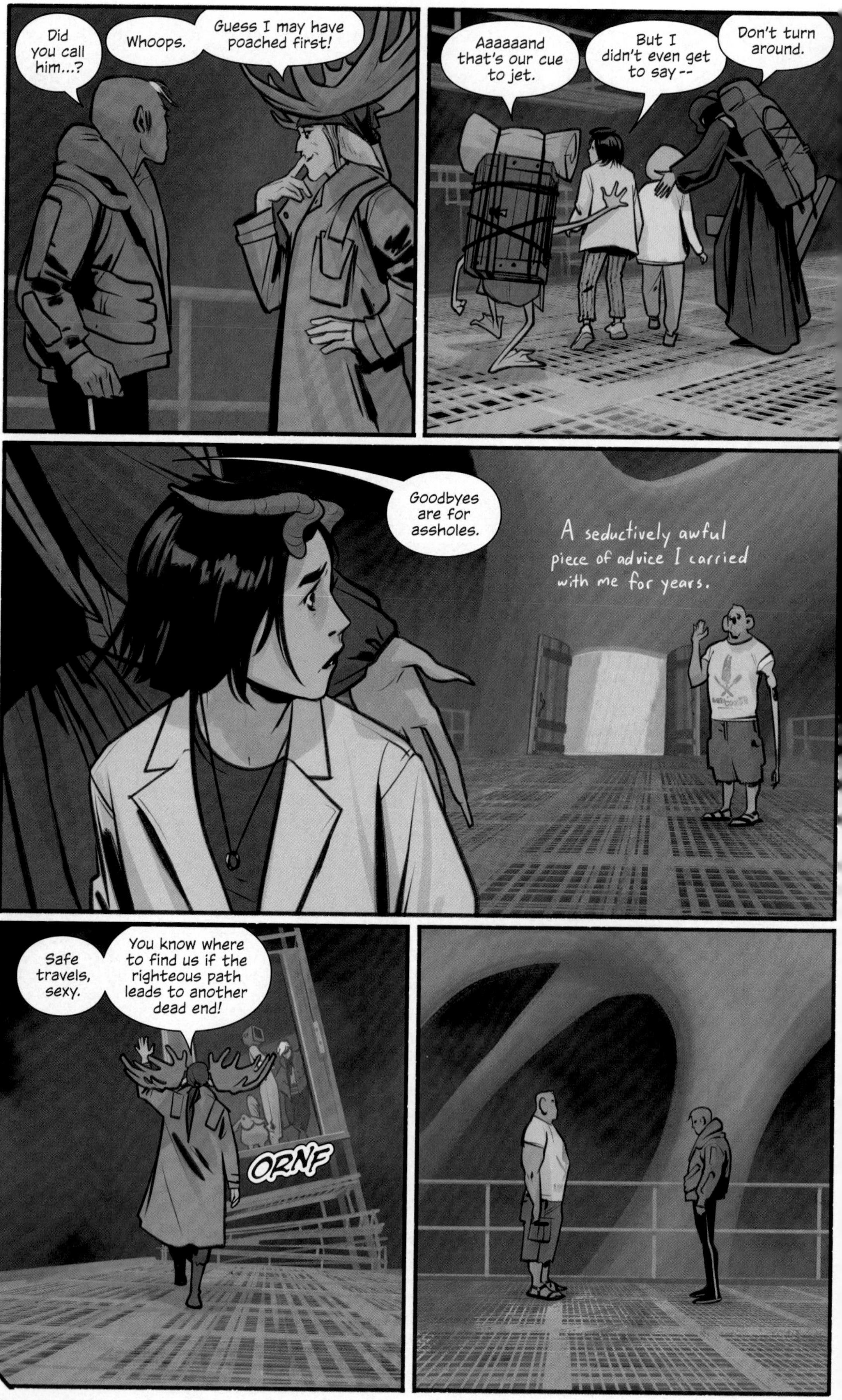
Did you call him...?
Whoops.
Guess I may have poached first!
Aaaaaand that's our cue to jet.
But I didn't even get to say --
Don't turn around.
Goodbyes are for assholes.
A seductively awful piece of advice I carried with me for years.
Safe travels, sexy.
You know where to find us if the righteous path leads to another dead end!
ORNF

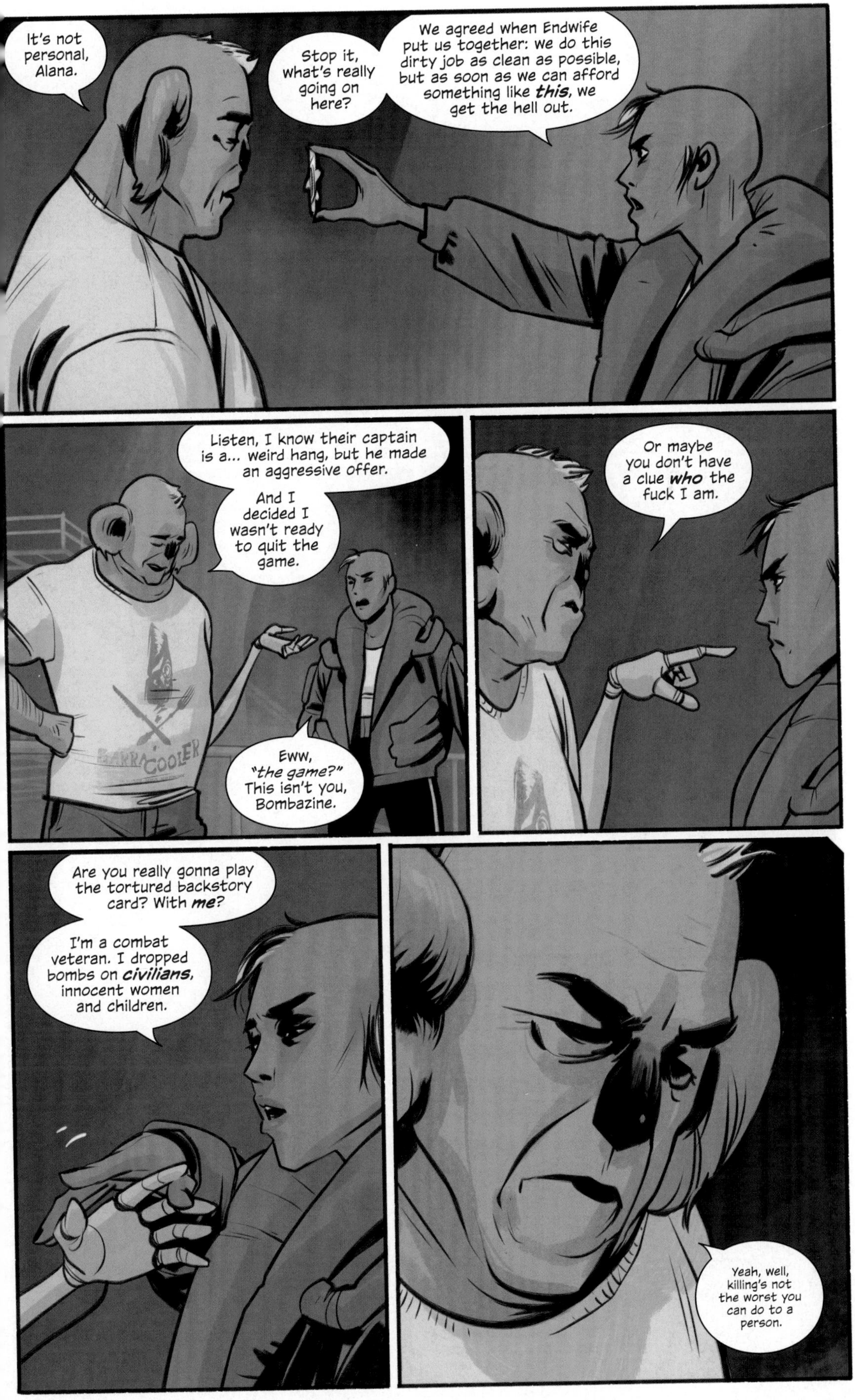

It's not personal, Alana.
Stop it, what's really going on here?
We agreed when Endwife put us together: we do this dirty job as clean as possible, but as soon as we can afford something like *this*, we get the hell out.
Listen, I know their captain is a... weird hang, but he made an aggressive offer.
And I decided I wasn't ready to quit the game.
BARRACOOLER
Eww, *"the game?"* This isn't you, Bombazine.
Or maybe you don't have a clue *who* the fuck I am.
Are you really gonna play the tortured backstory card? With *me*?
I'm a combat veteran. I dropped bombs on *civilians*, innocent women and children.
Yeah, well, killing's not the worst you can do to a person.

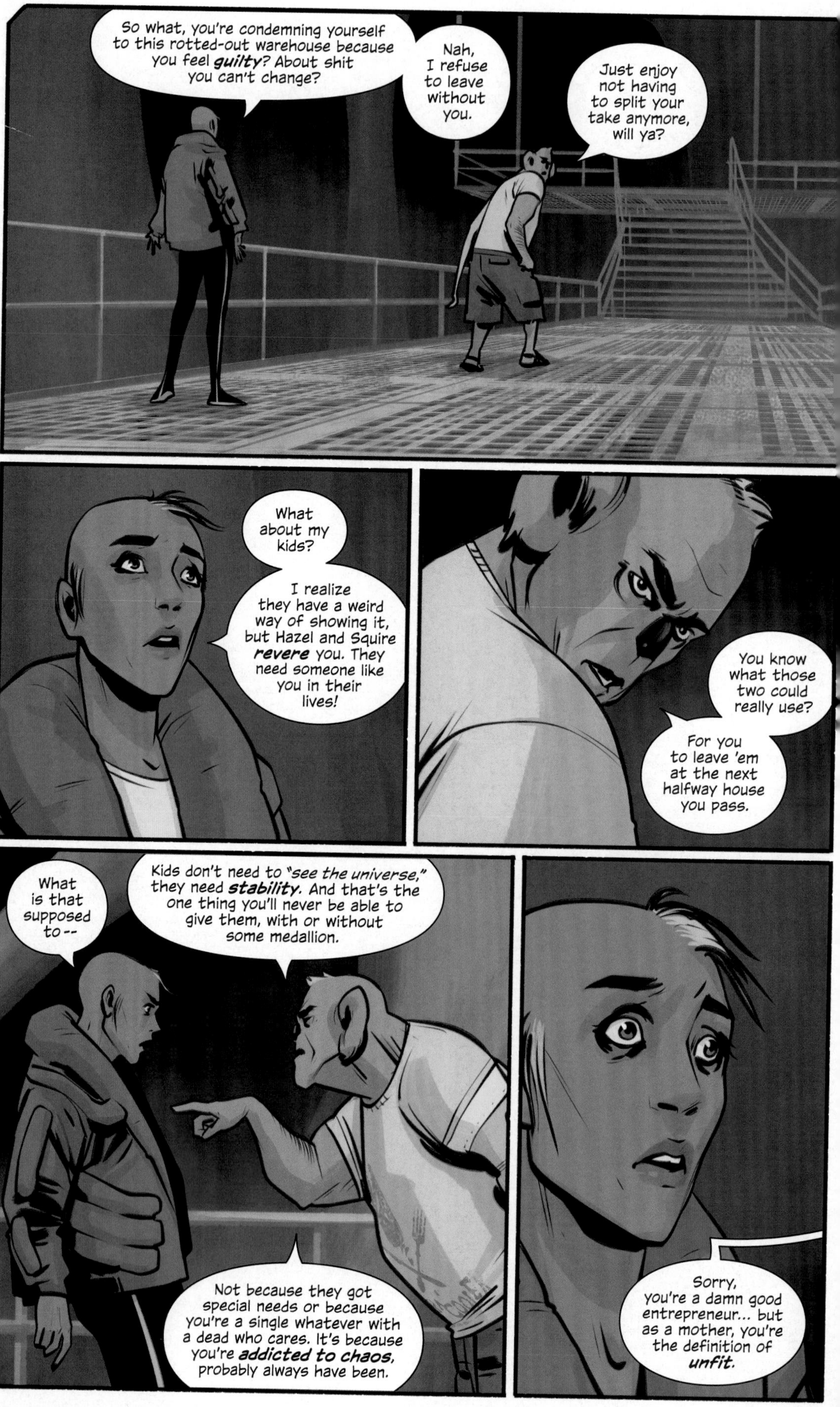

So what, you're condemning yourself to this rotted-out warehouse because you feel *guilty*? About shit you can't change?
Nah, I refuse to leave without you.
Just enjoy not having to split your take anymore, will ya?
What about my kids?
I realize they have a weird way of showing it, but Hazel and Squire *revere* you. They need someone like you in their lives!
You know what those two could really use?
For you to leave 'em at the next halfway house you pass.
What is that supposed to --
Kids don't need to *"see the universe,"* they need *stability*. And that's the one thing you'll never be able to give them, with or without some medallion.
Not because they got special needs or because you're a single whatever with a dead who cares. It's because you're *addicted to chaos*, probably always have been.
Sorry, you're a damn good entrepreneur... but as a mother, you're the definition of *unfit*.

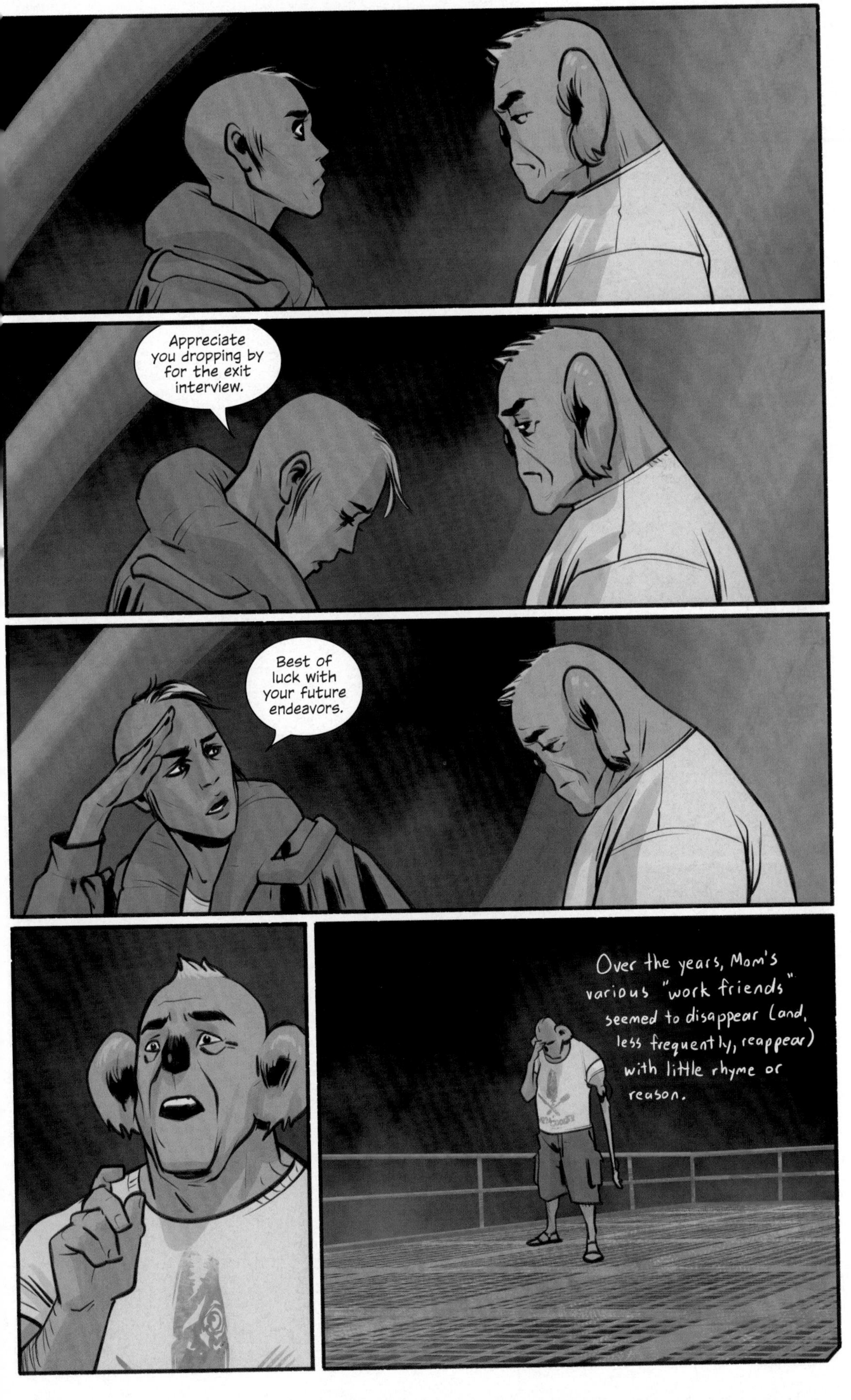
Appreciate you dropping by for the exit interview.
Best of luck with your future endeavors.
Over the years, Mom's various "work friends" seemed to disappear (and, less frequently, reappear) with little rhyme or reason.

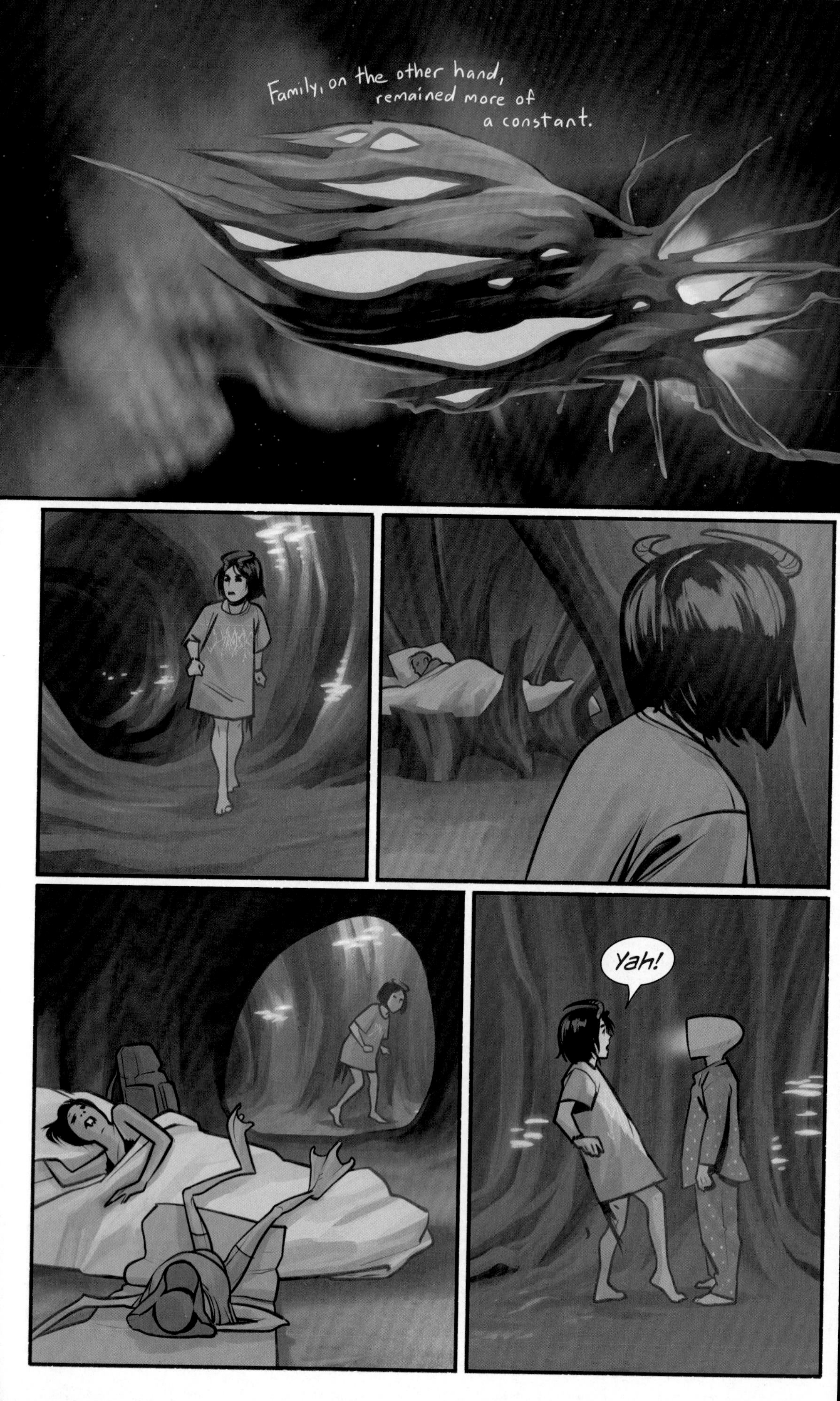
Family, on the other hand, remained more of a constant.
Yah!

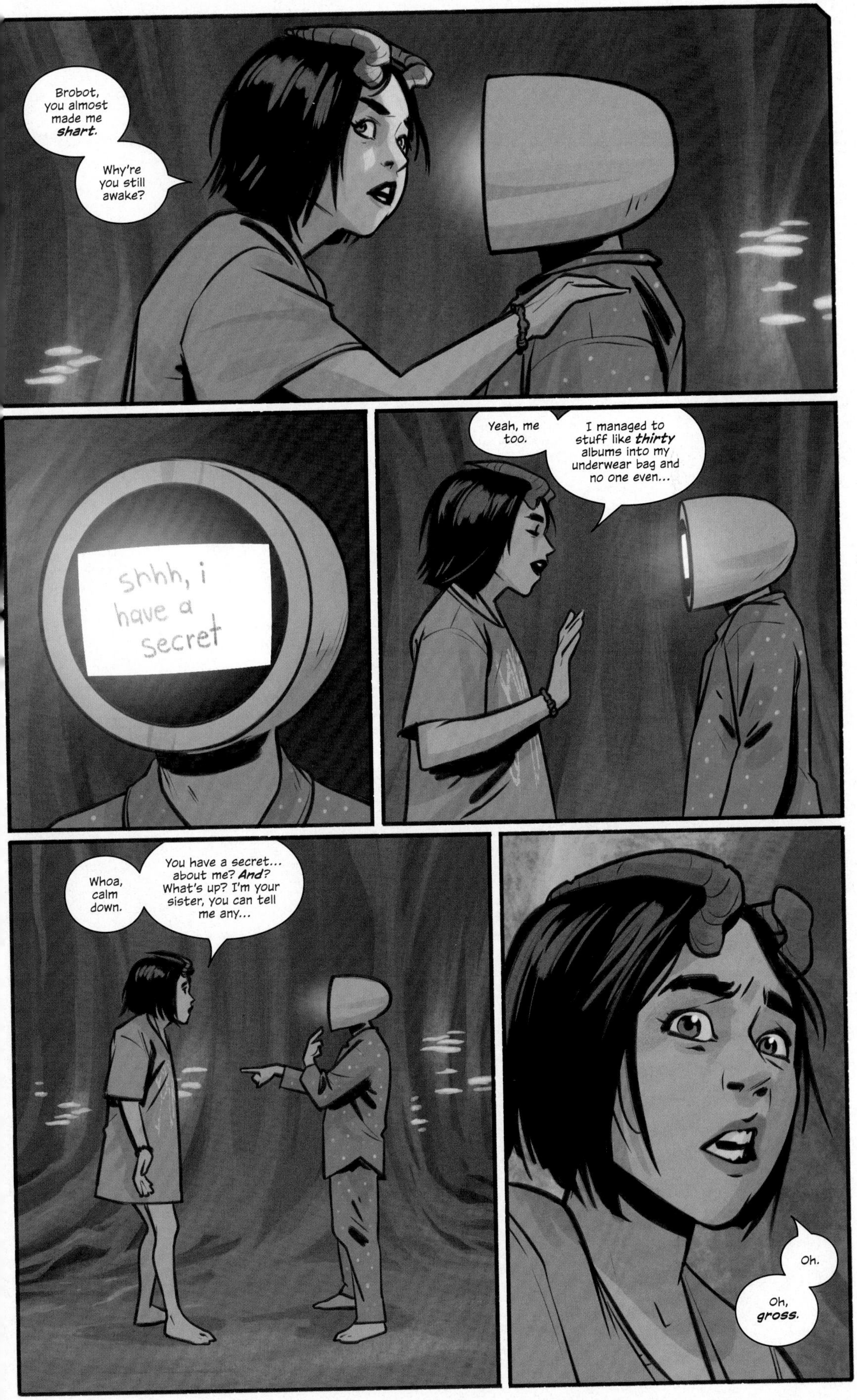
Brobot, you almost made me ***shart***.
Why're you still awake?
shhh, i have a secret
Yeah, me too.
I managed to stuff like ***thirty*** albums into my underwear bag and no one even...
Whoa, calm down.
You have a secret... about me? ***And***? What's up? I'm your sister, you can tell me any...
Oh.
Oh, ***gross***.

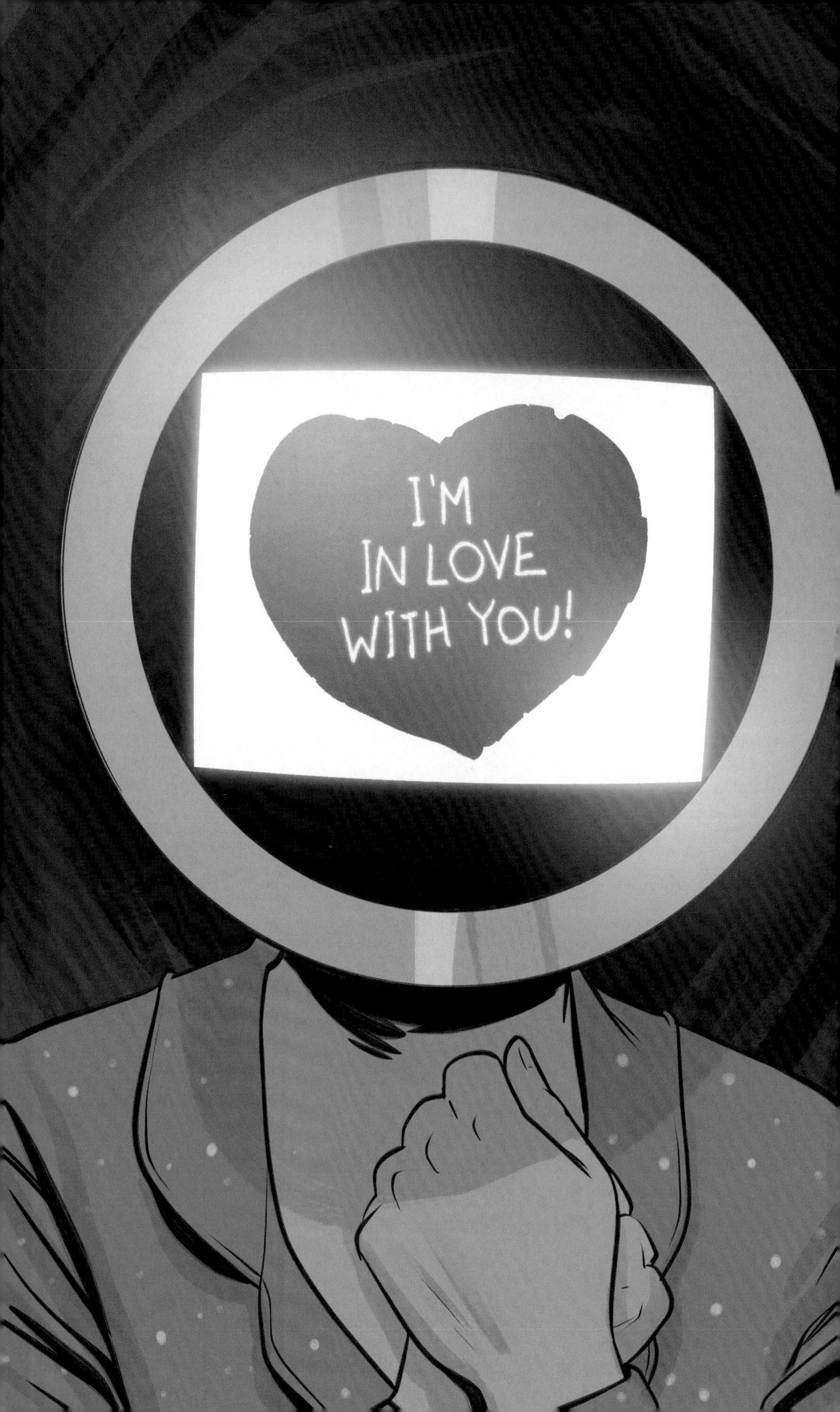
I'M
IN LOVE
WITH YOU!

end chapter fifty-nine

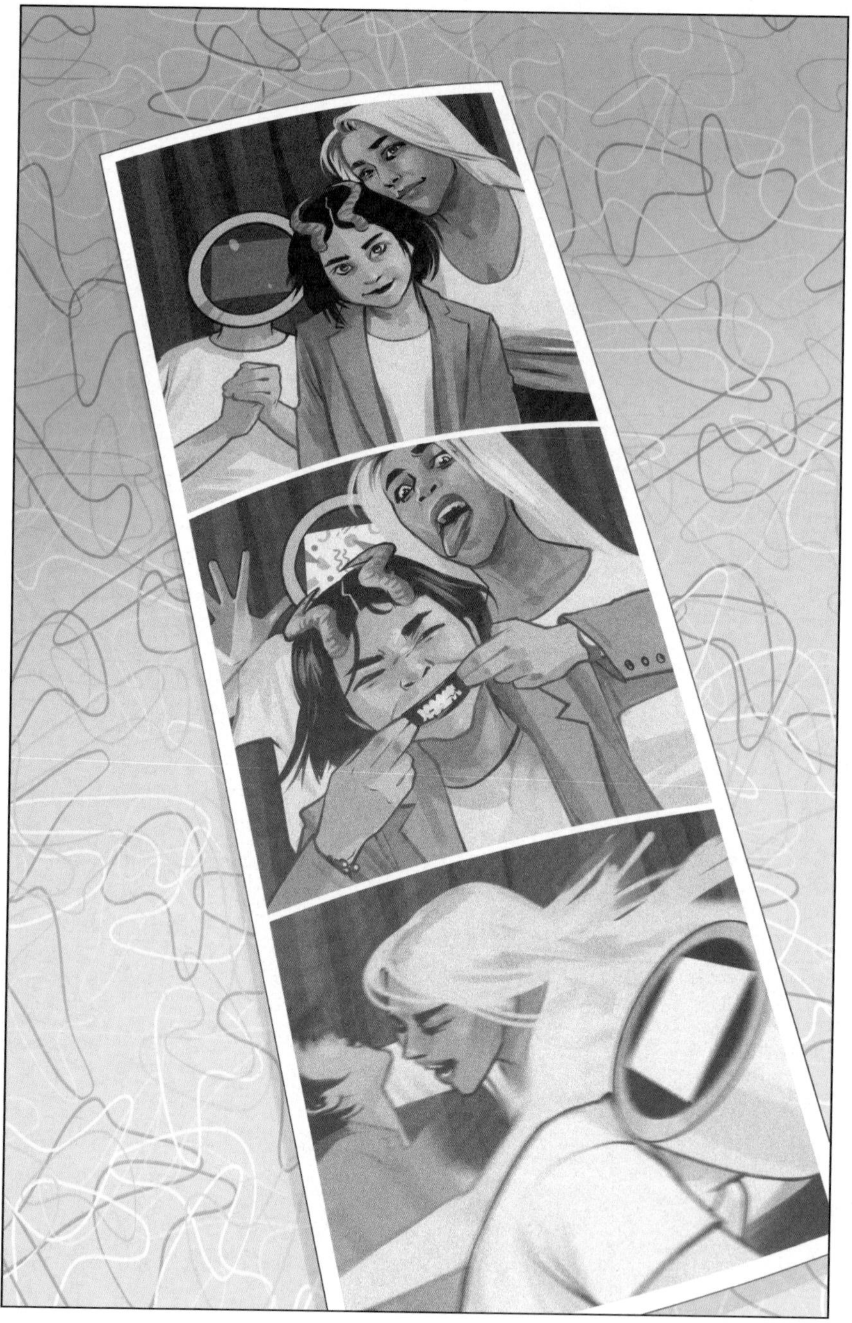

CHAPTER
SIXTY

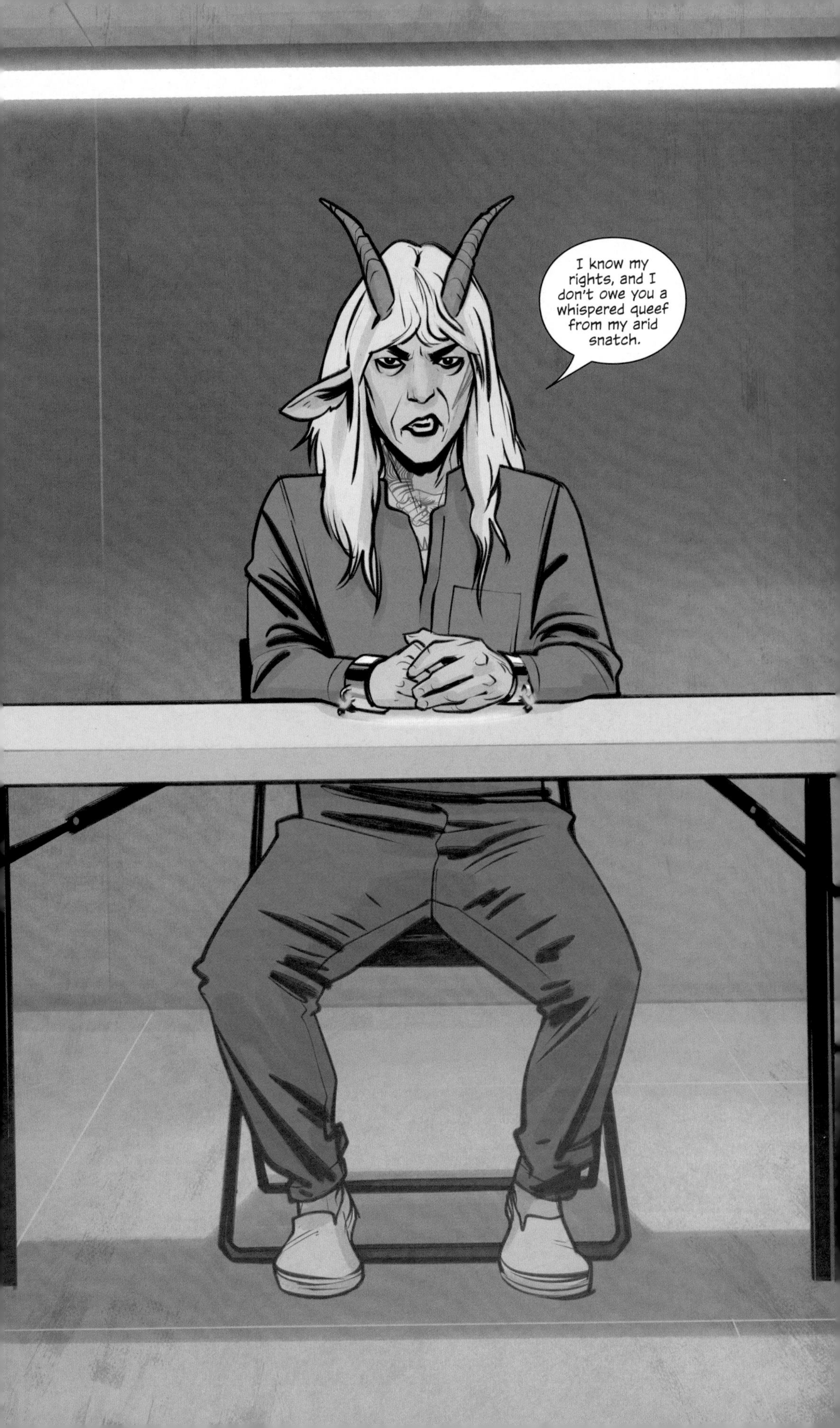
I know my rights, and I don't owe you a whispered queef from my arid snatch.

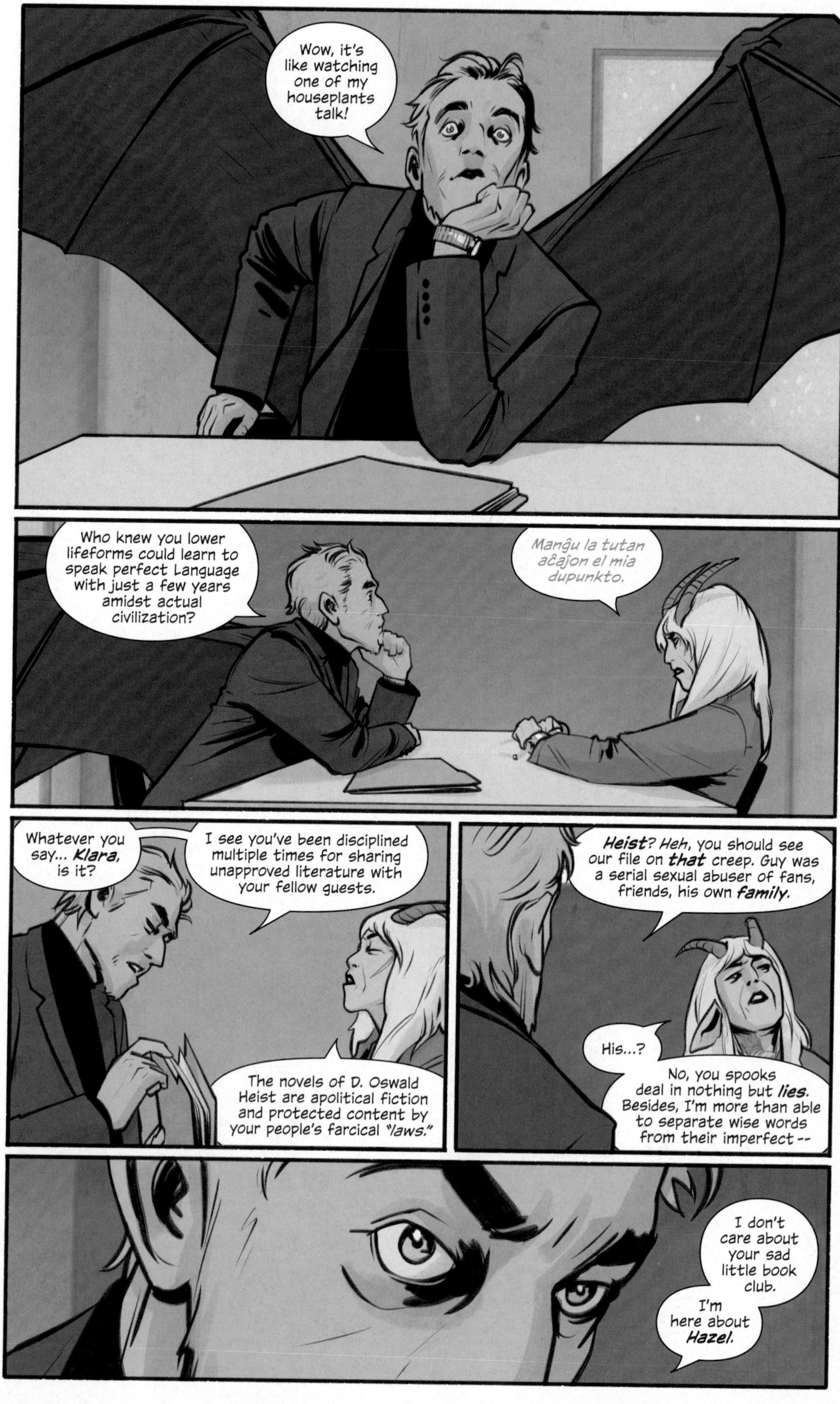

Wow, it's like watching one of my houseplants talk!
Who knew you lower lifeforms could learn to speak perfect Language with just a few years amidst actual civilization?
Mangû la tutan acâjon el mia dupunkto.
Whatever you say... Klara, is it?
I see you've been disciplined multiple times for sharing unapproved literature with your fellow guests.
The novels of D. Oswald Heist are apolitical fiction and protected content by your people's farcical "laws."
Heist? Heh, you should see our file on that creep. Guy was a serial sexual abuser of fans, friends, his own family.
His...?
No, you spooks deal in nothing but lies. Besides, I'm more than able to separate wise words from their imperfect --
I don't care about your sad little book club.
I'm here about Hazel.

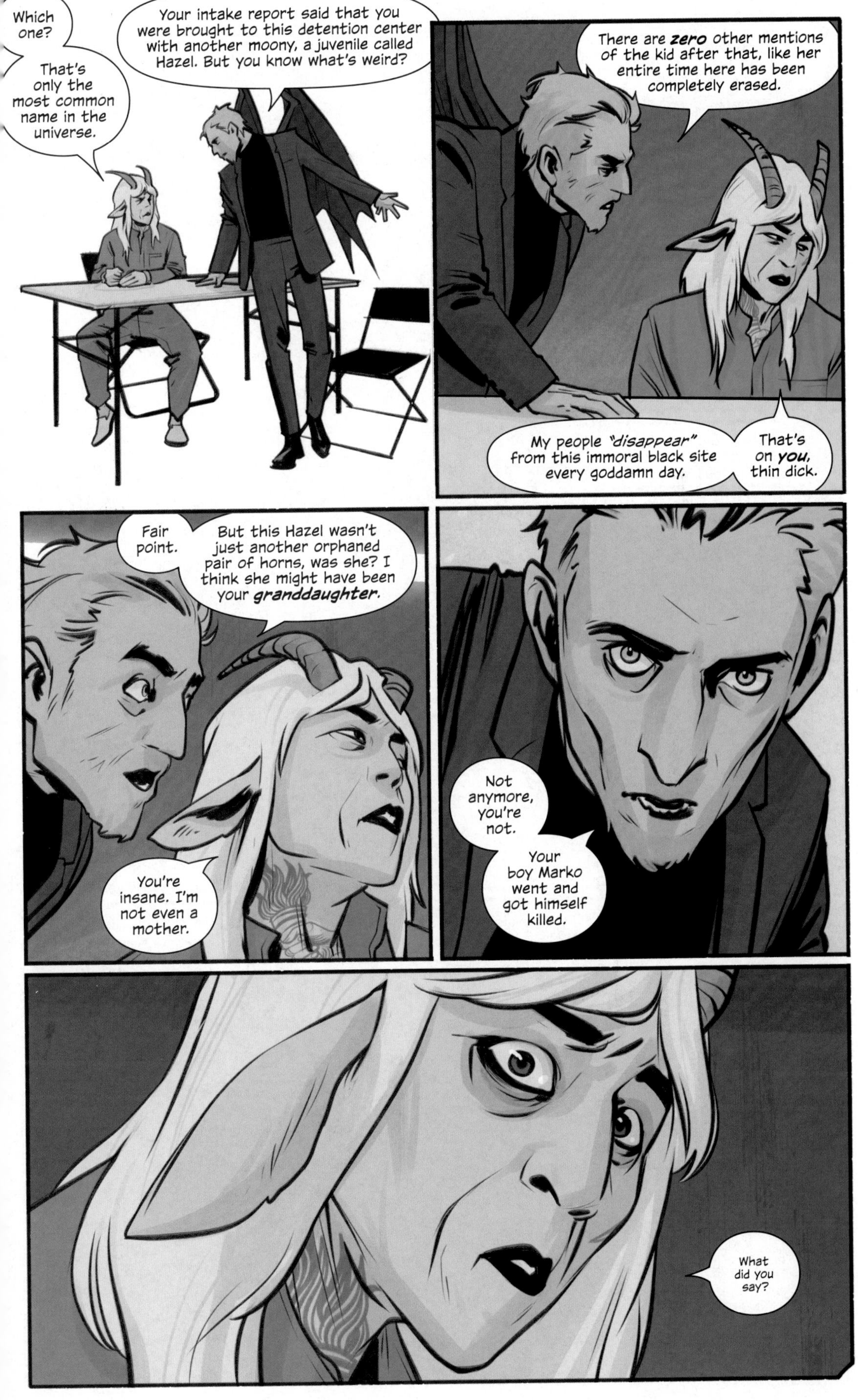
Which one?
That's only the most common name in the universe.
Your intake report said that you were brought to this detention center with another moony, a juvenile called Hazel. But you know what's weird?
There are **zero** other mentions of the kid after that, like her entire time here has been completely erased.
My people *"disappear"* from this immoral black site every goddamn day.
That's on **you**, thin dick.
Fair point.
But this Hazel wasn't just another orphaned pair of horns, was she? I think she might have been your **granddaughter**.
You're insane. I'm not even a mother.
Not anymore, you're not.
Your boy Marko went and got himself killed.
What did you say?

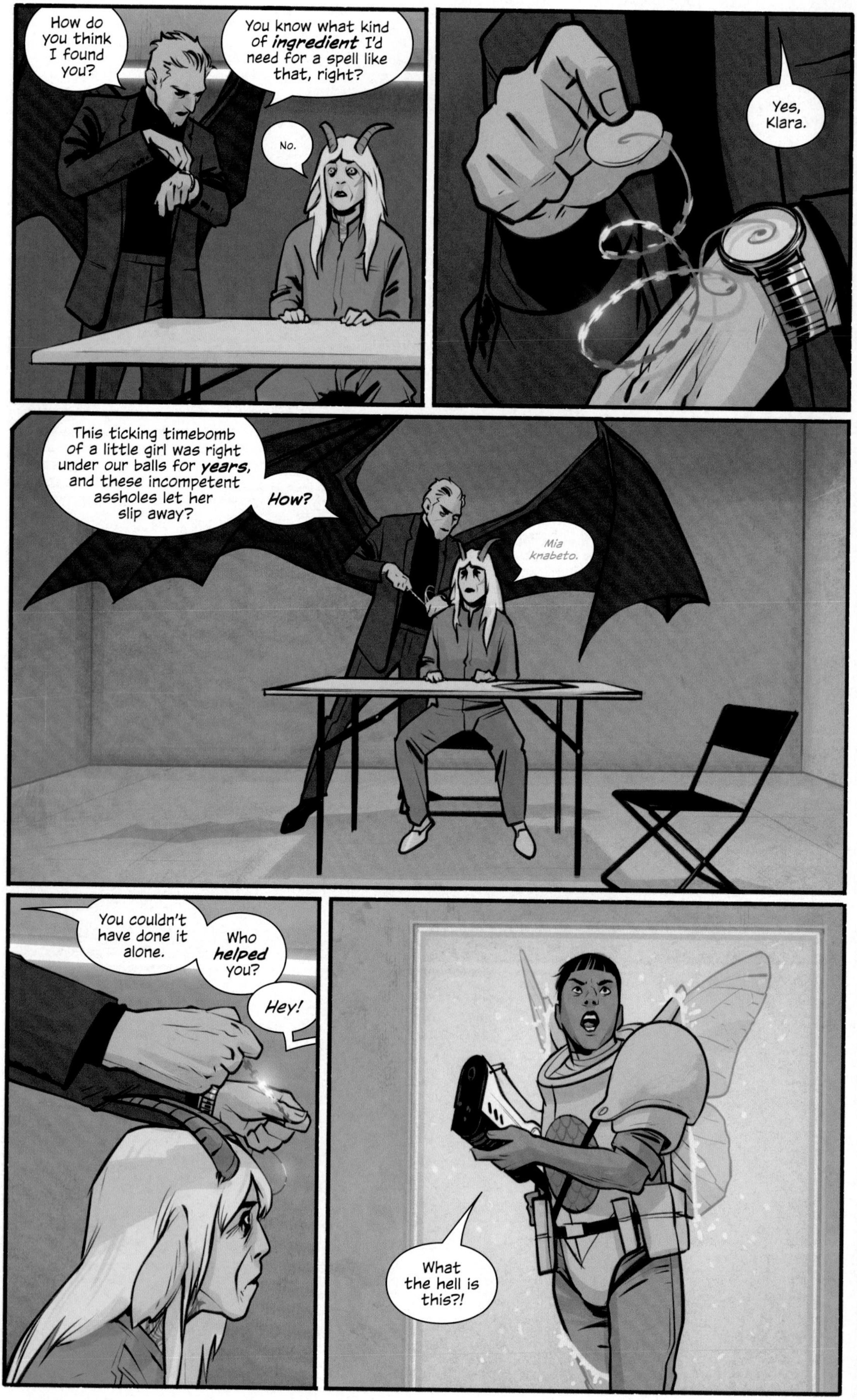
How do you think I found you?
You know what kind of ***ingredient*** I'd need for a spell like that, right?
No.
Yes, Klara.
This ticking timebomb of a little girl was right under our balls for ***years***, and these incompetent assholes let her slip away?
How?
Mia knabeto.
You couldn't have done it alone.
Who ***helped*** you?
Hey!
What the hell is this?!

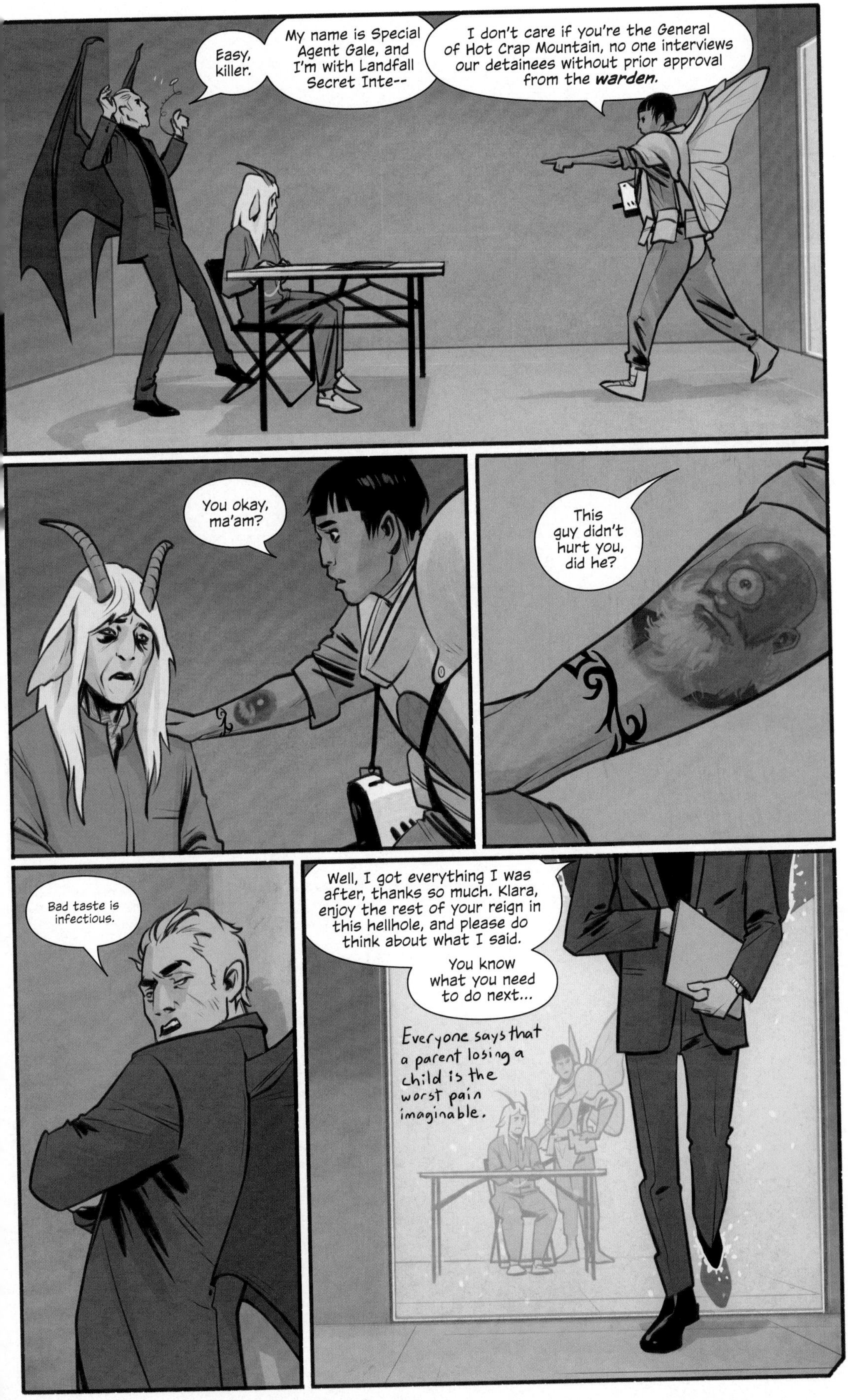

Easy, killer.
My name is Special Agent Gale, and I'm with Landfall Secret Inte--
I don't care if you're the General of Hot Crap Mountain, no one interviews our detainees without prior approval from the ***warden***.
You okay, ma'am?
This guy didn't hurt you, did he?
Bad taste is infectious.
Well, I got everything I was after, thanks so much. Klara, enjoy the rest of your reign in this hellhole, and please do think about what I said.
You know what you need to do next...
Everyone says that a parent losing a child is the worst pain imaginable.

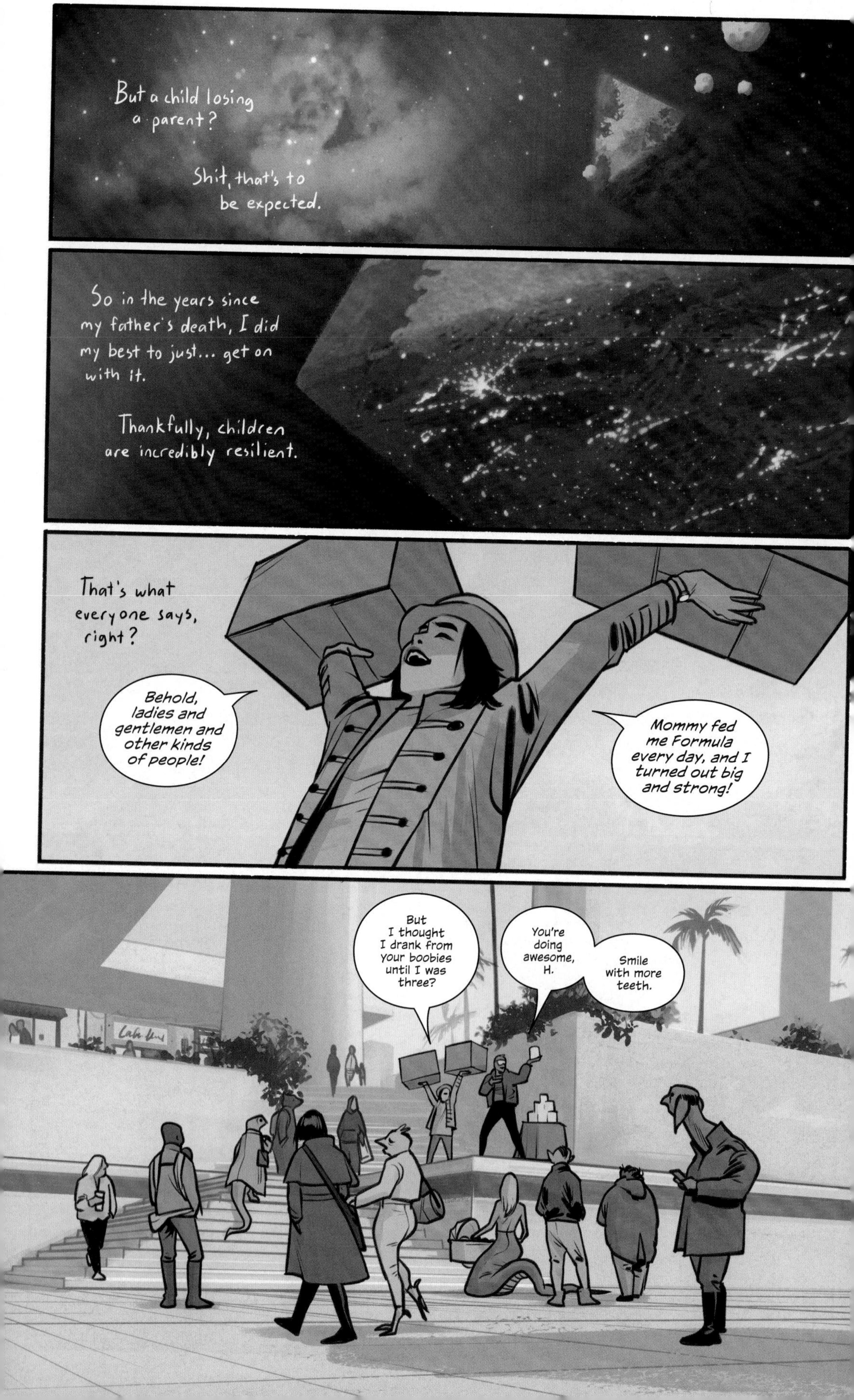
But a child losing a parent?
Shit, that's to be expected.
So in the years since my father's death, I did my best to just... get on with it.
Thankfully, children are incredibly resilient.
That's what everyone says, right?
Behold, ladies and gentlemen and other kinds of people!
Mommy fed me Formula every day, and I turned out big and strong!
But I thought I drank from your boobies until I was three?
You're doing awesome, H.
Smile with more teeth.

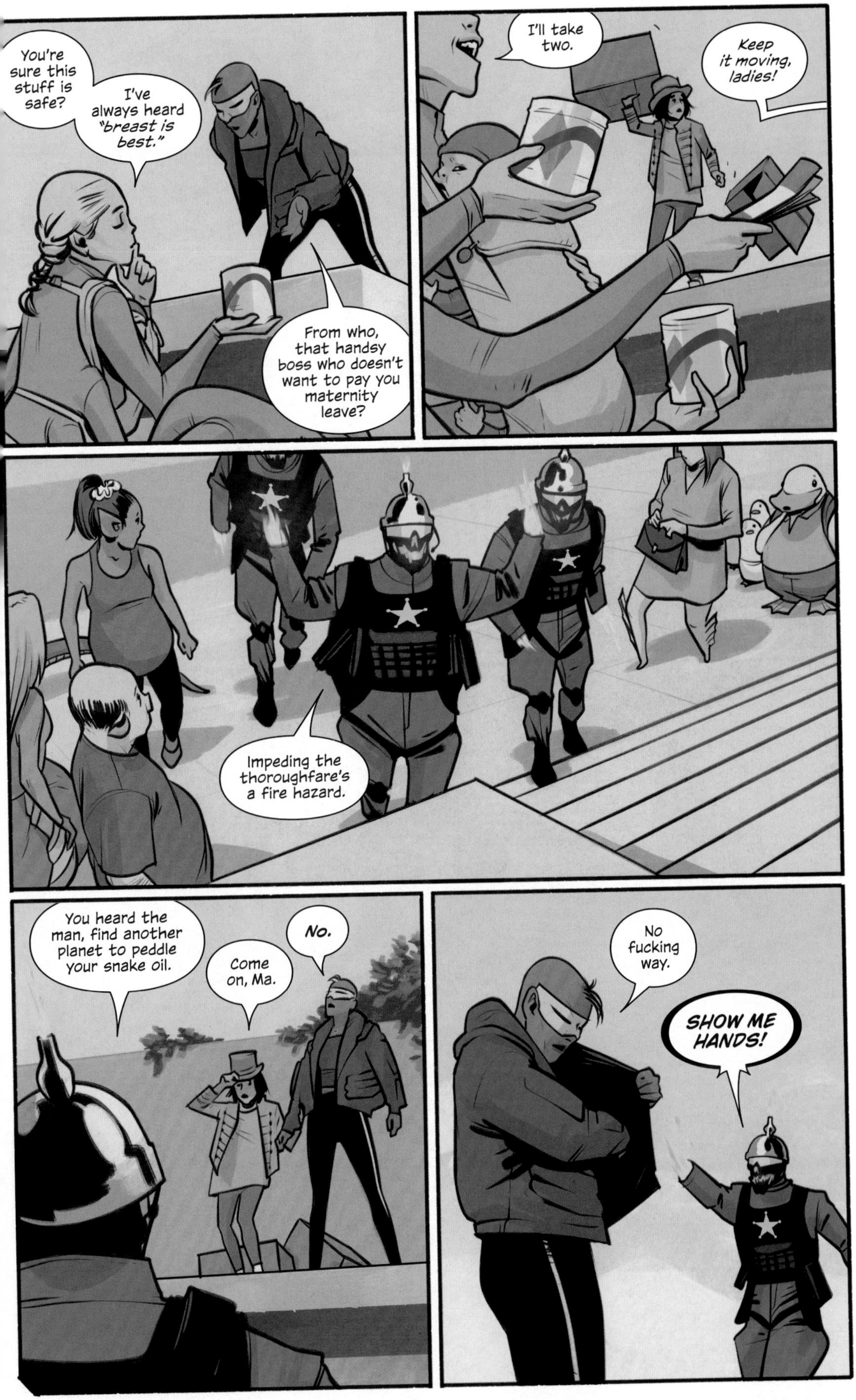
You're sure this stuff is safe?
I've always heard "breast is best."
From who, that handsy boss who doesn't want to pay you maternity leave?
I'll take two.
Keep it moving, ladies!
Impeding the thoroughfare's a fire hazard.
You heard the man, find another planet to peddle your snake oil.
Come on, Ma.
No.
No fucking way.
SHOW ME HANDS!

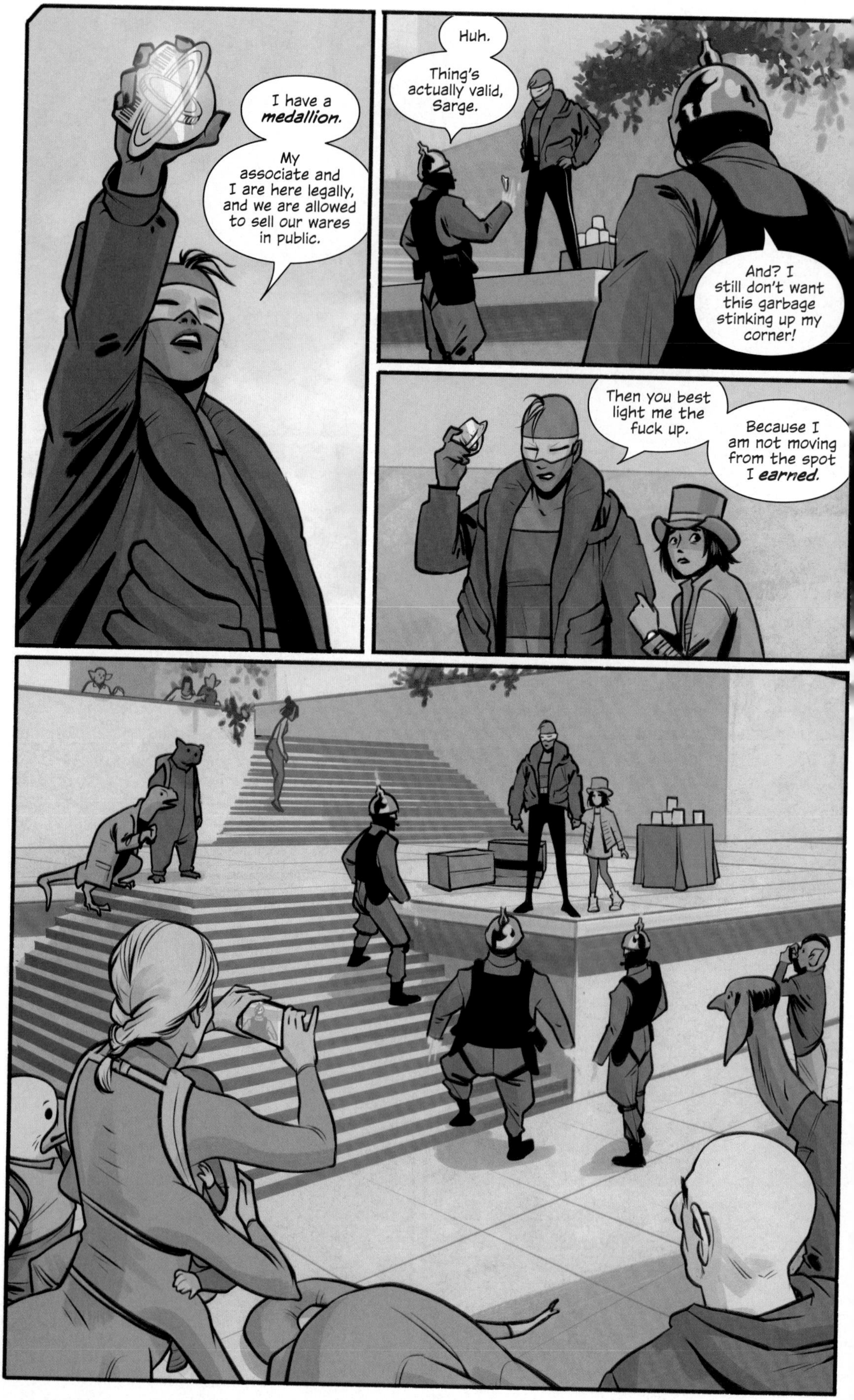
I have a *medallion.*
My associate and I are here legally, and we are allowed to sell our wares in public.
Huh.
Thing's actually valid, Sarge.
And? I still don't want this garbage stinking up my corner!
Then you best light me the fuck up.
Because I am not moving from the spot I *earned.*

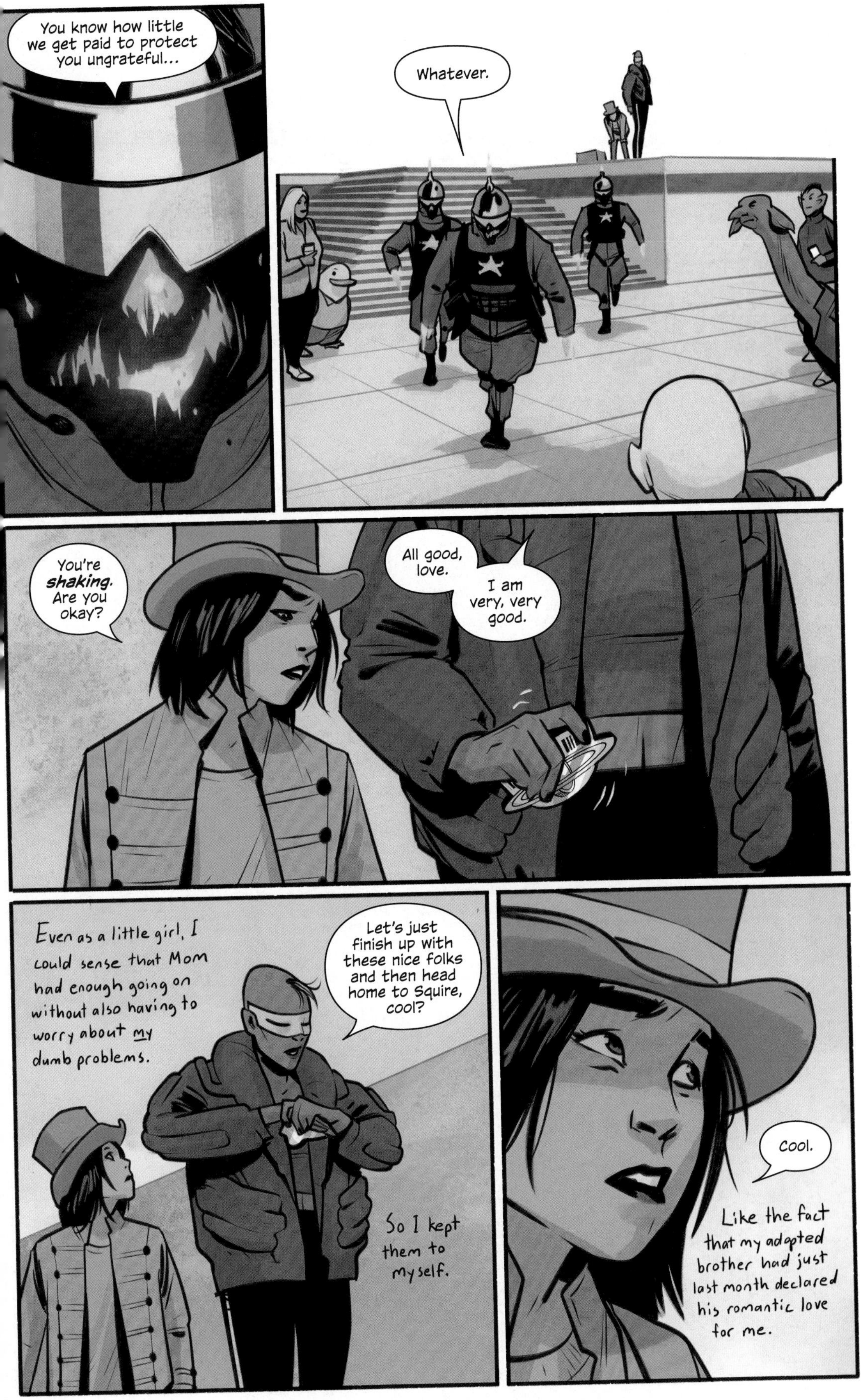
You know how little we get paid to protect you ungrateful...
Whatever.
You're *shaking*. Are you okay?
All good, love.
I am very, very good.
Even as a little girl, I could sense that Mom had enough going on without also having to worry about MY dumb problems.
Let's just finish up with these nice folks and then head home to Squire, cool?
So I kept them to myself.
Cool.
Like the fact that my adopted brother had just last month declared his romantic love for me.

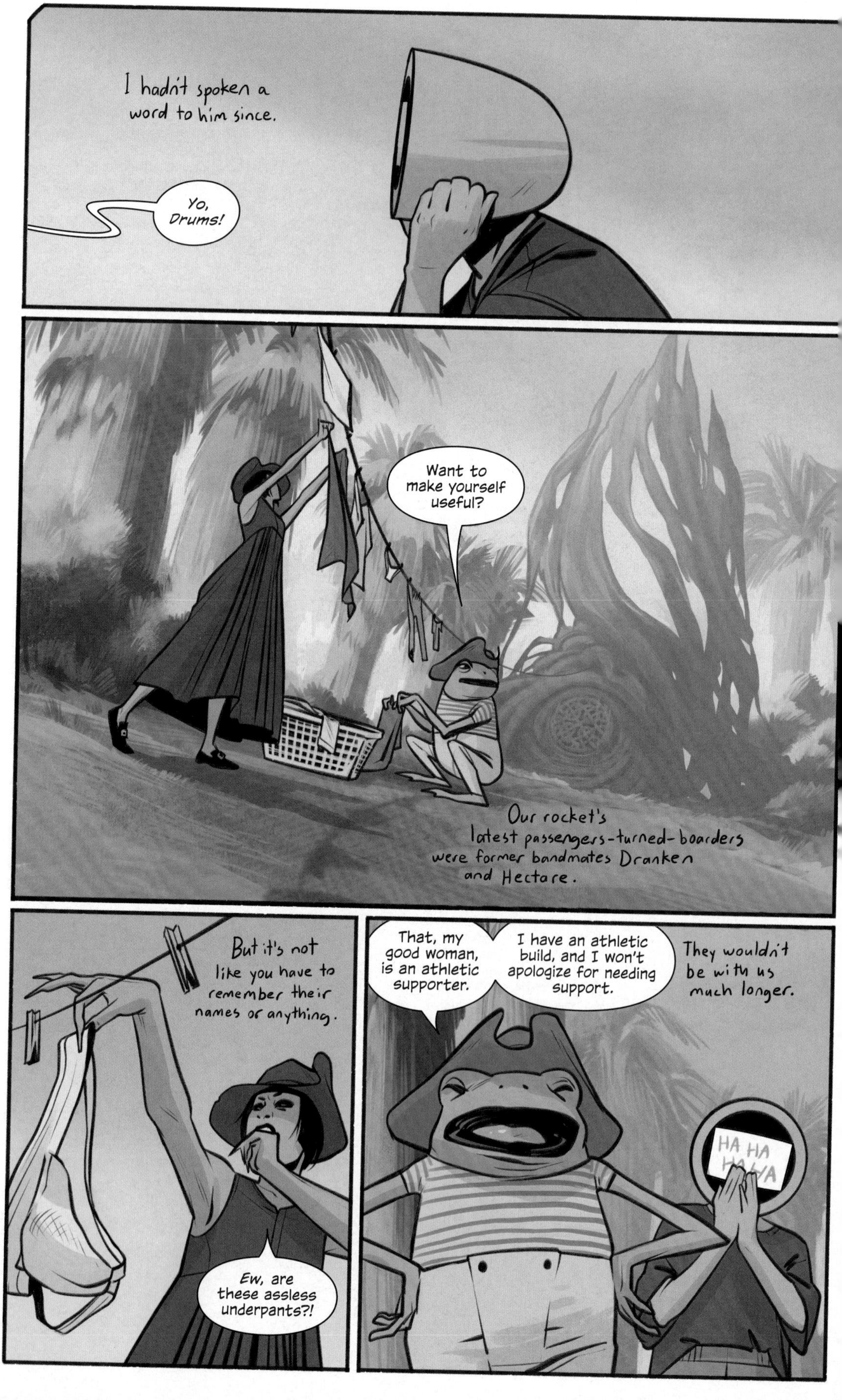
I hadn't spoken a word to him since.
Yo, Drums!
Want to make yourself useful?
Our rocket's latest passengers-turned-boarders were former bandmates Dranken and Hectare.
But it's not like you have to remember their names or anything.
Ew, are these assless underpants?!
That, my good woman, is an athletic supporter.
I have an athletic build, and I won't apologize for needing support.
They wouldn't be with us much longer.
HA HA HA HA

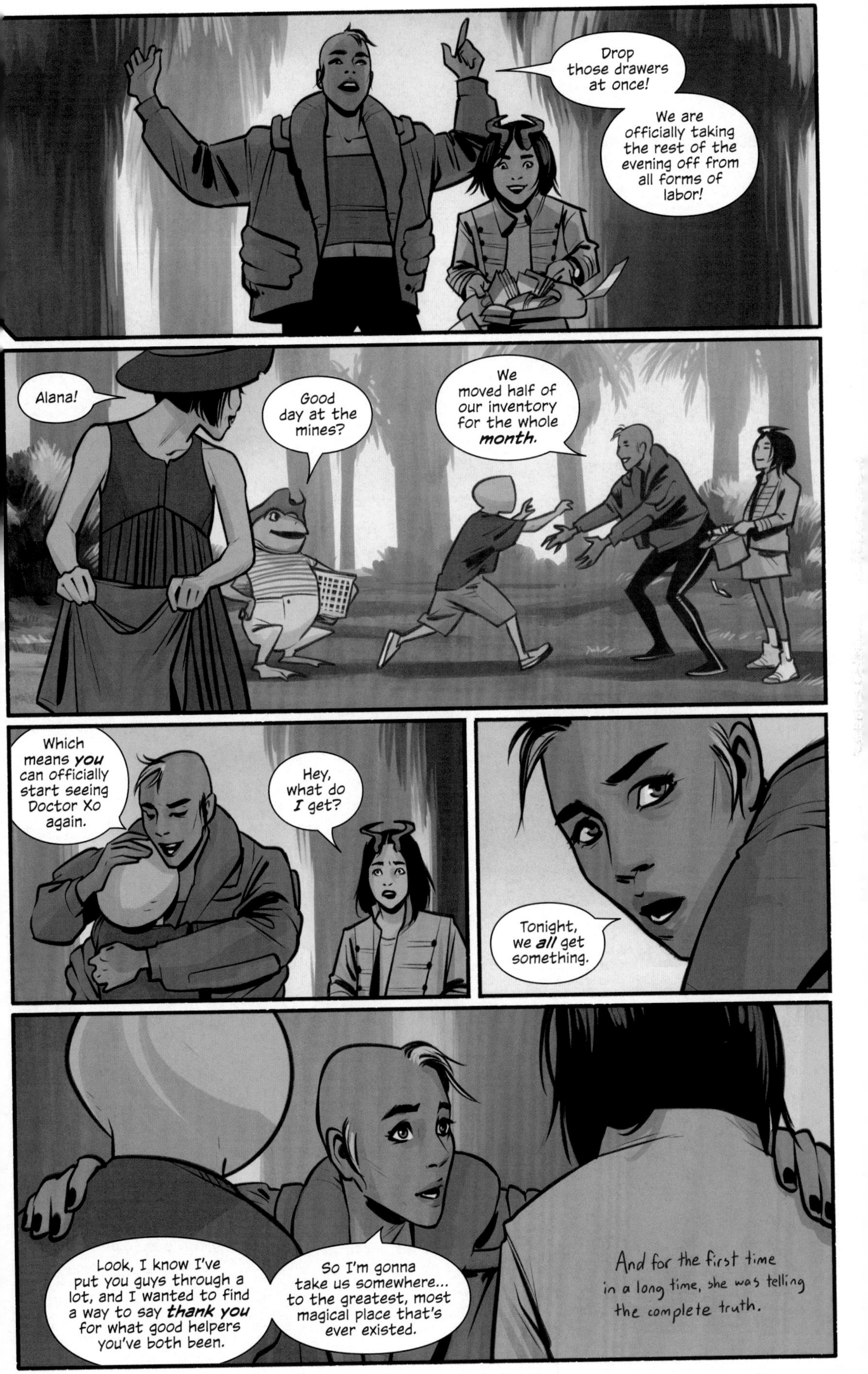

Drop those drawers at once!
We are officially taking the rest of the evening off from all forms of labor!
Alana!
Good day at the mines?
We moved half of our inventory for the whole *month*.
Which means *you* can officially start seeing Doctor Xo again.
Hey, what do *I* get?
Tonight, we *all* get something.
Look, I know I've put you guys through a lot, and I wanted to find a way to say *thank you* for what good helpers you've both been.
So I'm gonna take us somewhere... to the greatest, most magical place that's ever existed.
And for the first time in a long time, she was telling the complete truth.

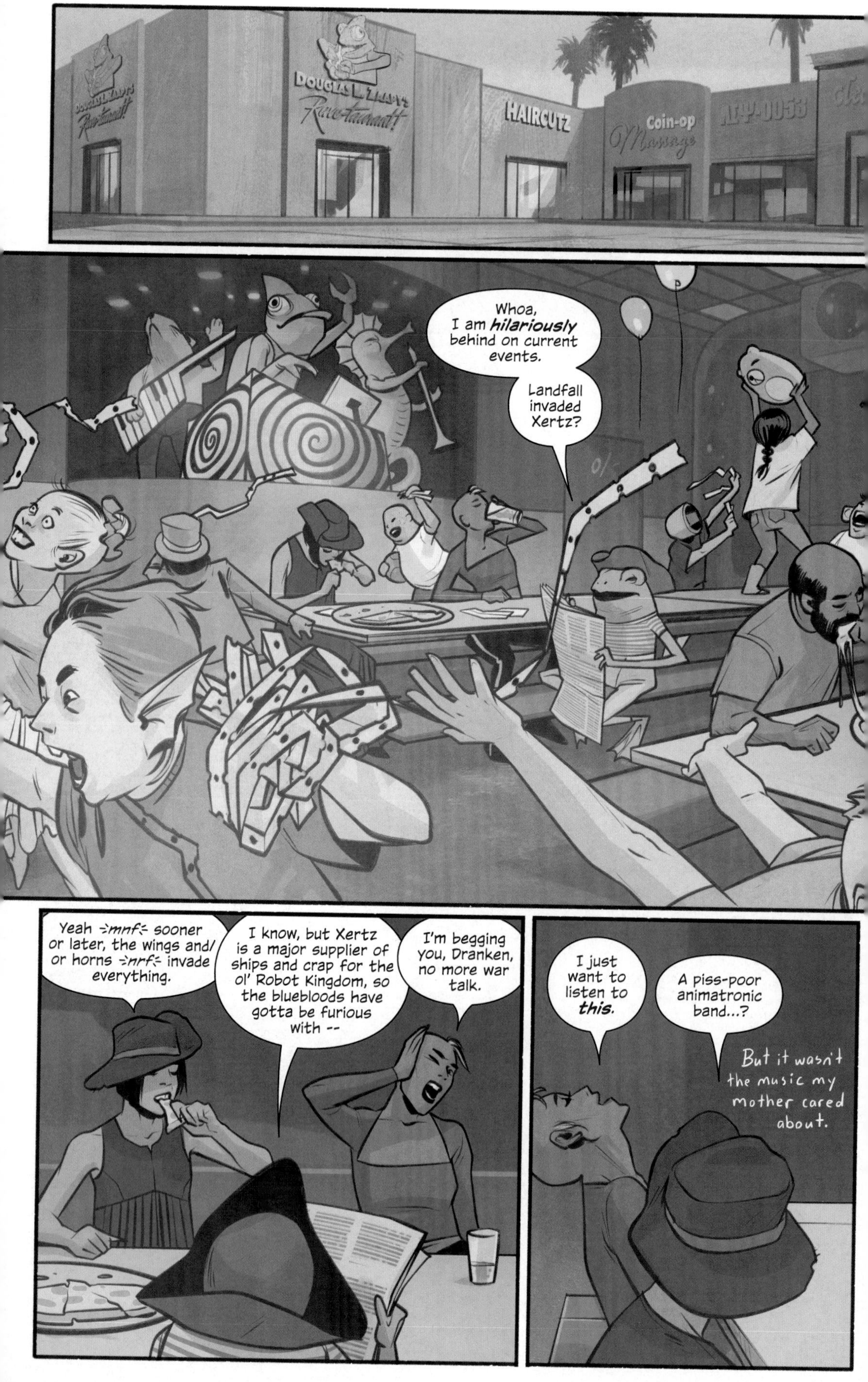
HAIRCUTZ
Coin-op Massage
Whoa, I am ***hilariously*** behind on current events.
Landfall invaded Xertz?
Yeah ⇒mnf⇐ sooner or later, the wings and/ or horns ⇒nrf⇐ invade everything.
I know, but Xertz is a major supplier of ships and crap for the ol' Robot Kingdom, so the bluebloods have gotta be furious with --
I'm begging you, Dranken, no more war talk.
I just want to listen to ***this***.
A piss-poor animatronic band...?
But it wasn't the music my mother cared about.

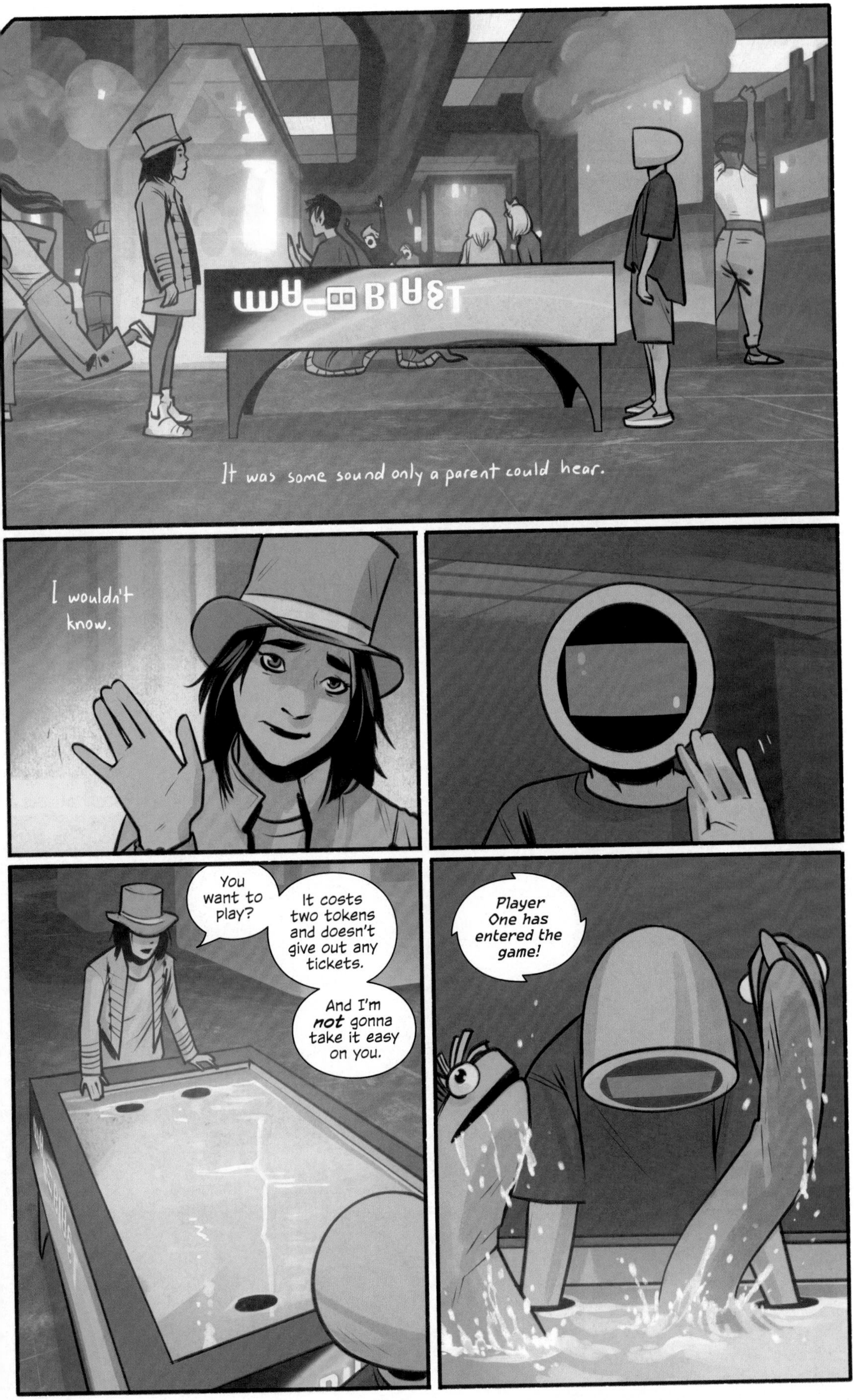
It was some sound only a parent could hear.
I wouldn't know.
You want to play?
It costs two tokens and doesn't give out any tickets.
And I'm **not** gonna take it easy on you.
Player One has entered the game!

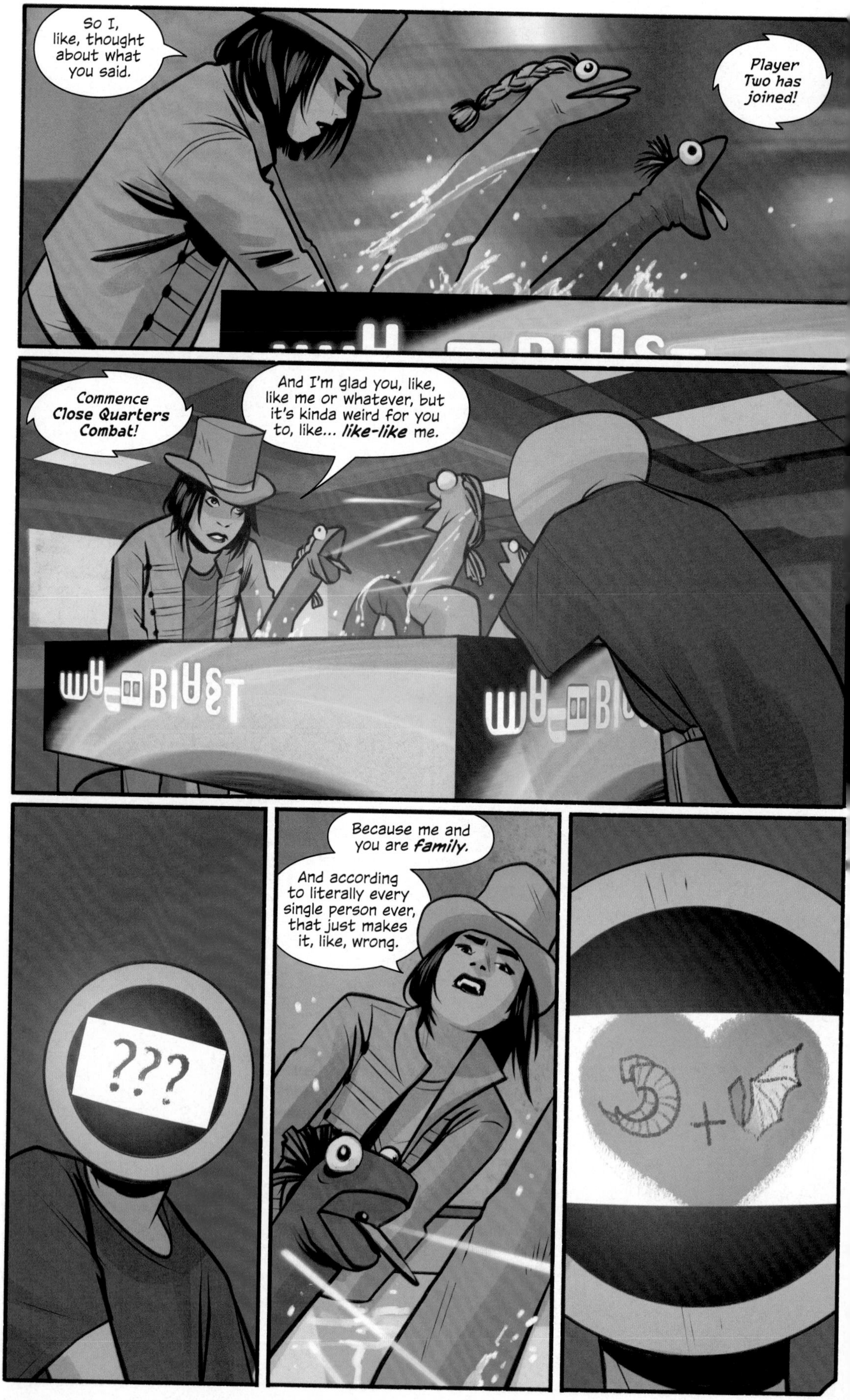
So I, like, thought about what you said.
Player Two has joined!
Commence Close Quarters Combat!
And I'm glad you, like, like me or whatever, but it's kinda weird for you to, like... like-like me.
???
Because me and you are family.
And according to literally every single person ever, that just makes it, like, wrong.

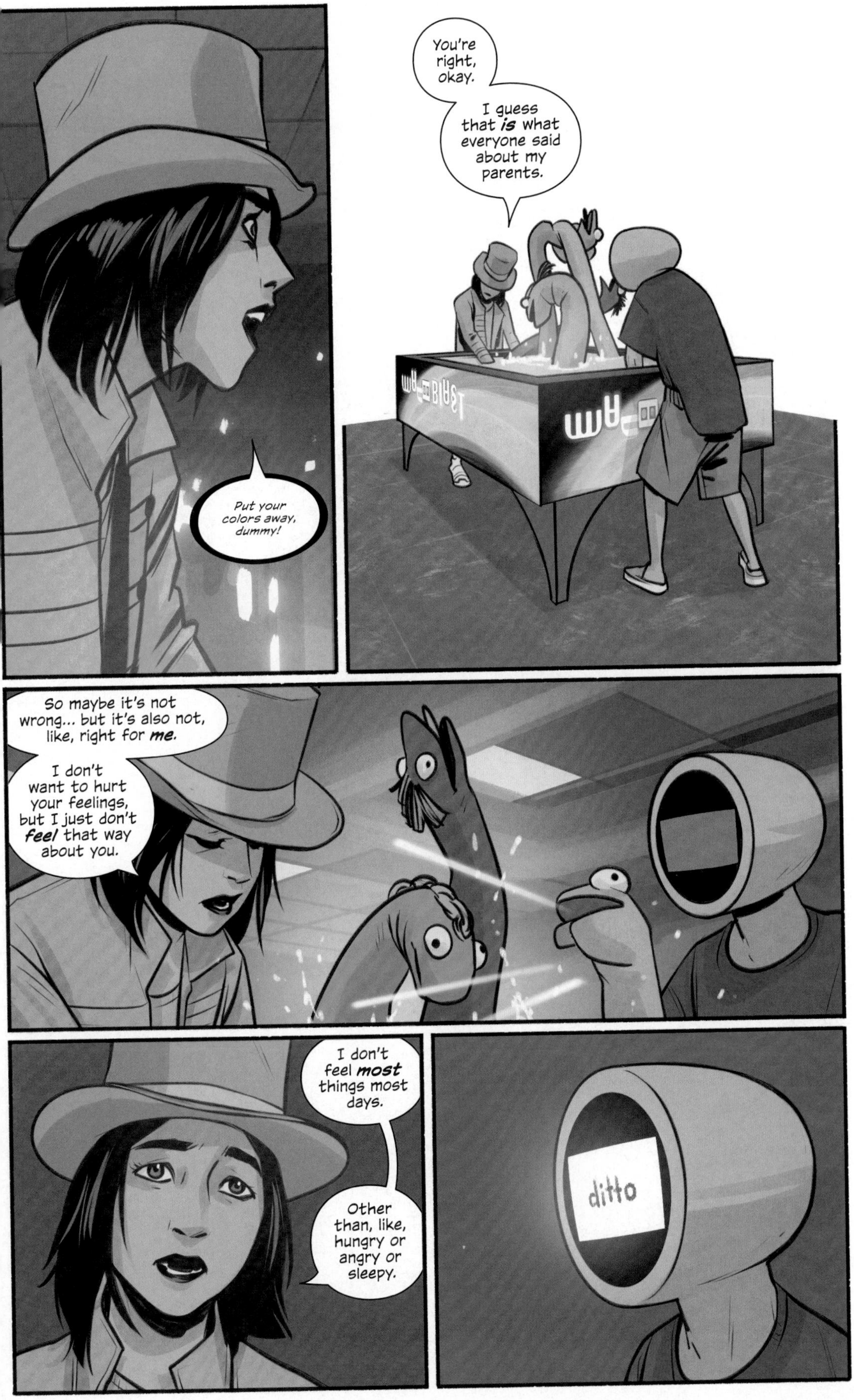
Put your colors away, dummy!
You're right, okay.
I guess that *is* what everyone said about my parents.
So maybe it's not wrong... but it's also not, like, right for **me**.
I don't want to hurt your feelings, but I just don't ***feel*** that way about you.
I don't feel **most** things most days.
Other than, like, hungry or angry or sleepy.
ditto

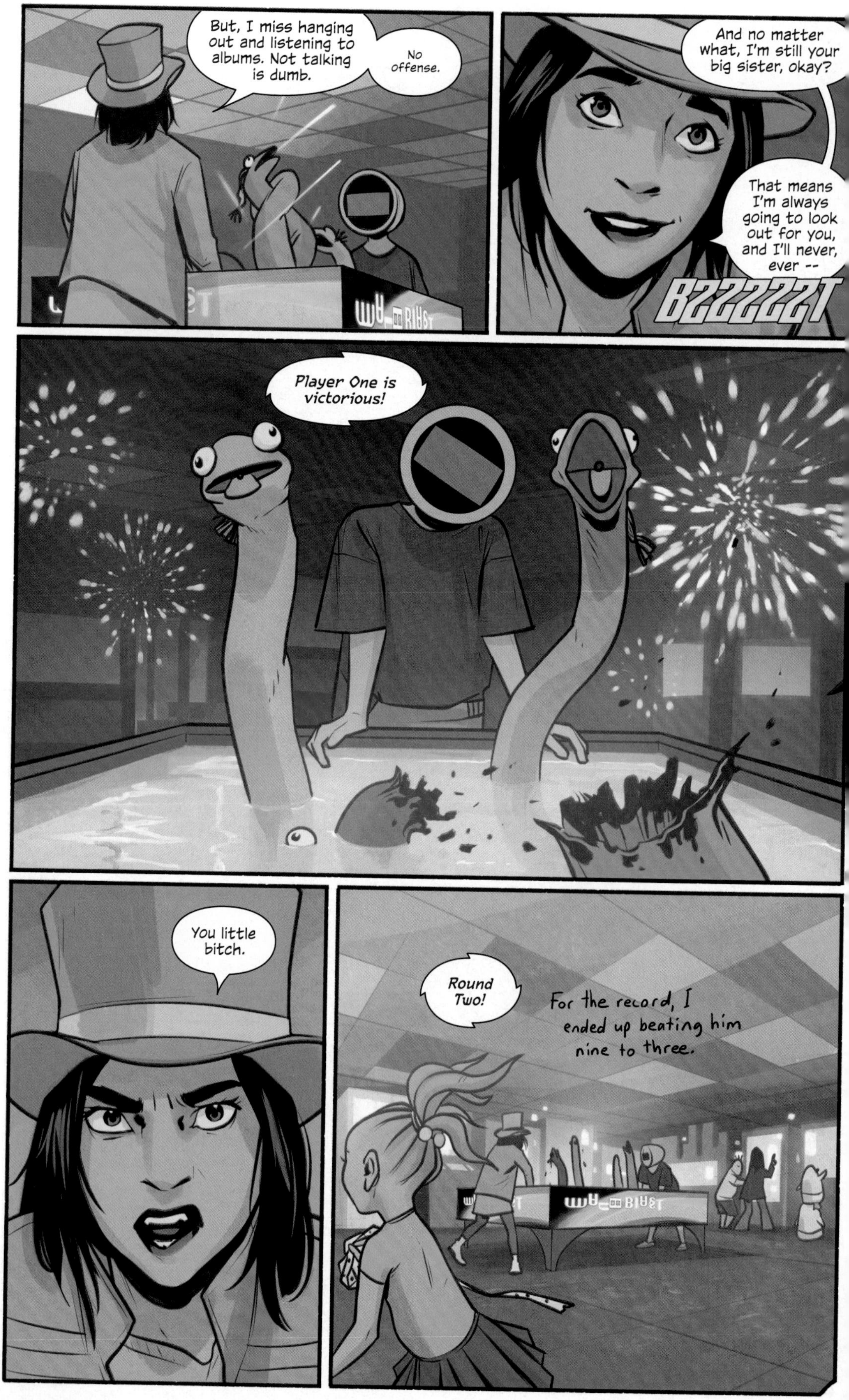

But, I miss hanging out and listening to albums. Not talking is dumb.
No offense.
And no matter what, I'm still your big sister, okay?
That means I'm always going to look out for you, and I'll never, ever --
BZZZZZZT
Player One is victorious!
You little bitch.
Round Two!
For the record, I ended up beating him nine to three.

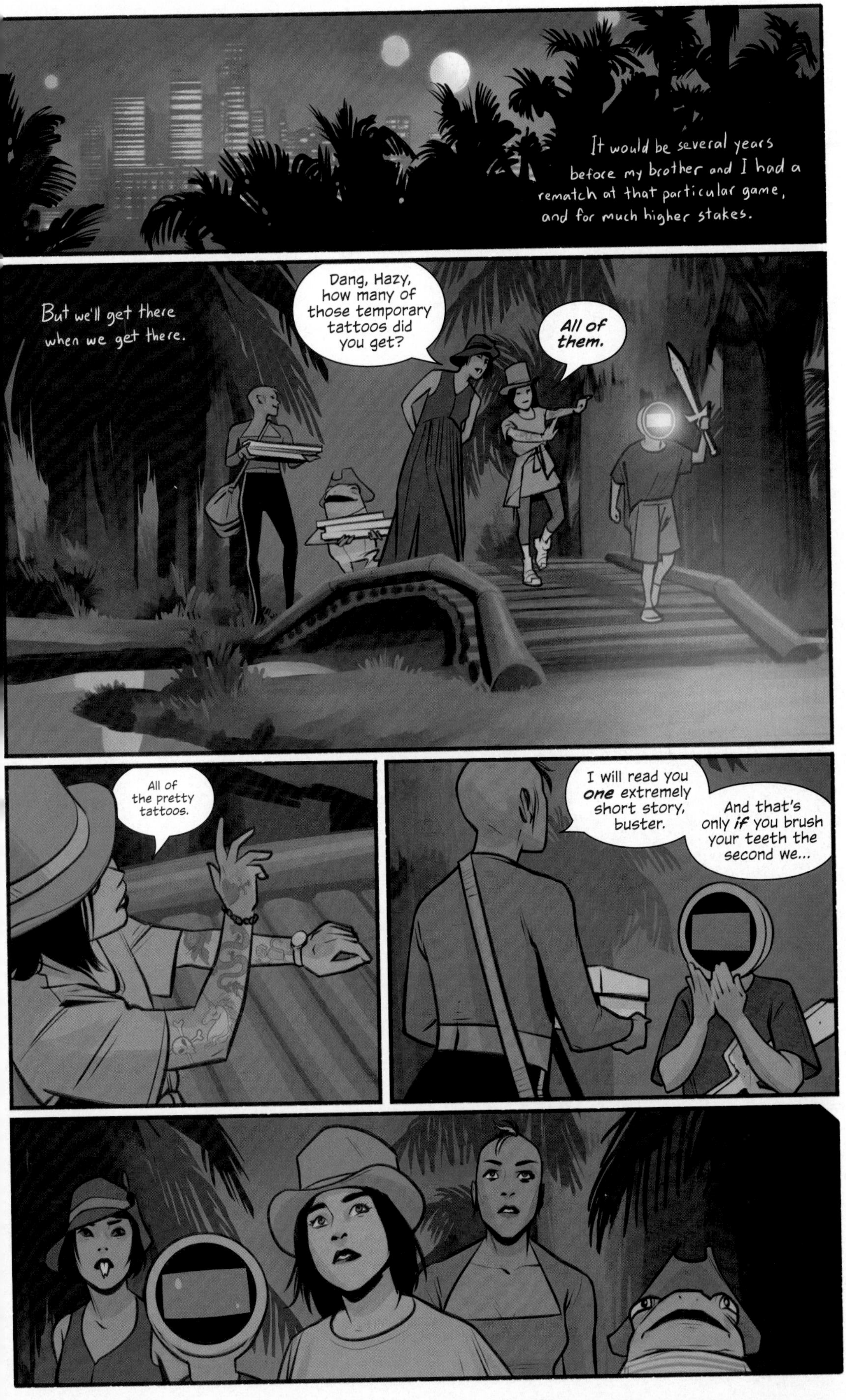
It would be several years before my brother and I had a rematch at that particular game, and for much higher stakes.
But we'll get there when we get there.
Dang, Hazy, how many of those temporary tattoos did you get?
All of them.
All of the pretty tattoos.
I will read you one extremely short story, buster.
And that's only if you brush your teeth the second we...

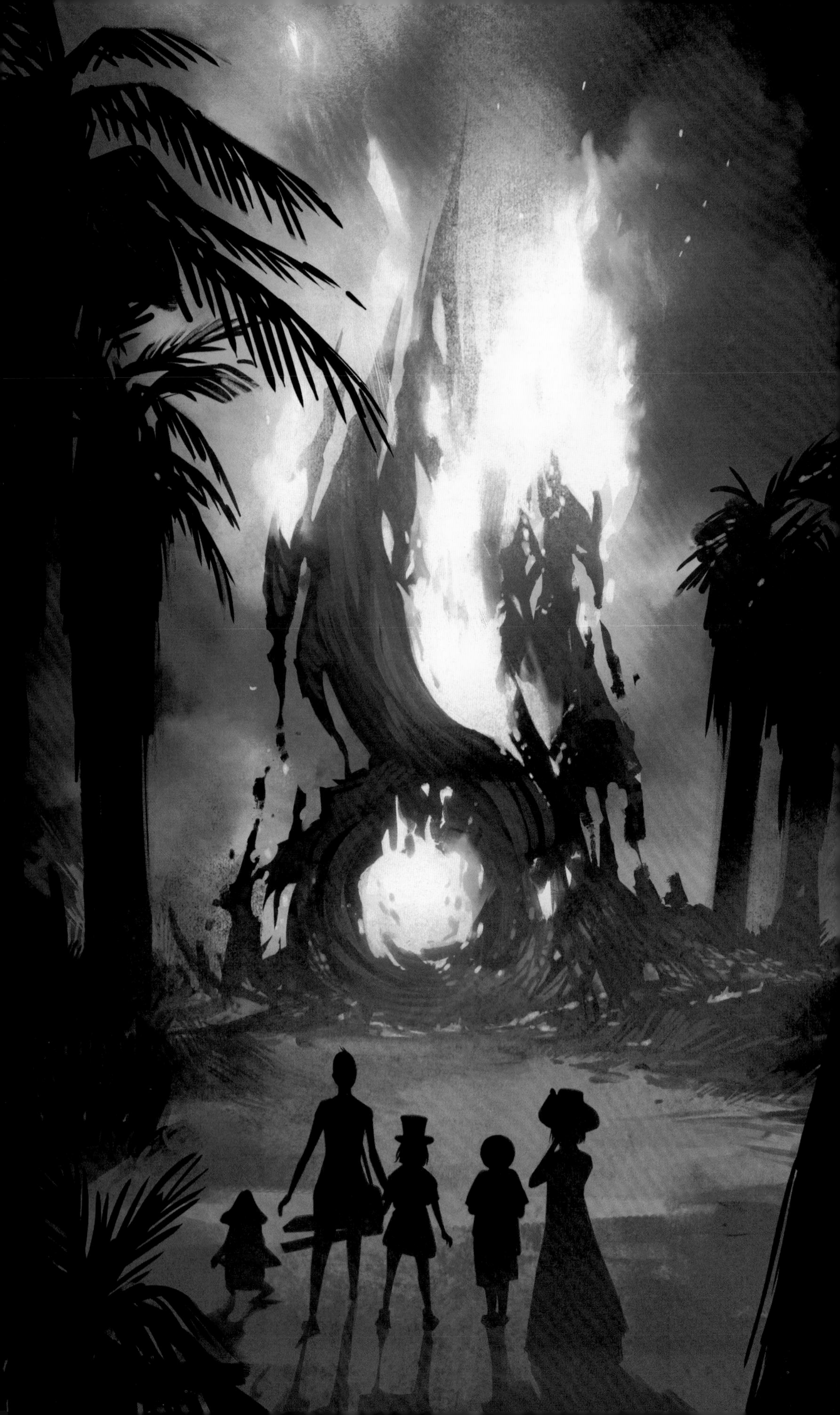

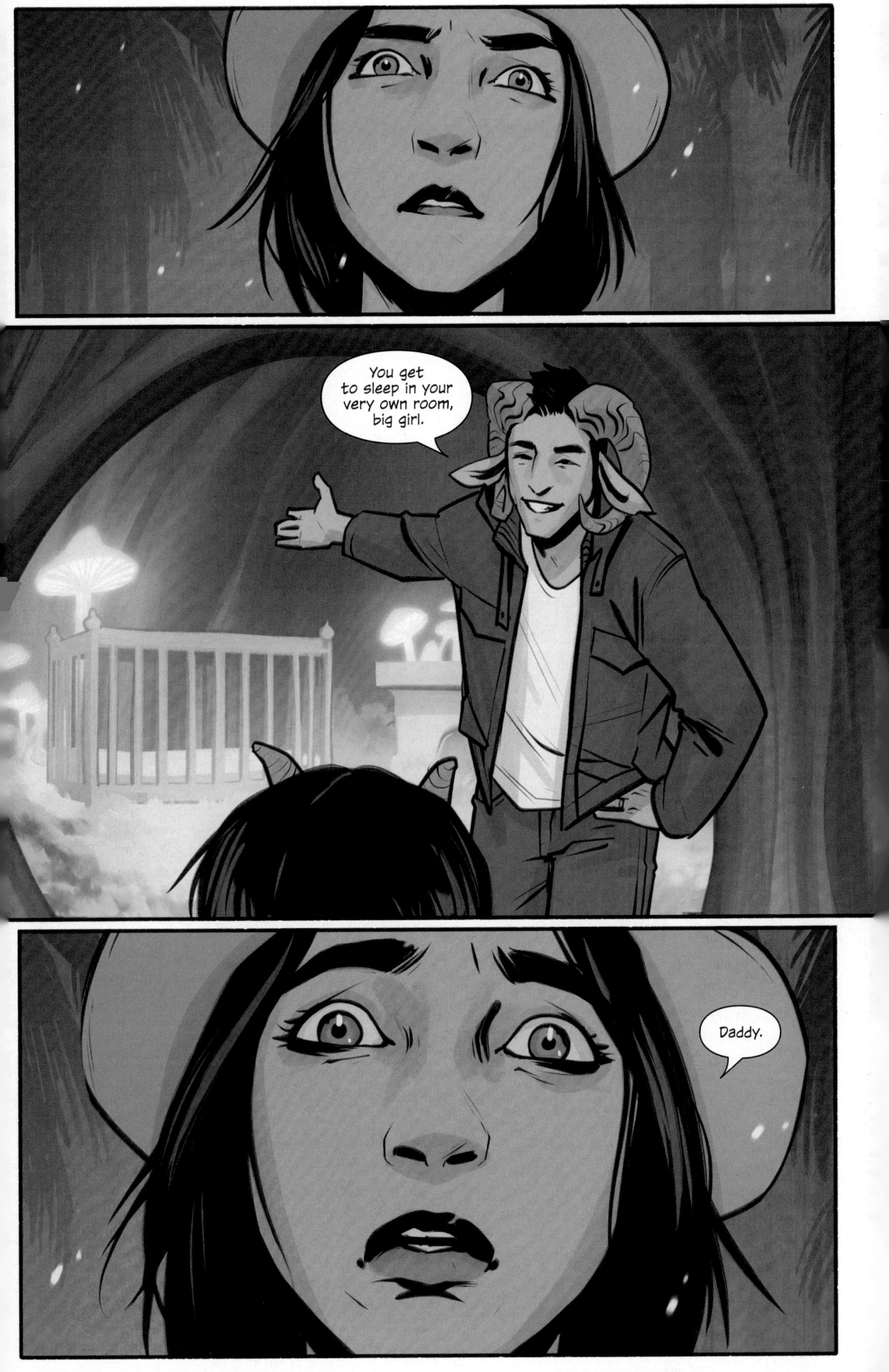
You get to sleep in your very own room, big girl.
Daddy.

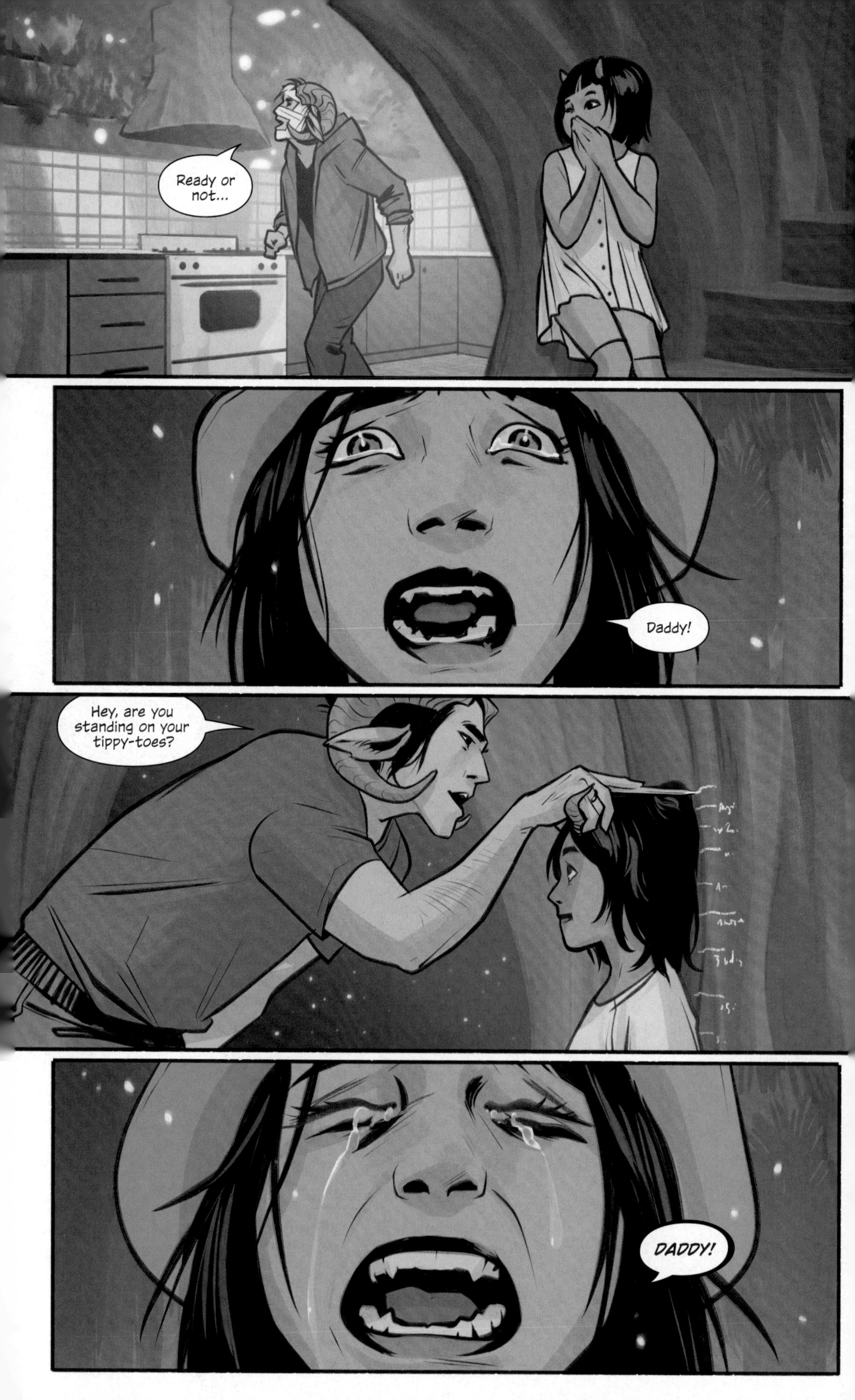
Ready or not...
Daddy!
Hey, are you standing on your tippy-toes?
DADDY!

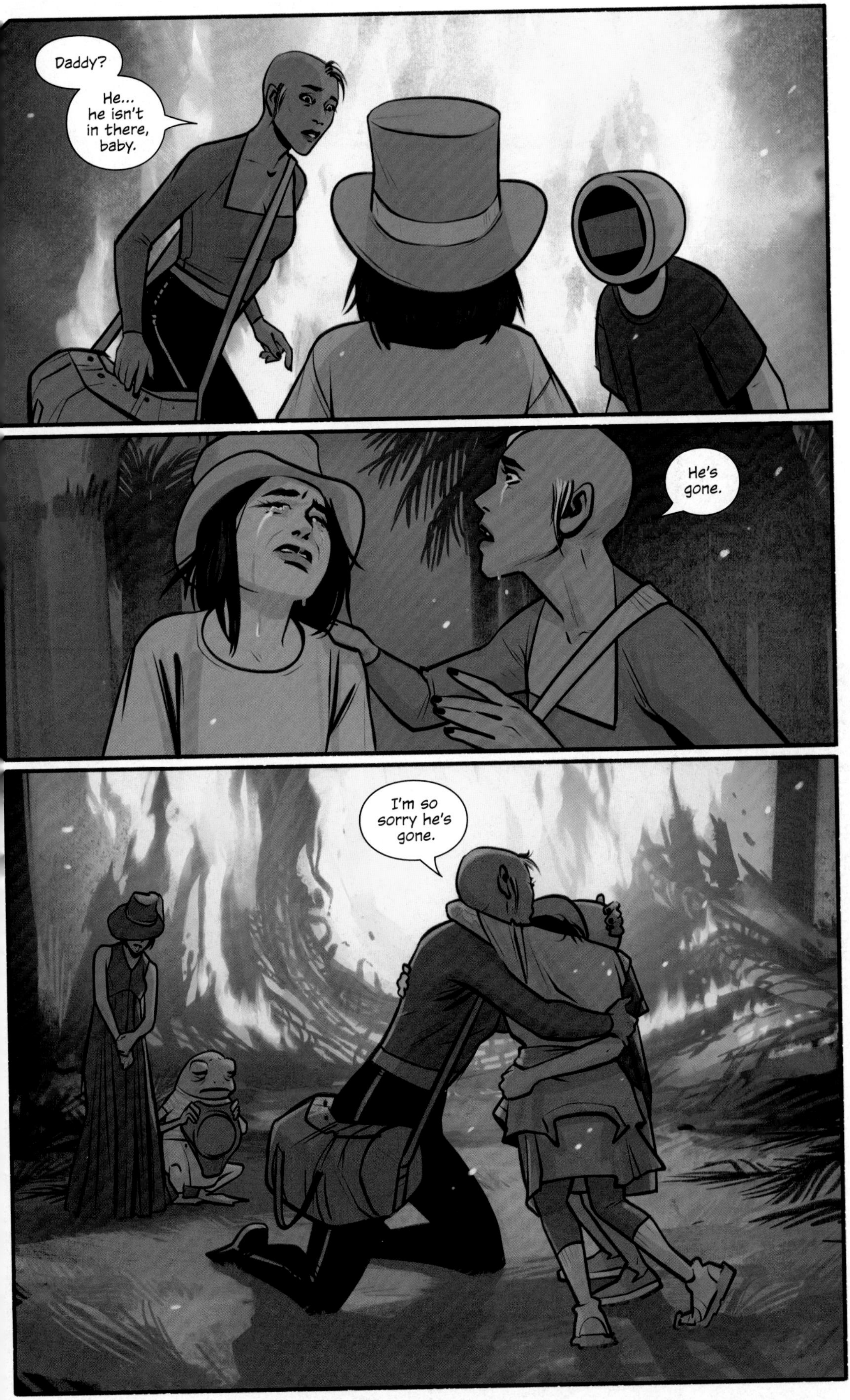
Daddy?
He... he isn't in there, baby.
He's gone.
I'm so sorry he's gone.

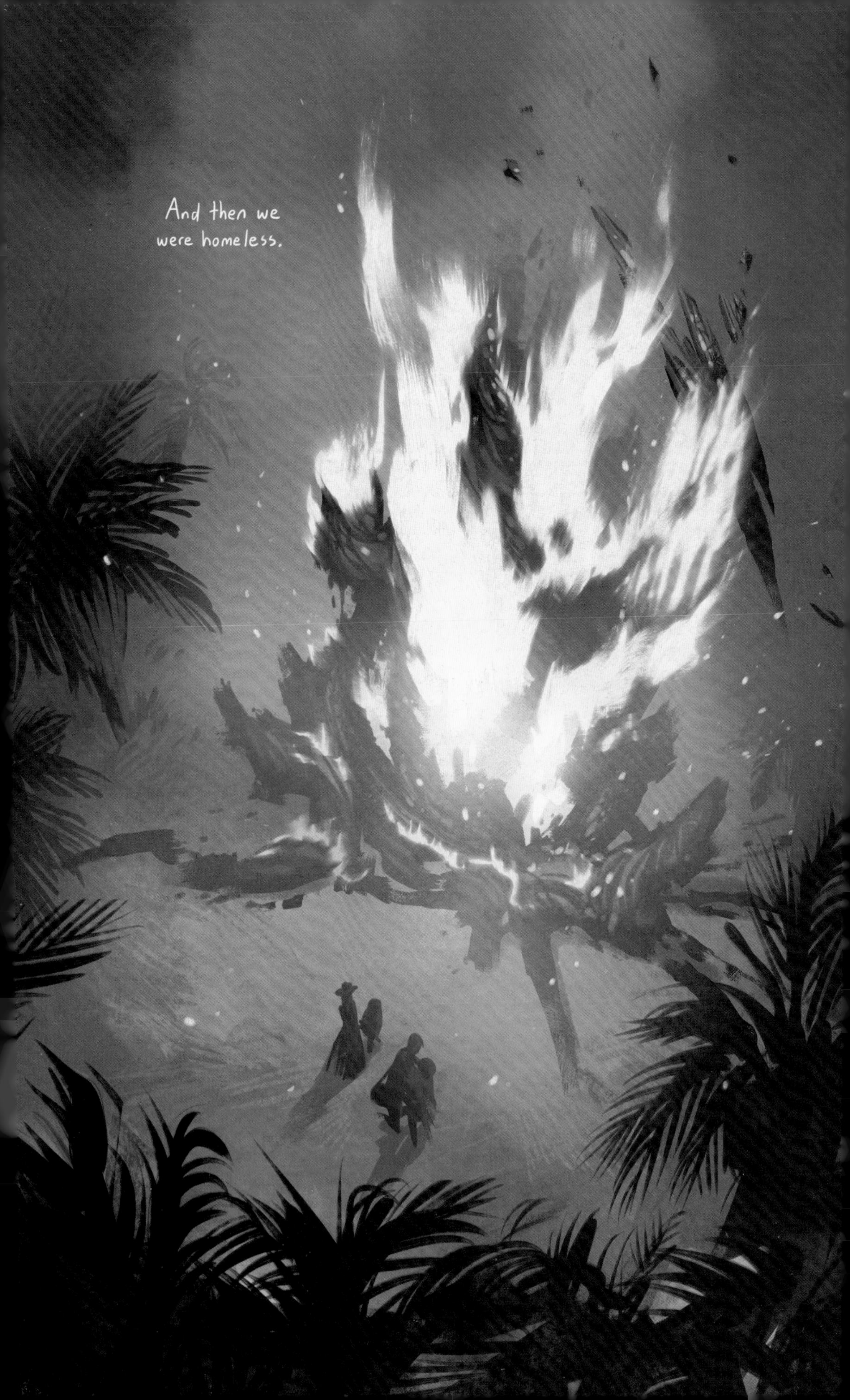
And then we were homeless.